Greyslaer

Complete-All 6 Books in 1 Volume

Greyslaer
Complete-All 6 Books in 1 Volume
A Novel of the American War of Independence
in the Mohawk Valley

Charles Fenno Hoffman

LEONAUR

Greyslaer
Complete-All 6 Books in 1 Volume
A Novel of the American War of Independence in the Mohawk Valley
by Charles Fenno Hoffman

First published under the title
Greyslaer Volumes 1 & 2

Leonaur is an imprint of Oakpast Ltd

ISBN: 978-1-78282-078-9 (hardcover)
ISBN: 978-1-78282-079-6 (softcover)

http://www.leonaur.com

Publisher's Notes

The views expressed in this book are not necessarily
those of the publisher.

Contents

To
WILLIAM DUER,
OF OSWEGO,
THESE VOLUMES ARE INSCRIBED
BY HIS EARLY FRIEND,
THE AUTHOR.

*"There is a divinity that shapes our ends,
Rough hew them how we will."*
Shakespeare

Why, peers of England,
We'll lead 'em on courageously. I read
A triumph over tyranny upon
Their several foreheads.

Ford.

'Tis a generous mind
That led his disposition to the war;
For gentle love and noble courage are
So near allied, that one begets another.

Cyril Tourneur.

This lady in the blossom of my youth,
When my first fires knew no adulterate incense,
Nor I no way to flatter but my fondness,
In the best language my true tongue could utter,
And all the broken sighs my sick heart lend me,
I sued and served. Long did I love this lady.

Massinger,

BOOK FIRST
THE BORDER RISING

CHAPTER 1

Forest Haunts and Sylvan Company

Away, away, to forest glades,
Fly, fly with me the haunts of men,
I would not give my sunlit glades,
My talking stream, and silent glen,
For all the pageantry of slaves,
Their fettered lives and trampled graves.

The Indian, by J. Lawrence.

Our story opens amid the depths of an American forest. It was midsummer; the bright green of June had departed from lea and meadow, and the brooks, even where their course lay through some grassy orchard, half sheltered by the spreading fruit-trees, had shrunk and dwindled in their channels; but here, amid the dank shadows of primeval woods, their currents still danced along with all the freshness of springtime. Here, too, the shrubs upon their banks still wore the delicate tints of early summer; for the canopy of dense foliage above them shut out the scorching heat. The birds of song, which, in the opening and closing year, are seldom heard in our deep forests, had now left the clearings, which they delight with their warbling in the mating season, and flitted through the cool and verdurous aisles that opened around on every side; now glancing sportively around the seamed and columnar trunks of the mossed trees, and now skimming high in air, but still sheltered by the cloistering architrave of interlacing boughs above them. It was noontide, but the freshness of early dawn and the mellow gloom of deepening twilight were commingled in those forest glades.

By the foot of an ancient tulip-tree, where a spring bubbled from beneath a rock, which its gnarled roots entwined, sat two men, who seemed the fitting tenants of a spot so wild. The one, a military veteran of about fifty, brawny and broad-shouldered, with freckled face and sandy hair, was dressed in the full garb of a Scottish Highlander, save that a jacket of green cloth, laced and guarded with bars of silver, like the uniform of a modern European trooper, was superadded to the tartan drapery that marks the ancient costume of his country. His companion, who wore a similar uniform jacket, was, in the fashion of his other garments, apparelled not unlike him; if a belted hunting-shirt of dressed deerskin, with fringed leggins of the same, and a scarlet blanket richly embroidered at the corners with porcupine quills, may be supposed to bear any resemblance to the kilt, hose, and plaid of the Scotchman, whose *skene dhu* was imitated by the terrible leg-knife, worn beneath the beaded garters of his companion. With the exception of a tomahawk secured in the *wampum* sash of the latter, both were in other respects similarly armed with pistols and *yaeger*.

But the accidental resemblance in the fashion of their equipments, which extended even to the ornamented tobacco-pouch worn at the belt of either, ceased altogether with a full survey of their persons, when contrasting these men together. There was nothing of the Celt or Goth in the swarthy lineaments of the American forester. Rising to his feet, while his blanket, dropping from one shoulder, set forth a chest of the finest proportions, he stood at least three inches taller than the European; while his lithe and well-rounded limbs fell at each motion into those easy attitudes which, among those who call themselves civilized, are seldom exhibited in their full grace by any but mere children, and which were in striking contrast with the angular movements of his sturdy and soldier-like companion.

"Well, *sachem*, what see you now?" said the Highlander, as the Indian, lightly planting one foot on a mossed root that pushed through the rotten sod, stood, with keen eye and dilated nostril, gazing intently into a deep glade of the forest.

"I looked for the return of one of my runners, but it was only a moose which stirred the leaves," he replied, quietly resuming his seat.

"A moose? ah! I've heard of that kind of deer. They tell me that they are famous fellows when at bay. But you should hunt a stag among old Scotia's mountains to know what sport is, Sachem. You never got as far, though, as our heathery hills, when you visited King George."

"There was game afoot here that would not have let me linger in the Highlands, even had I reached them."

"Ah! but even to have set foot upon the bonny purple heather, though but for once in your life, would have been something; and yet, perhaps, 'twere better not; it might have made you discontented with these gloomy forests that cover up your whole country."

"I saw many bald men among the counsellors of my British father; but the naked crowns of the Sagernash did not put me out of conceit of the long locks of an Iroquois," replied the forester, dryly. And then, continuing in a more animated strain, "I have not always, even in my own land, dwelt among these forests, which you think so gloomy. I have wandered for months over meadows laughing with sunshine and flowers, where the purple heather of which you speak, unless it out-bloom in richness all that I have seen in an English garden, were but a dull garniture for the delicious fields. And yet, though the prairies seemed so fascinating, when in early youth I followed over them the war path of the great Pontiac, their charms appear to me now but as the feeble and holyday work of Nature, when compared with a temple like that in which we stand.

"Look there," he cried, pointing upward to the sweeping cone of a pine that towered some two hundred feet towards the heavens, upon the lowest branch of which, still a hundred feet above the soil, an eagle was at the moment lighting, while the frayed bark, slipping from beneath his talons, floated long in air before reaching the ground. "Look at yon royal pine, Major MacDonald; such trees as that will grow but once in any soil! they are the production only of Nature in her prime; and, as one of her doomed children that must soon pass away, I would fain linger near them with my people until the last is gone."

"*Doomed, sachem?* tut, tut, not a bit of doom about the matter; we'll soon drive the rebels from the ancient seats of your tribe; or, should the worst come to the worst, why not leave this wild land? You have the king's commission in your pocket, and can still follow his majesty's banner wherever a trumpet shall sound."

"Never, never!" rejoined the Indian, mournfully; "I have been tutored in your schools; I have worshipped in your churches; I have feasted and slept in your dwellings; I have fought side by side with your warriors in the field; I have mingled with your courtiers in the palace, and your counsellors in the cabinet: but, my ways are still not your ways, nor has the heart of Thayendanagea been ever for a moment estranged from his tribe."

"Why, then, did you lead them to take a part with us in this quarrel, which, you told me but yesterday, must eventuate in the ultimate success of the rebel arms?"

"Why? why did not my countrymen accept the overtures of the French king, when Frontenac made his descent upon the cantons with a powerful army, and our allies, the Hollanders, at whom, through us, Ononthio struck the blow, were too feeble to aid us save with their wishes? why, until your country men, by their acquisition of this province, became heirs of the friendship we had sworn to the Dutch, did we stand by Quidar in his quarrel with England to the last? Why? why did you, Major MacDonald, who have now, with hundreds like yourself, taken up arms for King George, why did you become an exile by fighting against him when a stripling?"

The Scotchman sprang to his feet, and paced the turf in agitation for a moment; then, turning short in front of the other, exclaimed, as he clasped the hand of the noble Mohawk in both of his own and wrung it cordially,

"Captain Brant, you are a true and loyal gentle man, every inch of you; worthy to have been out in the Forty-five with the best of us; and if——"

"Hist—crouch," interrupted the *sachem*, lightly pressing the shoulder of MacDonald, who, obedient to the motion, sank on one knee beside him.

"I see him," whispered the Highlander, glancing in the direction whither his companion pointed; "a sable roan! A most noble charger; his rider must be near."

"*Yo-hah!* a horse of eighteen hands! there are not many such in the depths of an American forest Look again, brother soldier."

"*Jesu Maria!*" ejaculated the European, in a tone that might be thought to partake as much of alarm as of wonder, if the suspicion had not been belied by the flashing eye with which he instantly brought his *yaeger* to his shoulder, while the muzzle was as quickly averted by the hand of the Mohawk striking up the barrel.

"An old hunter looks at his range as well as at his mark," said Brant, in reply to an inquiring glance of the other; and the hasty Scot, looking again beyond his quarry, saw, for the first time, a half-naked Indian standing immediately in his line of fire.

"I must have those antlers to match a pair from the peat-moss in my brother's hall," he murmured, in a tone of disappointment.

"They shall be yours, but we must not wake these echoes with our firearms. Leave my runner yonder to deal with the moose, and we shall be certain of a savoury broil this evening."

The deer-stalker, or *still-hunter*, as we would term him in this country, seemed to be fully aware of the neighbourhood of his chief, and the precise point where he lay; for, gliding now like a shadow from tree to tree, and more than once fitting an arrow to his bow, as if about to shoot, while continually approaching the moose, he managed to place himself so that the two witnesses of the sport could not be harmed by the shot. The animal, in the mean time, pestered by the August flies that are so annoying to the larger tenants of the forest at this season, kept moving hither and thither within a small circle, pausing ever and anon to browse for a moment; and still, while feeding, making the dry branches crackle with his incessant trampling.

At last he seemed to be more contented, as he got his feet into a marshy piece of ground, from about his legs, as his hoofs broke the yielding soil. The Scotchman, who now, for the first time, had a full view of his huge uncouth form, could not sufficiently admire the ease with which the moose used his ungainly but flexile snout, to twist off the branches near him, while lazily catching at those within his reach.

But now the movements of the still-hunter equally claimed the attention of the lookers-on of this quiet but exciting kind of woodland sport. The stealthy savage, by flitting from tree to tree in the manner we have described, occasionally drawing his body, like a wounded snake, along the ground, had gained a fallen and decayed trunk within twenty paces of the moose, and, lying concealed behind this natural rampart, was watching, with keen eye, the fitting moment to launch his fatal shaft.

At last the moose, having stripped the boughs immediately in front of him, yet unwilling to change his position, threw back his broad antlers upon his shoulders, and, twisting his neck obliquely as he caught at a weeping birch that drooped over his left shoulder within reach of his uplifted muzzle, presented his throat as a fair mark for the arrow of the hunter. The bow twanged, and the barbed flint was driven, with unerring aim, through the neck, severing the swollen artery, and burying itself deep in the vertebrae at the base of the scull. The stricken animal uttered a terrific snort of rage and agony, plunged, reared, and, wheeling on his hind legs, made a desperate charge at his assailant, but fell dead at the feet of the Indian, just as the undismayed fellow was in the act of bounding forward to encounter him with his tomahawk.

"A good shot, Harrowah," cried Brant, moving leisurely from his covert; while the more ardent Scot rushed, with drawn dirk, towards the fallen moose, as if still hoping to have a hand in the death of so noble a quarry. But the bright eye was already fixed in death, though a muscular motion in the long and drooping muzzle made the Highlander quickly withdraw the hand which he had placed on that uncouth appendage.

"By Saint Andrew," he cried, "but you have an ugly face to claim kindred with the dun deer of my own heather."

"Yet, major, we foresters think that the woods afford no choicer morsel than a moose's muzzle; and your Frenchman of Canada will serve you up a stew of it that will shame the mock-turtle of a London coffee-house."

"Eat that hideous black thing?" said the Scot, with no feeble signs of aversion; "I've dined often upon horseflesh while serving in Tartary, but I'd as soon sup upon the trunk of an elephant as make a meal off that frightful big lip. Zounds! the thing quivers as if it were still alive; like the tail of one of your American serpents, which, they tell me, never dies till sunset."

The still-hunter stood, in the mean time, with folded arms, gazing listlessly upon the scene, until, giving a sort of grunt in reply to an order from his chief, delivered in his own language, he addressed himself to the care of the carcass. Selecting a smooth-barked beech for the operation, he prepared one of the lower limbs, by the aid of props, to sustain the weight of the animal. But the sleight of the slim hunter, and the united strength of his two stalwart companions, were all put in requisition to trice up the ponderous carcass, after the splinters, by which it was suspended, had been passed through the tough sinews of the gambles. The head was then severed from the trunk, and swung by the palmated antlers to the crooked arm of an ancient oak; and the body, after being flayed to the loins, and relieved of all superfluities, was wrapped in its own hide, and raised still higher from the ground, to be out of the reach of beasts of prey, until otherwise disposed of.

"I will send some of my people to bring the meat to camp before nightfall; and now, Major MacDonald, let us learn what tidings the runner brings us."

With these words the *sachem* moved to the spot where the reader was first introduced to him and his companion, and where blanket and tartan, lying where they had been dropped by the roots of the shadowy tulip-tree, offered inviting seats for the councils of this sylvan *triumvirate*.

Chapter 2

Frontier Factions

They left the ploughshare in the mould,
Their flocks and herds without a fold,
The sickle in the unshorn grain,
The corn half garnered on the plain,
And mustered in their simple dress,
For wrongs to seek a stern redress;
To right those wrongs, come weal, come wo,
To perish or o'ercome their foe.

M'Lellan.

The information brought to his chieftain by the Mohawk runner, though of deep import to more than one actor in the scenes we are about to describe, will hardly be intelligible to the reader, unless he revives his historical recollection of the political intrigues that distracted the important province of New York, as the drama of the Revolution was gradually unfolded along her far-spreading borders.

The long possession of the fur-trade, and the frequent Indian wars incident to the pursuit of this hardy and precarious branch of commerce, had at an early day given an adventurous and enterprising character to the population of this province. Their military spirit had been well tested in the arduous campaigns of the old French war; they had borne no feeble part in the conquest of Canada; and when the fall of Quebec, in consummating the glory of Wolfe, brought peace to the land, it found almost every man capable of bearing arms a soldier. While, therefore, the different parties of Whig and Tory were almost equally balanced in the province of New York throughout the Revolution, that memorable political struggle found fewer neutrals here than in any state of the Union; all men were eager to bear arms on one side or the other, and it is this circumstance only which will account for the great numbers that fell in battle, when the inferior degree of population, as compared with that of several of the other colonies, is considered.

But, bitter as were the political animosities existing in every part of this province, both before and after a recourse was had to arms, yet the spirit of faction called out in no district the same stormy feelings as now distracted the valley of the Mohawk. The elements of civil dissension had been long brewing in this beautiful region, where such a diversity of origin, of interest, and, we may add, of religion, existed among the heterogeneous population, that the soul of discord might well have been roused even in times the most peaceable.

Here had been the ancient seat of the most powerful and civilized, yet most warlike nation of aborigines, upon the northern part of this hemisphere, a large remnant of which still retained their possessions in the immediate neighbourhood of the European settlements. Here the sturdy and adventurous Dutch trader had at an early day been tempted to abandon his precarious means of livelihood, and sit down to cultivate the rich alluvial lands that had been readily granted to him by the grateful Mohawks, who had ever been treated as brothers by his countrymen during their sway over the province. Hither the German soldiers of Queen Anne's Protestant allies had in large bodies followed their European neighbours to settle upon the extensive tracts, granted to them when New York first took its modern name in passing to the British crown. Here, side by side with these brave mercenaries, or perched, rather, upon the northern hills that overlooked their fertile meadows, hundreds of Catholic Scotch Highlanders, with many Irish soldiers of fortune, the exiled followers of the last Stuart, had established themselves; while successive families of the Cameronian countrymen of the former had found their frugal homes upon the uplands south of the river, whose cultivation had been rejected by those who preceded them in gaining an interest in the soil.

The diversity of feeling which this difference of origin, of language, and of religion may be presumed to have created, was still farther enhanced in its effects by the difference in tenure through which the broad domains of the valley were held. For while the majority of the old "*residenters*" were freeholders, constituting a large and independent yeomanry, yet among those of British descent there were extensive feudal proprietors, holding their patents immediately from the crown, who could number a powerful array of dependants; and some of whom (as was actually the case with Colonels Butler and Johnson both before and during the war) commanded regiments of militia, raised exclusively among their own tenantry.

There was one feature common to this heterogeneous people, which will hardly be thought to have reconciled the jarring elements of strife, though capacitating them for acting in unison under some circumstances; and this was that, throughout the valley, there was scarcely an individual who had not been in some way trained to the use of arms.

The threatening storm of civil war had at an early day found both patriot and loyalist upon the alert to enlist the principles, the prejudices, or affections of their neighbours upon the side that either was determined to espouse. The leading gentlemen of Tryon County, whether Whig or Tory, kept up in deed for a long time the most friendly relations towards each other, so far as outward seeming was concerned. Both parties affected to be actuated by the greatest zeal in preserving the peace of the country, and particularly in all their public conferences agreed to act in unison in preventing the Indians from taking any part in the impending controversy, should a fatal issue be ultimately joined between them. But the acts of either faction seem sufficiently to have belied their words from the first.

Secret clubs and committees were organized upon the one side; and many of the wealthy upon the other, keeping open house for their partisans, made their hospitality a cloak for the dangerous councils that were rife at the festive board. The country was traversed by mounted men, bearing tokens from one disaffected family to another. Travellers upon the highways were stopped by the myrmidons of either party, and their papers examined by these border regulators with the coolest assumption of authority; and as, on the one side, the great landed proprietors soon commenced fortifying their houses and arming and drilling their tenantry, so, among the smaller freeholders on the other, several of the influential Whigs ventured to reorganize the militia in their own districts, and officers were deposed and others appointed, according to the peculiar tenets and wishes of the people.

This last innovation had been attended with some danger; though in one instance, Sir John Johnson, the leading magistrate of the county, met with a signal discomfiture when rashly intruding upon a party of villagers whom a lieutenant, elected by themselves, was engaged in drilling. The baronet chanced to be taking a drive with his lady when he came upon this squad of young soldiers; and incensed at seeing a man in the uniform of an officer who he knew did not hold the king's commission, leaped from his barouche, and advancing upon the patriot lieutenant, rebuked his presumption with great insolence, and called upon his comrades instantly to disperse. Swords were drawn, and Sir John, being the more skilful fencer of the two, disarmed his youthful opponent, but was ultimately compelled to retire from the levelled muskets which were instantly presented at his life, when he at tempted to push his advantage, by seizing the young man and securing him as a traitor to the king taken in open arms.

Convinced, by this and similar scenes, of the unpopularity in that part of the province of the cause which he had espoused, the zealous baronet addressed himself to the promotion of his royal master's interest in another quarter; and, in defiance of the implied stipulation existing between both parties of the whites, that the Indians should not be permitted to take a part in the family quarrel, as it was called, he proceeded to avail himself of his connexion with the tribes, to influence them to raise the tomahawk against his political opponents. His brother-in-law, Colonel Guy Johnson, the superintendent of Indian affairs for all the provinces of British America, readily lent his powerful aid to the furtherance of these intrigues; and the vigilant Whigs, while keeping a wary eye upon the powerful Tory families in their neighbourhood, soon became aware that Indian runners were continually passing and repassing between the settlements and the straggling troops of warriors that hovered on their border. The moose-hunter was one of a hundred similar agents of frontier diplomacy, that were continually traversing the country between Guy Park, the seat of the Indian agency, and the different council-fires, or outlying bands of the Six Nations.

Sir John Johnson's numerous tenantry of Scotch Highlanders were already in arms at Johnstown, where the baronet had fortified his large mansion with several brass fieldpieces; and the different cantons of the Iroquois, with the single exception of the Oneidas, were known to be so favourably disposed toward the royal cause, that the only question was now, how to unite the whole force, both European and aboriginal, so as to make it most effective, and overwhelm at its first outbreak the least movement of rebellion; this, however, required no feeble energies to accomplish.

The yeomanry of the valley had long regarded Sir John Johnson with a suspicious eye; alike from the baronial state that he affected upon his princely domains, and the insolent and dictatorial assumption with which he more than once intruded upon their popular assemblies. Colonel Guy Johnson, the superintendent of the Indian department, was held in hardly less aversion than his kinsman, and the celebrated Joseph Brant, or Thayendanagea, as he called himself, who filled the important post of secretary of that department for "all his majesty's provinces in North America," had, from his political connexions, lost much of the confidence of his old friends. Brant, indeed, though living upon the most intimate terms with many of the leading Whigs of Tryon County, was always suspected to hold himself in readiness for employment more congenial to the tastes of an Indian warrior, who, amid all the allurements of a European court, and when surrounded by every luxury and embellishment of civilized life, had made it his pride and his boast that he was a "full-blooded Mohawk."

That haughty chief, who, whether at the entertainments of princes and nobles, in the saloons of fashion, or the palaces of royalty, had always persisted in presenting himself in the peculiar costume of his people, seemed to have brought home but little from his European intercourse with the learned and the polite, save a strong feeling of attachment to the British crown: a sentiment of feudal loyalty, which, notwithstanding his early New England education, had become strangely grafted upon the peculiar love which he bore to the ancient republican institutions of the Five Nations. He seemed to regard England as the only muniment of their freedom, and was willing to render a cordial allegiance to her as the price of the protection; and while, in his intercourse with the whites, arrogating to himself a full share of that assumption which induced his semi-barbarous countrymen to call themselves the *Ongi-honwe*, or "men who surpassed all others," he was still willing to look up to the head of the British Empire both as the fountain of public honours and the guardian of his country's welfare.

But while this aspiring and sagacious sachem saw that the safety of his people and his own pre-eminence as a chieftain depended upon their siding with the royal cause—for at a very early day he foretold the blighting influence which this great overshadowing republic would bring upon the aborigines when its independence was fully established—yet his private partialities were from the first at war with the dictates of his ambition and his policy. He had been educated in one of the leading Whig families of Connecticut; he had fought side by side with the colonial troops in "the old French war;" and though he had derived preferment, fortune, and influence from his connexion with the officers of the crown, yet his old friends and neighbours in the valley of the Mohawk were adherents of the popular cause; and, save among the powerful family of the Johnsons, his nearest and dearest friends, the comrades of his hunts, the companions of his youth, were banded together against the party which he had joined. What wonder, then, that when the storm of revolution was about to burst upon his native valley, Brant should shrink from imbruing his hands in "the blood of its inhabitants, sprung from the same soil, though of a different lineage from himself?

These considerations will sufficiently account for the noble Mohawk so long endeavouring to temporise with the patriot party; and, when finally taking up arms with the loyalists, presenting himself with a few followers, instead of bringing his whole power into the field, after having already made a proud display of his warriors in his celebrated pacific interview with the republican general, Herkimer. It would appear, however, from some of his numerous letters still extant, that true Indian policy was not a little mingled with the unwillingness he showed to procure the gathering of the tribes, when all of the Iroquois confederates, with the exception of the single canton already mentioned, were eager to lift the hatchet for the mother country.

Brant thought that the family quarrel was of doubtful duration, and he was unwilling that the brunt of it should fall upon his people until England had tried what she could do to repress the rebellion in the province of New York, without having recourse to the aid of the Indians. He left it, therefore, for Colonel Guy Johnson to collect the warriors of the Six Nations, while he, with a chosen band of his own Mohawks, hovered near the border, watching the turn events might take, and still secure in the deep forests where we have first introduced him to the reader.

These mountain wilds, which are now chiefly embraced in the counties of Montgomery, Herkimer, and Hamilton, still preserve much of their savage and romantic character; but, at the day of which we write, they were almost inaccessible to any but an Indian or a hunter of the border. Here the chieftain held his woodland court, until the issue should be fairly joined between the high parties that now so threateningly lowered upon each other; and here he awaited the fitting moment, when the contest should be fairly begun, to make the most advantageous descent upon the lower country, and, by some brilliant exploit at the first outbreak of Indian hostilities, make good his haughty claim to be considered as the great captain of all the Indian nations that should take up arms on the side of the crown.

In the meantime, however, Sir John Johnson had assiduously kept up his influence with the wary but aspiring *sachem*; not only by a constant correspondence; not only through the various Indian runners who were continually bearing messages between himself and Brant,[1] but also by placing near him a zealous and sagacious Scotch officer, who, being made the bearer of a commission of captain in the royal army, which had been politically bestowed upon Brant, made his way to the camp of the gratified Mohawk, and remained among his people under the easy pretence of wishing to become initiated in the wild sports of the aborigines.

Leaving these two partisans of the royal faction to discuss the tidings which had just been brought them by the moose-hunter, let us now learn their nature by shifting the scene to the valley of the Mohawk, and proceed with the action of our story.

---

1. "The Indians conveyed letters in the heads of their tomahawks and the ornaments worn about their persons."—*Campbell's Annals of Tryon County*.

CHAPTER 3

The Liberty-Tree

Deep in the west, as Independence roves,
His banners planting round the land he loves,
Where Nature sleeps in Eden's infant grace,
In Time's full hour shall spring a glorious race.

                                        Sprague.

Rumours of the first blood shed at Lexington had reached the valley of the Mohawk; but the length of time it required in those days to traverse the intervening country, prevented the story from being soon confirmed in all its particulars; when, one after noon, it was noised abroad that a messenger, direct from the scene of action, would address the friends of liberty at a meeting to be held in front of the stone church at German Flats. The occasion was deemed a good one, by the leading Whigs of the neighbourhood, for carrying into effect a favourite political ceremony of the day, which should at once mark their own adherence to the popular cause, and, by its boldness, encourage and confirm their wavering friends. To further which intention, placards and notices were industriously circulated, inviting the people to "assemble unarmed, for the purpose of peaceable deliberation, and also *to erect a liberty-pole!*"

The yeomanry of the valley had been frequently thus convened of late, to pass some vote of censure upon the acts of the British *ministry* (for here, as elsewhere throughout the provinces, during the early stages of the Revolution, the name of the king was studiously omitted in all the attacks upon his government); and, like well-schooled fencers closely practised in mock-combat, the thoroughly organised community was versed in political discussion and habituated to public business, long before its ability for self-government was tested in a real struggle with established power. But the measure now in contemplation was a direct assault upon the dignity of the crown; and the call "to assemble unarmed for the purpose of *peaceable deliberation*" was too flimsy a covering for the treasonable deed to which it was meant only as a precursor—the raising openly the great emblem of rebellion.

Many, therefore, shook their heads, and stood aloof from those who, they thought, were rashly precipitating matters to a crisis. Some doubted whether an immediate revulsion of public feeling might not result from carrying proceedings at once so far. Some actually felt this revulsion, and stood prepared to co-operate with the Tory magistracy in crushing so daring an outbreak of faction. But others, who, from the first, had counselled more daring measures, and had lately hung back in disgust at the cautious, and, apparently, reluctant movements with which they thought their leaders had impelled the ball of revolution, were now emulous to spring forward and take their place among the most active in hurrying it onward. While others, again, knowing no other principle than the love of change, no impulse save that of curiosity, were urged, by the novelty of the occasion, to be spectators of a scene, where, if sympathetic excitement should impel them to become actors, circumstances would determine the part they should play.

Such an assemblage was the true field for a popular orator to prove his powers; and tradition still tells of the eloquence which wrought upon those materials, and moulded and moved the mass as one man, on that day. Tradition, too, tells especially of one speaker—a youth of scarce twenty summers—a shy student from Schenectady, who, fired by the impassioned appeals of older and more practised orators, burst through the bashfulness of inexperienced youth, and, leaping upon the rostrum, poured forth a flood of eloquence that hurried along the most sluggish natures upon its irresistible tide.

"Who," said a bystander to a sturdy hunter, who, with mouth agape, and eyes riveted, as if by magic, upon the speaker, stood leaning upon his rifle near, "who in all natur is that springald with sich a tongue?"

"Why, Adam, is it you, man, that axes me who young *Greyslaer*, of Hawksnest, is? You've seen me teaching the boy afore now, when he came up to Johnstown in his hollowdays, and, thof he be grown a bit, you ought to know my old scholard."

"Lor! Balt, that ain't the bookish chap that you larnt the rifle to? The bold younker that stood the brunt, when scapegrace Dirk de Roos got into that scrape in old Sir William's time?"

"I tell you it is, though," said the woodsman, proudly; "and a right proper shot I made of him. You see, now, how he plumps his argerments right into the bull's-eye of the matter."

"Sarting! he does make a clean go-ahead of it. But when did he come up here to mix in our doings?"

"He? why, man, he's been here this four week, and came up too with the Congress's commission in his pocket, to raise a company. Who but him was it that Sir John raised a rumpus with at the training last week? Ah! if the boy only had as good laming with the sword as he has with the rifle, the baronet could never have filliped it out of his hands so sarcily as he did."

"Oh! yes, I heerd of that, Balt, as also how you came near having your heels lifted higher than your head, for threatning to blow Sir John clean through if he did not let the stripling go."

"I'd like to see the day when any of Sir John's folks would try to back that brag of his'n. I'd a mounted him upon the spot only for making it, but the people said 'twas only words, and I must not mind sich, and go and make further fuss, seeing we had got young Max out o' his hands. But hist! what's the lad saying now?"

"I mistrust that that's the Yankee messenger he's introducing to the people," said Adam, in a modest whisper; for the hunter had gained tenfold in the respect of the simple yeoman since this popular display of his pupil.

"Behold," cried the speaker, interrupting himself in the midst of a bold apostrophe to Liberty, whom he pictured as hovering over the land with wings that shadowed it but for a moment, until she could alight in peace and safety: "Behold the harbinger of her first triumph! fevered with haste, worn with impatient travel, he comes, like the victorious courier from Marathon of old, to tell of Freedom's bloody dawn at Lexington. Up, man, up, and tell a tale that never can grow old, but freshens from the frequent telling;" and, suiting the action to the word, the youth, carried away by the enthusiasm of the moment, seized the courier by the wrist, and dragged the embarrassed man forward.

"Now that awkward loon, Adam," said the hunter, "will make a botch of the hull business. A murrain on the Bosting folks that sent a critter what couldn't speak."

"Why, Balt, I guess they want all their speakers to hum, and raaly I don't see but this chap has done all in natur that was required of him, in coming here so quick. It wan't judgmatical in young Max to expect more from him, and pull the fellow up there to gape about like a treed 'possum."

The orator appeared himself to be instantly aware of his error, and, even while the worthy Adam was commenting upon it, had, with ready tact, turned the poor fellow's confusion to advantage. "What!" he cried, "bewildered, my friend, by the crowd of heads you see below? This stout array of gallant yeomen, the bone and sinew of our land, numbers not half of those devoted to our cause, that will soon pour from every glen and mountain near; men with tongues as slow as yours to boast their deeds, but having still the iron will to work them; men with arms as strong as yours to raise the tree of Liberty, and hearts as true to guard it."

A deafening shout of applause burst from the multitude almost before the last words had passed the speaker's lips. The stout-limbed New Englander, changed at once from a shamefaced rustic into the hero of the scene, threw up his head, broadened his chest, and displayed his stalwart frame with honest vanity. Then, as if wit had been suddenly born of praise so well applied, he leaped from the scaffold, and seizing a tall hickory, which, freshly deracinated, was held erect by some labourers near, he bore it, amid the plaudits of the crowd, to a hole that had been previously prepared, and, spurning the aid of some tackle erected upon the spot, tossed the heavy sapling from his shoulders, and planted it pointing to the skies.

The centre of attraction was now changed, as the crowd collected around the spot, while those who stood nearest were active in throwing earth and stones around the roots, to secure the tree in its position. The preconcerted act of rebellion for which they had chiefly met was fully and successfully consummated, but any farther measures which might have been contemplated by the leaders of the assemblage, were at this moment summarily discomfited.

The trampling of hoofs, and the dust arising from a large body of horsemen at a turning of the road, gave the first intimation of the approach of the royalists, while proclaiming that they came in sufficient force to crush any violent outbreak of insurrection. There was a momentary panic in the assemblage, and, before they could recover from the surprise, Sir John Johnson, with a large body of retainers armed with sword and pistol, rode into the midst of the unarmed multitude. He was followed by Colonels Claus, Butler, and Guy Johnson, a civil magistrate by the name of Fenton, and other Tory gentlemen of the county, each backed by a strong party of followers similarly armed, who successively drew up in military array so as nearly to encircle the astounded Whigs.

"What mummery is this?" demanded the haughty baronet, glancing round fiercely at those who stood near the Liberty-tree, while more than one, over awed by his bearing, attempted to slink away in the crowd. A stout Whig, by the name of Sammons, stepped boldly forward to make reply; but, before he could ascend the stage to place himself upon a level with his mounted adversaries, Sir John had thrown himself from his horse, and occupied the place from which Greyslaer and the Boston emissary had descended a few moments before. Without noticing the movement of Sammons, he at once commenced haranguing the people with great vehemence. He appealed to the ancient love they had borne his family, rehearsed the virtues of his father, once so popular throughout the valley, and exhorted them still to sustain the established magistracy, which had ever kept their best interests at heart.

Finding, then, that the attempt to address their affections and re-kindle the faded ashes of loyalty met with no response, he endeavoured to awaken their fears. He dwelt upon the strength and power of the king, and painted in strong colours the folly of opposing his officers and revolting against the crown. But the assemblage was still mute; the approving plaudits of his own partisans called forth no echo from the moody and stubborn Whigs.

Irritated at their sullen obstinacy, Johnson now turned disdainfully from the "motley crew of would-be patriots," as he in derision termed the multitude generally, and poured out his invective upon their leaders. The shrewd New England features of the Bostonian next caught his attention, and the sharp eye of Sir John instantly detected something in the man's air or apparel which might have escaped any gentleman but the owner of beeves and hemlock forests, whose revenue depends so much upon the trade of a tanner.

"Who," he asked, scornfully levelling his finger at the stout yeoman, "who are the real leaders of your mongrel crew, the vultures that ye bring hither to hatch the egg of treason, that creatures as foul and contemptible have thrust into our nest of peace and loyalty? An itinerant New England leather-dresser! a vagrant peddler of rebellion! that could only retail his wares to such offscourings of society as many I see around me, if men whose education should teach them better, had not misled the gallant yeomanry, that I grieve to find in such disgraceful company. You have had your musters, too, your military gatherings, your array of fools, that would fain play the soldier, with such a beard-less stripling as that to lead them. I know the boy!" cried he, with a smile of scorn, pointing to Greyslaer, who stood with folded arms and compressed lips, as if with difficulty restraining the ire that boiled within him. "I know the boy; I knew him in old Sir William's time, who was once dear to all of you; he was whipped then by my father's overseer for plundering an orchard! Pity that the lash had not—"

"Liar and villain!" shouted Greyslaer, springing forward toward the stage.

"Seize the traitor!" cried Sir John, striking at the youth with the butt of a loaded whip. Actively evading the blow, Greyslaer succeeded in getting one foot on the scaffold, but the next instant the sturdy baronet had fastened a grip upon his throat, and flung him backward into the arms of one of his myrmidons, who quickly placed himself astride the prostrate stripling.

"She must keep quiet now, or te tirk will pin her," said the brawny Highlander, who held him thus in durance, smiling grimly the while at the in effectual efforts of Greyslaer to free himself, in spite of the drawn dagger that flashed before his eyes. The trusty Gael, in the mean-time, might have felt less comfortable in his position, had he known that he was covered by the deadly aim of the hunter Balt, whose cool discretion prevented him from firing, save in the last extremity.

The benignant Mr. Fenton pressed near to Sir John, as if about to intercede in some way, but the arrogant soldier heeded not his well-meant offices. An indignant murmur arose among the Whigs at wit-nessing this scene; and, upon a slight movement made among them, weapons were drawn, and a low browed, lank-haired, saturnine man, whose age might be somewhere about thirty, a trooper in Colonel Butler's train, spurring to the front, snapped his pistol in the face of a bystander. He was instantly reprimanded in sharp terms by his supe-rior.

"What! fire on an unarmed man, Walter? Shame on ye for one wearing the king's livery! May I eat hay with a horse, if I suffer such a thing among my riders, Watty."

"We shall have to cut these rebel throats sooner or later," replied the man, doggedly, "and it matters not when the business is begun."

"Shame, shame," cried Mr. Fenton.

"Walter Bradshawe," said Greyslaer, without making an effort to rise or gain any advantage to protect himself from the consequences of what he was about to say, "you, though so much my senior, were for months my mate at school. I knew you, too, as an aspiring attorney's clerk in my first years at college; your political career has since made your name common in the mouths of all men, and there must be others here who know you full as well as I; and when I say that, as boy and man, you were ever a brute and a ruffian, there's not a man present that can gainsay my words."

"Tut, tut, boys," cried Colonel Butler, restraining a fierce movement of his subaltern, "may I eat hay with a horse, but this is a foolish pair on ye here. There's trouble enough without your brawling, and you may soon have an opportunity of fighting out your quarrel in the name of king and country, without troubling older people with your capers."

A glance of deadly hatred from Bradshawe, which was returned with one of utter scorn from his quondam schoolmate, was all the reply the young men made to this speech. In the meantime, notwithstanding the dismay which the sudden appearance of the armed royalists had inspired, there were no signs of dispersion among the patriot assemblage. A few craven spirits had, indeed, slunk away, but their absence was more than supplied by a number of sturdy countrymen, in the guise of hunters, who, with rifle on shoulder, came straggling into the scene of action, as if brought thither only by accident or curiosity. The Tories, who had trusted only to their arms to give them a superiority over the party, which from the first outnumbered them, began soon to be aware that they were fast losing their only advantage; and Colonel Guy Johnson, acting in his capacity of a county magistrate, saw that it was true policy to close by an act of civil authority the duties which had been entered upon with a less peaceful mission. He therefore addressed the people anew, but in terms more soothing than those which had been adopted by his kinsman the baronet; though, like him, he commenced by trying to awaken their old feelings of feudal attachment to his family.

He spoke of the affection which they had always borne to his father-in-law, Sir William Johnson, now but a few months deceased, and who was believed to have been brought to his grave from anxiety of spirit at the perturbation of the times, and the struggle between loyalty and patriotism, as the crisis approached when he should be compelled to decide between his king and his country. He said that he saw many around him who were the old friends and playmates of his youth, and who, till the last, had always been cherished guests at his table. And he appealed particularly to the influential families of the Fondas, the Harpers, the Campbells, and the Sammonses, several members of which were afterward so distinguished in the border war of Tryon County, to unite with him in his exertions to prevent the effusion of blood among their mutual kindred and neighbours. Finally, after regretting the necessity of placing young Greyslaer in the custody of the sheriff until he could be tried by his country in fair proceedings at law, he made a signal to Sir John, who had already placed the prisoner on horseback in the midst of his retainers, and bowing politely to the company, the complaisant colonel moved off in the rear of his retiring party.

The people, in the meantime, either too much confused by the unexpected events which had succeeded each other, or confounded by the fair and polite words which had last been addressed to them, made no movement to the rescue. But the sound of the retiring troopers had scarcely died upon the ear, before a deep murmur of disapprobation pervaded the assemblage. Some reproached each other with pusillanimity in having looked so calmly upon the scene which had just been enacted before them. Those who were armed were told that they should never have permitted one of their friends to be thus torn from among them.

And those who had been instrumental in getting up the meeting without providing for such an exigency, were rebuked by the riflemen, who had come last upon the scene of action, because they did not direct them what part to take when the difficulty came on, of whose origin the newcomers were themselves ignorant. These mutual bickerings and recriminations, however, which only temporarily suspended the unanimity of council, resulted at last in a general call for immediate action. Everyone agreed that young Greyslaer must be at once delivered from the hands of the Johnsons, who, notwithstanding their promises, would doubtless seize the first opportunity of transporting the youth to Canada, where, if his fate were a no more cruel one than perpetual imprisonment, he would be at least utterly lost to the cause.

The hunter Balt, who had stood moodily looking on without taking any share in these discussions, seemed to catch new life from the determination, when announced.

"I don't know," said he, looking round, "whether or not ye all mean to stick to what you say; though I hope so, raally. But I do know, that if young Max Greyslaer be not as free as any man here, afore one wilted leaf of this tree falls to the ground, I'll water it with the best blood of the best Tory in the county! That's right, Adam, jist empty another gourd upon the roots, the poor thing looks thirsty."

How the hunter's vow, and the resolve of his excited compatriots, were carried into effect, may be best told in another chapter.

CHAPTER 4

The First Shot

From man to man and house to house, like fire
The kindling impulse flew; till every hind,
Scarce conscious why, handles his targe and bow,
Still talks of change.

Hillhouse.

It was the middle watch of a summer's night. The shadows lay deep on fell and forest; but above, the waning moon shone bravely out in the blue heavens. The night was calm; so calm, so still, that the murmur of myriads of insects grating their wings amid the leaves, made, as it were, "a silence audible." As the moon gradually approached the horizon, leaving the stars only to gladden the welkin, this creeping symphony appeared gradually to have its concord broken in upon by sounds which, though similar in character, did not completely harmonize with the others. A humming noise, like that of a huge beetle booming through the air, first broke the tiny chorus.

It was answered by the harsh discord of a locust, who seemed to rap his wings with angry impatience, like some old fellow jostled by his mate in the midst of a nap. His ire was reproved by a pert young katydid, whose shrill tones indicated that her wings were only half grown, and that the froward thing must be the earliest of the season. Then followed sundry orchestral croaks of a tree-toad, which in turn were replied to by the deep diapason of some sturdy bullfrog. At last the feathered tribe seemed preparing to join in this nocturnal concert. The timid and delicate note of the night-sparrow, rising distinctly fine from a clump of maples, was answered by the shrill and petulant cry of the whippoorwill from the lower boughs of a broad-armed oak, that stood singly in an open glade of the forest.

With the last call the woods became suddenly mute, but the next moment the spot was alive with a dozen dusky figures that glided from the adjacent thickets towards the trysting-tree.

"Well answered, my mates," cried an active woodsman, leaping from the oak into the midst of them; "are we all together? I see nothing around me but hunting-shirts. Ah! all right," he added, as some thirty men, in parties of three each, came cautiously forward from blind by-path and tangled forest lair, where the hunters had answered each other's signals while guiding the rest to the place of rendezvous.

One of the last comers, who were all in the ordinary dress of citizens or plain farmers, now advanced to the first speaker, and, catching his hand, said, while wringing it cordially, "Most neatly managed, my sturdy Balt. You have brought us safely and quietly together when I apprehended the worst from the outlying spies of Sir John's Indian rabble. And now, gentlemen, as you have chosen me your leader in this business, I pledge my life to its accomplishment under the present auspices."

"Why, you see I told you, Major Sammons, that we hunters didn't live among the Injuns for nothin', for where'd be the use of consorting with the red skins if you didn't catch some of their edication from the cunning varmints? And you've all seen tonight that the woods afford calls, jist as many and as good calls as a bugle has, for making men act in concert, where they can't see a signal no how. But now my say's over; and let's hear the crowing of the game-cock of Caughnawaugha—axing your pardon, major, for the freedom."

"Are we all armed?" said Sammons, glancing around the group; "Colonel Fonda, you and young Derrick de Roos have, of course, your side-arms with you."

"Ay, ay, sword and pistol both for me. But carry on, carry on, major, we are all ready, man, and up to anything; carry on, carry on." The gay youth who thus spoke with so little show of deference to his seniors, was a curly-headed, fair-faced gallant of about three and twenty. His features were frank and good-humoured, and certainly prepossessing in the main, though something of sensuality, if not of dissoluteness, in their cast, slightly vulgarized by broadening their natural recklessness of expression.

"Peace for the nonce, mad Dirk," cried Sammons, somewhat impatiently. "Kit Lansingh," he continued, turning to a tall and modest-looking young hunter in a green rifle frock, "you are a model for such younkers to dress their manners by. Captain Vischer, Helmer, Veeder,

I see you are prepared. Ah! Adam, that was well thought; you are not used to a sword, and your pitchfork may do good service. Bleecker, you must lay aside that fusee, or draw the charge; not a shot must be fired unless Balt and his hunters, who are to cover *our* retreat, should find it necessary to use their rifles. Doctor, we'll trust you with your pistols; but, remember, they must remain in your belt. Clyde, your axe is well thought of; but where's Wentz with his crowbar?"

"Black Jake has the crow, and I've brought along this suckling trip-hammer with me."

As the brawny blacksmith answered thus, he raised a ponderous sledge from the sod upon which it rested, and threw it into the hollow of his arm as carelessly as if it were some light bauble he was handling.

With these, and a few more brief and rapidly given directions, the Whig leader soon marshalled his zealous forces, a large proportion of which had come a day's journey or more through the woods to the place of rendezvous, some two miles west of Johnstown.

A short walk of a few minutes found the party in the immediate neighbourhood of Sir John Johnson's fortified mansion, when a halt was ordered for the purpose of adopting some new precautions in making the circuit of the building.

"Now, major," whispered Balt, approaching the ear of the leader, "if you'll only say the word, we'll make a clean business of it at once. Here are fifty as good fellows as you'll find in old Tryon. Sir John has but a hundred of his Highlanders with him; and when I pick off that sentinel whose blunderbuss gleams agin the casement yonder, you've only to dash right into the hall and take the bloody Tory, with all his papish crew."

"The time is not yet come for that, my worthy fellow," answered Colonel Fonda, who overheard the request; "Sir John is an old neighbour of many of us. His father was the friend of my father; he was born here in the valley among us; his mother was one of our own people; he may yet think better of his course, and determine to act with his countrymen against the tyrannical ministry."

"The colonel says right," rejoined Sammons. "And though Sir John has already dealt harshly with me and my brothers during the troubles, yet I am not the man to hurry him on to his fate, and make him irretrievably commit himself on the wrong side of the quarrel. No; let us pass on, my friend; we came only to rescue Max Greyslaer, and we will harm no one save those who interfere in the attempt to liberate him."

And adding aloud some words, which were intended as much to regulate the over-excited zeal of his younger followers as to repress that of the daring woodsman, he dismissed the subject by giving the order to advance. Throwing, then, the old mill that was in use in Sir William's time, between themselves and the hall, the party followed down the rivulet north of the house, till they reached the little bridge, memorable for Sir John's horse having fallen dead upon it while spurring vainly to reach the bed side of his dying father, a few years before the period of our story; and shortly after the whole band entered the village of Johnstown.

The slumbering inhabitants little dreamed of the bold deed that was meditated in the midst of them, as the conspirators glided through their silent streets. The party reached the jail, which stood in rather an isolated position near the southeastern corner of the town, and no one was yet disturbed. They drew up in the shadow of the building, stationing themselves before an iron wicket within a few yards of the main entrance; the hunter Balt, at the instance of his leader, advanced to the outer door to try the effect of a parley with the jailer. A rap with his ponderous knuckles upon the oaken door brought only a hollow echo from within; and Balt, after vainly waiting a moment or two for a more satisfactory answer, applied his lips to the keyhole.

"Mike, Michael," he cried; "Michael, I say! the blasted paddy's asleep. Jake, move hither with your crowbar—softly though—he hears."

"I hear ye, ye loon ye; what the de'il d'ye want with Mike at this hour of the night; a murrain upon ye!"

"Mike, my good fellow, I come with a message from the hall, and you must let me in instantly."

"From the hall, eh? ye landloper; I'll hall ye, if I get hold of your ugly self the morrow. Sir John doesn't often send midnight messages to old Mike in these times; you've come on a fool's business, and that's your own, misther."

"I know, I know you, foolish Mike; but there's been a rising below of the Whi—, I mean the rebels. Yorpy, the half-breed, has just brought the news from Caughnawaugha, and Sir John wishes to move young Greyslaer to the hall for safer keeping."

"Let him send the sheriff, then, or a sargeant's guard of his Scotchmen; the lazy loons have nothing better to do than play sodger there from one week's end to the other. Deil a bit will Michael open jail till he does. So clear out wi' ye, or I'll unchain the dog through the

36

wicket."

As the sturdy jailer pronounced these words, a deep-mouthed mastiff, who had hitherto been snuffing impatiently beneath the door, uttered a fierce growl, and seeing, with the sagacity of his race, that no exit was to be had this way, ran round to the wicket and commenced barking furiously at the party which was crowded near it.

"Curse the brute," said Balt; "will no one stop his mouth with a pitchfork?"

"Balt, your profanity would bring a blight on the most righteous cause," said the leader, sternly; "stand back, and let Jake heave the door at once with his crow; no time is to be lost."

A sinewy *mulatto*, whose muscles, long exercised in the toil of a journeyman blacksmith, seemed to have assimilated to the tough material in which he worked, moved to the spot and struck the crowbar between the door and the lintel. But the blow, though repeated for the second and third time, seemed to produce but little effect, until his master, rushing forward, threw his whole weight into his gigantic sledge-hammer, in the same moment that the *mulatto* summoned all his force for one more effort. The door went down crashing inward, while poor Jake, who pitched himself fairly within the entrance, was saluted on his sconce by the jailer with a huge bunch of keys, which would have crushed the scull of any other than a negro, and which made Jake measure his length upon the floor.

"Harm not the faithful Irishman," cried Colonel Fonda, arresting with his hand the uplifted hammer of the blacksmith; "the brave fellow has only done his duty."

"Thank yere honour," answered Mike, making a reverence as he felt his heart touched in the right place, and quietly submitting to be secured by the overwhelming force which surrounded him; "thank yere honour kindly; rebel or no rebel, ye're jist the gintleman that Mike would take service under, if Sir John was not a kind of third part countryman, and me beholden to him upon the top o' that, yere honour," added he, raising his voice, as the colonel, who had seized the jailer's lantern, now gained the top of the staircase.

"Max, my boy, Max Greyslaer, where are you?" shouted Balt; "whistle but once from your perch, my young hawk o' the mountain, and—ah, Jake, your toothpick's the thing;" and, interrupting himself, as he suddenly clutched the crowbar from the negro, he dashed in a panel of the first door near him, and the liberated young patriot was the next moment overwhelmed with the congratulations of his friends.

Elated with their success, but still conscious that these lawless proceedings might recoil severely upon themselves, the band of Whigs unanimously determined to seize the sheriff, who had been the willing instrument of the Johnsons in depriving Greyslaer of his liberty, and hold him as an hostage for their own safety. This gentleman, a brave and zealous loyalist, chanced to be absent from home, passing the night with his friends at the hall. But his house was left in charge of one of his myrmidons, equally determined in character with the sheriff himself.

This redoubtable fellow, of German parentage, and who, under the name of Wolfert Valtmeyer, or Red Wolfert, as he was more generally called, became afterward the terror of the border, was a hunter by profession; and, though impatient of restraint, reckless of temper, and wholly undisciplined in character for the ordinary purposes of social life, he was well suited, not less by his remarkable strength and activity, than by his hardihood and love of daring enterprise, to fill the station of a bailiff among the frontier community around him. In this capacity he had, in former years, been frequently retained upon an emergency, when his services were temporarily in demand; but the life of a free hunter was so dear to him that he could never be persuaded to undertake the permanent duties of a sheriff's officer. Indeed, the love of his personal liberty and freedom from all responsibility was so strong in Valtmeyer's bosom, that it seemed to leave room for one only other sentiment—a grasping desire after gold to procure him immunity from labour, and the free indulgence of his lawless pleasures.

Wolfert Valtmeyer, being such as we have described him, was not long in making up his mind which of the two contending civil factions to side with. For, while property, and the consequent means of rewarding his services, was in his county chiefly on the side of the Tories, he was already indebted to some leading individuals among this party for rescuing him from punishment as a felon, and conniving at his escape to a distant part of the country. Rumours of his death were subsequently put in circulation, while all legal investigation gradually died away so completely, that Valtmeyer now ventured, amid the confusion of the times, to steal back to his old haunts, and even offer his secret services to the magistracy of the county. Though the difficulties with the crown had so lately commenced, yet he had already given signal proofs of his zeal in sustaining the royal cause; nor was he wanting in courage and conduct upon the present occasion.

The house of his principal being sufficiently far from the jail for

Valtmeyer not to overhear the commotion that had already taken place, he was awakened in the dead of the night by the angry shouts and imprecations of the crowd that rushed thither, and called from beneath the windows for the sheriff; but, undismayed equally by the suddenness of the attack and the strength of those who came in such force to assail the person whom he represented, Valtmeyer only greeted the uproar with a muttered oath or two, as he prepared to meet the occasion.

"*Heilege Kreuz Donnerwetter!* but I will make the hide of one hound smoke for it;" and, growling thus, he leaped half naked from his bed, snatched a loaded pistol from its case, and threw open the window-sash. "Now, *verftuchter kerl*, look well to thyself," muttered the ruffian, as he singled out for his aim the leader of the party, who was standing in the porch apart from his followers. Raising his voice then, and at the same time imitating, as nearly as possible, that of the absent sheriff,

"Is that you, Sammons?" he cried.

"Yes," was the prompt reply.

"Then take that for a d——d burglarious rebel."

A ball whizzed past the head of the sturdy Whig, and buried itself in the doorpost beside him. "This," says the historian, "was the first shot fired in the Revolution west of the Hudson."

Though happily uninjured by the bullet, yet it glanced so near that the patriot leader recoiled as it grazed his temples, and his followers, thinking that he was about to fall, forgot, in the quick thirst of vengeance, the order they had received from his lips an hour before. A dozen rifles were instantly discharged into the open window, but a scornful shout from the bold Tory within told that their fire was ineffectual. A tumultuous rush at the door was the next movement of the infuriated crowd. It was quickly burst open, and the fate of Valtmeyer turned upon a single cast. The foremost of the assailing party were already upon the staircase, and making their way to his bedroom, when the report of a distant cannon proclaimed that their volley of firearms had been heard beyond the precincts of the village, and that the Tories would soon be upon them.

"Back men, back; heard ye not our signal for retiring? 'Tis the alarm gun fired at the Hall by Sir John. Balt, Adam, down with ye at once! Lansingh, Greyslaer, call off our friends, or we shall have the bluff Highlanders upon us to spoil our night's work before we regain the woods."

"Don't ye hear the major, Squire Dirk?" cried Balt, throwing his arms around that rash youth, who still attempted to push through the crowd and mount the stairs in the very teeth of the order that had just been given by his leader; and lifting young De Roos fairly from his feet, the stalwart hunter urged the others before him through the door, and was himself the last to retire from the scene.

CHAPTER 5

Evening Visitors

Our fortress is the good green wood,
Our tent the cypress-tree,
We know the forest round us
As seamen know the sea;
We know its walls of thorny vines,
Its glades of reedy grass,
Its safe and silent islands
Within the deep morass.

Bryant.

"I rayther guess," quoth Balt, when the party had all, by different routes, arrived at last at their place of rendezvous in a moonlit glade of the forest, "I rayther guess that we've stirred the game right in airnest this night, and the best thing we can do to morrow is to commence running balls for a good long hunt."

"Our sturdy friend speaks truly, gentlemen," said the leader of the party, gravely, "and Heaven only knows how the 'long hunt,' as he terms it, may terminate,"

"Be the issue what it may," exclaimed Greyslaer, in tones of deep fervour, while his earnest eye kindled with enthusiasm, "the game's afoot, and whether it lead to freedom or the grave, we must hence-forth follow the chase."

"Why the devil, Max, do you put on the phiz of a parson when using the lingo of a sportsman?" cried the gay Derrick de Roos. "It becomes the old cocks, who have drawn apart to prose under the tree yonder, to look sermons, as well as preach them; but for us, man, for mettlesome chaps like us, why—

We hunters who follow the chase, the chase

41

Ride ever with Care a race, a race,
And we reck not, &c., &c."

And the rattling youngster, to the great delight of old Balt and some of the juniors, and the equal annoyance of Greyslaer and other more thoughtful members of the party, ran through a verse or two of a popular hunting song, long since forgotten.

"Well, Mr. de Roos," said Colonel Fonda, coming forward from the group, in whose councils Greyslaer seemed to be taking an active part, from the impatient glances he from time to time cast over his shoulder at the singer, from whose side he had in the meantime withdrawn; "well, sir, we have determined to take decided measures for ascertaining the real state of the county, and putting our friends upon their guard, and your father's house is spoken of as the place of our next meeting on Thursday night."

"The old man will be proud to entertain your friends and mine, Colonel Fonda; and yet," added the young man, with a degree of hesitation that showed more considerateness than might have been expected from *his* conduct a moment before; "Hawksnest is the property of my father's ward, Max Greyslaer there; and, after what has passed this night, an overt act of rebellion by the present ten ant, in harbouring traitors, as the Tories call us, might make poor Max forfeit his acres, in case the ministry get the better in this family quarrel; some of the grasping rogues begin already to talk of sequestrations and such matters, you know."

Greyslaer, upon overhearing these remarks, advanced, and whispered to his friend, "If you be not quizzing, according to your wont, Dirk, I congratulate you upon the seasonable return to gravity which your speech evinces. But, gentlemen," he continued, raising his voice as he turned to his other compatriots, "I shall consider your confidence withdrawn from me, as one unworthy to share it, if the hint suggested by my friend De Roos—I doubt not in all kindness—be allowed to have a moment's weight with you. My honour is already committed in the cause you have espoused; my life I here pledge to it, and he can be no friend to Max Greyslaer who holds his fortune dearer than his life or his honour!"

These words, not less than the spirited tone in which they were pronounced, terminated at once all doubts as to the propriety of the step that was meditated; and the discussion, as well as the events of the evening, seemed at an end. The hunter Balt, who had lounged about the while, without venturing to intrude his advice upon those more fitted by education than himself for council, now brightened up, and shook off the air of listlessness that had crept over him. He struck the butt of his rifle smartly upon the sod, and surveying it affectionately for a moment, as he held it thus at arm's length perpendicular to the ground, as if to catch inspiration from the gaze, he with becoming gravity thus delivered himself:

Well, I only wanted to see folks get through with their parrorching, for you see I'm no great hand at making a speech; I've been here to your public meetings and there to your public meetings, and I never felt in my heart as if natur called upon me to say anything; for when natur does call, and right in airnest, she apeaks out of the mouths of hunters as well as of babes and sucklings. She doesn't care, I say, much, when she's right in airnest, what sort o' tool she works with; jist as I've seen a good hunter, who had got out of powder when ravin distracted hungry, bring down a buck as slick with a bow and arrow as if it had been his own rifle, and that, too, when he had never used the ridiculous thing in his life afore. Well, as I said, I'm tired of this etarnal parrorching about the country's troubles; I only wanted to see folks begin to make a raal thing of it, and then Tender-Tavy—I call the iron crittur after this fashion, gentlemen, partly out o' respect to Miss Octavia, old Deacon Wingear, the tavern-keeper's darter, and partly because the barrel is of so soft a natur that I can chip it with my hunting knife. I say, that when once there was a raal rising of the Whigs, then this here rifle—

Interrupting himself at the word, Balt clapped to his shoulder the reputable weapon of which he spake, and glancing along the barrel as it gleamed in the moonlight, beckoned with his forefinger to a shadowy figure that stood motionless beneath a spreading chestnut within the range of his fire, "Come in, ye varmint, come in, ye lurching mouser from old Nick's pantry, ye pisoned scum of the devil's copper caldron; come in, ye scouting redskin, or Tender-Tavy shall blow a hole through ye."

"Fire not, Balt," cried Greyslaer and De Roos, both leaping at the same moment before the levelled gun; "'tis the noble Oneida Teondetha." And the two young men bounded forward with outstretched arms to greet their Indian friend.

"Bah! only an Oneida," said the rifleman, dropping his piece in a tone of sullen disappointment; "I wouldn't harm the boy, pervided he comes as a friend; but, youngsters, though you seem to be so mighty fond of him, when you know as much of the woods as old Balt, you'll larn that the less one has to do with an Injun the better. *Let every man stick to his colour*, is my motto."

The momentary flash of anger that distorted the smooth and bland features of the Indian, showed that he partially understood the disparaging words of the white hunter; but the disturbed expression passed away as the gentlemen of the party, unheeding the rude remarks of Balt, advanced with eager cordiality successively, and gave their hands to the new comer.

"And what news brings my young brother from his people?" said Greyslaer, addressing the Oneida in his own language.

"The song of evil birds has been heard in the lodges of the Ongwi-Honwi. The Oneidas only, of all the Six Nations, have shut their ears against it. Their hearts bleed to know that the rest of their countrymen are bent upon rooting out the sons of Corlaer from the land. The Oneidas will not help to destroy a people born on the same soil with themselves. Their wise men say, it were better at once to extinguish the great council fire that has burned for centuries at Onondaga, and thus dissolve the league of the Aganuschion. The Oneidas are unwilling to take up the hatchet against their former brothers, whether red or white; but they warn you that Thayendanagea has sold the Mohawks to the Sagernash king, and that they now walk with your enemies."

"What! Brant actually up in arms!" exclaimed a dozen voices, when Greyslaer had interpreted the information to his friends.

"He flits along the border like a foul bird in scent of carrion. He watches the smoke of your lodges; and, if their hearth-fires be unguarded, he will swoop like that night-hawk upon your women and little ones," replied the Indian, as a dusky bird pounced greedily upon a swarm of gnats that hovered near.

"The wily knave must be looked after instantly, gentlemen; we must lose no time in collecting information respecting his movements, and determine upon active measures at the next meeting of our friends. But as yet we are all in the dark. If you, Mr. de Roos, will take a scout of a dozen men with you, and bring us some tidings of this dangerous chieftain, it will give more shape to our proceedings. This friendly Oneida will doubtless, with Balt and some of his comrades, volunteer—"

"Axing your pardon, colonel, Balt don't go scouting with an Injun in the party. Tender-Tavy doesn't know much difference atwixt one copper face and another, and she'd be jist as like as not, in a dark swamp, to mistake that sleek chap for one of Brant's people, and go off of herself. So there's an eend o' the matter." And the woodsman, crossing his legs, leaned moodily upon his rifle, with an air of dogged determination to which there was no reply.

"If Balt chooses," said Greyslaer, "I would rather have him with me, as I shall find difficulty in getting my company together without assistance in time for the meeting."

"I don't see that, capting, as folks are now engaged in harvesting, and you'll find them pretty much, here and there, in bunches, helping one another. But I feel sarcy-able in persuading some of your wild chaps to come along, that I guess won't move from their homes at this season for your order, no how."

"For God's sake, then, go with Greyslaer, you self-willed old bear. Let's to other matters, gentlemen," cried De Roos, impatiently.

"If I am an old bear, I never hugged you to harm you, young squire, when I used to carry you as a petted brat to see me shoot pigeons from a bough-house; besides lots of dandling in other ways that you've had in these old—paws!"

"True, true, my excellent friend," answered De Roos, good humouredly, while with difficulty restraining a laugh at the ludicrous words and accompanying gesture with which the stout-fisted woods man concluded his mortified appeal to the better feelings of the other. "I spoke but in jest, Balt, or, at least, too hastily. And now, carry on, boys, carry on; Kit Lansingh, Helmer, Bleecker, Conyne, which of you lads are ready to take duty under my command, for twenty-four hours, while we look after Brant up by the Garoga lakes?"

Twenty voices instantly replied, all expressing their readiness to go upon the scout; and De Roos's only difficulty was, to select from the number those best suited to such an expedition.

"Well, gentlemen," said Mr. Sammons, who was only the temporary leader of the party, and whom we ought, perhaps, according to the worshipful custom of our country, still to distinguish by his militia title of major, "I believe we now all understand each other, and had better disperse to our houses; those of us who live near will see if they cannot furnish a bed to our friends who have come from a distance on the good errand of this night. Perhaps, though, Mr. de Roos proposes a night march with some of you?"

The young partisan needed not the hint to spur his zeal, but, warmly seconded by his followers, he drew off at once, and took his way through the woods with his party, trolling as he went a voyageur's song of the Mohawk boatmen, in which his favourite slang phrase seemed to make the burden of the chorus:

Carry on, carry on, 'tis the word that will bear,
From one bright moment pass'd to another as fair,
So lift the canoe, lads, and traverse the brake,
Though we're leaving the river we'll launch on the lake;
The portage is made, boys, the forest is gone,
Now bend to your oars, carry on, carry on.

The low-voiced chant of the retiring party soon died away in the distance, and their departure was the signal for breaking up the assemblage, and the other patriots soon dispersed, the majority taking their route towards Caughnawaugha, and others moving off in different directions, two and three together, until Balt and Greyslaer were soon left the only tenants of the spot.

"It wants yet some hours of the dawn, capting, and I propose sleeping them off in the woods, because it's the best way of getting an airly start in the morning. And we may perhaps have a good deal of footing to do about among the farms on the off settlements tomorrow, afore we can get your men together. But this here is no sort of place to camp in, with the trails of fifty men leading to it on all sides. There's a dry swale on the other side of yon hill, where one of my old shanties is probably yet standing, and we'll jist take ourselves there as soon as may be.

"I used to have shanties like this all about among these hills wherever my traps were set, though none so near the settlements as this," continued the hunter, when they had gained a rocky dell, where the frame of a wretched wigwam, partially covered with birch bark, was discernible to Greyslaer after he got within a few feet of it. "You see, now, capting, the comfort to a man who shanties out as much as I do, of having a home all fixed and ready for you. Here, now, is dried venison in my katchy (*caché*), under those leaves, if the wood-mice haven't got at it. There, too, I've laid away some—but darn those gnats, I must make a smudge afore we do anything else."

With these words, Balt proceeded to strike a light; and kindling first some dry leaves, he scraped the moss from a moist stump near, and covering up the flame with the damp material, the thick fumes of his "smudge" soon caused the insects to disappear. Greyslaer, in the mean time, had stretched himself upon some hemlock boughs, spread out beneath the shed of bark, which was barely ample enough to keep off the dews of night; and having refreshed himself upon the fare which the hunter drew from his *caché*, he observed to Balt, as the latter threw a fresh handful of leaves upon the smouldering flame, "That a hunter's fire was a sort of company for him, when passing a night in the solitudes of the wilderness."

"Jist the best sort of company a man can have, capting, if he would exercise a free and independent privilege of choosing his own. They say, you know, that the devil hates all flames save those that are kindled by himself; and in my hunts among the wild hills away to the north of us, I never shanty out without a large fire, even in midsummer. I may be kind o' particular in this matter, but ever since I got so terribly scared five years ago, I always love the light of a big fire to sleep by."

Greyslaer, instantly suspecting that the bluff woodsman, like many a man equally bold, was the victim of superstitious terrors, asked, with some curiosity, what it was that had thus inspired him with a fear of sleeping in darkness, when Balt, after a preliminary hem or two, thus told his story.

"Why, you see, I had gone clean up to Racket Lake to make out a pack of deer-skins for a Scotch trader at Schenectady, hoping to get a few beaver, at the same time, on my own account. Well, I might ha' been in the woods a week or more, engaged about my consarns, when, one day, after trampoosing over a pretty smart space of country, looking after my different traps, and, not having seen a single deer through the livelong day, I came, about nightfall, to a bark shanty, where some hunter had made a pretty good camp for the night, and left it standing. I was tired and disappinted; and, as I hadn't spirit enough left in me even to skin a chipmunk, if I hadn't a' found this lodge I should have laid myself down, like a tired hound, and slept anywhere.

"But now I began to think that all sorts of luck hadn't left me, and I spunked up and looked about to see how I could best make myself comfortable for the night. I had shot a brace of ducks during the day, and the first thing to do was to build a fire and cook 'em. But, as I had left my hatchet at the camp from which I started in the morning, thinking to return there and sleep, it cost me a heap of trouble collecting such dead branches as I could lay my hands upon, and dragging 'em together before the shanty. And here was a pretty how-de-do when I got 'em there; the man that built the shed must have been a born nateral to choose such a place for it. For, instead of picking out a patch of firm airth whereon he might build a fire judgmatically, he had laid the logs right down on a piece of deep, mucky soil, made up of old roots, rotten leaves, and sich things as go to make up a soil only fit to raise toadstools, ghost moccasins, or timber so spongy and good for nothing, no one can tell why natur produces it.

"Well, true enough, his fire had burned right down four feet deep into the ground, through such truck as that; and I, of consekins, must either remove the shanty, or go to work to get rid of the hole, before building my fire, if I expected to get any heat from it; and the night was pison cold, I tell ye. So, having no shovel to fill up the pit with airth, and ne'er an axe to fell a tree across it, I goes mousing about, in the dark, after old rotten stumps and fallen trunks, whose mossy wrappings keep them damp through and through the year round, and slimy roots, which, if they hadn't snakes under them to nibble my fingers while tearing them up in the dark, yet felt, for all the world, like raal sarpents in the handling. All sich like truck that I could lay my hands upon, I managed, with pretty hard work, to drag together, so as nearly to fill up the hole, and, placing my dry wood upon it, I lit my fire.

"Well, after eating one of my ducks, I dressed and roasted the other, so as to have him ready for my breakfast in the morning; and then, as I put my feet to the fire and laid myself down to sleep, I felt right comfortable. I slept and I slept, and I don't know for how long, but it must have been a pretty likely nap, howsomdever. Long enough for my fire to burn so low as to get pretty deep down the hole. But the first thing that I remember, before I waked and diskivered that, was my dreaming of being chased by wild Injuns, who came whooping and yelling after me as if crazy to get my scalp. '*Howh*,' '*howh*' '*howh*,' the sound went clean down into my ears; and, waking with a start, I saw a pair of bright black eyes glaring at me.

"Had I used my own judgmatically, I might have diskivered that these belonged to a great antlered buck that was standing with his fore feet fairly upon the ashes of my fire, which made his eyes gleam unnaterally as he looked straight into mine. But, half awake, and flurried as I was, I snatched up a brand and flung it, with all my might, into his face; and then, as the poor brute scoured off, '*howh*,' '*howh*,' '*howh*,' a pack of wolves came ravening on his track; *tramp, tramp*, I heard them, nearer and nearer, until, fifty in number, they dashed furiously by my fire, making the bushes fairly *winkle* as their black troop swept howling on.

"Sarting, capting! I trembled like a leaf that time, I did, until the opposite mountain threw back the last shrieking echo from its side. I don't think I ever knew exactly what a raal scaring was afore that night; but, since then, I always keep up light enough to let inquiring varmint see that it's Balt the hunter who is sleeping in the neighbour-hood, with Tender-Tavy by his side. What, capting, snoring already! Well, if my story has put the lad to sleep, it hasn't been wasted to no purpose, howsomdever."

And with these last muttered words, after mending his "smudge" with a few handfuls of fresh moss, the good-natured hunter lay down, and was soon dreaming with his comrade.

CHAPTER 6

Preparations for a Foray

Fiercely they trim their crested hair,
The sanguine battle stains prepare,
And martial gear, while over all
Proud waves the feathery coronal.
Their peäg belts are girt for fight,
Their loaded pouches slung aright,
The musket's tube is bright and true,
The tomahawk is sharped anew,
And counsels stern and flashing eyes
Betoken dangerous enterprise.

Yamoyden.

Let us now return to the wild-wood scenery of our opening chapter. The events recorded in those which have followed it, were, as the reader will readily imagine, the tidings which had been brought to Thayendanagea by the Indian runner. The daring acts of the Whigs had equally awakened the indignation and the alarm of the royalist, and the message from Sir John declared the country to be in a state of actual revolution, and called upon Brant, as an adherent to the government, to move at once with his power to its support. It conveyed, too, some slight reproach for the coolness with which he had hitherto held himself aloof from the troubles which an armed force might have awed into quiet; and hinted that the best service that the chief could now render to approve his loyalty, would be to seize upon some prominent disaffected persons of the county, and hand them over to the king's magistrates as hostages for the conduct of their friends and kindred. The heir of Hawksnest, especially, was mentioned as a fierce zealot and turbulent young demagogue, whom it was well to remove from his present sphere of mischief as soon as possible.

The task thus enjoined upon Brant was a favourite proceeding with the Tories throughout the war of the Revolution, and was often but too successful in its results. In the province of New York, hundreds were, from time to time, suddenly and secretly torn from among their friends, and carried away to captivity or death. Nor was there any feature of the civil war, during that painful seven years' struggle, more appalling than this. The boldness of the act—for it was frequently practised in the most populous districts, in an armed neighbourhood, in the very capital of the province itself—struck dismay into the families of those who were thus abducted, and the cruel doubt and mystery which shrouded their fate was not less frightful; for while some, with shattered constitutions and spirits broken by confinement, returned from the prisons of Canada after the war was over, yet many were never heard of by their friends from the moment of their disappearance, and their destiny is enigmatical to this day.

Nor was it only the influential partisan or his active adherent that was thus subjected to this hideous, because secret, danger. The hostages, as they were called—the victims, as they were in reality—were taken, like those of the secret tribunal in Germany, from either sex and from any class of society. The homes of the aged and infirm—of the young and the lovely, were alike subject to the terrible visitation. The gay guest, who waved a blithe *adieu* to the friends who were but now planning some merry-meeting for the morrow, was seen to mount his horse and turn some angle of the road in safety, but the steed and his rider were never traced afterward. The hospitable, festive host, who left the revel for a moment to cool his temples in the evening air, and whose careless jest, as he passed to the porch without, still rung in the ears of his impatient friends, never again touched with his lips the glass that had been filled for him in his absence. The waking infant cried vainly for the nursing mother, who had left it to be watched by another for a moment. The distracted bridegroom and fierce brother sought vainly for the maid, whose bridal toilet seemed just to have been completed, when, by in visible hands, she was spirited away from her father's halls.

"We begin our career of arms together with a painful duty, Captain Brant," said MacDonald, after the chief had expressed his determination to move instantly upon the settlements in the direction of the Hawksnest. "I think I have heard you speak of having been upon friendly terms with the present tenant of this property, who, if I mistake not, was one of your nearest neighbours upon the river side."

"I mean not in any way to harm old Mr. de Roos; but this met-tlesome young Greyslaer must be re moved, or he will only qualify his neck for the halter by stirring up more treason. I shall attempt to decoy him from the house, or, failing in that, will surprise it with so strong a party as to make resistance hopeless; and we shall merely ruf-fle the nerves of his friends a little in seizing the springald," replied Brant, coolly.

"Are there no females in the family?" asked the European, with some anxiety.

"Yes; there are two, a pair of sisters, mated in love as closely as the kissing blossoms that tuft a single twig in April; but no more matched in character than is the oriole, whose lazy nest swings from the bough beneath him, with the eagle, whose majestic wing is circling yonder mountain. Yet the pale girl, whom they call Tyntie, is a fair and gentle lady, and her kindness has been owned by more than one woman of my own kindred. But Alida, that queenly, stag-eyed creature—surely, captain, you have heard of the beautiful and haughty Alida de Roos; she for whom my madcap son has conceived so strange a hatred."

"Of which of his sons speaks the noble Thayendanagea?"

"Of that dark and dangerous boy whom Bradshawe has spoiled by encouraging in his wild doings; of him who nearly compromised his father's honour and a chieftain's name by consorting with the ruffian Valtmeyer."

"Valtmeyer? surely, this is not the lady whom Valtmeyer wronged so deeply, when Bradshawe saved his neck from the gallows?"

"The same."

"I have heard the story," said the Scotchman, musingly; "I have heard the dreadful tale. But, after being outraged so cruelly, I should have looked rather for her resemblance in the fragile, fading girl of whom you first spoke, than in the blooming creature you describe as her sister."

"Miss de Roos was scarcely more than a child when the affair hap-pened. Years have passed since then. Time will do much with sorrow, pride, perhaps, more. But, if you had ever marked the bright and glassy glare of Alida's ayes, you would have thought of those whom we In-dians believe have become the tabernacles of another spirit than that which first possessed the body; and such a spirit, 'tis said, no mortal grief can overshadow."

"A beautiful superstition to assuage the horrors of lunacy, but too fanciful for truth. I have heard, indeed, of men with souls so haughty that they would never entertain a grief, if its memory were linked with shame to themselves or lineage, especially if the consciousness of unmerited obloquy or the keen hope of ultimate revenge buoyed up their sanguine nature. But with a woman of blighted honour—"

"You may hold there, MacDonald. That proud girl could never be made to believe that aught of reproach has assailed her name; though her slim sister, they say, faints at the sound of Valtmeyer's name, and has pined away from the moment the ruthless villain crossed Alida's path."

"Good God! was there no brother, no kinsman to look after this horrible business?"

"Not one save the old father, who lived so retired that the story never reached his ears; for Alida was off on a visit to some friends in a distant settlement when the abduction took place. Her brother, young Derrick, then but a child, was with Greyslaer, his father's ward, at school at Albany. And he has turned out such a fiery fellow since he came to man's estate, that no one now would dare to hint the matter to him."

"And had the family not one friend to lift an arm in such a quarrel? and yet indeed it were a delicate business to meddle with," said MacDonald, doubtingly.

"They had two," answered Brant, with some hesitation; "two friends to whom the country people looked for dragging the offender to justice. One of them, Walter Bradshawe, who was said to be wooing the young lady at the time. But he never moved in the matter, save secretly, to use his influence in Valtmeyer's favour."

"The base mongrel! And what said men of such a recreant?"

"His conduct was known but to few, and those said it sprung from a mean spirit of vengeance for having been rejected by the lady. But this may have been mere calumny, for parties were running high at the time; Bradshawe was never popular, and being a candidate for public office, his character was roughly handled."

"You have said the De Roos family had two friends they might have looked to. Had the other one, then, no influence with the magistracy of the country?"

"He had," said Brant, again hesitating, with some emotion, before he made his reply; "he was connected with them both by alliance, by political position, and by official station; and were not the honour of his blood involved in the inquiry, no feeling of paternal

53

tenderness would have prevented him from cutting off his misbegotten offspring with his own hand. And yet the Spirit above us knows I love that wayward boy." The chieftain seemed now deeply agitated for a moment, and then turning suddenly, so as to fix his eagle glance full upon the eye of his companion, he added, in a stern and almost fierce tone, "I have answered your inquiries, sir, from no mere prating spirit that feeds an idle curiosity. You have formed a sudden intimacy with Au-neh-yesh; I would warn you, as a gallant soldier of the king and a friend of the Mohawk, against the son of my own bosom. But though the unnatural boy has twice attempted his father's life, yet one whisper that attaches infamy to the blood of Thayendanagea will bring veng—"

"Spare the threat, noble *sachem*; your secret is ever safe with me. I cannot be too grateful for the confidence you have this day reposed in me; yet I cannot think there is anything of malignancy, much less of meanness, in the character of Isaac Brant, or Au-neh-yesh, as you prefer calling him. God forbid that I should attempt to palliate his unnatural conduct towards his father. But phrensied as are the passions of youth, yet—"

"Enough!" said the chief, in a tone so emphatic as at once to cut short the discussion; and then striding forward impatiently, as if to get beyond the reach of a reply from his companion, he added, in a low and tremulous, but still distinct voice: "The friend of Thayendanagea will bury this subject for ever in his own bosom."

A few moments afterward the two partisans reached the clearing upon the Sacondaga, where the principal warriors of Brant had taken up a strong position in an elbow of the river, fortifying their camp with mounds and palisades after the military custom of the Six Nations.

The day was now long past the meridian, and the chieftain lost no time in making his preparations for a movement upon the settlements of the "German Flats" on the morrow. After a brief harangue to his followers, he drew out a select band of warriors, his son Au-neh-yesh being one of the number, for the proposed expedition; and straightway commenced the fantastic pageant incident to the setting out of a war-party at the commencement of an Indian campaign; while Mac-Donald, surveying the spectacle with a curious eye, was not a little surprised to witness the almost childish zeal with which Thayendanagea took his full part in the savage mummery. A strange and bombastic metamorphosis seemed to have come over the reasoning companion with whom he had hither to been acquainted; so changed, indeed, did the whole man seem within one brief hour, that the wondering Scot could scarcely recognise in him the person with whom he had lately walked conversing.

"This Mohawk," said MacDonald, mentally, "with all his talents and attainments, can never be given as an instance of the capacity of his race for civilization. The man seems to have two natures; or, rather, the artificial character, produced by education, is as distinct from his Indian nature as if it belonged to another person. And if they do ever mingle, it is only as I have sometimes seen the blood of a European veining, without suffusing, the cheek of a half-breed."

This opinion of the shrewd Scotchman seems to have been subsequently borne out by the singular incongruities which characterized the career of the remarkable person of whom it was pronounced; and the historian of the times still hesitates in what light to regard him who is described by many of his contemporaries "as a mere cruel, coarse-minded savage," at the very time when the chief enjoyed the friendship of some of the most chivalric hearts, and could boast an intimate correspondence with some of the most polished minds of Europe.

The sun had got low in the heavens by the time the warriors were all arrayed for battle, and the important task of putting on the war-paint concluded. His level beams shot through the tree-tops on the opposite shore, and glancing luridly upon the broad stream that flowed in front of the Iroquois camp, lighted up a grotesque array of forms and faces, mirrored in every variety of attitude in the tranquil river.

"Good!" said an Indian, who had just completed his barbaric toilet, and still lingered, surveying the result, with childish gratification, in the tide that rolled at his feet, "very good; Squinandosh is a great man. The Sacondaga is a happy stream, to reflect a face so terrible as his. Go, river, and bear his image in thy current while men tremble along thy shores as they see it float by. Go, river, and tell the great lake into which thou pourest, that thou hast seen Squinandosh."

"Who is greater than Kan-au-gou?" cried another, rising with solemn gravity from the position in which he had crouched, "the bravest of the men who surpass all others. He paints not, he, to make his features terrible, but to hide the countenance, from which, if seen, his enemies would fly so fast his bullets would never overtake them."

"Behold, Au-neh-yesh! look well upon the tall one," said a third warrior, with the same Homeric diffidence of self-praise. "It is the blood of fifty white warriors that sprinkles his forehead. I hear their widows and children howling after their scalps, which shall dry in the smoke of his lodge; but what hand shall ever reach up to the scalp of him who walks with his head among the clouds?"

One youth, more sentimentally given, seemed to regret only that there were no fair ones present to yield their admiration to the gallant figure that he made in his own eyes. Rejoicing in the possession of a bit of broken looking-glass, this animated personage paused ever and anon to elaborate his toilet with some additional grace, as he strutted about like a bantam cock, exclaiming: "Where are the maids of the Mohawk, who love to look upon such a man as 'Le-petit-soldat?' Where is Tze-gwinda, the fawn-eyed girl of the Unadilla, and she whose feet move like a tripping brook, when the hawks-bells tinkle around her slender ankles in the dance, the laughing Ivalette? Where Waneka, of the willowy form, and 'Cherie,' whose eyes outsparkled those of Ononthio's daughters at Montreal? Where is she whose foot-falls leave no print behind them on the greensward or snowdrift; she who steals upon men's hearts they know not whence or how, where is 'The Spreading Dew?' Let each of them come, look upon 'Le-petit-soldat,' and sigh to be the squaw of such a warrior."

"The Little Opossum is a great painter," added yet another of these heroic worthies; "none but a medicine can find out his secret for mixing colours. Owaneyo has not yet breathed in the nostrils of the man that is meant to kill him. This island has but one such warrior. Who but 'The Little Opossum,' can kill 'The Little Opossum?'"

As the night closed in they lighted their torches, formed of the pitchy knots of the yellow pine; and their barbaric boasting grew still more extravagant as they tossed them wildly in the war-dance. But here the demoniac forms, the distorted features, and ferocious gesticulations, as they moved in savage measure to the deep roll of the Indian drum, gave at least a fiendish dignity to the scene in the eyes of the European. It seemed as if the yawning earth had released a troop of demons from below to practise for a while their mad antics in the upper air; and the Briton shuddered as he thought of such a hellish crew being let loose to work their will upon his rebellious countrymen.

There was a heavy rain during the night, and many of these gallantly-apparelled warriors, who slept in their war-dresses, looked sadly bedraggled, after an hour's march through the dripping forest the next morning; but their appearance was still sufficiently formidable to awaken the admiration of the martial Scotchman; and their military order, their silence, and precision of movement, in obedience to each command of their leader, when they were once fairly started upon the war-path, struck him as characterizing a race who were soldiers, both by nature and education.

But among no martial people of whom history preserves a record were there severer disciplinarians than among those semi-civilized tribes which are known by the generic name of the Iroquois; a stern and stoical people, whose peculiar institutions and Spartan-like character—for their discipline extended to all the relations of life—have been so ignorantly confounded with the loose customs of the more mercurial races, the mere barbaric tribes that are still scattered over the northern and western parts of this continent. Many, indeed, have denied the superiority of the Six Nations over other aboriginal races, and questioned the degree of civilization which they had reached, because it was not progressive; because the era of the Revolution found them with the same social habits that are ascribed to them by the earliest writers who make mention of the Iroquois.

But if that anomalous and remarkable feature of the respect paid to women[1] among them were wanting to confute this position, how, it might be asked, how can that nation be progressive in civilization which makes war the end of all its efforts for improvement, instead of keeping prepared for it merely as the means of preserving the blessings of peace? which encourages agriculture, and builds granaries, only for the supply of armies, and explores the navigable waters of a vast continent, not for the purposes of trade, but to secure the transportation of those munitions which may enable its forces to keep the field through a succession of campaigns? Yet such was the policy which enabled the Six Nations to carry their conquering arms through every region that is now comprehended in this widespread Union; and which made them formidable, not only to the wild tribes far west of the Mississippi, but to the Frenchman of the St. Lawrence, the Englishman of the Chesapeake, and the Spaniard of Mexico.

The Scottish soldier listened with thrilling interest to the wild and warlike tales of distant forays, as Thayendanegea beguiled the march by dwelling upon the former glories of his people. Their religion and laws were frequently the subject of his inquiries; and, strange and un-

---

1. The written treaties of the Five Nations, preserved among the government archives, always open with, "We, the *sachems* and principal *women* of the Five Nations," &c.

57

couth as many of their observances appeared to him, he had travelled too widely over the earth to judge peculiar usages by the narrow standard of his own national customs. The partisans talked next of the civil war, whose outbreak, so long threatening, seemed now at hand; and the sagacious and comprehensive views of the chieftain were not thrown away upon his experienced companion, though more than once a strange discord was struck in the bosom of the latter by the ferocious sentiments that gleamed through the polished language of his Indian comrade.

MacDonald, though a soldier of fortune, had never been engaged in quite so disagreeable a business before. For, though upon the same side with a majority of his Catholic countrymen, yet there were great numbers of Cameronian Scotch acting with the Whigs; and, Jacobite as he was, he felt that there was a difference between battling with an opposite faction at Culloden and cutting the throats of countrymen who, like himself, had come to find a peaceful home in a strange land. This not unnatural feeling of compunction was brought out more strongly by a fierce reply which Brant made to some observation of his about the relations of friendship in which the chieftain had recently stood towards those with whom he must now come in immediate collision.

"And what," said the Mohawk, "what are private ties in times like these, when those of nations are so rudely severed? Do you expect an Indian to play the woman, when you white men have forgotten all the claims of blood and kindred in this strange quarrel with each other? If the wolf devour his own whelps, why should the panther spare them, merely because they are tenants of the same forest with himself?"

But the night has again closed in around us, and the prowling Indian has reached the fold he would plunder.

CHAPTER 7

The Rifling of the Hawksnest

A crash! They've forced the door, and then
One long, long shrill and piercing scream
Comes thrilling through the growl of men.
              'Tis hers!
                        Dana.

The Farmer's Homestead, from which the estate of Greyslaer took its name, lay upon the banks of the Mohawk, immediately at the mouth of one of those wooded gorges through which the tributaries of the river descend from the mountains of Montgomery to unite with the parent stream. The broad, low-eaved mansion reposed in a rich alluvial meadow, amid a clump of weeping elms; the luxuriancy of whose foliage betrayed the neighbourhood of the brook that watered their roots; and which, descending impatiently amid the copses of hazel and wild cherry, from the upland in the rear of the house, glided slowly and noiselessly through the green pastures, as if unwilling at the last to merge its current into the broader stream beyond.

"Here," said Thayendanagea to his European friend, when, having stationed his band in the under wood that lined the sides of the gorge, he began to move cautiously toward the house, accompanied only by MacDonald; "here is the Hawksnest of which I have spoken, and within an hour we will clip the wings of the wildest of the falcon brood."

The two royalists now approached the house with the most stealthy caution, and by glancing from one outbuilding to another, keeping always within their shadow, they at last attained a position in which, screened behind a trellis covered by gourds and hop-vines, that sheltered the cottage-like porch, they could easily look into the low windows of the mansion.

The scene thus witnessed brought so vividly to mind the recollections of his early home, that the British officer again shrunk from the stern task in which he had consented to share. The window opened into a large room wainscoted with black walnut, whose dusky panels were relieved here and there by the glimmer of a brass-mounted press, or an antique *beaufet* with its attendant service of painted china, and other furniture of European manufacture, which had probably been brought from his fatherland by the first owner of the dwelling. There was no carpet upon the floor of the apartment, which seemed to be a sort of hall, or common sitting-room of the family, and a large ducking-gun supported upon a magnificent pair of antlers over the fireplace, with other appointments and trophies of the chase, indicated the predominant tastes of its customary male occupants.

But there were traces also of the presence of woman in this rural household, in the framed needle-work that adorned the walls, the vase of freshly-gathered flowers upon the mantelpiece, and, above all, in the general air of neatness that pervaded its simple arrangements. Nor did MacDonald long doubt to whom these slight but indubitable evidences of feminine taste were owing, when he gazed upon the occupants of the apartment. These were an aged man and his two daughters. A white-haired patriarch, who sat a little aloof from the table, at which a slight-made, invalid-looking girl was seated, reading aloud, while the other, a dark-eyed, luxuriant beauty, stood reeling some coloured worsted from the back of a chair.

The glow of health, the purple light of youth, the pride of rich, resistless womanhood, seemed all mantling in the cheek and animating the person of the latter; and when the European gazed upon her haughty, intellectual brow, her mouth, whose ripe and melting softness was still redeemed from all weakness of expression by something wayward and aspiring even in its smiles; when glancing from her white and exquisitely turned shoulders, just touched by the light which polished her velvet bodice, he looked to the noble contour of her person, brought out as it was by the position in which she stood, with one fairy foot upraised upon the lower rung of the chair before her, the portrait of more than one proud dame of princely courts rose freshly radiant to his view; while the pale, passionless-looking girl, upon whom the old father gazed with eyes of such affectionate interest, seemed the far fitter tenant of an abode so obscure.

"It is, indeed, a cruel duty, *sachem*, to disturb such a home as that," he whispered to his companion.

"Yes, but still it is a duty," muttered the Indian, sternly.

"And yet not necessarily ours tonight; the young man whom you seek is evidently not at home; for see, now, the tall girl has laid aside her work; they are preparing for family prayers, yet Greyslaer is still absent."

"Speak lower," said Brant, in a suppressed tone, which sounded like the hissing of a serpent in the ear of the other; "that tall girl could wield the souls of a hundred rebels with her eyes! She must be placed out of the way till these fanatic boys of the same traitorous household recover their senses. Nay! murmur not at this decision; a hair of her head shall not be injured. But, hist, what noise is that?" he added, turning round as he retired a few paces from the trellis, which interposed its leafy curtain between him and the window.

"It is only some of your followers; you told them to approach for the seizure, the moment that the rising moon should cast her first beam above yon clump of maples."

"Yes, but she yet lacks a hand's breadth of gaining the top of the sugar-bush, and that tramp is never made by an Indian *moccasin.*"

As the chieftain spoke, the sharp crack of a rifle, followed instantly by the wild whoop of Indian warfare, rang out on the night air, while a young warrior, whose approach had been hitherto unobserved by Thayendanagea himself, stood suddenly before them.

"A party of Corlaer's fighting men! but we outnumber them. Our warriors sent me to ask leave to fight, but the foe has stirred their covert before the message could reach my father."

"And where was Au-neh-yesh, not to know of their approach?" fiercely asked the chief of his son, in their own language.

"Au-neh-yesh watched upon the hills above the waterfall; Kan-au-gou in the fields below. The sons of Corlaer came up the bed of the running water, and Kan-au-gou must have mistaken the plashing of footsteps on one side for the ripple of waters on the other."

"It is well; let our people stand fast till they hear my signal from the hill behind them, and then disperse as best they may."

The chieftain spoke, and Au-neh-yesh disappeared on the instant. "And now, Captain MacDonald," said Brant, "we have not a moment to lose in securing our captive, while my young men keep the rebels at bay. Nay, I pledge myself to the girl's safety," he added, with a gesture of impatience, observing still symptoms of reluctance in his coadjutor.

But the feat, so often afterward, during the war, accomplished by

61

Brant with such consummate address, was fated, in the present instance, to a more serious result than could have been anticipated.

Of the different parties of Whigs, who, according to previous concert, were to rendezvous at the Hawksnest this evening, that of Greyslaer was the only one which, for reasons that will be hereafter mentioned, moved to the proposed conference. It was well that the band was better armed and better ordered than were most yeomanry corps at the commencement of our civil struggle, and that they were commanded by one who, on this night, gave as signal proofs of his quickness of resource and ability as a partisan soldier, as he had formerly shown evidence of high moral courage upon the occasions we have already noticed.

The twenty-four hours which had elapsed since his deliverance from the myrmidons of Sir John Johnson, Greyslaer knew afforded sufficient time for that vigilant loyalist to obtain information of the proceedings of the patriot party, and to adopt measures to prevent the proposed meeting. This, in the excited state of popular feeling, could scarcely be effected by an open exercise of his authority as a magistrate. A stroke of address in seizing the rebel ringleaders, or the cutting off the different parties in detail, by way laying them on their approach to the rendezvous, seemed the only movement that could serve his purpose. Fearful, therefore, of an ambuscade, Greyslaer had exercised the greatest caution in approaching the scene of danger.

Marching warily along the banks of the river, until he came within half a mile of his destination, he had turned aside upon reaching the mouth of the tributary before mentioned; and, making the bed of the smaller stream his highway, had struck inland towards the hill, so as, by a serpentine course, to approach the house from the rear. These precautions, however, would only have served to throw him into the midst of Brant's party, which, intent upon the operation which had brought their chief to the spot, lay concealed upon the banks of the brook where it first descended to the lowlands, if the military foresight of the young partisan had not added another safeguard to his march by throwing out a picket upon either side of the stream.

The worthy Balt, who chanced to be one of the two persons detailed upon this duty, used always to quote his deeds of this night in illustration of a favourite assertion of his, that a true woodsman always knew, by instinct, when an Indian was within fifty yards of him. Certain it is, that he had not proceeded in advance of his comrades a hundred yards up the stream, when a faint whistle, like that of a woodcock settling in a cornfield when a summer shower has lured him from his favourite morass, caused an instant halt of his party. The call was answered by an Indian, who, rising slowly from a brake, showed his shaven crown, for a moment, in the moonlight, and then slunk back to his cover, as if having, for the instant, mistaken the call of a real bird for the signal of some comrade come to relieve him at his post.

Some three minutes were now passed by Greyslaer's party in breathless attention for another signal. These were so skilfully employed by the woodsman in gliding towards his foe, that they measured the mortal existence of the unhappy Indian. A short and desperate struggle, a smothered cry, and the crashing of branches, as a heavy-body rolled through the thicket into the water, finished the career of the warrior Kan-au-gou.

"Thank your stars, boys, that your lives are not trusted to such a stupid lout as that," whispered Balt, joining his party the next instant. "Capting, that chap was painted for a war-party, and you may depend there is more vermilion in the neighbourhood. The red devils must be beyond the rifts upon the hill above us; God knows how many of 'em; but the best thing we can do is to change our course, and strike straight through the fields to the homestead, where we can stand a siege, if the worst come to the worst."

Greyslaer nodded approval, and instantly gave the necessary order; while his men silently deployed from the bed of the stream, and ascended the bank, preparatory to making a swift movement across the meadows to the house. Two fields, separated by a high rail-fence, laid "worm-fashion," intervened between them and the homestead, and it was the sound of their feet, in running across the first field, which caught the quick ear of Thayendanagea, and in the same moment alarmed his ambushed followers. Au-neh-yesh, by the order of one of the chiefs, had bounded off, on the instant, to communicate with the *sachem*, and had nearly reached the house, when, casting his eyes behind him, he beheld Greyslaer's party in the act of surmounting the division-fence we have mentioned.

Without waiting to select his man, he instantly fired upon them, and the shot produced at once the effect intended by the keen-witted savage. The whites, finding themselves thus at tacked in the direction of the house, deemed that it was already in possession of the enemy. They faltered in their advance, and then, as a tumultuous yell burst from the thickets on their flank, they formed in the angles of the serpentine fence, as the nearest cover at hand, and poured their fire upon the advancing foe. The Mohawks recoiled on the instant, and both parties lay now protected by their cover, with a broad strip of moonlit meadow between them, into which both were afraid to venture, contenting themselves with keeping up a dropping fire upon each other, as the gleam of weapons betrayed here and there an object to aim at.

The situation of Greyslaer's party seemed now precarious in the extreme.

"The Redskins are surrounding us, captain," said one of the brave but undisciplined yeomanry. "We had better back out by crawling, in the shadow of the fence, to the bushes on the riverside in our rear."

"Rayther," said another, "let us go ahead, and make a clean thing of it, by charging through the varmint in front, and gain the heavy timber in *their* rear."

"Now my say is, boys," quoth Balt, "just to do neither one nor t'other."

"What, then, do you counsel, Balt? for we cannot long maintain ourselves where we lie, if the Indians are in any strength," said Greyslaer.

"Why, the bizness is a bad one, anyhow you can fix it, capting; but I think I understand the caper on't. Don't you see—sarve you right, Bill; I told you they'd spile that hat afore the night was over, if you would pop up your head above the rider instead of firing atween the rails—don't you see that we've only had one shot from the house, while the old fence is already pretty well riddled from the hillside? Well—elevate a little lower, Adam, if it's that skulking fellow by the big elm you're trying for—well, then, as I was saying, it's pretty easy to guess where the strength of the redskins must lie; and I don't see that we can do better than streak it right ahead for the house, and trust to legs and luck for getting safe into it."

The suggestion was too much in accordance with Greyslaer's feelings not to be eagerly caught at by him. Indeed, so overpowering was his anxiety for the beloved inmates of the mansion, that nothing but considerations of duty toward the party who had trusted themselves to his guidance, had hitherto prevented him from dashing forward to his destination at all hazards. But if he had still hesitated as to the course to adopt in the present exigency, all doubt as to his movements was at once dispelled in the moment that Balt finished speaking.

A sound of terror, the shriek of woman in distress, with the hoarse cry of age imploring mercy and assistance, rose suddenly from the dwelling, chilling the blood of some, and making the pulses of others leap with mad and vengeful impatience. And it was then that, bursting simultaneously from their cover, the red man and the white could be seen urging their way with rival fleetness towards the same goal, for the moment apparently regardless of each other's neighbourhood; pausing not to strike down a competitor in the race, but striving only who first could reach the bourne. The one thirsting to share in the massacre that seemed in the act of perpetration; the other burning with fierce impatience to arrest or avenge the butchery of his friends.

A light and agile youth, a fair-haired boy of sixteen, was the first that gained the door of the mansion; but even as he planted his foot upon the threshold, his head was cloven asunder by an Indian tomahawk, and, with limbs quivering in death, his body rolled down the steps, while the exulting savage who dealt the blow leaped over it brandishing his fatal weapon. But his triumph was short. Greyslaer was close upon him, and, as he strained every nerve in rushing forward, he came with his drawn rapier so impetuously upon the Indian, that the point was driven through his back deep into the panel of the door, which burst open from the shock.

Leaving his friends for the moment to make good their entrance as best they could, by opposing their hunting-knives and clubbed rifles to the tomahawks and maces of the Indians, who instantly mingled with them in wild melee around the porch, Greyslaer rushed forward to the sitting-room of the family. He shrunk aghast at the sight of horror which told him that he had come too late. The master of the house lay stunned and senseless upon the floor. Alida, the beautiful Alida, had disappeared; but her fair-haired sister lay weltering in her blood, while a gash across her forehead, with the tangled locks drawn backward from her brow and the print of gory fingers fresh upon the golden tissue, called Greyslaer's eye to a savage, who shook his scalping-knife at him with a hideous grin of disappointed malice as he sprang through the open window. But there was no time now for grief to have its way. The din of the conflict still rose fresh behind him, and Greyslaer turned to the succour of his friends whom it might avail.

"Powder, powder, capting!" shouted Balt, who this moment presented himself. "There's a big redskin keeping three of our men at bay with his tomahawk; I must use him up at once, to give the rest an opportunity of making a rush from the outhouse; our best men are still outside. Bedlow and Boonhoven are both down; but big Hans, the miller, yet holds the door stoutly, and Bill Stacey has gone up with his axe to drop the gutter from the eaves upon the redskins that are hammering at the windows. Ah! there's the tool for my purpose," he added, seizing the ducking gun from the chimney, and throwing down his half-loaded rifle; while Greyslaer had, in the meantime, secured the window through which the ferocious Au-neh-yesh had a moment before made his entrance and escape.

Greyslaer now rushed to support the man who was holding the door against odds so stoutly; while Balt ascended the staircase, freshly priming the ducking gun, and adding a handful of buckshot to the already heavily charged piece as he went. He gained a window in the same moment that Greyslaer, sallying out from the house sword in hand, cut down the sturdy warrior for whom Balt had prepared his charge. A dozen Mohawks instantly rushed forward to avenge the fall of their comrade. But the heavy piece of Balt did good service in the moment, or Greyslaer's career would have been cut short for ever. A shower of buckshot drove them quickly to regain their cover.

"Now, boys," shouted the woodsman, "make a rush for the house, while the red devils digest that peppering."

The handful of outlying whites did not wait for the invitation to be repeated, but rushed pell-mell within the porch so furiously as to bear down each other in the hall, while the sturdy miller made a liberal use of his foot in pushing aside their bodies while shutting the heavy oaken door.

Furious at being thus foiled, the brave Mohawks made a simultaneous rush towards the entrance, when, at that instant, the rude and ponderous gutter, loosened from the eaves, descended with a crash upon their heads; and, with a wild howl of grief and dismay, the survivors of their party drew off their wounded and disabled comrades, and left the stout yeomen masters of the field.

Book Second

CHAPTER 1

The Ruined Homestead

The father gazed in anguish wild,
He pressed the bosom of his child:
There beat no pulse of life.

Yamoyden

The human heart has no more bitter grief than that which springs from the recollection of unkindness toward those who, loving us when living, are now, by the barriers of the grave, placed for ever beyond the reach of our remorseful recollection. But love—whether it be the love of kindred, or the wilder, warmer passion, that more generally bears that name—is ever humble and self-chiding when absent from its object. The heart then forgets the frailties that may at times have shaken its esteem; it softens in degree the faults which have so severely tried its regard, that it cannot but remember them; it pardons every offending quality, that may often have tasked its forbearance, and threatened even the continuance of its tenderness; it imputes to itself all the blame that it has ever attached to the beloved object; and finds an excuse for each caprice of the one who may have trifled with it, in its own unworthiness, to inspire true affection.

It was not unnatural, therefore, that the young Greyslaer, when he surveyed the desolation that had come over the home of Alida, and thought of her as torn from that home, a captive, dependent upon the mercies of the half-civilized Mohawk—it was not unnatural that, while every humane and generous impulse of his heart should be called into action, the more subtile emotions of latent tenderness should also quicken afresh in his bosom.

"She loved me not, she never would have loved me," said the youth, mournfully; "yet, God knows, I would have laid down my life for her.

69

Yes, coldly as she received me the last time I crossed this threshold, and forbidding as I for months have found her whene'er we met, I would give worlds for one haughty and impatient glance, checking my ill-timed assiduities, could she but now sit there in safety to receive them. So noble, so gifted, so gentle, to be torn thus—*gentle?* No, Alida, the word befits not thy proud and aspiring nature! Yet why should I hold her high spirit in reproach, because I may at times have chafed at its imperiousness, and thought that it looked too insolently down upon such a thing as I am? What am *I*, that I should aspire to the love of such a being? What guerdon have I won from glory, what deed of nobleness have I achieved, that I may aspire to mate myself with one whose queen-like step should be upon the neck of emperors?"

And the young man strode to and fro across the apartment with disordered pace and gesticulations that became the extravagance of his language; while desperate resolves and bitter self-reproaches were so wildly mingled in his speech, that one who had never before witnessed the fantastic mood of a lover, would have deemed that, if not the immediate instrument of the calamity that had overtaken his mistress, yet the preferring of his unwelcome suit must be in some way the cause of her disastrous fortunes. But when was there a lover who was not an egotist, or who did not believe that the dream which wraps his senses must somehow shape the destiny of her who inspires the infatuation; who can be made to think that the current of his feelings, like the ocean tides, may reflect the image without influencing the actions of their mistress? But Greyslaer, though the first burst of feeling will ever have its way in one so young in years and new to sorrow, was not a man to waste the moments that were precious, in a lover's idle rhapsodies; nor, indeed, had he given way to even this transient weakness, until he had done all that could be at present accomplished for the distressed household.

The bereaved father, when first brought to his senses, and enabled to recall his share in the events of the night, left little doubt, by his testimony, as to the disposal that had been made of Alida. But the narration was so loose and unconnected, as wrung piecemeal from the broken-hearted old man, that we have ventured to enlarge and connect his relation, in order to make it intelligible to the reader.

The shot and shout which heralded the conflict had struck dismay into the family engaged in the peaceful avocations we have described at the opening of the last chapter. The invalid girl had the moment before laid aside the book which she had been engaged in reading aloud; and her sister, taking a Bible from the chimneypiece, handed it to her father to close the evening with the customary religious service before retiring.

"It would be provoking," remarked Alida, while opening the good book on the table before him, "if some of Derrick's rough comrades should not have heard that the night of the rendezvous was changed, and come and rouse us an hour hence from our slumbers! There's one gallant I wot of, Tyntie," added she, passing her hand archly over the head of her sister, "who would not be sorry for the omission, if it but gave him an excuse for showing his new uniform at Hawksnest."

"Pshaw, sister, you know that young Harper is no more to me than any other young man of the valley that comes to our house. But I am sure that tonight I should be glad to see him or any of the bold friends that Dirk has collected around us in these stormy times. Brave as you are, I don't believe you would have been sorry if, instead of the boy they sent with the note, wise Max Greyslaer had been the bearer of it."

"The striplings are alike to me," said Alida, without noticing the faint smile of the invalid. "As for Greyslaer, he had to go south to the Reinhollow Settlement to get his friends together; and they would have eaten us out of house and home, if we had to keep his hungry hunters over the morrow. But, silly one, think you that, if there were danger, Derrick would have kept aloof himself? Father, let me look again at his note! See, there's nothing to alarm us here," pursued she, reading the missive aloud:

"We shall not disturb the repose of your house tonight, my dear father, as the proposed meeting of the *friends of the king and constitution* is deferred. The ministerial malignants are abroad. Johnson, indeed, still lies, with all his power, at the hall; but his tool, Joseph Brant, has got together some vagabond Mohawks at the north, and has prepared to move tomorrow towards the river. He claims that he and his miscreant followers represent the sentiments of the whole Six Nations; and we are going westward to intercept his march, and seize his person, before he can communicate with the other Indians and work us farther mischief. I always told you, honoured sir, that this precious specimen of the civilized savage would go with the British ministers in their tyrannical attempts to enslave us, and I will make your quondam friend confess as much before tomorrow night, if—"

The sudden report of firearms, followed immediately by the appalling war-whoop, broke off the farther reading of the note, and struck dismay into the defenceless household. The timid Tyntie, pressing her hands to her temples, as if to shut out the fearful sounds, bent her head down to the table, cowering like a frightened bird, hopeless of escape when the fowler is upon her. The old man clasped his hands, and uplifted his aged and prayerful countenance with a look of mute but anxious pleading. Alida only, of the three, seemed to retain the power of action. Pushing the table impatiently from her, she stood, for a moment, with flashing eye and dilated form, and senses all alert, as if, Penthisalea-like, the sounds of approaching combat were music to her soul. Then, as the turmoil of the strife rose nearer and clearer, she cast a hurried look of anxiety at the helpless beings by her side, and rushed to a window to gain intelligence of the extent of the danger.

It was the same window beside which Brant and his Scottish accomplice had planted themselves; and, as impetuously throwing up the sash, she leaned far out to catch a view of the grounds beyond the end of the house, the sinewy arm of the chieftain encircled her waist in a moment, and, incapacitated from resistance alike by surprise and the position in which she stood, she was lifted from her feet by a power that was equally rapid and resistless, and placed in the arms of MacDonald, who, moved but not melted by her shrieks, hurried from the spot with his captive. As for Brant, he had only delayed for a moment to pinion her arms by securing the ends of his knotted baldric, which, unobserved by MacDonald, he had thrown over her shoulders in the moment he seized her person, and then he bounded through the open window into the apartment.

"Joseph Brant!" cried the old man, raising the palms of his hands like one startled by an apparition, and averting his head as if to shut out the conviction of the character in which his former neighbour now presented himself. "Joseph Brant, my enemy!"

"Thayendanagea, your ancient friend," replied the chief, advancing with outstretched hand.

"Off, off, perfidious and ruthless villain. If a father's vengeance could renew the strength in these withered limbs, you durst not—"

"By the eternal spirit of Truth above us, not a hair of your daughter's head, old man, shall come to harm. 'Twas but to prove to you Alida's safety in the hands of Thayendanagea that I have betrayed my share in this night's business; for that, and to assure you of your own, is all—"

"Yes, as the hound protects the hind from the knife of the hunter, when he has driven her into his hands. Off, dog of an Indian, off, wretched mercenary; or, if your power to save be equal to your will to slay, protect yourself at this moment." And seizing a tall andiron from the fireplace, he brandished aloft his awkward weapon, and rushed upon the chieftain. with passion, the feeble old man had summoned all his remaining energy to deal a single blow at the spoiler of his household; and as Brant leaped lightly aside from the descending blow, he fell forward, striking his hoary brow with stunning effect against the iron instrument, which came between his head and the floor.

At this moment, Alida, escaping from the care of MacDonald, presented herself at the window, with the Indian Au-neh-yesh in close pursuit behind her. The ferocious young savage had already raised his tomahawk to strike, and it was only the menacing cry of his chieftain and father which saved the life of the maid. A few hurried words from him told Brant that there was now no time to be lost, if he would secure the only prey yet in his power. He tore the shrieking girl from the window-sill, to which she clung; and lifting her like a child in his arms, rushed through the garden and up the wooded hill in the rear of the house.

The young Mohawk turned to bear back the command of his *sachem* to his party, but catching a glimpse of Tyntie's prostrate form, who still lay lost in the swoon into which the first alarm had thrown her, he could not resist his ferocious propensities, while the tumult of the strife, which at this moment rose nearer and nearer, urged their gratification. He sprang forward, buried his tomahawk in her brain, and, twisting his fingers in her long tresses, had already drawn the scalping knife from his girdle, when Greyslaer's sudden appearance compelled him to seek safety in flight.

The other incidents of the assault have been already detailed to the reader in the previous chapter. The note we have mentioned, which still lay open upon the table, for the first time acquainted Greyslaer with the altered intentions of his friends. But, under existing circumstances, he determined to remain at the Hawksnest, and await their corning on the following day. An attempt to rescue Alida with his present handful of men would, he soon acknowledged, be worse than vain; but he did not abandon the idea, until, by a close examination of the ground, he had made a tolerably accurate estimation of the number of followers Brant had with him, and his means of securing an escape to the upper country. He was even able to trace the footsteps of Alida herself in several places.

But a dog belonging to the household, which had been unchained to assist in the examination, and had proved himself eminently useful in striking the Indian trail in the first instance, and shown his sagacious sympathy in their search by uttering a sharp howl when they first lighted upon the traces of his mistress, disappeared soon afterward amid the darkness of the forest, and the use of the lanterns in groping about added nothing farther to their discoveries when the aid of the animal was withdrawn.

In the meantime, the patriot party took every precaution to secure themselves against a surprise during the night. The windows of the house were strongly barricaded, sentinels were posted, and a shed, with other slight outbuildings, which might cover the approach of an enemy, were levelled with the ground. The body of the unfortunate Tyntie was consigned to the care of a couple of female slaves, whose vociferous grief over the gory remains of their young mistress almost drowned the deep mourning of her stricken-hearted father, who had to be forcibly torn from the body and carried off to another chamber.

After a night made tedious by broken slumbers and harassing dreams, confusedly alternating each other, it was with no slight feeling of relief that Greyslaer hailed the approach of dawn. The summer landscape wore a Sabbath-like stillness, as he gazed upon it from his open window, while inhaling the fresh breeze of morning. The mist-wreaths curling up from the river were the only objects moving, and even these stole off as gently as if fearful of breaking the silence by a more rapid motion; creeping now around some imbowered islet, pausing now to twine for a moment amid the leafy festoons of vines and branching elms upon some jutting promontory, and now circling the brow of one of those cliffs whose craggy and frowning summits give its only feature of sternness to the soft and lovely vale of the Mohawk, and at once dignify and diversify its exquisite landscape.

The heart of the young patriot bled to think that a scene so fair and smiling must be given up to the cruel ravages of war. Of a war too, which, while presenting itself in the worst form of that scourge of humanity, brought with it the threatening horrors of many a savage massacre, superadded to the dire calamity of armed discord among those who call themselves civilized.

"And what," thought Greyslaer, "what are the private griefs of one solitary being like myself, to the sorrows of the thousands whose fate is wound up in this impending struggle; what weighs the present doom of all of us, when balanced in the scales of Omniscient Benevolence, against the welfare of the millions yet unborn, whose destiny hangs upon the success of our endeavour. God of Heaven! but it is a gallant game, a noble stake we play for. But those that come after us! will they prize it when won, will they cherish the glorious guerdon, and remember the deeds and the men who made it theirs? Will they love each rood and inch of their blood-bought patrimony, where every acre that was sown with the dragon teeth of despotism produced its hero? Will they too rear a race of men, fit to be the second crop of a soil so generous? Will the free-born dames of those days, will the mothers that tutor them—alas! if their mothers were to be such as thee, Alida, who could doubt their high-souled nurture!" But the thoughts of the youthful Greyslaer became less coherent, as they assumed a softer character, nor need we follow the reflections of the ardent young patriot, as they became merged in the vague musing of the less sanguine lover.

As the day wore on, and the hour of the expected return of the younger De Roos to his father's house drew nigh, Greyslaer shrunk from witnessing the harrowing impression which the desolate house hold must make upon his friend. Derrick came not, however, in the manner that was painfully anticipated by those who dreaded the shock of surprise that seemed to await him. Ill news flies fast, and the story of his ruined homestead was soon spread over the country; and when the young De Roos, returning from his bootless quest of Brant, first fell in with his friends and neighbours flocking to the scene of disaster, he soon learned the dark story from the agitated females, who were hurrying, in company with their fathers and brothers, toward the Hawksnest. Leaving another to take charge of his own immediate party, the horror-stricken young man threw himself on a fresh horse that was proffered by a kinsman, and, striking the spurs into his flanks, dashed furiously forward.

"Where is she? Where are their bodies?" he exclaimed, foaming with impatience as he leaped from the saddle and rushed into the house, as if the mad energy of his grief could even yet rekindle life in the bosoms of the dead.

"My son, my son!" cried the old man, moving a step toward Derrick, then tottering, and sinking helpless into the chair from which he had risen,

"My father!" screamed the youth, in a wild tone of delight and grief, most strangely mingled. "And did the wretches then spare your gray hairs; are all, then, not gone?"

"All! look there, look there, Derrick! They left my aged blood to chill in my veins through time, if horror might not curdle it; but those young pulses have ceased to beat forever." And the frame of the youth trembled like that of a woman as his father pointed to the narrow cot where, stark and stiff, but still composed, in the decent attire of a Christian grave, reposed the remains of Tyntie, his younger sister. His features were as pale as those of the corpse as he advanced to its side and raised the napkin which covered the face. He started. "What, Tyntie, my poor, my gentle girl! And was thy delicate thread of life, that might have snapped so easily—so nearly worn, too, that any moment might have severed it—was that frail thread thus rudely riven asunder?" He spoke mournfully, but there was no bitterness in his grief; and nascent hope and burning anxiety were depicted in his countenance as he turned hastily to his father, in a hoarse and tremulous whisper:

"Alida—Alida, my father?" His agitation was too great to utter more.

"She was borne off by the villain Brant, unharmed as we think and trust," said Greyslaer, advancing. "I waited but your arrival, Derrick, to reinforce my rifles and start in pursuit."

A complete reaction now took place in the feelings of the mercurial young De Roos. Rumour, who flies on magic wings, generally, too, exercises a magical power in exaggerating the tidings that she bears. The dismayed youth had heard in the first instance of the total destruction of his house; indeed, there had been tales of burnings as well as massacres; and when he rode so furiously homeward, it was not until he beheld the quiet smoke ascending from the hall of his infancy that he hoped even to recover the bodies of his kindred for Christian burial. To find his father living, and Alida, his favourite sister, his pride and his delight, still not numbered with the dead, wrought such a change in his mind, that every object around him wore a new aspect.

The world, which a few moments before seemed so drear and gloomy, that the very idea of drawing out his desolate existence for an hour was accompanied by that suffocating sense of pain intolerable, that most men, perhaps, have sometimes known—the world, the young and half-tried world around him, seemed now almost as fresh and fair as ever. With buoyant step he hurried out to meet his approaching friends, and, as the wagons of the gathering yeomanry drove into the courtyard, it would have seemed, from the congratulations that passed among the females, whom sympathy or curiosity had brought to the house of mourning, that every cause of grief were for the moment removed.

All the particulars relating to the last hours of the young girl, who thus far had been the chief sufferer by these events, were now told over and over, amid frequent exclamations among the females, while the incidents of the flight were recounted with not less animation by the men who participated in it, as they clustered around some mounted rangers, who, being among the newcomers, were now engaged in grooming their horses at the stable. The fate of the brave fellows who had fallen, and who, few in number, chanced to be mere hangers-on of the community, with no near kindred to lament them, was by their acquaintances and comrades sincerely deplored.

As the evening drew on, many of the party dispersed, some to seek a supper and bed with the nearest neighbours, none of whom dwelt within a mile of the Hawksnest; and others to seek a berth for the night in the barn or some other outbuilding, where they might be ready for attendance upon the funeral on the morrow. Greyslaer, in the mean time, having taken counsel with the friends of Alida's family, it was agreed that he and Derrick should leave the care of the ceremonial to a near kinsman of the latter, while, selecting a chosen party of followers, they should set out together an hour after midnight to follow up the trail of Brant.

Chapter 2

Death's Doings

And he looks for the print of the ruffian's feet,
Where he bore the maiden away,
And he darts on the fatal path more fleet,
Than the blast that hurries the vapour and sleet
O'er the wild November day.

Bryant.

It was through the lenity of MacDonald, in releasing the bonds of his captive the moment he discovered her arms were pinioned, that Alida had succeeded in making her single attempt at escape, which we have already seen was futile. The worthy Scotchman was deeply chagrined at having in any way participated in the business of the night, which he deemed affected his character both as an officer and as a gentleman; and now, while hurrying toward the Indian station, he did not hesitate to express his regret that the lady had not succeeded in regaining the protection of her friends. Thayendanagea seemed in nowise offended with the bluntness of his language, as the major denounced in no measured terms the Indian system of making war upon women and children, answering only very dryly that that was a question for the moralist, which he would be happy to discuss with his friend when they should be at leisure to talk over the whole subject of war, with Sir John's chaplain to make a third party in the discussion. "But, Major MacDonald," said he, "I could tell you that in regard to the position of this young lady which entirely vents her case from being included in the question you have raised."

"You have already told me the considerations of policy which prompted the act; but, *sachem*, there is but one policy which should ever govern gallant men when the welfare of women is concerned.

78

Our humane civilization teaches us that war is an honourable game, at which the noble and the far-descended should play with the lavished lives of their inferiors, the wail of whose desolated kindred can never reach the ears of the upper classes, to whom alone the prize of glory in any event may fall; pardon my interruption, but that, Major Mac-Donald, is the real purport of what you would say. You would shudder at the bare thought of one of England's high-born dames being torn from her luxurious home to a prisoner's dungeon; and the horror of her being tortured at the stake would darken the recollection of the most brilliant successes in war.

"But the wretched children, whom you doom to grow up in poverty and contempt by making them fatherless; the lacerated hearts of thousands of widows, whose existence you protract by your reluctant bounty, after rendering that existence miserable; these are never remembered to cast a shade over the tale of a victory. Call you this humanity, which embraces but the welfare of a class within its mercies? Call you this consideration for woman, which regards the rank rather than the sex of the sufferers? The sex? Great Spirit of the universe! have I not read of your gallantry, your *tender mercies* toward them in the storming of towns and castles? *I*, an Indian, a *savage*, have seen your own records, the white man's printed testimony to these abominations of his race; but the breath of life is not in the nostrils of him who has seen a female insulted by her Iroquois captor."

MacDonald listened to the tirade of the chieftain without caring to contradict what he said; and, by way of cutting short the discussion, and changing the subject to one of a less abstract nature, he admitted that if war were an evil, not the least *summary* way of putting an end to it was by the Indian mode of making all who were interested in its result indiscriminate sharers in its horrors. "But I have yet to learn, *sachem*," said he, "why the welfare of this young lady is not involved in the question?"

Brant smiled grimly, and pointed to a litter of boughs carried by a couple of Indians, whereon reposed the form of Alida, wrapped in his own mantle. "Could a father," he said, "care more gently for his own daughter than do I for the Lady Alida? Could that feeble old man, with his rash, hot-headed son, have given her the safe shelter she may find, in times like these, beneath the roof of Thayendanagea? The devil is unchained, I tell ye, Major MacDonald, and there are wild men enough beside Indians to do his bidding in these parts."

"Why," said MacDonald, in a tone of surprise and pleasure, "why

79

did you not hint this to me before? You spoke but of taking the lady as an hostage! Had I thought that so generous a concern prompted—"

"Nay, speak not of generosity. Perhaps, after all—though her safety is best secured by the act—it was but as an hostage that I did seize my captive. But I mean her as an hostage to restrain far more dangerous spirits than the mad-cap De Roos, or the dreaming enthusiast Greyslaer. There are men—men bearing the commission of the king, who bring the ferocious nature of outlaws to our cause; men whom you and I would scorn to act with, save in a cause so holy; and in the mad dance of devilish passions which the convulsion of the times will let loose, they must be restrained by other powers than those of official authority. There is one man who—but this is not the time to speak of him; let us urge onward to our destination."

That time never came with Brant, who seemed to have forgotten the promised solution of his dark and mysterious language when they arrived at the Indian station; nor did MacDonald, who soon after departed with an escort through the woods to Johnstown, understand, till long afterward, the bearing of what the chieftain said upon events disclosed in the sequel; and which may be best unfolded in the regular course of our story, which recurs again to the scene of our last chapter.

It was about the hour of midnight that the younger De Roos, taking Balt to guide him upon the Indian track, quietly withdrew to the hillside with his followers; where, after some ten minutes' impatient waiting for Greyslaer, they took up their line of march through the forest without him.

Greyslaer, in the meantime, rising from the pallet whereon he had snatched a brief repose, descended the staircase, and already had his hand on the outer door, when a deep moaning in the room adjacent to the passage arrested his attention. A feeble light streaming through an aperture showed that the door was ajar, and, with cautious and subdued steps, he hesitated not to enter.

It was the chamber of the dead.

The flickering taper upon the hearth revealed the figure of an old woman in a gray cloak, whose attenuated and sallow features looked still more ghastly from the scarlet hood which was thrown back from her forehead and rested upon her shoulders. She sat upon a low wicker chair, with one of her feet upon a footstool, and the other with the toe stiffly upturned, and the heel resting on the floor, thrust out so far beyond her dress that its shrivelled proportions showed like the stark limb of a skeleton. Her cheek supported upon her bony fingers, with the closed lids of her sunken eyes, showed that her vigil had been badly kept; and Greyslaer, pained at the thought that the remains of the gentle Tyntie should be left to such a watcher, turned from the forlorn old crone to the coffin in which the body had been laid.

It was empty. But, before he could rally his thoughts to account for a circumstance so astounding, the moaning sounds which had first drawn him to the chamber again caught his ear. He turned, and beheld a sight both piteous and awful.

In a shadowy corner of the room, removed as far as possible from the slumbering guardian of the dead, sat the venerable father of the murdered maiden, folding her stiffened corpse in his arms, and pressing it to his bosom with a tenderness as passionate as if he thought that the pulses of parental affection which beat within could rekindle those of life in his departed daughter. The shroud, with its formal drapery, still veiled the lineaments of her clay-cold form; but the napkin that shielded her throat, and the fillet or muslin band that covered the gash in her forehead, while keeping the long locks smoothly parted beneath it, had escaped from their place; and the golden tresses, floating loose, mingled with the gray hair of the old man, as he madly kissed the frightful wound through which her gentle spirit had been dismissed to heaven.

The agonized parent, who had thus crept, in the dead of the night, to hold this awful communion with his child, seemed wholly unconscious of the presence of Greyslaer, who would fain have slunk away in silence as one who, by unwitting intrusion, profaned some hallowed mystery; but his power of volition seemed taken away, and he still continued to stand, in spite of himself, as it were, with eyes riveted upon the heart-rending spectacle. At length the mute anguish of the old man found vent in words. The colour went and came strangely over his ashen countenance; while his features writhed as if it were difficult for them to assume the new expression of malevolent and vindictive feeling they had now for the first time to wear.

"Brant, cruel Brant," cried the wretched parent, "the God—the Christian's God, whom I aided in teaching thee to worship, may forgive thee this, but I—I never can. A parent's curse the curse of a bereaved and stricken heart, be, oh God, upon—" A burst of sobs, that for a moment threatened to suffocate him, cut short the blasphemous appeal; but history, in the tragic fate of Brant's own family, has shown how deeply the malediction wrought in after years; and the old man, like one startled by a spell himself had evoked, seemed, with the prophetic eye of approaching dissolution, to foresee the working of his curse. He shivered as with a grave-chill; and, dropping now upon his knees, with the lifeless face of his daughter upturned upon his bosom, mutely pleading toward heaven, he essayed in prayer to beseech a pardon and recall his words. But his quivering lips refused to syllable a sound. A sudden and subtile agony seemed on the instant to travel through his limbs and rack his aged frame; and then, while unresistingly permitting Greyslaer to take the body from his arms, he sank unconscious upon the floor.

Calling the old woman to his aid, Greyslaer, with the tender care of a mother, lifting the fragile form of her child in which life still feebly hovers, again consigned the body to its formal receptacle; and, while the crone busied herself in readjusting the grave-clothes of the maiden, he turned to raise her wretched father from the ground.

But the sorrows of the old man had ceased forever; the thread of his feeble existence, protracted only, as it seemed, beyond the usual length, to be interwoven at the last with more than usual misery, had snapped beneath the tension of an agonized spirit. He had been called away—after a long life of blameless benevolence and Christian meekness, he had been mysteriously called away in a moment of contumacy toward Heaven. He departed, indeed, with a prayer upon his lips, but his last-uttered words were those of imprecation. He had been called, though, by a God of mercy!

It was with a sad heart that Greyslaer, after climbing the hills to strike the trail of his friends, succeeded at last in overtaking them after an hour's rapid walk through the forest; nor, for a long time, could he find the heart to break to Derrick de Roos the mournful event which he had just witnessed. The blow was better received than he had anticipated. The grief of the warm-hearted but mercurial young man was indeed, in the first instance, passionate to a degree that was outrageous; but, as it found an immediate outlet in words—for, in the madness of his mood, he poured out such a torrent of curses upon Brant, the author of his sorrows, as to shock the better-disciplined mind of his friend—the first paroxysm soon passed over.

When this violent burst of emotion had had its way, he seemed, by a versatility of feeling not uncommon in persons of his keen but transient susceptibility to the impression of the moment, to be almost reconciled to the event. And his words characteristically betrayed this condition of his mind. He stood a few minutes, distracted between the natural wish to return and aid in the last obsequies to his father, and an eager impatience to hurry on to the rescue of his sister, and, at the same time, strike instant vengeance upon the desolator of his household.

"Yes, I will proceed," cried he, at last; "and now Alida—the only living object that remains for my care—must at once be got out of the clutches of these hell-hounds. Perhaps, too, after all, my dear Max, it is better that the old man departed as he did. There will be wild work doing in the valley for years to come; and the kind heart of my father already bled for the distracted state of the country, as he used to pray that he might never live to witness the scenes of havoc and of bloodshed that must soon ensue. Strange! and I used to think it but an old man's dreaming. Yes, yes, Greyslaer, it was better that he should be removed at the first outbreak of the storm, than that those gray hairs should be left to be still farther bleached by its peltings, and bowed down to the grave at last, without his ever beholding the bright days to come that you and I may yet witness."

And, with the wonted buoyancy of his gay and not wholly unself-ish nature, refusing thus to entertain a grief where regret was una-vailing—with the sanguine hopes of youth gilding thus quickly the clouds of a new-sprung sorrow, the young man seemed to dismiss the subject for the present, whatever may have been his after-emotions. Constitutionally reckless and unreflecting as he was, it would be doing injustice to De Roos, however, to say that his step was as buoyant as before, though he again strode stoutly forward with his comrades.

CHAPTER 3

The Forest-Trail

He skims the blue tide in his birchen canoe,
Where the foe in the moonbeam his path may descry;
The ball to its scope may speed rapid and true,
And lost in the wave be thy father's death-cry.

Sands.

"Well, Squire Dirk," said Balt, breaking a long silence, and speaking for the first time since the party had got fairly on the move once more, "I mistrust that your Injun friend there, Teondetha, or whatever be the chap's name, that you and Capting Greyslaer are so thick with, I mistrust that he didn't help you much, arter all, in finding out old Josie. I'll warrant me, now, the sarpent's one of Brant's own crew, sent out to mislead our people. Whereabouts did the Oneida leave your party?"

"What!" exclaimed Greyslaer; "surely Teondetha did not desert you. I'll answer with my life for the fidelity of that Indian."

"And so, twenty-four hours since, would I with mine," said Derrick, sorrowfully. "I've known Teondetha much longer than you, Max; he was here at Mr. Kirkland's missionary school while you were getting your college-training at the east. With our bows and arrows we used to watch the stone walls for chipmunks when boys together; often have I taken off my stocking for him to bag the flying squirrel, as he climbed to the hollow bough of some tall chestnut, while I thundered with the back of his tomahawk upon the decayed trunk below. And in later years, when he came down to Guy Park with his tribesmen to receive the government presents, many a hunt have we had in these woods together. But one knows not who to trust in times like these; there's Brant himself was for years my father's friend, though I never liked the haughty *sachem*." The last words suggested as-

84

sociations so bitter that the young man was for the moment overcome by his emotions, and then, regaining his composure, he resumed, still in a mournful tone: "Certain it is, Greyslaer, that Teondetha separated from us in the forest, but whether from accident or treachery I am unable to determine."

"Well, a painter is always a painter, an Injun always an Injun, no how you may tame 'em; and I don't quarrel much with the crittur because he chose to sort with his own kind. No man's to be blamed for sticking to his colour, for that's human natur through and through, any way you may fix it. I'm not mad with him for that I'm only mad with myself that I didn't shoot him down jist by accident, as it might be, afore he got fairly into our councils."

"Balt!" whispered Greyslaer, in a low but stern voice, for he did not wish to mortify the faithful woodsman before his comrades; "to me, Balt, and to our cause—to all whom you call your friends, I believe you to be a good man and true; and, as such, I would peril my life with you or for you; but, Indian or white, by the God that made me, if you ever practise such a piece of treachery upon breathing man, you shall die the death at my hands. I will pistol you upon the spot."

"Wh-eu-gh! and what would old Balt care for that, if, by shooting one of the red devils, he could save your scalp or squire Dirk's! You're boys, both on ye, and don't know the natur of an Injun. But I tell ye, Capting Greyslaer, as I suppose I must call ye, it isn't fair and comely, it isn't treating me in a likely manner, to use sich hard words to me, considerin its only two days gone that I let ye put down my name on your muster-paper there, as making myself a raal sodger under you; I might better have let the cause go to the devil, or have gone and taken service in Bradshawe's battalion with wild Wolfert Valtmeyer, rayther than to be spoken to so like a dog—I might. I almost wish I was shut of the business of sodgering altogether, if sich talk as that is to be my wages."

"If those are your sentiments, my good fellow," said Greyslaer, stopping short in his walk, as the two pursued a path together a little apart from the rest of the band, "if you really wish to side with the Tories and shed the blood of your countrymen, I will strike your name off this paper in an instant, and you have full liberty to go where you please." And Greyslaer drew the muster-roll of his company from his bosom, as if about to give his last and most valuable recruit a fair discharge.

"Well, that beats natur; that's raaly the worst thing, arter all. The

85

boy talks jist as if he could get along without me. Ah! ye green sprin-gald ye! ye callow fledgling! ye yearling that would gore with your horns yet in the velvet! ye, with yere book- larnin, yere speechifying, yere marchings and counter-marchings, yere shoulder-firelocks, and yere right foot, left foot, ye'd make a pretty how-de-do in times like these, with only sich a mad loon as Squire Dirk to counsel and guide ye! I tell ye what, Capting Max Grayslaer, I've holpen your edication in some things that may cause ye to make a figure in sich times as these, with someone to look after ye; but, though ye want now to get shut of me, as if I was an old granny of a Yankee schoolmaster dogging his urchins in the holydays, I'm d——d if I give ye up till I've seen the eend of ye. Put that in yere pipe and smoke it, my laddie! and now go ahead as soon as ye choose, for where *your* trail is there old Balt will follow."

"A hopeful subject I have here for a disciplined soldier," said Grey-slaer, mentally. Amused, provoked, and, at the same time, touched by the petulant freedom and stanch fidelity of his follower, he silently abandoned the altercation, and pocketing the muster-roll with an em-phatic "*umph!*" that said everything to Balt, once more pursued his way with the doughty hunter.

"How do you know, Balt," said he, after they had walked on for some time in silence, moving through the forest as nearly as possible in a parallel line with the main body of De Roos's band, from which two corresponding flankers had been thrown out upon the opposite side, "how do you know that Valtmeyer has taken up arms with the Tories under Bradshawe?"

"How do I know? why I had it from Red Wolfert himself only the day before yesterday, when I left you to go and look after farmer Stickney's tall sons. Two likely fellows they be, too, those boys, Syl and Marius Stickney, though Bradshawe has got 'em clean safe into his following by this time."

"What do you mean?"

"I mean to say that Valtmeyer beat me at 'lectioneering, that's all. I could only promise the boys liberty and equality of human rights if they'd turn out with our people, as they promised they would at the last training; but Wolfert promised he'd burn down their barn if they did, and he carried the day arter all."

"The pitiful scoundrels!" exclaimed the young officer, indignantly.

"Yes, capting, seeing as how they promised, they ought to have come, if it was to a den of rattle snakes. But the barn is full of grain, and the old man had his say, for Wolfert threatened to return a couple of horses on his hands that he had just bought with some broad pieces for Bradshawe's use?'

"Do you think that Valtmeyer would really have burned the barn?"

"*Sarting!* and mayhap the housen too. He hates a white man like pisin, and has jined Bradshawe jist to work out his grudge agin his own kind and colour. *He* burn a farmer's barn? I'd like to see the day of the week when Red Wolfert Valtmeyer wouldn't like a pretence for doing of that."

"And does Valtmeyer think that these two Stickneys will keep their faith more truly with his people than they have with ours?" said Greyslaer, not incuriously.

"Sarting they will," replied Balt, shaking his head. "I never knew a Connecticut chap yet but what stuck to his bargain when it was once made clean out and out; the snarl of the thing is to find out what they consider a raal bargain complete. I rayther mistrust it's only when they put their names right down in black and white upon paper. Wolfert, I know, made them do this, he seemed so tarnal sure of his men forever and aye. But here we are at Damond's run, and the squire had better order a halt, as we must be within half a mile of the Fish-House clearing."

In the moment that Balt spoke, a faint signal from the extreme right, which was repeated by De Roos from the centre, reached the ears of Greyslaer and the flankers at once; closing in, the whole party united upon the banks of the rivulet, at a point where it first commenced its descent from the upland. Taking his orders now from De Roos, for Greyslaer was only acting as a volunteer upon the expedition, Balt ascended a tall hemlock to reconnoitre the point to which they were approaching, and where it was presumed that Brant lay with his followers.

"How many fires do they count?" cried De Roos from the root of the tree.

"Fires? Devil the one!" muttered the scout, in a tone of sullen surprise and chagrin. "A fool's errand we've come upon. They've shut themselves up in a block-house and stockade upon the banks of the river, and our night's bizness is done for."

"Can we not decoy them from their defences?" asked Greyslaer, anxiously; "it would be madness to assault their palisades without artillery, and it would be folly to wait until cannon can be transported through woods like these we have traversed tonight."

"Easy enough to get some of the critters out, and pepper 'em for the fun of it," said Balt; "but that wouldn't help us in retaking Miss Alida. By the etarnal thunder! but there's some of the varmint now, pushing off in a canoe to gig trout or examine a fish-wier, I don't know which; but I see by the light of the pine knots in the bow that they push along mighty slow, as if looking for something at the bottom of the stream. I have it, I have it, capting; I have it, squire;" and, as if some rare device had struck him on the instant, Balt straightway descended the tree. "We can captivate those chaps complete, I tell ye, if they only move a little further downstream, where yon woody mound shoulders the current. I know the ground here all to pieces. Those maples, whose round tops are just now slicked up by the moon, cover a thick undergrowth that will conceal us in creeping along the shore, and we can cut off the Injuns from the fort as soon as they turn the pint."

"Ay, but how do you know they will turn the point?" said Greyslaer, who, standing upon a rock round which the runnel gurgled, looked down the defile through which it travelled to the river, and caught a glimpse of the moonlit landscape below.

"Leave that to me, if chance don't fix it," replied the woodsman; "and now, Squire Dirk, as you command here tonight, jist let old Balt order the position of all of us before we move farther."

"If you know the ground, as you say you do, Balt, you are the proper person to guide us in our operations. I give you full power to act, if you will only secure me a chance of trying my *yaeger* upon the miscreants."

"Well, well, that shall be cared for, only don't be too headysome, or you'll spile all. I want to take the Redskins alive, and get some tidings about Miss Alida; and, if one be a chief, we may exchange him. We must divide into three parties to make sure of our object; I want five of our stoutest men to creep with me to the water's side, to the bend south of the mound, where we must secure the canoe-men, if anywhere. You, squire, must throw yourself, with the strength of the party, to the north side, so as to cut off the Injuns from the fort with your rifles if they escape from our hands and attempt to return to it. Capting, I'm sorry I cannot give you more lively work at the outset; but, if the thing comes to a fight, you will have a sodger's share of it where I'm going to place you. We must trust to your spunk and headwork in getting us out of the scrape if my plan fails; and you must take a position, with half a dozen men, where you can see what's going on, and bring us off safely if the worst come to the worst; and if the fire of Squire Dirk's party draws a sally from the fort, we shall see hot work, I tell ye. There's a ledge of bald rock to the left yonder, that puts out from the ridge we are on, about a hundred yards from this. That cliff commands the whole valley below, and there is a deer runway leading up from the water-side to its base. That way lies our retreat. A half hour hence the moon will touch the cliff, whose edge is still in deep shadow from the hemlock thicket that covers it; so you must gain it at once, and lie there close as a hunted opossum to a gray log. If we are pursued, you, capting, know as well as I do what follows; we'll—"

"You will lure the chase to the base of the rock, make a detour to my rear, and leave me to deal with the rascals in front. Exactly, Balt; I comprehend your plan completely; and its details are worthy of a veteran partisan."

"I don't know what sort of a chap that may be; but if it mean an old bushfighter, there's no man in all Tryon County, not even Red Wolfert himself, but must knock under to old Balt in expayrience." And, with this harmless ebullition of vanity on the part of the woodsman, the council of war was broken up. The party was divided agreeably to his suggestions, and the three bands immediately afterward separated, and sped with silent haste to their different destinations. Greyslaer, having but a short distance to move with his handful of followers, soon gained the position indicated by Balt; and throwing himself upon the ground, with his feet hanging over the rocky ledge, he cast a thoughtful eye over the sleeping landscape below.

The moon was in her last quarter, but the atmosphere was so clear that her waning beams lighted up the scene with a splendour that is rarely witnessed in other climes. The Sacondaga, which near this region, at the present day, winds through green meadows grazed by a thousand cattle, was, at the time of which we write, thickly wooded along its banks. The luxuriant foliage of primeval forests impended in billowy masses over the devious water, which only showed to view in shining intervals, like the broken links of a silver chain. A few cleared acres only, around the Indian stockade, let the moonlight down more broadly upon the stream, where the burned and blackened stumps stood grimly marshalled along the water's edge, like the dwarfish opponents of the girdled trees, whose tall, stark stems, and jagged and verdureless array, bounded the opposite sides of the clearing.

The stockade itself lay a deformed and shapeless mass of logs in the midst of this desolate area; and the eyes of Greyslaer, as he watched the twinkling lights which ever and anon revealed the floating canoe upon the river, reverted continually to this sullen den, in which he thought Alida was immured. He imaged to himself the lady of his love as looking out with the cheerless spirit of a captive upon the few dreary acres of the Indian clearing, which could alone meet her eye from her forest-walled prison-yard; he thought of her love of nature and exquisite taste in rural refinement, as seeking vainly for solace in that circumscribed, uncouth, and mutilated landscape; and then he thought—so idly does the mind wander in such a mood—he thought, reverting to the white man's "improvements," characterized by similar features to those of the scene before him, he thought whether utility could not in any way work out her ends, by some less unsightly and devastating process than the ordinary one of clearing a new country.

"And must the prodigal soul of man, too," said he, mentally, "must the primal freshness of all things earthly be thus wastefully converted to their final ends? Must the soil of virgin nature be thus encumbered with the wreck of its beauty, thus enriched with its own blasted luxuriance, turning again to earth, ere it gather strength to bear things that are truly precious? Must the wild heart of youth, redolent of hope and high affections, moving with each generous impulse like this plumy forest to the breeze, must it also give up its first noble, natural growth of feelings, and become barren and desolate, like yon blackened clearing, before, like that, it can bear fruits fit for the best purposes of social being? . . . .

"The wild Indian, too! Is he subject to the same mysterious law, or has Nature a different dispensation for her own immediate children? Doth *age* alone ripen his mind, and by gradual and kindly means steal from him the pledges of life's morning promise, and lead him to an inviting grave with youth, all glorious, eternal youth, still glowing beyond its portals? or doth he too, like us, grow old before his time, with faculties quickened by suffering and matured by pain? Doth he, bewildered by conflicting passions like ours, and misled by stumbling reason, chase the phantom Hope where'er she leads? or doth rather a narrow but subtle instinct deter him from the vain pursuit, or guide him with unerring finger to fruition?"

"But what boots this vain dreaming?" cried he, interrupting himself impatiently, as a cloud, at that moment obscuring the moon, snatched the scene which had awakened these reflections from his view. "What matters it that our scheme of existence should be as vain and uncertain as the landscape that but now glimmered below me, when death, like yon cloud, may come at any moment and obscure it forever!"

As the last thought passed through the mind of Greyslaer, and even before language could have given it shape and utterance, it seemed as if the chilling image of death had but presented itself as the precursor of the reality. A sharp, stunning blow, that came with such force, glancing along his ribs, as to turn his body completely round, drew a sudden exclamation of pain and surprise from him. "Hah! God of Heaven, what's that!" he cried, clapping his hand to the wound as he rolled over upon the rock, struggling to gain his feet. But the effort was vain. He became dizzy on the moment. He tried to shout to his comrades, but the voice seemed drowned in other sounds. A fearful yell, that rung confusedly in his ears, like the spirit call from another world, swallowed up the feeble cry. But still he seemed not dead, for a strange sensation, like that of falling into a fathomless depth, yet called out the exercise of volition. His hands groped about as if clutching at something to hold on by, and then he lay in utter unconsciousness, with the cold moonlight streaming on his motionless form.

CHAPTER 4

The Hunter's Ambuscade

Again upon the grass they droop,
When burst the well-known whoop on whoop;
And bounding from the ambush'd gloom,
Like wolves the savage warriors come.

Street.

The plans of the hunter Balt, when he was permitted to arrange the movements of his party for the night, were well laid in every respect save one; the omission, on the part of De Roos and his forest counsellor, to keep up a communication with Greyslaer, either by messengers or signals, to be available in case they met with any obstacle to the consummation of their design. The unfortunate issue of the ambuscade was mainly attributable to this oversight. "The attempt," they argued, "must either be fully successful, when we shall rejoin our comrades without molestation, or, if we are interrupted by a sally from the fort or other untoward occurrence, the report of our firearms will soon show Greyslaer how things are going." In guerilla warfare, however, so much often depends upon an instantaneous change of the mode in which you would effect your design when carrying any given piece of strategy into execution, that the most perfect concert of action should be observed if you would avail yourself of their flexile councils without endangering your brother partisans.

The two parties, led severally by Balt and De Roos, gaining the bottom of the hill upon which they had left the ill-starred Greyslaer, separated near the base of the promontory before described, and betook themselves to their appointed stations. De Roos posted himself, with his men, in a swamp that fringed a little bay a few hundred yards below the Indian stockade, from which it was divided by the river, which was here about a rifle-shot in breadth. The promontory extended out into the stream upon his right, and the canoe, which was the object of attack, was just turning this headland as he reached his position, and might be said to be thus already cut off from the fort had he dared to fire upon her. But Balt, who gained the shore, amid tangled vines and thickets of elder, upon the lower side of the promontory, awaited there his opportunity to seize the fishermen in a more peaceable manner.

Placing his followers in a copse near the mouth of the brook already mentioned, he proceeded cautiously to a clump of chestnuts near, and selecting one fit for his purpose, he cut off a stick about two feet in length from a green sapling, and, after rolling it between his palms for a few moments, succeeded in drawing out the woody part from its bark casing, forming thus from the latter a hollow tube, which might answer the purpose of a speaking-trumpet. Placing one end of this to his mouth, and bending his body so as to bring the other within an inch of the ground, and partly to smother the sound he intended to produce from the instrument, he drew from it a deep discordant noise, not unlike the distant roaring of a bull. The call almost immediately brought a reply, both from the hillside and from the water. From the hills it came back in a wild bellowing, that was evidently that of a real animal answering a beast of its own kind. Upon the water it was replied to by the Indians, who, equally deceived by sounds that seemed to indicate their vicinity to a moose-deer buck, or bull moose as our hunters call it, attempted, by putting their closed fists to their mouths, to mimic the cry and lure the animal to the waterside, where the torches in the bow of the shallop would enable them to fix the buck at gaze, and to approach sufficiently near to destroy him with their fishing-spears.

Guiding their birchen vessel now into an eddy of the stream by a scarcely perceptible motion of the paddle, they approached with care the spot where Balt and his comrades lay. But the next moment, exchanging some words with each other in a low tone, which made them inaudible to those on shore, the steersman gave a flirt of his paddle, and the light bark swung round again to the centre of the stream. Here the Indians paused, as if listening intently; and the wary Balt, fearing, now that their attention was fully awakened, to repeat the same lure, which might fail to deceive them when so near, resorted to another less easy of detection.

He took a cup from his hunting-pouch, and, stooping down to

the brook, dipped up the water and let it fall again into the current, to imitate the plashing footsteps of an animal stalking along the bed of the stream. The Indians had drawn out toward the channel of the river, in order to give the supposed moose a wide berth between themselves and the shore, where, as he waded out to lave his flanks, a cording to the custom of the animal at this season, they would hold him to advantage in the deep water. But as the plashing sounds which they had just heard grew fainter, as if the moose were retiring from the river side, they abandoned this expectation, and, mimicking his bellowing cry once more, they gave the canoe a direction toward the cove, and glided silently into the mouth of the brook. Their glaring torches shone double upon its shallow and pebbly bottom, and lighted up the overhanging thicket with a ruddy glare.

"Captur, but slay not!" cried Balt, leaping into the frail shallop with a force that drove his feet through the flimsy bottom and anchored it to the spot, at the same moment that an Indian in the bow was vainly attempting, with his long spear, to push back into the parent stream. A blow from the hatchet of the woodsman snapped the shaft, leaving the barbed end quivering in the bank, and the other a harmless weapon in the hands of the Indian, who was instantly secured by his opponent. Not so, however, with his two comrades; one of those, who held the steering-paddle, threw himself backward over the stern, floundered with mad desperation through the shallow water, and, diving like a duck the moment he attained that deep enough for swimming, struck out for the opposite side of the river, which he gained in safety. The remaining Indian was not less successful in his attempt to escape. This man, a warrior of powerful frame and great prowess, deeming himself surrounded, leaped from the canoe at the first alarm, and charged into the midst of his enemies; grasping his fishing-spear by the middle, so as, at the same time, to protect his person and prevent the long shaft from becoming entangled in the underwood, he levelled a yeoman with a blow from either end at the first onset, and, seizing a rifle from one of the men as they fell, bounded off, unharmed, into the forest.

"Old Josey himself, by the Etarnal! there's no Injun breathing but he could have done that," cried Balt; "we have let the head-devil of them all, boys, slip through our fingers, and we shall have the hull kennel of hell-hounds let loose upon us in an instant. We must lose no time in crossing from these parts, or our scalps will fly off like thistle-down; we must make a diversion, too, or we'll lose our prisoner." And, binding the hands of his only captive with a tendril of grapevine, the hunter hastily consigned him to the care of his comrades, and told them to move down along the banks of the river as rapidly as possible, without attempting to regain the place first designated as a rendezvous. With these hurried directions, Balt sprang forward to give in person the necessary warning to De Roos, whom he met mid way, hurrying with his men to join him.

"Turn, Balt, turn, or the dogs will be on our trail in a moment; I've seen a dripping savage emerge like a musquash from the water on the opposite side, where a dozen canoes are drawn up before the station, and we must put the rapids between them and our party as quickly as possible."

"What, risk our only prisoner, squire? when I've sent my men that way with him, hoping that we could lead off the pursuit toward the cliff, where the capting awaits us."

"It will never do," said De Roos, still keeping his party in motion; "Greyslaer will get sufficient warning to retire in time, seeing the movements around the fort; and as for our joining him, it is too late. My men have already seen one armed Indian skulking between them and the hill, and we may be at this moment surrounded by a hundred."

As these words passed hurriedly between the commander of the expedition and his unlucky adviser, Balt, who had for the moment allowed his course to be turned, and himself borne along with the rapid march of his comrades, stopped short, exclaiming, "On, then; on, Squire Dirk; you may have changed our plans for the better, and the capting, may hap, would consider your retreat sodger-like, seeing so many lives are at stake; but I cannot leave him to take his chance of first hearing of it from the Injuns themselves."

With these words, only the first of which were heard by De Roos, Balt broke away from his comrades, and ran back until he reached the brook which the retreating party had crossed a few moments before; turning then, and following up its current as the readiest highway that offered, amid the heavy forests through whose glooms its course occasion ally made an opening toward the moonlit sky.

"Tarnal crittur! she's hid her vixen face," he exclaimed, as, looking upward through one of these openings, he saw that the planet was obscured. "Shine out, old lily-white, shine out, for shame, upon the Redskins, or they'll cross the river and be upon the capting afore I can stir his kiver."

The prayer of the woodsman was quickly answered. The moon,

indeed, shone out but too soon, for the sharp crack of a rifle, followed by the war-whoop, and answered by a brief and irregular discharge of firearms, showed that her reappearance, instead of being the harbinger of safety, had been but the signal for onslaught. Rushing forward, the hunter gained the top of the hilly ridge whereon he had left Greyslaer, and was moving with hasty but cautious steps toward the shelf of rocks where that luckless officer had taken post with his party.

"The capting, the capting, what have ye done with the capting?" cried Balt, as he met Greyslaer's men in full flight from the spot.

"Run, Balt; for your life, run; it is all up with Captain Max! a rifle from the woods, below the cliff picked him off the very moment the moon got high enough to bring his body out of shadow. The woods are alive with Redskins, and our legs must save us now if we would live to avenge him."

An incessant whooping, that each moment came nearer and nearer, seemed to prove the truth of what the man said; and with a light heel but a heavy heart, the sorrowing woodsman turned and fled with the rest; muttering imprecations on himself the while for having left for a moment, amid such scenes, his commander, friend, and *protégé*.

De Roos, in the meantime, hurrying along with his prisoner, followed the course of the Sacondaga, which here runs in a northeast direction for a few miles, and then, leaving it abruptly, struck due south, making for the nearest settlements upon the Mohawk. The approach of morning found his party in the neighbourhood of Galway; and crossing the highway, or trail as it might rather be called at that day, between Saratoga and Johnstown, he made a sweep to the south of the latter place, and, striking due west, passed Stone Arabia, famous afterward for the gallant fight and subsequent slaughter of the brave Colonel Brown and his regiment, reached the Mohawk at Keeder's Rifts, equally noted in the border-story of after years. The retreat, considering that De Roos had not only to escape from his Indian foes in the first instance, but that he carried his prisoner through a district, the great portion of whose scattered inhabitants were as yet either lukewarm patriots or zealous adherents of the Johnson party, was creditable to his address as a partisan.

Worn down with fatigue and long watching, Derrick and his companions were rejoiced to find shelter and refreshment in the hospitable mansion of Major Jelles Fonda, a faithful officer and confidential friend of the father of Sir John Johnson, but who, having now sided with the patriot party, was exposed to the vengeance of the royalists, which was afterward so terribly wreaked upon his house hold by the devastating hand of the stern and inexorable son of his friend.

The Mohawk captive, during the route, had borne himself with dogged indifference to his fate, obstinately refusing to answer any of the questions with which De Roos, who spoke his language, plied him, whenever occasion offered, during a brief halt of his party. Refreshments were now placed before him, but he refused to partake of them, replying only to the repeated invitations of his captors by glancing, with a look of mute indignation, from their faces to the bonds by which his right arm was still pinioned, the left having been temporarily released to enable him to feed himself. This silent appeal, however, produced no effect upon his wary captors.

"If the scoundrel is too proud to help himself with one hand, let us see if fasting won't bring humility with it," said one.

"The cunning cat! he only wants to get his claws free to use them," cried another; "but he can't come the mouser over us with his mock dignity."

De Roos, who had been looking at the accommodations of his party for the night, at this moment entered the room, and ordered a guard of three men to repair with the prisoner to the kitchen, which was assigned them as their quarters. He at the same time handed the Indian a blanket, wherewith one of the females of the family had provided him, and, for the first time since his capture, a gleam of pleasure shot athwart the dusky features of the Mohawk as he stretched out his left hand to receive the boon. Indeed, he folded it about his person with as much care as if he took pride as well as comfort in his new acquisition; nor had he completely adjusted its folds to his satisfaction, before a corner of his new mantle had more than once swept the edge of the table, as he brushed along its sides, while making his way out of the apartment.

The kitchen was not entirely vacant when the prisoner and his guard reached their quarters. For, besides several negro slaves, which at that time formed an essential part of the household of every opulent farmer in the country, there sat in the chimney-corner a shabby-looking wayfarer, who, in those days of infrequent inns and open hospitality, had been allowed a stall for his horse and a shelter for himself during the night.

The dress of this man, which was a sort of greasy doublet, or fustian shooting-jacket, of dingy olive, with breeches of the same; shoes without buckles, and a broad-leaved chip hat, having a broken pipe stuck beneath the band, marked him sufficiently as belonging to the lower order of society. For, while among our wise fathers a man's apparel was always thought more or less to indicate his social position, a traveller's especially, who presumed to take the saddle without being either booted or spurred, would be set down as near akin to a beggar, who had his horse only for some chance hour. Some, however, beneath the neglected beard and generally sordid appearance of this wayfaring horseman, might have detected features which, if not those of a true cavalier, belonged at least to the class which was then generally supposed exclusively to furnish such a character.

The man's look was sinister, if not decidedly bad; but there was a degree of haughtiness mingled with his duplicity of expression, and the intelligent and assured air of his countenance was far above the rank which his coarse habiliments would indicate. He started as the Indian entered the apartment; and as the name "Au-neh-yesh!" escaped his lips, the emotion seemed for the instant to be sympathetic with the prisoner. It was so slight, however, upon the part of the Mohawk as not to attract observation. He moved at once toward the kitchen fire, and, though it was a summer's night, threw himself on the floor with his feet toward the ashes, and, covering up his head in his blanket, seemed soon to be forgetting the cares of captivity in soothing slumber.

Two of the men to whose custody the prisoner had been consigned soon afterward imitated his example, and stretched themselves upon a flock-bed in a corner of the apartment, while the third paced up and down the room, to keep himself awake while acting as sentinel over the prisoner. The slaves, with the exception of a single old negro, had all slunk away, one could hardly tell how; and this worthy, with the sinister-looking traveller, were left as the only waking companions of the sentinel. The traveller, too, at last, after ruminating in a drowsy fashion for some time, expressed his intention of seeking a bed in the haymow, and, procuring a stable-lantern from the negro to look after his horse in the first instance, withdrew from the apartment. In passing through the door, he fixed his eyes earnestly upon the sleeping Indian, and his face being thus averted from the passage-way, he stumbled awkwardly, so as to make his tin lantern clang against the lintel so sharply as to startle both the sentry and his prisoner, though the slight movement which the latter made beneath his blanket was not observed by the soldier, who turned to close the door behind the retreating traveller.

"What tink you of dat trabeller-man, massa?" said the old negro, with a knowing look, as soon as he heard the outer door closed after the other.

"Think of him? why I don't think of him at all, Cuff; that sleeping hound by the fire is enough for me to trouble myself about, after trampoosing for twenty-four hours on a stretch, with not even a loon's nap at the end of it."

"Trabeller-man hab mighty fine hoss, massa! Him look as like as two peas to de boss dat Wolf Valtmeyer bought last week for Massa Bradshawe, and drew to here, mighty like dat same boss, massa."

"Well, what of that? you don't take the chap for a horse-thief, do you? He's more like some travelling cobbler, that's going his circuit through the settlements."

"He be bery like a cobbler, certing," said the complaisant negro; and then, after musing a few moments, added, "He be bery like lawyer Wat Bradshawe too, massa."

"I never saw that rip, Cuff, though, if the traveller has heard as much of him as I have, he wouldn't be beholden to you for discovering the likeness."

"Lawyer Wat has shaked hands wid de debbil, certing!" said the negro, shaking his head mysteriously.

"Why do you say that, Cuff?"

"'Cause he no fear de debbil."

"Why, what the devil do you know about him, you old curmudgeon?"

"Hab not old black Violet told me of his doings long ago, when he was but a boy? Let Cuff alone to find out de secret; he know all about Massa Bradshawe, and he know how to keep de secret too."

"Now, Cuff," said the soldier, stopping short in the middle of the room, "you see that Injun there! Well, he's a real Injun juggler, and, unless you tell me instantly your secret, as you call it, I'll stir up that fellow with the butt end of my rifle, and he shall fill this room with fiery serpents in a moment."

The poor superstitious negro recoiled with horror at this alarming threat. He had all the awe of his race for the red man, who, having never been reduced to subservience by the white, is regarded by the docile African partly as a wayward, wicked, and disobedient child, who refuses to be guided by those who have a natural right to authority, and partly as a hybrid, heathenish mortal, in whose paternity the devil has so large a share that the Indian is unfitted to take a part in the ordinary lot of mankind.

"Why you see, massa," said he, beginning at once, with trembling lips, to tell his story, "it was when old Dinah, the black witch, that perhaps you have heerd tell on, was living. She used some times, of a winter's night, to be let in at de house of Massa Walter's papa, where she slept by de kitchen fire, but always went up de chimbley on a broom stick before de morning. Violet herself say—and Violet live at de house for many years—Violet say she often let Dinah in, but she nebber in her life see her go out, 'cept one morning, and den she went out a corpse; and she die wid pains and aches, oh horrible! so Violet say—"

"The devil take Violet; out with your story; what had Wat Bradshawe to do with the business?" cried the impatient soldier, thinking matter might be forthcoming from this kitchen gossip that would reward him by adding something worth repeating to the many strange stories that were told of Bradshawe throughout the country.

"What Massa Walter do?" exclaimed the negro, lowering his voice; "why, who but he dat kill de old woman! Massa Wat, he watch Dinah go up de chimbley, he see dat de black witch always slip off her skin, and hang it up behind de pantry-door before she go up. So he watch him chance, like a mad boy he was; he go to de dresser, take de casters, put pepper, mustard, and plenty salt on de skin; him chuckle, laugh, say 'he make de *debbil* ob de old woman.' Well, de witch come back, slip into her skin, she kick, she holler, she fall down in fit, and so she die, and dat de end ob Missy Dinah."

"Why—you—tar—nal—old—black—fool!" said the soldier, with a ludicrously indignant expression of baffled curiosity. "You—you— you jackass—you. I've more than a mind to stir up this Injun juggler, to show what real deviltry is, Cuff, for making me listen to such heathen stuff as that."

As the soldier spoke, he advanced so near to the sleeping Mohawk as to strike him with his foot while heedlessly throwing it out to annoy the apprehensive negro. He had better have alarmed a coiled rattlesnake. For a knife, as deadly as the fangs of a serpent, was the next moment plunged in his bosom as the captive leaped upon him. A window was thrown wide open by some unseen hand in the same moment. The negro stood speech less with horror; and, before the slumbering comrades of the unfortunate sentinel could rouse to avenge him, his scalp was filched from his head by the carving-knife which the Indian had secured beneath his blanket while brushing past the supper-table.

He shook his gory trophy in the affrighted eyes of his half-awakened foemen, and bounded like a deer through the window.

In the morning there were no traces to be found either of the young savage or the suspicious-looking itinerant.

CHAPTER 5

The Indian Leech

Thus error's monstrous shapes from earth are driven;
They fade, they fly but truth survives their flight;
Earth has no shades to quench that beam of heaven;
Each ray that shone, in early time, to light
The faltering footsteps in the path of right,
Each gleam of clearer brightness, shed to aid
In man's maturer day his bolder sight,
All blended, like the rainbow's radiant braid,
Pour yet, and still shall pour, the blaze that cannot fade.

Bryant

The wound of Greyslaer had been given precisely in the manner described by the panic-struck fugitive, though both he and De
Roos were mistaken in thinking that their party was surrounded. A
large body of Indians had indeed crossed the river, under the shelter
of the cape or headland, during the few moments that the moon
was obscured; but this was after De Roos was in full retreat: and the
"skulking savage" who had so alarmed his followers, as well as the
sharpshooter who had subsequently picked off Greyslaer, and struck
a panic into his party in turn, was no other than the single *desperado*
who had so gallantly achieved his escape from the canoe. This formidable warrior—for, as Balt surmised, it was no other than "old Josey,"
or Thayendanagea himself—was aided by fortune, not less than by his
own address, in escaping the perils of the night. Foiling by his prowess
the ambushed foes that attempted to seize him, he had, in the first instance, after breaking from their hands, struck directly across the neck
of the promontory as the shortest way to the station.

He had nearly gained the little bay on this side, where he would

102

take the water to swim to the opposite shore, when, discovering the position of De Roos's band by hearing some of the outlyers whispering together, he made a detour to turn their flank. The gleam of his rifle soon after betrayed his vicinity to them, as was indicated by a movement of alarm among them; and, perceiving that he was observed, he widened his circuit by striking inland toward the hill. This route brought him immediately beneath the projecting ledge whereon Greyslaer was reclining.

Deeming himself now surrounded by foes, the chieftain thought that it only remained for him to fight his way through them as best he might; and when the moon, after being a few moments obscured by a cloud, shone out, bringing the form of Greyslaer above him in clear relief against the sky, Brant discharged his piece and raised the warwhoop. His fire was returned with a volley from the bushes, where the whites lay within a few yards of their officer; but their shot were thrown away, for the darkness that reigned below the cliff prevented them from taking aim at their unseen assailant. The single war-whoop of Brant was the next moment echoed back by a tumultuous yell from the nearer side of the river, and the dismayed borderers, hearing no order from their insensible leader, concluded that he was slain, and sought their own safety in instant flight.

The darkness of the woods rendered pursuit in effectual. The forest rung for a while with the impatient yells of an Indian chase, and then, before an hour had passed away, the lonely whoop of some solitary savage, hailing his comrades after a reluctant and disappointed return, was all that met the ear These last sounds, had Greyslaer had sufficient consciousness to comprehend them, would have told him of the safety of his friends, however precarious might be his own. The wounded officer, upon reviving from his swoon, found himself stretched upon a pile of skins in an Indian *wigwam*, with a noble-looking Mohawk, a man of majestic figure and commanding aspect, standing near, with eyes bent keenly upon his own. Greyslaer made a movement as if to lift one of his hands, and was about to speak, but the Medicine-man— for such the Indian seemed by the talisman which he wore around his neck, as well as other emblems and equipments of the aboriginal leech, or conjuror's trade, that marked his appearance—motioned the youth to remain silent and quiet.

The sage then, baring the wound by stripping off some moss or lichen with which the blood had been temporarily stanched, proceeded to dress it. This he did, with the assistance of a withered old squaw, who stood by, holding the various preparations in her hands, while ever and anon she bowed reverently to the muttered charm of the operator. When this part of his medical treatment was carefully completed, the magician administered a draught with the same solemn and superstitious ceremonial; and his patient soon after slept.

The slumbers of Greyslaer must have been long and refreshing, for he found himself so much revived upon awaking as to feel a disposition to rise. But upon the first indication of such an intention, his ears were saluted by a shrill and discordant cry from the old squaw, who sat crouched among the ashes, watching a brazen kettle, into which from time to time she cast certain roots and herbs, muttering some gibberish to herself the while. Her call was answered from without by a gruff "*umph*," as of some voice chiding her shrewish cry; and straightway the mat which formed the only door of the lodge was raised, and the benignant features of the Medicine-man were seen at the entrance. He advanced to the couch of Greyslaer, and placing his hand upon the forehead of his patient, while he gazed upon him thoughtfully for some moments, seemed to be at length thoroughly satisfied with the results of his treatment thus far, for straightway he began to engage him in conversation, speaking English at the same time with an ease and fluency that astonished the soldier-student.

"*The Spirit* hath not yet need of thee in another land, young man. *He* leaves thee here yet a while, to repent of thy wickedness in aiding to drive his red children from their country."

"*I* drive them? I love the Indians!" said Greyslaer, with spirit. "It is only those who make themselves the slaves of a foreign king, to aid in enchaining my countrymen. It is only the murderous Brant and his renegade crew upon whom I would make war."

"Darest thou, young man, speak thus of the great Thayendanagea? and yet it fits thy presumptuous years to pass in judgment upon the deeds of a *sachem* who hath sat in council with the wisest of thy race."

"The *great* Thayendanagea!" scornfully repeated Max. "A presumptuous half-breed! whose demi-barbarous vanity has been tickled by sharing in the mummery of European courts. A degenerate hound, that has exchanged the noble instincts of his forest training for the dainty tricks of a parlour-bred spaniel. *He* sit in council! the poor tool of profligate Tory partisans, who will use him to enslave his people when they have destroyed mine."

The eyes of the Medicine-man shot fire as Greyslaer, feverish per-

haps from his wound, spoke romantic student, and whose clerkly employment as secretary of Guy Johnson had not raised him in the eyes
of the aspiring young soldier; while recent events made Max regard
him as a crafty, cruel, semi-civilized barbarian, who brought the name
of "Mohawk" into abhorrence and contempt. Greyslaer had his eyes
fixed upon the rafters above him while thus warmly and disdainfully
inveighing against the cap tor of Alida, and he did not, therefore, observe the agitated movement with which the Medicine-man carried
his hand to the knife which he wore in his girdle, though, from the
excitement under which he spoke, it is doubtful if even such observation would have restrained his heated expressions.

The magician took two or three turns through the narrow apartment before he trusted himself to reply, which he did at last with
calmness and dignity.

"Young man, you speak falsely, though probably unknowingly, in
calling Joseph Brant a half-breed; and, were you not intrusted by him
to my care, you should die on this ground for so vile a slander. Thayendanagea is a Mohawk of the full blood. And if any gainsay this truth,
Brant, much as he holds your European usages to scorn, will—I take
it upon myself to say meet any rebel officer of his own rank in private
quarrel, after the foolish fashion of the whites. For the rest—" and
here a strange and undefinable expression of emotion passed over the
swarthy features of the speaker, who seemed to hesitate for words to
express his mingled feelings—"for the rest, the *sachem* would, I know,
forgive you for the love you seem to bear his race; and it may be true
that he has done ill in linking the fortunes of his tribe with those of
either party of the whites. The carrion birds might have quarrelled
over the carcass, but the eagle should never have stooped to share their
wrangling, if he would soar with untainted plumage."

"Your tribesmen, noble Mohawk, if indeed you be an Indian," answered Greyslaer, touched by the proud yet feeling tone with which
the last words were uttered, "your red brethren had indeed better keep
aloof from us, alike in war or in peace, for they seem to acquire only
the worst attributes of civilized life by attempting to mingle with us as
one people: and their share in this struggle must—"

"Ay, you speak well, young man," interrupted the Indian, now
wholly thrown off his dignified reserve of manner by what appeared
to be a theme of great excitement with him; "if your vaunted civilization be not all a fraud, your perverted learning but a shallow substitute
for the wisdom of the heart, your so-called social virtues but a loose

covering for guile, like the frail thatch of leaves that hides the traps of an Indian hunter; if your religion be not a bitter satire upon the lives of all of ye; if, in a word, all your conflicting teachings and practices be indeed reconcilable to *Truth* and pleasing to *The Spirit*, then hath he created Truth of as many colours as he hath man; and his red children should still rest content with the simple system which alone their hearts are fitted to understand."

Greyslaer was precisely at that age when most men of an imaginative cast of mind mistake musing for philosophizing, sentiment for religion; and with that ready confidence in the result of one's own re flections and mental experience which is the darling prerogative of youth and immaturity of thought, he did not hesitate to assume the attitude of a teacher in reply to the last remark of the Indian. "Truth, noble Mohawk, hath ever been, will ever be the same. But the truths of the other world, as well as of this, are often wrapped in mystery. God has, in two dispensations of light from above, revealed to mortals so much of his holy truth as the human mind was fitted to receive.

"The first revelation was like a dawn in the forest, where the young day shoots its horizontal rays beneath the dusky canopy of tree-tops, and, glancing between the columned trunks, streams upon the path of the benighted wanderer of the wilderness. That *matin*-light—those holy rays of the virgin morn of true religion—I am willing to believe, illumined the lake-girdled mountains of the Iroquois hunter as well as the cedar-crowned hills of the Hebrew shepherd. It shone alike, perhaps, upon the path way of either, if indeed they were not one and the same people.

"But the realm of glory to which that pathway led; the snares that beset it; the solace and refreshment that lay within reach of the traveller, alternating his perils, these it required a second revelation to bring to light; when the sun of righteousness, fairly uprisen, should throw the blaze of noontide into that forest, revealing now, in stern reality, its yawning caverns, its precipices and pit falls; now touching with mellow beauty its mossy resting-places, or sparkling with cheerful radiance upon its refreshing wayside-waters; and now bathing with glorious effulgence the region beyond the wilderness, where lay the final rest and reward of the wanderer. The good men of my race, therefore, preach not a new Truth to the Indian! they seek but to share with him that broader light which has been vouchsafed to us regarding the same one Eternal Truth."

The Mohawk listened with an air of deep respect to the earnest language of the youth, but his own feelings and prejudices were too deeply excited to permit the discussion long to preserve the abstract character which Greyslaer attempted to give it.

"I spoke not against the truths of Christianity," said he; "for they may have their sanctuary as well in the desert and the forest as in the city; I spoke not, I say, of the pure light of Christianity, which your mobbled faith no more resembles than do the stained and distorted rays that struggle through a dungeon's window resemble the beams of the noontide sun. The holy teachings of your Master come to us like those unwholesome airs which, travelling out pure and invigorating from the skies, are polluted and made pestiferous by traversing some noxious marsh before they reach the unfortunate mortal who is doomed to breathe them. It is your vaunted social system from which I recoil with loathing. Your so-called civilization is, in its very essence, a tyrant and enthraller of the soul; it merges the individual in the mass, and moulds him to the purposes, not of God, but of a community of men.

"It follows the guidance of true religion so far only as that ministers to its own ends, and then it turns and fashions anew its belief from time to time, to suit the 'improved' mechanism of its artificial system. In crowded Europe the evil is irremediable; for man the machine occupies less room than man the herdsman or hunter; but your mode of existence is not less a curse to ye—the white man's curse, which he would fain share with his red brother! But have I not seen how it works among you? Have I not been to your palaces and your churches, and seen there a deformed piece of earth assume airs that become none but the great Spirit above? Have I not been to your prisons, and seen the wretched debtor peering through the bars? You call the Indian nations cruel! Yet liberty to a rational creature as much exceeds property in value as does the light of the sun that of the smallest twinkling star! But you put them on a level, to the everlasting disgrace of human nature. I have seen the white captive writhing at the Indian stake, and rending the air with shrieks of agony; strange that the unhappy man did not endeavour, by his fortitude, to atone in some degree for the crimes com mitted during the life thus justly shortened.

"I have witnessed all the hideous torments that you ascribe to such a death, and yet I had rather die by the most severe tortures ever inflicted by the Indian than languish in one of your prisons a single year! Great Spirit of the Universe! and do you call yourselves Christians?

Does the religion of him you call your Saviour inspire this spirit and lead to these practices?"[1]

Greyslaer, who listened with curious attention to this strange harangue, as coming from the lips of an Indian, was completely bewildered by the fluency and energy with which the magician delivered his tirade, and he scrutinized his features and complexion, as if expecting to discover the lineaments of some disguised *renegado* white, who, with talents fitted for a better sphere, had, induced by caprice or compelled by crime, banished himself from society, and assumed the character of one of the aborigines. But the natural and easy manner in which the object of his suspicions turned the next moment and addressed the Indian woman in her own language, not less than the veneration with which the squaw received his behests, dispelled the idea, while little opportunity was given him for making a more minute examination. The Medicine-man, smiling blandly, as if he read what was passing in the mind of his patient, approached to his side, and telling him that he was now about to consign him to the care of others, asked Greyslaer, as the only return expected for any service he might have rendered him, to curb his tongue hereafter in speaking of Joseph Brant!

Before the patriot officer could reply, the magician had turned upon his heel and gained the door; but, as if struck with an afterthought, he instantly returned, and, ere Greyslaer was aware of his intention, he had bared his arm to the shoulder, produced a stained flint from his pouch, and branded an uncouth device, that made the skin smart with pain as the blood oozed through.

"He who loves the Redman may die by rifle or tomahawk, but he will never be disgraced by the scalping-knife or tortured at the stake if he shows this mark to the followers of Thayendanagea!"

And, before Greyslaer could find language to express his astonishment, either at the act or the words which accompanied it, he was alone with the old woman, who busied herself in reverentially picking up and putting away the mumming tools of his profession which the pseudo magician had flung upon the ground as he disappeared through the door.

---

1. The crude sentiments of this "Medicine-man," as thus spoken, seem, by some coincidence or other, to have been afterward partially repeated by Thayendanagea, and in nearly similar words, in a letter to a correspondent of the chieftain. *Vide Stone's Life of Brant*, vol. ii.

CHAPTER 6

The Squaw Camp

A swampy lair, walled round with sullen hills,
Whose jagged rocks upheaved their splintered crests,
Frowning above the fray of wrestling limbs below;
A wild morass, whose tangled thickets hid
The blessed sunshine from its oozy pools,
Save where some grassy tussock, cinctured by a rill,
O'er which the fragrant birch and spicewood drooped,
Let down the quivering light upon its floor.

Ms. Poems.

The above lines describe, not inaptly, the scene to which the wounded prisoner had been carried for safety and seclusion. The lodge in which Greyslaer lay helpless upon the bed of pain, stood, among several others in the wilderness, remote from the station where the warriors of the Mohawks were collected; and, from the pleasant murmur of female voices, and cheering call of children at play, which met his ear when returning strength enabled the wounded officer to be more observant of things around him, he soon became aware that his present *domicil* must be none other than the "Squaw Camp" of Thayendanagea; a lonely fastness where, in time of war, the women and children of his tribe were sequestered for safety.

Eager to catch at anything to vary the monotony of slow convalescence, and prompted by that thirst for sunshine and the breeze which gives such a yearning to the sick man's spirit, Greyslaer would fain have expressed his desire to be lifted out in front of the lodge. But, ignorant of the Mohawk language, he found some difficulty in making the old squaw, who, as his only nurse, affected to regulate all his movements, understand his wishes. Her consent to the step, however, was obtained without any great difficulty, and she transported the invalid beyond the porch by dragging his pallet of skins, with the patient upon it, to the outside of the *wigwam*.

A rivulet, bounded upon the opposite side by a wall of vines and briers, which in their turn were overhung by tall aspens, intermingled with the swamp-ash and dusky tamarack, rippled against the mossy bank whereon he lay, and hid its wanderings in mazy thickets beyond. The hammock whereon the cluster of wigwams which formed the camp had been raised, seemed to afford the only spot firm enough for such a purpose amid the spongy and quaking morass that spread around on every side. And this grassy esplanade was so limited in extent, that a clump of witch-elms growing in the centre cast their drooping branches nearly to the middle of the stream that bathed the wild flowers on its edges.

Beneath one of these trees was collected a group that instantly arrested the earnest gaze of the captive officer. A merry crew of children, which seemed to have been confided to her care, were playing with a large, solemn hound that reposed at the feet of a slim Indian girl. The girl, leaning against the tree, with one pretty foot upraised upon its straggling roots, sat weaving a baldric of silk and *wampum*, whose gaudy strings lay partly on the green sod beside her, and were partly held in long beaded cords by a noble-looking woman that stood behind her, playfully twining the gay tassels in the raven locks of her companion.

The face of the larger and more commanding maiden was averted from his gaze when her person first caught the eye of Greyslaer; but her snowy hand, resting for a moment upon the nut-brown neck of the Indian girl, sufficiently revealed to him the neighbourhood of one of his own race and colour; perhaps a countrywoman; perhaps, indeed—he could scarcely repress a cry of joy at the thought of the bare possibility—perhaps Alida! The proud and commanding mien proud, even though something mournful in her air was blended with the half sportive act in which she was engaged—was surely that of Alida. The same dejection or listlessness of manner, call it which you will, it was true, might characterize any female captive so situated; but the scenes which Miss De Roos had recently passed through would best mark her as the victim of present melancholy.

So Greyslaer thought, and his surmises were almost ripened to a certainty when he looked again, at the hound. He thought he beheld in him the cause of an outcry which had been more than once raised near his cabin, as the shrewish squaw beat off a dog that from day to day persisted in thrusting his nose under the blanket which formed the door, and smelling round as if in search of an acquaintance. The invalid had himself noticed the intrusion as pertinacious, but believed the offender to be merely one of the wolfish mongrels that hang round an Indian camp. It was like recognising an old friend to discover his mistake. "Brom!" he called, in a low voice; the hound raised his ears. "Brom!" he repeated, in the same suppressed tone. The dog shook off the urchins that beleaguered him as he sprang to his feet and looked anxiously around. "Brom, my poor fellow!" said Greyslaer, somewhat louder, and the hound bounded upon him, devouring him with caresses.

"Down, sir, down," he cried, extricating himself with difficulty from this overpowering outbreak of affection, and turning to look for the fair mistress of the animal. But Alida, if it were indeed she, had disappeared on the instant; and the Indian girl, collecting her work together, was preparing to follow her companion.

The wounded Greyslaer, whose situation prevented his moving, was filled with grief and vexation when, unheeding every gesture by which he attempted to arrest her attention, the Indian girl also flitted from the spot. He sank back, exhausted with agitation, upon his couch of skins; and believing almost that his fevered senses had deceived him, turned the next moment to look for the dog, to see if he too had been spirited away. The hound had couched down a few yards off, where he sat watching his new-found acquaintance. He wagged his tail, and approaching as he caught an encouraging look from Greyslaer, proved, by rubbing his cold nose against the hand of his friend, that he at least was a substantial thing of earth.

"Why, old Brom, are you still true to your mistress's friend, while she flies his presence as if he were an evil spirit?"

The dog looked as if he had every disposition in the world to comprehend what was said to him, but, like most dogs who fail in such endeavour, gave no

"But here comes my termagant nurse, and you must walk off, my poor fellow."

As the youth spoke he warded off a blow which the truculent dame aimed at the hound with a stick which she seized from the ground, and which Greyslaer, snatching from her hand, shook at her in a threatening manner, to show his displeasure, before casting it into the stream near him. The worthy Brom, meanwhile, either understanding the last words which had been addressed to him, or unwilling to create scandal by causing a domestic broil in Greyslaer's establishment, wisely abstracted himself as fast as his legs could carry him. It is a curious fact, that a well-bred dog, who has been happy in his associations with the polite of our species, will never fly at a woman or child; and Brom, though he preferred running to fighting in the present instance, curled his tail so erect upon his retreat, that no suspicion could attach to his valour. Turning round when he had gained a discreet distance from the virago, he paused for a few moments, and looked back upon her with a countenance more in sorrow than in anger before taking up the lazy trot with which he finally disappeared behind a remote *wigwam* of the group.

The young officer was not at a loss to account for the conduct of the white lady in *apparently* avoiding him, if she were here a captive like himself. But, assuming her to be such, he could conceive no satisfactory reason for her discouraging every kind of communication between them. Yet such seemed really to be the case when, a few days after his first transient glimpse of her person, his eye again encountered her figure, as, with the luxurious laziness of an invalid, he loitered in the cool shade, musing upon his situation. His strength, which had rapidly improved within the last few days, enabled him now to move toward the lady; but the eager cry with which he pronounced the name of "Alida" warned her of his approach; and its earnest and anxious repetition only added quickness to the speed with which she eluded his pursuit.

The dispirited Greyslaer began now to doubt whether or not the fair captive, for such both the dress and complexion proclaimed her to be, were really Miss De Roos. And yet, while it would be equally strange for any other of his countrywomen to practise a similar avoidance, considering the situation of both parties, and how much a good understanding between them might tend to facilitate their mutual escape, the circumstances under which Alida had been carried off, and the presence of her favourite dog in company with the mysterious maiden, seemed sufficiently to prove that the white lady could be no other than Miss De Roos.

Another suspicion which passed through the mind of Greyslaer was hastily dismissed as un worthy both of Alida and himself, considering the perils which he had encountered to restore her to her friends. It was, that the coldness with which she had ever frowned upon his boyish suit actuated her conduct in their present situation.

"She is unwilling," said he, bitterly, "to receive succour at my hands. Nay, she is indifferent to the disaster which has overtaken me in attempting to rescue her; and regardless, perhaps, as to what may be my fate as a wounded prisoner in the hands of these savages; and yet she lacks not humanity! Surely, am I less than naught to her?"

We have said that Greyslaer repelled these unworthy suspicions, and so he did, indignant that a thought demeaning to his mistress should have found a place in his mind, much less shaped itself into words. He repelled it, but in vain, for the same ungenerous thought recurred again and again, with withering effect upon his already depressed spirits.

Alas! what a blight does that thought bring over a young, ardent, ingenuous mind! The thought that it hath lavished its wealth of loving upon one who not only can make no return, but who cares not, recks not how prodigally the treasures of the heart may be wasted; who regards the most generous sacrifices of disinterested feeling as mere in cense upon the altar of vanity; who derides the idolatry of true affection, and holds the deepest throes of devoted passion but as idle sallies of youthful extravagance that have no claim upon her sympathy, that can never awaken her gratitude! Such, however, is too often the recompense of the misplaced affection that knows not how to conceal or regulate its own overflowings.

Ingratitude, however, is not, therefore, the special fault of the sex! It is human nature, not woman nature, which sets lightly by a homage which has never been solicited, and which is paid without stint! When that homage is pertinacious and un seasonable, it becomes irksome and offensive. The attentions of love that we do not reciprocate, however pleasing to our vanity at first, cease to flatter when passion increases to infatuation. The idolatry which springs from too extravagant an appreciation of our character or personal qualities, seems akin either to folly or madness, and we no longer value the good opinion which is the offspring rather of a heated fancy than of a judgment which we can respect.

But though these chilling laws of reasoning human nature admit of but little mitigation, yet Alida de Roos was of too magnanimous a spirit to apply them in full to one who loved her, if not wisely, yet with all truth and nobleness; and seeing in her youthful admirer all the qualities to awaken a sister's tenderness, she mourned his infatuation with a sister's sorrow. Love him she thought she never could, even if her heart had not been preoccupied by an emotion that closed it completely against such a sentiment. Her haughty and aspiring mind had hitherto detected no qualities in Greyslaer's character which could touch it to gentle issues. It was only as the refined but visionary student, the romantic cherisher of vain and speculative dreams, such as float around a young enthusiast who knows the world through books alone, that Greyslaer had hitherto appeared to the lady of his love. The play of his polished fancy, the allurements of his cultivated intellect, had interested her in studying the character of a stripling who, some years her junior, and continually thrown in her society as the most intimate friend of her brother, did, not unnaturally, attract her kindly regard.

But while, with less mental acquirement upon her own part, Alida perhaps over-estimated that of which Greyslaer could boast, yet her esteem for his talents and accomplishments was full as nearly allied to pity as to admiration. She admired the qualities in themselves, but she thought that their possessor, in this instance, was deficient in the power to make them useful either to himself or to others. She thought the character of Greyslaer was wholly unsuited to the country and the circumstances amid which his lot was cast. He possessed the requisites, among other scenes and other times, to grace a fortune or uphold an honourable name; but he lacked the stirring qualities to win either by his own exertions. He was, in a word, one whose impracticable, feeble, or misapplied energies doomed him to mediocrity in life; a mediocrity which, by the comfortable respectability that she believed would attend it, gained nothing in the eyes of a woman whom poverty or peril would never have prevented from sharing the destiny of the man she loved.

'Twas strange! yet the acute-minded Alida de Roos seemed never to dream that the wild devotion which the student bore her was what absorbed all the salient energies of his soul; that she was the bond that kept its pinions from mounting; that idolatry for her alone had robbed ambition's shrine of Greyslaer's worship; that love—love only—all-absorbing, all-devouring love, had delved the grave in which his youth's best promise was swallowed up! The bitter reflections of the lonely prisoner were destined to a more early and agreeable relief than he had anticipated. An hour or more had passed away, and Greyslaer still sat beneath the weeping elm, now moodily gazing upon the stream that twinkled through the bushes near him, and now casting a fierce and impatient glance upon some lounging Indian, an aged or broken-down warrior of the band, who had been left by the chief for the nominal protection of the camp.

At last an object of more agreeable interest presented itself in the shape of Brom, the stag-hound. Greyslaer had not seen the dog for some days; and surmising that the friendly animal had been kept out of his sight by design, he was at once struck with the peculiarity of his conduct now, as the hound, instead of bounding eagerly forward to fawn upon him, exhibited the coolest indifference to the call of his friend. The sagacious Brom went wandering hither and thither, smelling idly along the ground, and, though gradually coming nearer, making his approaches after such a careless fashion, that Greyslaer was in doubt whether the brute knew him or not. He whistled, and again called him by name; but the dog, raising his head, looked vacantly around him, and then resumed his course, without adding either to the rapidity or directness of his steps. At last, getting within a few yards of his friend, the worthy Brom appeared to be for the first time aware of his neighbourhood, though not until he had first passed by, and, as it seemed, thrown a chance look over his shoulder, which induced him to turn and come gravely forward, as not wishing to cut an old acquaintance by design.

Amused with "the airs" of the dog—for in happier days Greyslaer had frequently seen him put on the same whimsical dignity for less cause than might have given Brom offence at his last visit to the *wigwam*—the young man took the head of the hound in his lap and patted it kindly. Brom only acknowledged the caress by rubbing his head against the knees of his friend, as if his collar were too tight for him; and, placing his hand under the clasp to loosen it, Greyslaer felt beneath it a scroll of birchen bark, whose smooth and flexible texture allows it to be written upon and folded like paper. Agitated with joy at the discovery, the surprise of the youth did not, however, prevent him from instantly concealing the missive in his dress; while the wise Brom, apparently contented with the interview, went smelling and loitering on his way around the camp, as if his tour was one of idleness altogether.

The note, as read by Greyslaer the moment he had attained the interior of his lodge, from which his quondam nurse and present amiable housekeeper was happily absent, contained only these words, written with charcoal:

An hour after midnight, be near the fallen sycamore which crosses the brook within a few paces of your *wigwam*. The Indian girl will conduct you to an interview with

A. D. R.

115

CHAPTER 7

The Haunted Rock

And in the mountain mist, the torrent's spray,
The quivering forest or the glassy flood,
Soft-falling showers or hues of orient day,
They imaged spirits beautiful and good;
But when the tempest roared, with voices rude,
Or fierce red lightning fired the forest-pine,
Or withering heats untimely seared the wood,
The angry forms they saw of powers malign;
These they besought to spare, those blessed for aid divine.

Sands

"And what fears The Spreading Dew in this place, that she would have me now choose another for her to lead the white man to, that I may hear tidings of my friends?"

"This rock whereon we sit, lady—for Teondetha told me thou wert a chieftainess among thy people—this rock is sacred to the spirit that watches over true affection. Here the young hunter breathes the vow that binds his fidelity forever. And she that hearkens to it here, if listening but from girlish levity, or induced by maiden prankishness to break it afterward, she withers from the earth like a plant plucked from the garden of the blessed, and sent to shrivel mid the fires of the Evil One."

"But, foolish girl, I mean not to mislead this youth," rejoined Alida, in the Mohawk tongue, which, like many a lady near the border at that time, she spoke with ease and fluency. "Is the soul of my young friend so full of Teondetha, that she thinks every man, like him, a lover?"

"The image of her true warrior, though ever present to The Spread-

116

ing Dew, still leaves room for all good spirits, and their ruler, Owaneyo, to be remembered. The brown-haired captive loves my blue-eyed sister; and if he be no more to her than she says, it were mockery to the spirit to bring him here."

"And by what means got you the idea that this young man thinks of your friend save as a country woman in captivity like himself?"

"Thou speakest with two tongues, lady; and I, though the talk of the white man is strange to me, can do the same. The brown-haired warrior is a friend of the Oneidas, and can use the tongue of Teondetha; and, even if words had not betrayed his secret, as he implored me to look first to your safety, lady, when you came not to the spot to which I led him upon the opposite side of the camp yesternight, should I not have known how it stood with him? Doth not the breeze know why the flower trembles when it fans it? And held I not the captive's hand while I spoke of you, when guiding him through the thicket's depths?"

"It is too late now, my gentle sister, to change our place of meeting," said Miss De Roos, who saw that it was equally impossible to reason the girl out of the conviction which she had lately adopted, or the superstition which was so intimately ingrafted with her forest faith. "I must see the youth tonight, and upon this spot, or we must abandon the interview altogether; and even now I hear the sound as of someone leaping from bog to bog in the quaking fen around us."

The Mohawk girl hesitated no longer. Anxiety for the fate of Teondetha's friend, wandering in darkness amid the spongy and treacherous morass, laced everywhere among its blind thickets with deep and sloughy pools, urged her to spring forward and guide him in safety to the Haunted Rock; and in a few moments Greyslaer had penetrated the copse of tamaracks that girdled it, and gained the firm and broad platform whereon his mistress stood. The Indian maiden, from considerations of delicacy that in such matters seem common to her sex, however uncultivated, instantly glided away; and the lovers, if such they may be called, were left alone together.

And now, young gallant, so lithe of foot and bold of hand, so ready in speech and act, alike amid man hood's councils and warrior fray, where lurks thy smooth tongue, thy nimble wit and stout endeavour, that have already proclaimed thee *man* among the ablest of thy fellows? Why do thy knees tremble, and thy quivering lips refuse to lackey thy laggard thoughts to utterance? Why tak'st thou not the outstretched hand the maid in friendliness accords thee? Why fall thy muttered syllables like broken drops feebly distilled from some slow-thawing fount ain? Is it the Divinity of the place that awes thee? or doth thy spirit quail before an earthly presence?

"Greyslaer," said Alida, solemnly, for her woman's heart was touched by the agitation which overwhelmed her lover, and the bright stars shining down upon the spot revealed the paleness of his cheek. "God! he knows that I would spare you the pain my words may inflict to-night; I sought this interview for a far different object from that to which I now see that it must—that it ought, perhaps, for your future happiness, to tend. I blame myself in not inviting such an explanation between us long ago. Be a man, Max Greyslaer, and shrink not at what I am about to say. You love me?"

"To idolatry, to madness," cried the young man, in a hoarse whisper of passion, while his thronged feelings, rushing tumultuously to find vent through his lips, seemed nearly to suffocate him as he flung himself upon his knees before Alida.

The lady recoiled against a blasted tree that grew nearby, and, overcome for a moment, could only mutely motion to him to rise. He sprang to his feet, and stood with folded arms before her. "Alas! alas!" she said, at length recovering herself, "you need not have told me that. And yet, the God of Heaven be my judge, I dreamed not till this night that your regard was of so deep a nature. But you are yet young, Greyslaer; love cannot exist without hope, and this fancy will soon pass away, or be transferred to another more worthy of your esteem; to one who can reciprocate your affection."

"Yes! when the last year's stubble shall sprout with a second spring; when that scathed tree against which you lean shall shake off the moss that drinks up its sap of life, and be clothed anew with verdure of its own; when—"

"Hold, Max, hold; this is the very phrensy of passion. I cannot listen to you longer, unless you show some regard for my feelings by repressing the vehemence of yours. Oh! Max Greyslaer, if you knew how deep a cause I have for grief in which you cannot share, you would from this moment cease to add to my sorrows by urging this misplaced, this most unhappy passion."

"You unhappy, Alida?—forgive me for thus calling you. You the victim of a secret sorrow? *You*, with that smooth cheek; that rounded, pliant form; that brow on which—no, no, the hand of grief hath never left its wasting fingers there, nor hollow care enshrined himself in such a tenement; you but mock me, Alida; or, rather, you would thus, in mercy, crush my ill-starred passion. But, Miss De Roos, you know me not! If the presumption of my love offend you—"

"Oh! not offend me," tearfully murmured the afflicted girl.

"If the madness of my love offend you," pursued Max, unheeding the low-voiced interruption, "you may teach me to curb, to smother, to bury in my inmost soul the feeling that consumes it; but there, there it will burn forever. The heart of Greyslaer can know no second love."

"This is too, too much! It will drive me mad to speak it; yet nothing else will extinguish his un happy infatuation. Max Greyslaer, hear me. I have long since given you the regard of a sister. I have watched you alike in your studies and your sports, with the pride and the interest of an elder sister; and a sister's fondness would have followed, could I have shut out the painful conviction that it was not with the affection of a brother you regarded me. This interest in your welfare alone would impel me to leave no step untried to root out this fatal passion from your heart. But since the wild avowal of this night; since the declaration of desperate feelings you but now betrayed, I feel, though most innocently the cause of them, that you have still deeper claims upon my sympathy, that you have new ones upon my gratitude. I feel that there is but one way to break the miserable chain by which you would link your fate with mine, and give you back to the higher and happier destiny for which, by every circumstance save this one only, you are fitted. Nay, thank me not; I acknowledge you have a *right* to my confidence."

She paused, and the features upon which the domestic sorrows of the last few weeks had left no feeble impress, became agitated with an expression of pain, which even the recollection of that night of horror at the Hawksnest had failed to trace. Greyslaer himself awaited what was to follow; and her words, as she resumed, were spoken in a tone low but clear, firm but in expressibly mournful. "There is," she said, "there is but one man living, Greyslaer one as vile, sordid, ruthless, and malignant as you are gentle, generous, and noble—one only other who shares the secret you have this night wrung from me."

"And he is—"

My husband!"

The wretched girl, whose lofty spirit was still farther wrought up by the high and magnanimous sentiment of generosity which sustained her for the moment, swooned the instant she had pronounced the words. The weakness, however, quickly passed away, as, at a cry of alarm from Greyslaer, the Indian maiden bounded from the covert, and applied some cool glossy leaves, wet with the dews of night, to the brow of the sufferer.

The blow was better received by Greyslaer than could have been expected or hoped for by her that dealt it. He was indeed astounded and petrified by the first announcement; but all consideration for himself seemed the next moment merged in concern for his unhappy mistress.

"Lady," he said, dropping on one knee before her, and with an air of deep respect pressing his lips to the hand which she did not attempt to withdraw, "you spoke truly, lady, when you said my fate was linked with yours; but you erred in believing that aught could sever the chain, though it might lead me to destruction. As a lover, after what I have heard this night, you shall never know me more. But you have still left me something to live for, in taking away the only hope that could make existence happy. You have given me back to myself, but from this moment I am more completely yours than ever. The romantic dream of my youth has passed away, the madness of my misplaced and boyish love is over; and here, by the cool light of manhood's enfranchised reason, here upon this planted rock, with yon bright heaven as witness of my vow, I swear, while the pulses of life beat within me, never to leave nor desert you until I unravel this hideous mystery, and break the spell in which some fiend has manacled your soul.

"Nay, shrink not, dearest lady, as if my sworn service might prove intrusive. How or why these devilish meshes have been woven around you, I ask you not to explain until I have in some way approved my faith and loyalty. But be it when or where you choose to make the revelation; be the deed what it may, you claim in return for the precious boon of your confidence, if human hand can work it, it shall be done at your bidding."

A light as from a maniac's eye glared in that of Alida as the young man rose slowly up before her after this wild and solemn adjuration.

"No, no, Greyslaer," she cried, shaking back the long tresses which had fallen in disorder over her neck and shoulders. "No, Greyslaer, thou art not yet dear enough to me to share the fruition of the hoarded hope I have lived upon for years. Alida's own hand shall alone avenge Alida! For what else have I cherished the strength of this useless frame; for what have I forgot my woman's nature, and shared your schooling in feats of arms with my brother? Think you it was an idle caprice of my sex, or the perverted taste of an Amazon, that made me choose pistol and rapier, instead of needle and distaff, for my amusement? No, Max Greyslaer; my hand, as well as my heart, hath been schooled for years to the accomplishment of one only end, and they will neither of them fail me at my purpose. That is, if this poor brain hold out."

And, pressing both hands to her temples, the unfortunate young lady looked so bewildered for a moment, that Greyslaer could hardly resist the conviction that her intellects were disordered. Yet, if such were indeed the case, how, he thought, could her mind be so well balanced in regard to all other subjects? In reference to this one, too, her reason, though disturbed, was not clouded; the agitation of the fountain did indeed hide its depths from view, but the water was bright and limpid still.

If it be true, however, "that great wit to madness nearly is allied," while gleams of insanity have been discovered in minds which have exercised a wide and enduring influence over mankind, and, mastering their disease till the last, have left in death the wisest of their survivors doubtful as to the suspicion that has attached to them; then might a far more experienced observer of human nature than young Greyslaer be at fault. Nor, indeed, were it just to conclude, only from what he had witnessed, that the senses of Alida were deranged. The sentiments which she had just uttered were indeed abhorrent to the nature of her sex, to her Christian education, and all her early associations of refinement. But while the excitement under which she spoke would sufficiently account for her momentary air of wildness, there was none of the incoherence of distraction in her speech; and as for nature and education, the first had been shocked, overthrown, and changed by the outrage which trampled upon it, and the last the last— is but an artificial barrier, that at once gives way when the former has become perverted.

While these reflections, or others not unlike them, passed hurriedly through the mind of Greyslaer, the lovely subject of them seemed too busied with her own conflicting thoughts to observe the earnest and anxious gaze that was riveted upon her countenance. At last, as if shaking off the load that weighed upon her spirits, and recovering from the attitude of dejection that for a moment bowed her commanding form, she said, in a calm voice,

"I would, Mr. Greyslaer. that you could forget what has passed between us this night. I have been hasty in permitting you to commit yourself to take an interest in my affairs which they do not deserve at your hands. I have thought of the mischievous consequences of yielding you a more full and complete confidence; and it would be ungenerous in me to claim your active sympathy for the blind and partial revelation of my sorrows already made. I beseech you to remember only the friendly interest with which I requite your regard, and to forget all else that has passed between us."

These formal words, which struck chillingly upon the ear of Greyslaer, were pronounced in that measured tone of superior self-possession with which a master-spirit may sometimes address an inferior, blended with the air of kind authority which considerate age will put on when conversing with inexperienced youth. But, though she knew it not yet, the ascendancy which the generous and haughty-souled Alida had hitherto exercised over the mind of her lover was gone forever; and Greyslaer made her feel that it was so in his reply.

"An hour ago, Miss De Roos, and I was, perhaps, the rash and doting boy you think me. Rash in aspiring to the hand of one so gifted as yourself, doting in that I dared to tell you of my passion; but though I still bear you a regard passing the love of kindred, however near, *boy* I am no longer. The day-star of my youth has set for ever; the destiny of my life is written; for good or for evil, 'tis henceforth twined with yours. If you repent the share you may have had in thus determining my fate, if it be a generous concern for my welfare that prompted your words, your anxiety is thrown away. It is too late for *you* to recede; and I—I have thrown my cast, and am determined to stand the hazard of the die!"

"And how," said the lady, with an irresolute, uneasy air, that perhaps betrayed a mingled feeling of jealous pride, of growing self-diffidence, and newly-awakened respect for the lofty and decided tone the youth assumed so unexpectedly, "how, Greyslaer, am I to avail myself of any service which you might render me'?"

"By designating the villain at whose life you aim, and leaving me to avenge your injuries."

"Speak you in earnest, Max Greyslaer? Do you think me, then, capable of such ignoble and cold blooded selfishness? so ignoble as to place my mortal quarrel in the hands of one who is a stranger to my blood; so selfish as to requite affection by imposing a task that may lead to death?"

"Well spoken, young missus, like a gal of spunk as you are," exclaimed a harsh voice nearby, while a brawny ruffian, leaping from the thicket, and striking the rock with a short Indian war-club as he gained his footing upon it, placed himself between Greyslaer and

Alida. "What, ho! younker," he cried; "you would add to the account that is chalked up agin you already, would you? God help you in his own way; but, unless the devil fail wild Wat afore then, you will find him a hard reckoner; that is, if your carcass first escape a roasting at the hands of the bloody Mohawk."

"Standoff, ruffian," muttered Greyslaer, choking with passion, as he saw the savage-looking fellow circling the waist of Alida with one arm, while, weaponless and feeble from his recent wound, he felt himself incapable of protecting her.

"Fair words, fair words, if you please, my young master; I come here only to rescue this lady from Indian captivity; and, as the Redskins are still my friends in the main, I should be sorry to rob the stake doubly by knocking you in the head."

"Oh, Max," murmured Alida, who had hitherto stood as if paralyzed with horror, "strive not with this dark and terrible man, who even now has stepped, as from the grave, between us."

"And so you, too, eh, my *fraulein*, thought, like many others, that Red Wolfert had kicked the bucket, because I took Wat's advice, and cleared out for a while, to save my neck, till things should blow over. But times have changed, my spanking lass; tall fellows hold up their heads once more, and I come here to exercise the rights of one of them over Mistress—"

"Speak, speak but one word, I pray you, Alida! Is this horrible ruffi—is this your husband?"

"*Dunder und blixem*, and suppose I be," cried the man, catching the words out of the mouth of Alida, whose senses seemed too much benumbed to make a ready reply. "Don't you see how the gal wilts like when I look at her, and who but her natural husband should make a woman cower?"

"In the name of the devil, who are you, that speak so fitly in his tongue?" said Greyslaer, making a wary movement toward the man, in the desperate hope of clutching from his hand the short mace with which he dallied.

"A clerk of St. Nicholas, who will despatch you with a message to his employer if you move a step nearer, *verfluchter kerl.*"

"If you be the fiend himself, here's at you," shouted Greyslaer, bounding furiously forward. The contest was too unequal to leave a hope of success for the invalid youth, had he succeeded in closing with his antagonist; but the latter, to whom the now senseless Alida seemed no encumbrance, as he actively leaped aside, laughed to scorn the vain efforts of his assailant, who still pressed impetuously upon him. His words, however, betrayed his growing irritation, as, backing step by step toward the edge of the rock, so as still to keep the full swing of his arm while the youth attempted to close in upon him,

"*Gemeiner hund,* madcap, idiot, dolt, take that to quiet you," he cried, at last dealing a blow that brought Greyslaer instantly to the ground.

Valtmeyer, for the ruffian was no other than that redoubtable outlaw, waited not to see how durable might be the effects of the blow, but, plunging into the bushes, he glided along a slippery log with his burden, thridding the morass like one accustomed to its dangers. Stricken down, and stunned for the moment, Greyslaer was slowly regaining his feet, when the first object he beheld was the Mohawk maiden, gazing, with clasped hands and bewildered eyes, toward the thickets into which the outlaw had disappeared. His towering form, his sallow features, his long beard of grizzled red, and aspect altogether foreign and hideous to her sight, made him no unfit personification of those evil spirits of the forest which the Indian girl would naturally paint, as the very reverse in appearance from the smooth-cheeked warriors of her race; and the simple sylvan maiden, as she breathed a prayer for the ill-fated pale sister of her sex, thought that the offended genius of the place had permitted some fiend to intrude within his hallowed circle, and punish on the spot the first violation of the Haunted Rock.

CHAPTER 8

Tory Councils

The sachem spoke:
Resentment rising, seemed to choke
The words of wrath that forth had broke;
But conscience lent her bland relief,
And calmly spoke the injured chief.

Sands.

The calamity which had overtaken the family of the Hawksnest, the mysterious fate of Miss De Roos, and the presumed death of one so popular as young Max Greyslaer, excited the deepest sensation through the Valley of the Mohawk. The two political parties which divided the district were as yet by no means fairly in the field against each other; and the warfare of words being still carried on for a season before a final appeal to arms was had, recrimination rose high between either faction.

The patriots did not hesitate to charge the Tories with being the instigators of this ruthless attack upon the peace of a private family, while the loyalists, affecting to be equally indignant at the outrage, taunted the Whigs with being the first to bring the laws of the country into contempt by their own factious conduct. The catastrophe, however, seemed in one respect to have a salutary effect. It opened the eyes of both parties to the horrors of a civil war. Both seemed willing to pause and await the effect of circumstance in preventing their being farther embroiled; and both united with apparent sincerity in passing public resolutions against the employment of the Indians to strengthen either side, whatever the issue might be, and whenever that issue might be finally joined. But the ball of Revolution was in motion; and though its course might be for the time more noise less, neither its momentum nor its accumulating forces were diminished.

The organization of party, and the dangerous tampering with the Indian tribes, went on as industriously as ever; the Whigs displaying the greatest coolness, foresight, and address in the one respect, while the Tories were equally successful in the other.

Months, in the meantime, passed away, and the operations of either began to show results which must produce a crisis. The civil authority passed into the hands of the patriots, who found an excuse for a stern exercise of that authority in sending General Schuyler, with a large body of militia, to disarm the disaffected, in the same moment that the predominant influence of the Tories in Indian politics was fully consummated. The tribe of Oneidas, after long nobly withstanding both threats and cajoling, were at length driven, by the intriguing arts of the latter, to detach themselves from the confederacy of the Six Nations, and assume that neutral position which was afterward only abandoned for a warm espousal of the patriot cause.

It was Christmas morning; and the sun, which shone through the sacred grove of Onondaga, touched with gold the pendant icicles which drooped from the heavy boughs that had wailed for a thousand winters around the ancient citadel of the Ongi-Honwe, The adjacent lake, whose frozen surface was freshly covered with virgin snow, smiled in the glad light of the morning, whose early rays were glinted back from bush and thicket, that were all clothed with the same dazzling mantle. A few shreds of smoke ascending straight upward into the clear blue sky was the only object stirring amid the bright and tranquil scene.

But for this faint indication of the neighbourhood of man, the lonely stockade, that was dignified with the name of "The Onondaga Castle," seemed wholly deserted; and he who gazed within would have looked in vain for the imposing assemblage of patriarchal sachems which, in the previous century, was likened to the Senate of Rome by Frontenac, when that adventurous Frenchman, like another Brennus, intruded with his armed followers into the great council of the Aganuschion.[1] One lonely female was the only occupant of the building.

The stranger, who was aware of the consideration in which the

---

1. "The national council (of the Six Nations) took cognizance of war and peace, of the affairs of the tributary nations, and of their negotiations with the French and English colonies. All their proceedings were conducted with great deliberation, and were distinguished for order, decorum, and solemnity. In eloquence, in dignity, and in all the characteristics of profound policy, they surpassed an assembly of feudal barons, and were, perhaps, not far inferior to the great Amphictyonic Council of Greece."—*De Witt Clinton.*

sex were held among the Ongi-Honwe, and who knew that this rude building contained the great national altar of their confederacy, might at first have mistaken the woman now before him for one of those pious devotees who successively, for ages, watched the sacred central council-fire of the Aganuschion. But the mean features and apparel of the withered old crone, as she sat crouched in the ashes, would soon, upon a close survey, have proved that she could not claim to be numbered among "the principal women of the Six Nations."

"*Wah!*" exclaimed the hag, as, with a crooked stick, she vainly pushed a wet and blackened ember toward the smouldering ashes; "could not the fools leave enough of the fire that has burned for a thousand winters to warm these old bones with? May the Evil One broil them on his own for meddling in the quarrel of Corlear[2] with the Sagernash! May their tribes be dispersed like these scattered embers! May they, like them, be trampled upon by—" Stopping short in her imprecation as she caught sight of a half-extinguished branch, which still lay smoking in the corner where it had been tossed, the crone hobbled toward it, and thrust it afresh in the ashes, applying, at the same time, the air from her wheezy lungs to rekindle the flame.

Her efforts were followed by a momentary ignition, indicated by a few sparks, that made her mutter still more angrily, as, to avoid them, she threw back her head, from which the long gray hair drooped in the ashes. The dying brand crackled feebly, sighed like a living thing, and expired.

"*A-rai-wah!* The Sacred Fire of Onondaga is extinguished forever!"

As she spoke the hag gathered her knees toward her body with one hand, and resting her shrivelled cheek upon the other, commenced rocking backward and forward, croaking a harsh song, in which lamentations and curses were so wildly intermingled that the eldritch dirge partook equally of the character of either.

But this wretched remnant of mortality was not the only mourner for the extinguished pride and power of the now broken Iroquois confederacy.

The Christmas sun shone merrily upon the frosted window-panes of Johnson Hall; gleamed upon the armour that decked its walls, and

---

2. "Sons of Corlear," or "The Children of Quidar," were the terms by which "The Six Nations" indifferently distinguished the inhabitants of the Colony of New York; and, though first adopted during the Dutch ascendancy over the province, we find them used in Indian treaties and speeches down to quite a recent period.

tinted with freshness the evergreens that festooned its ancient portraits. But here, as at Onondaga, its beams seemed to smile only as in mockery of man and his doings. Here were men, haggard and worn with long watching, grouped in disorder throughout the broad corridor. Some were engaged in anxious or angry debate together; some, as if wearied out with action or discussion, were stretched upon the oaken settles, regarding with dogged indifference the excited disputes of their comrades; and one, more swarthy of feature than the rest, a tall man of a fierce and haughty aspect, was striding impatiently to and fro, casting ever and *anon* a hasty look at the staircase, whose polished banister he repeatedly struck with his tomahawk in passing.[3] Twice he had ascended several steps, as if determined to seek above some person who had exhausted his patience in delaying an interview; and then pausing a moment as he thundered anew with his hatchet upon the stairs, he turned abruptly upon his heel, breathing indignation against those who appeared not to heed his savage signal.

At last a strong-framed man, hastily arrayed in a dressing-gown, accompanied by a Highland officer in full uniform, presented himself upon the landing of the staircase. The features of either were clouded; but of the two the former seemed to be labouring under the greater emotion. His look was agitated, but not alarmed; distempered, but not angry.

"Brant!" said he, with some severity, "at any other time I would not overlook this want of respect; I would not put up with this rudeness from any man breathing. But since we are all here companions in affliction together, a quarrel with so old a friend of my house would not become me."

"Companions together, Sir John? You honour the poor Indian by placing him in such company, even in your *speech*, though you can find no room for him in your *writings* when making terms with the enemy!"

"Speak, Alan MacDonald, and dispel these ungenerous suspicions of our friend! Tell him the circumstances under which we have been compelled to treat with the commissioners from Albany."

"I am wholly at a loss upon what particular point to answer Captain Brant," said MacDonald, coolly. "He seems already to be aware that we have accepted terms from General Schuyler, who is marching hitherward with three thousand men; and, unless report belies them,

---

3. The marks of the Indian tomahawk are shown upon the stairs of the hall to this day, (as at time of first publication).

with a hundred Mohawk warriors in his train!"

"Yes! a pack of frightened curs from the lower castle, with a hand-ful of naked renegades from my own people. The hungry offcasts from my tribe, who hope, with Schuyler's countenance, to make spoil of the blankets and provisions that are laid up here for our projected cam-paign. But tell me, Sir John Johnson, is the falling off of these wretches to excuse this desertion of your Indian friends, after entangling us in this contemptible quarrel? God of my people! that the power and glo-ry which thou hast suffered them to attain should be thus ruinously periled in a stranger's brawl! that the league of our ancient confedera-cy, cemented by the blood of a thousand victories, should dissolve like snowflakes upon the river, because, in an evil moment, we consented to interfere in a paltry dispute about a few halfpence of revenue be-tween some peddling foreigners, who would cut each other's throats for gain! Nay, sir, never lay your hand upon your sword! and you, ye prying knaves, unless ye stand back at mine or your master's bidding, shall be dealt with less daintily than the rebel general will handle ye. Back, I say, or my signal call shall fill this hall with those who'll flood it with your gore! By the valour of a Mohawk! but it were a good deed to call in my warriors, and supplant such recreants with men who will hold these walls against all odds till they crumble around them!"

And the indignant chieftain strode haughtily to and fro, as if re-ally balancing in his mind this mad procedure, while the baronet, too much incensed by the insolence of Brant to make any concession to his wrath, was yet too politic to trust himself with a hasty reply. The cool and discreet MacDonald now put in a word to sooth the exasper-ated mood of the demi-savage, as he considered the chieftain when thus excited.

"Captain Brant is too experienced a soldier not to be aware of the impossibility of maintaining our present position against the over-powering force which has been unexpectedly sent against us."

"And could not these heavy-limbed fellows have taken to the bush, and shared a hunter's fare for a few weeks, until the first burst of the storm should have spent its fury? Did you think, in taking up arms in a forest-land like this, where every rock is a fortress, every tree a citadel, did you think that the struggle was to be decided by the capture of a few towns and villages?"

"We did not, noble Thayendanagea," said Sir John, taking the words from the mouth of MacDonald. "Nor do we now believe that one compulsory compromise like the present is to terminate the resistance of the king's friends in this rebellious colony. Had we treated with the rebels for peace throughout the province, our brave Indian brethren would never have been forgotten in the treaty; but our capitulation refers only to the loyalists in this individual district. Our friends are still in arms in other parts of the colony; and even here the gallant gentlemen whom you see around you will yet again lift up the royal banner, or flock to it upon the first opportunity, if Thayendanagea keeps it flying in the field. I—I myself will lead them to—"

"Hold, Sir John! unless you would have your spoken promise give the lie to your written pledge. Remember that '*Sir John Johnson, having given his parole of honour not to take up arms against America,*' he can never—"

"Where, where do you find such words as those?" cried the baronet, hardly knowing what he said in his confusion.

"The *title* of the instrument runs thus, please ye, Sir John," replied Brant, coolly drawing a written document from his bosom, the preamble of which he began to read in a measured, sarcastic tone:—

Terms offered by the honourable Philip Schuyler, major-general in the army of the Thirteen United Colonies, and commanding in the New York department, to Sir John Johnson, baronet, and all such other persons in the county of Tryon as have evinced their intentions of supporting His Majesty's ministry to carry into effect the unconstitutional measures of which the Americans so justly complain:

"Do you mark the emphasis?" said the Mohawk, scornfully, while another storm seemed gathering on his brow, as, repeating the phrase, he went on:—

. . . . .of which the Americans so justly complain; and to prevent which they have been driven to the dreadful necessity of having recourse to arms: first, that—

"Pshaw! you have it there in the third article, and may read for yourselves if you have forgotten the contents of the document, when your signatures, confirming your acceptance of these terms, can scarcely be dry upon the original."

The chieftain, as he spoke, flung the paper contemptuously at the feet of Sir John, who comprehended, without looking at it, that it must be a copy of his terms of surrender, furnished by the politic Whigs to shake the loyalty of Brant.

"It is in vain, Captain Brant," said he, with sad composure, "to conceal from you the extent of our misfortunes. My poor services, in a military capacity, are indeed lost to the crown; and these brave Scottish gentlemen, though suffered to retain their side-arms, are placed by their parole in the same unhappy predicament as myself. But the king has many as capable servants as we, who may still assert their loyalty in the field; and if the fear of chilling their zeal in my royal master's cause induced me to withhold from you the extent of the rebel triumph, I know I shall be forgiven by so ardent and generous a partisan as Thayendanagea."

The tones in which his gallant friend spoke, not less than the words which he uttered, seemed instantly to change the mood of the stormy chieftain, who paced to arid fro for a moment before he replied.

"Sir John," said Brant, with feeling, "I have nothing to forgive. It is you of whom I should ask pardon. You are nearer to the great king than I am, and know best how much of his affairs to suppress and how much to reveal. I have always borne you the love of a brother; and for that, if for nothing else, you will forgive me for thinking you faithless when you were only unfortunate. But I have heard that within the last hour," he added, with that air of calm fatalism characteristic of the Iroquois, even while using the language of a European, "I have heard that which might well distemper me: the confederacy of the Aganuschion is broken. A formal assemblage of *sachems* at Onondaga has dissolved the league of the United Cantons that existed beyond the traditions of our race. Our Great Council Fire is extinguished, and the Six Nations, whose delegates consummated the fatal ceremony with the peaceful unanimity of a band of brothers, meet hereafter only as broken tribes arrayed in deadly hostility to each other."

"Not so, noble *sachem!*" cried the baronet, with brightening features. "It is only the Oneidas, with their adopted children, the Mohicans, who have seceded from the union. The whole Tuscarora tribe, the greater portion of the Onondagas, the fiery Senecas, and valiant Cayugas, are even now assembling under Guy Johnson at Oswego, and wait but for you, with your indomitable Mohawks, to lead them, in all their ancient pride of arms, upon the foe. The delegates of the loyal tribes attended the great central fire only to gain time and blind the lazy eyes of the Oneidas, who convoked the council. Their protest against the confederacy taking any part on either side in this war was not received. They declared their secession from the union, and the sacred fire of the united brethren was extinguished. But the act was illegal; for, as you know, the Mohawks were not represented in the council;[4] and the holy flame of union and power may again be re-lighted in a blaze of glory which shall illumine the land."

The eye of the Indian *sagamore* flashed with fierce delight; his mien assumed a lofty bearing, as of one who felt himself yet destined to be the leader of armies, while his nostril dilated as if already he snuffed the battle. These indications of strong emotion, however, passed away like a flash, even as Sir John pronounced the last words which seemed to have kindled them; and then the face of the Mohawk assumed that immovably stoical expression which rendered it impossible to surmise what was passing in his bosom, and which, upon the countenance of an Iroquois, always covered his deepest and most earnest thoughts.

It might be that vague dreams of ambition, which had heretofore passed through the mind of Brant; that plans of personal elevation at the expense of his less cultivated countrymen, which, in moments of temptation, had suggested themselves, and been indignantly discarded from his thoughts at the generous call of patriotism, or reluctantly abandoned from a conviction of their impracticability under the existing organization of the Aganuschion republic—it may be that these dark and aspiring schemes were busy within him now!

It might be—and the loyal, disinterested character of the man, his romantic love of his doomed race, and his pertinacious aversion to European civilization, while evincing in his own conduct many of its benefits, render this solution by far the most likely—it might be that that silent mien and fixed expression of countenance concealed the devotional communings of his heart—a patriot's thanksgiving for a people saved.

"Captain Brant looks grave," said MacDonald; "he thinks that the responsibility of his part has increased just in proportion that the chance of his playing it successfully with our aid has diminished by that aid being now withdrawn."

If a taunt were implied in this speech, it was so slight as to pass unheeded by Brant; but his heart was not inaccessible to the subtle

4. It may have been under some such pretence as this that the refugee Mohawks, who found a home in Upper Canada after the Revolution, ventured to dedicate a place there as the seat of "The Great Council Fire of the Six Nations," and call it Onondaga, while, in fact, all the confederates but themselves remained within the territory of New York, keeping the original Onondaga among their reserved lands till the present day. Red Jacket, the famous Seneca, stirred up a serious dispute about this exclusive assumption both of the national shrine and general name of his countrymen.—See Stone's *Life of Brant, vol. ii.*

appeal to his vanity which it conveyed.

"I see, I see," said he, casting his eyes in musing fashion upon the ground, and smiling grimly, as if it were impossible wholly to suppress the pleasurable thrill of pride which he wished to conceal. "The great king depends now upon the Indians to preserve this colony for him. Our warriors are to keep the rebels in check until the great king can send over such an army as shall make it safe for his loyal subjects once more to rise and help him! Good! very good! *He shall find that WE are to be depended upon.*"

The voice and manner of the *sachem* suddenly altered with the last words, as he raised his eyes and cast a stern and haughty gaze around. "Yes, gentlemen," he continued, in a more cool and lofty tone, "the largest, and the fairest, and most fertile part of this rich province is now left to the guardianship of one who, among yourselves, bears but the rank of an English captain; and I would have you know that it is not from ignorance of the value of the pledge, of the cost of protecting it, or of the opportunity of successfully treating with the Americans for the heritage which you are compel led to abandon, that I here, in the name of my countrymen, assume its charge. With you, Sir John Johnson, as the official representative of your sovereign, I might have made my own terms for the better defined security of our rights under the British dominion; but a Mohawk chieftain is no trafficker of loyalty. Your king shall learn how far he may depend upon the faith and valour of the Iroquois, and the future will reveal the measure of his justice to us in return.[5] Our *power* to serve the British cause remains to be proved. You at least, Sir John, can bear witness to the readiness of our *will*."

"He is a slave that doubts either," cried the baronet. "Though the terrible Virginian himself should take the field against you, his wisdom and his valour will find a match in Thayendanagea. And *I*, my noble friend, though prevented by fate from serving with you as a comrade in arms, I, while watching your glorious career, will console myself with the reflection that I have, by temporizing, preserved the services of these brave followers to my sovereign till they can be used with a

---

5. The difficulties with the British Government which imbittered the closing years of Brant, his neglected petitions, the invasion, alike of the property and the political rights of his tribe, and the forced necessity he was under of asserting his legal claim to the half pay of a British captain, might suggest some doubts as to the wisdom of his confidence in the justice of the crown. But have the Oneidas, who espoused the cause of the republic, fared better than the Mohawks?

hope of success hereafter."

The last words, which were addressed as much to the bystanders as to Brant himself, had their full influence in reassuring the spirits of the former; and MacDonald confirmed their effect by immediately adding,

"Sir John could certainly not better serve our cause in the present exigency than by securing him in the midst of the party which we wish to keep together. We are still strong in numbers throughout the district, and, while he remains with us, we shall never want a leader at the proper moment for striking."

"Your parole of honour!" said Brant, drawing himself up and looking with a lowering eye upon the company.

"Though given to outlaws, it shall never be broken but for cause," replied Johnson. "But the rebels, drunken with their first success, will soon supply us with legitimate grounds for disregarding the pledge they have wrung from us."

"Well, you white men know best how far ye may trust each other," observed the chief, with a significant and pitying smile, while, in drawing his mantle around him to depart, he muttered less audibly beneath its folds something still more contemptuous. His precise words were unheard, but their purport was sufficiently intelligible to rouse the ire of MacDonald, who mutely folded his arms when the chieftain stretched out his hand to exchange a parting salutation with him.

"Nay, Captain MacDonald," said Brant, "I part not thus with a brave comrade and tried soldier. It was of the white man's, and not the Scotchman's, faith of which I spoke, and you will pardon the prejudices of the Indian, however you would resent the suspicions of the friend."

"I am not so Quixotic, Captain Brant, as to proclaim myself the champion of my race," replied the other. "But, in giving you my hand, as I now do, I will venture to suggest that, if your knowledge of our usages disinclines you to practise European urbanity, you are not fortunate in your mode of recommending Indian courtesy—by your own example."

"Good!" said Brant, smiling. "Very good!" he repeated, shaking again the hand of him who had chastened him, while MacDonald, whose whimsical expression of countenance showed how much he was confounded at the odd impression which his pithy lecture had made upon his half-savage friend, followed his retreating figure with his eye as the Mohawk strode out of the apartment.

"The infernal strange dog!" cried the Scotchman; "I never know where the devil to find him."

"What, Alan," said Johnson, laughing, "is my red brother Joseph a puzzle to you? An Indian, man, is like a woman; you must follow his humours without attempting to regulate them. Brant's touches of civilization are like grains of wit in a madman's brain; they just suffice to mislead him who would discover some regular system of ideas in the lunatic's disordered senses. But, for all that, the fellow has sense and courage, and is as true as steel in matters of moment."

And thus ended this singular interview, which, commencing in a scene of passion, that, with its attendant grouping of strongly contrasted characters, might well exercise the pen of the dramatist, terminated, as do most romantic situations in real life, with commonplace occurrence and discussion; which, however actual in themselves, detract, it must be confessed, not a little from the poetic dignity of their relation. But "*these are the days of fact nor fable*;" and the legendary writer of our time must content himself with detailing mere familiar tradition, until another *Scott* shall arise to revivify the dry bones which it is our humble task to collect together, clothe them anew with all the attributes of breathing life, and make them walk the earth afresh, dignified, exalted, and adorned by the prodigal drapery of immortal Genius.

CHAPTER 9

The Borderers

When, lo, he saw his courser reined
By an unwelcome hand!—Earl Rupert.

There was a proud complacency upon the brow of the Indian chief when he found himself alone beyond the precincts of the Hall. The morning was cold, and the snow lay deep upon the ground; but while the latter offered no impediment to his devouring steps as he rapidly stalked along, the glowing thoughts within his bosom seemed to make him insensible to the former. His mantle was indeed wrapped closely around him, but it was from the tension of strong emotion that his hands were clinched in its folds. His open throat and lofty head, whose plumes tossed in the light breeze that swept the eminence from which he was descending, betrayed none of that sensibility to the elements which belittles the mien of the cloaked and cowering form that now confronts him in his path.

It is a half-frozen horseman, who shrinks in his saddle, as if he would thus make his weight as light as possible to his jaded steed. The proportions of his figure are concealed by a military *roquelaure* wrapped closely around him, and his face is so muffled up with furs as barely to permit his eyes to see the road before them; yet both are instantly recognised by the keen-eyed Mohawk. Some new emotion now agitates his features, and a look of sudden wrath has succeeded to that of calm and pleasurable pride. He stops short in his rapid walk, and plants himself in the centre of a little bridge that here crosses the highway, just as the mounted traveller has gained its opposite side. The horse recoils at the barbaric apparition in his path, and his rider, looking up for the first time, beholds the cause of his affright.

"Why, you d——d Indian scarecrow, what mean you by standing there to frighten cattle on the king's highway—wae, boy! wa—e gently, now, gently—stand out of my path, you stupid blockhead, or, God help me, I'll ride right over you." And, suiting the action to the word, the distempered and insolent traveller plunged both spurs into his horse, which bounded forward upon the bridge; but, quick as light, the sinewy arm of the Indian has grappled his bridle-rein, and, with starting eye and distended nostril, the mastered steed stands trembling.

"Why, Joseph Brant, my good fellow! who the devil expected to meet you here! You must for give my haste in speaking as I did, and I'll pardon this abrupt salutation in so old a friend, if you'll only loose my rein and let me push ahead to the Hall."

"There is time enough for that," said the chief, smothering his indignation at the man's insolent familiarity. "What news bring you from below?"

"Schuyler's within half a day's march, with three thousand Whig militia; that's all, my good fellow; and now let me carry the news to our friends. We must up stakes, I take it, from these parts, and go and lend a lift to the loyalists in the southern corner of the province: and now, my dear Joseph, I wish you a good-morning."

"Softly, softly, Mr. Bradshawe. There is no necessity for this great haste. Sir John is already 'in possession of all the news you can give him."

"He is? The devil! I met that arch-rebel Duer, with a brace of kindred Whigs, at a roadside inn last night—Yates and Glen, I think they were; and I half guessed that their venturing so far in the valley boded no good to our cause. Surely they cannot have brought the news, conveyed in the shape of a threat, from Schuyler?"

"They were commissioners to settle the terms of Sir John's surrender, and Schuyler's present advance to take possession of Johnstown shows how well they succeeded."

The countenance of the traveller grew dark as midnight while Brant thus briefly and coolly told him of the discomfiture of his party. The chief waited a moment for him to make some comment, but his astonishment was so great that he had not a word wherewith to reply; and Brant, in the same calm tone, went on. "These tidings seem to be somewhat strange to Mr. Bradshawe. He has kept himself aloof from his friends of late. It is at least four months since I heard of him in these parts."

"Yes, why, yes," said the other, confusedly. "Some business took me south last summer about the time the Hawksnest affair and subsequent disappearance of young Greyslaer put the country in hot water. None but you, Joseph, could have been at the bottom of that hubbub."

"I heard of Mr. Bradshawe in Schoharie," said Brant, dryly, and with an elevation of his eyebrows so slight as to be almost imperceptible.

"Schoharie? Oh!—ay—yes, I have been in Schoharie. I've just come, indeed, from down that way. I heard of this rebel rising while in Schoharie, and rode for dear life to warn Sir John."

"It is useless to seek him now upon such an errand; and if Mr. Bradshawe wishes to give his reasons for having so long kept out of the way of his political friends, I would advise him to take some opportunity when the baronet is in a happier mood."

"A d——d politic suggestion! Josey, you certainly are no fool. But where the devil are you leading my mare to?"

"Why," said Brant, with a careless laugh, "two such suspicious characters as we are should not be seen holding so long a talk here on the highway, when, by moving a few yards, we can throw that knoll between us and any travelling impertinents that may chance to pass. I would confer with you, too, Mr. Bradshawe," he added, more gravely, "where we are not liable to interruption."

"You are a queer chap, Brant. Leave you alone to have your own way. But here we are in the hollow; and now what have you got to say? Be quick, man, for I'm getting devilish cold."

"You will be still colder before I have done with you, Walter Bradshawe, unless you reply promptly to my questions."

"Why, my good Joseph, what the h—"

"Hold! no more of that, sir; blasphemous and vulgar-souled as you are, you can still ape the decorum of a gentleman when it suits your turn; and you shall perish here like a crushed hound in the snow, unless you practise it now."

"This to me, you d——d Indian dog!" cried Bradshawe, jerking his rein with one hand, and plucking a pistol from his holster with the other. But, before he could cock the piece, a blow from Brant's tomahawk sent it flying through the air into an adjacent snowbank, while in the same moment the *desperado* was hurled from his saddle, and lay prostrate at the feet of the Mohawk.

"One motion, one word, a look of insolence, and I'll brain you on the spot; that snow-wreath shall be your winding-sheet, and the April thaws will alone reveal your fate, if the wolves in the mean time spare that wretched carcass."

"Who the devil thinks of resisting, with knife and tomahawk both at his throat? Ugh—ugh, you have knocked all the breath out of my body. Gad! Brant, you inherit a white man's brawn from your Dutch grandfather. Hold! you Indian devil; don't murder me for squinting at a fact which all the country believes except yourself."

"They lie who say I'm other than a Mohawk of the fall blood," exclaimed the Indian, fiercely, but drawing back, at the same time, as if stung by an adder.

"Perhaps they do; but you'll not prove the genuineness of your blood by spilling mine," replied the other, picking himself leisurely from the ground. "Give me my other pistol, son of Nickus, and we can dispute the matter more upon an equality."

"Bradshawe, you are a brave man, and, as such, I cannot wholly scorn you; and were your honour but half as bright as your courage, you should—But enough of this. You will be wise, sir, now, in fooling no longer with my patience, but reply with directness to what I have to ask you. You are reputed to have sense, Bradshawe, and you see I am not to be trifled with."

"Why, as to my sense, *sachem*, it seems to have been pretty much at fault in dealing with you. I've always thought you a devilish shrewd fellow for one who was only quarter white man—nay, let that cursed knife alone—I say I've thought you so, that's a fact; though I may sometimes have laughed in my sleeve when you got on your high ropes, and put on quality airs like Sir John. I don't know how it is, however; I still believe you to be pretty much of an adventurer like myself; but, if you are not a lineal chief, as your enemies say, by G—d, you deserve to be a born aristocrat for the neat style in which you do the thing. I speak the truth, I do, by G—d. I could put it in softer phrase, as you know full well; for you have seen me humouring the shallow fools who ape nobility here among us provincials. But I talk to you as a man that can't be come over by flummery; and now go ahead with your questions, which, I suppose, relate to the De Roos girl that Red Wolfert snicked off so handsomely."

"Red Wolfert," said Brant, scornfully. "Wolfert Valtmeyer dared not have touched captive of mine but as the instrument of a more powerful scoundrel than himself; and you, Bradshawe, must answer for the acts of your creature. Where is Miss De Roos?"

"Where? Ask Wolfert. If I use the rascal now and then to farther our political intrigues, does it follow that I know aught of his amorous doings? I suspected that you would hold me accountable for his dealings with this wench; for it certainly was a bold flight for such a kite as Valtmeyer to strike at game like her."

"Beware, Mr. Bradshawe; there are limits to my patience, and you cannot deceive me. It was through your aid that Au-neh-yesh escaped from the hands of the rebels. He repaid you with information that you valued beyond aught else, for no scruple could prevent you from availing yourself of it to tear the young lady from the refuge in which I had placed her. You, and you only, with the ruffian Valtmeyer and my wayward and unhappy son for your instruments, have spirited away this girl, for whose safety both our friends and our foes hold me now accountable. Bradshawe, I tell you, if one hair of her head be injured, I will wreak vengeance so dire that men shall stand aghast when they hear of it. The tortures of the Indian stake shall be merciful to those which you shall suffer, till the hapless fate of Thayendanagea's captive is forgotten in the hideous punishment of her destroyer."

The voice of Brant was calm and low as he pronounced these words; but the ascendancy of his mind was now so completely established over that of Bradshawe, that, daring and reckless as he was, they fell with withering effect upon his spirit; and he even, for a moment, shivered like the criminal who has just heard his awful and irrevocable doom passing the lips of one who is endowed with all earthly authority to inflict the final sentence of a judicial tribunal.

"She is safe—I believe—I know—she is—she must be safe," stammered forth the bold borderer, who, for the first time in his life perhaps, felt conscious that his heart quailed and his cheek blanched beneath the eye of a fellow-mortal. "I left her last where I believed no earthly harm could reach her; and, so help me Heaven, *sachem*, there breathes no human being whom, with my life, I would sooner guard from injury than this same lady."

"Yes! as the cougar would protect the hare from the wolf that disputes his prey with him. Where left you Miss De Roos?"

The distressed air of mortification that now marked Bradshawe's features showed that he would gladly evade the question. He even turned his head quickly on one side, as if recourse to flight suddenly suggested itself upon the emergency. But the snowdrift that walled in the little hollow in which he stood shut out the desperate hope on that side. He turned his eager gaze to the other, but it straightway fell before the basilisk eye of the Indian, who, still grasping the bridle of Bradshawe's horse, stood with one foot advanced, and his right hand upon his knife, warily watching his victim. But the hand fell to his side, the foot was drawn back, and the deadly glare of his eye changed to a cold and stony gaze in the moment that the crest fallen borderer slunk back to his former dogged attitude of unresisting dejection.

"Where is the lady?" repeated Brant, between his clinched teeth.

"Take my secret, then, if I must speak—the Cave of Waneonda, where the stream which you Indians call the River of Ghosts holds its way far under ground beneath the forests of Schoharie, there in the—Hah! what sounds are those? May my tongue be blistered if its swiftness to betray has—"

"'Tis Schuyler's advancing column. I know the sound of his bugles," cried Brant, uneasily; and, even as he spoke, a squadron of troopers, who formed the advanced guard of the Republican forces, wheeled around an angle of the road, and came galloping forward in all the hasty disorder of newly-levied militia flushed with their first success in the operations of war.

Their common danger—for Brant and his recent adversary were, on personal as well as political grounds, equally obnoxious to the popular party in their district—impelled them to simultaneous flight. But even at such an exigency, when his life seemed on the point of being yielded up to the sabres of this lawless and hot-headed soldiery, the generosity of the chieftain did not desert him. "Save yourself," cried he to Bradshawe, in the same moment flinging his bridle into the hand of the royalist officer. "But remember! if you have deceived me here, you had better perish on this spot than live to meet my vengeance."

The last words were either unheard or unheeded by Bradshawe. He made no reply, but, leaping swiftly into his saddle, struck the spurs into his horse, and dashed across the fields, so as to turn the right flank of the advancing party, and place a hill between himself and the threatening danger. He had emerged from the hollow so suddenly that he gained a hundred yards almost from his starting-place before he was observed by the troopers. And it was well for him that such was the case; for, as his dark figure swept the snowy waste, it offered so distinct a mark for the yeomanry sharp shooters, that the volley which they fired, after vainly hailing him, must inevitably have proved fatal but for the distance.

The militiamen, as Brant had perhaps anticipated, instantly wheeled from the road, and with tumultuous cries launched in pursuit of the flying officer; and, though the chase was abandoned with equal sud-denness when they found themselves floundering through deep snowdrifts after a fugitive as well mounted as themselves, and who had soon placed a ridge of upland between himself and their fire, yet the circle which they made in again recovering the road enabled the stealthy Indian to glide unseen along a snowy swale, and shelter himself in a thicket of ever greens, from which he soon seized an opportunity to escape into the deep forest.

Brant did not retire, however, until he had first seen the march of the Congressional army, whose main body was now at hand. The forces were newly levied; but, though exhibiting few of the disciplined traits of veteran soldiery, yet the sturdy yeomanry wore individually that martial air which characterizes Frontiers-men skilled from their boy hood to the use of arms, alike in the wild forest- hunt and the Indian foray. The clump of cedars in which Brant had ensconced himself crowned a rocky knoll which commanded a turning of the road; and the stern though dejected mien with which he looked upon the pageant; the gaze, half sullen, half admiring, which he fixed upon the serried battalion, as banner, and plume, and fluttering scarf, and bright bayonet flashing in the frosty air, swept beneath his view, might have marked the chief as the personified genius of his fated race; a warrior prophet, who gazed admiringly upon the battle cloud whose thunders he knew must destroy his people.

Chapter 10

The Fastness

But see, along that mountain's slope, a fiery horseman ride,
Mark his torn plume, his tarnished belt, the sabre at his side;
His spurs are buried rowel deep, he rides with loosened rein,
There's blood upon his charger's flank, and foam upon his mane;
He speeds toward the olive-grove, along that shaded hill,
God shield the helpless maiden there, if he should mean her ill.

Bryant.

Bradshawe, after the interview which had been so abruptly commenced and broken off with Brant, lost no time in making his escape from the precincts of Johnstown, where the presence of the patriot forces made every moment fraught with peril to him. Indeed, after escaping so nearly from their hands, he was obliged more than once to make a wide circuit in order to avoid the straggling bands of Whig militia that seemed pouring along the roads, bent upon making their way to join the main column of Schuyler's army.

Schoharie was the point which he now aimed at making as quickly as possible; and as it was long before he could venture to cross the frozen river and turn his horse's head upon the direct route he wished to travel, the noble animal had occasion more than once to rue, the brutal temper of his master, as, chafing with impatience at each cause of delay that interposed, he now spurred hotly toward the bank of the stream, and now wheeled from its brink, or reined up sharply at some turning of the road. Here the rapids, or the evident weakness of the ice, prevented him from crossing; there the deep snow drifts, or the steep and slippery banks, prevented him from descending to the frozen highway; and now again there were appearances upon the opposite shore which deterred him from trusting himself upon the snowy waste, where his dark figure crossing over might be seen at a long gunshot, and tempt some idle patriot ranger, or officious "committee-of-safety" member to bring him to for a parley.

The immediate personal peril weighed not, indeed, a feather with him. But to be recognised and tracked in the snow to his ultimate destination might be fatal to the projects which he had now most at heart. The truth is, that, though Bradshawe had, when he found himself so hard pressed by Brant, designated the Cave of Waneonda as the present retreat of Alida, he was not himself perfectly assured that she was really there, though his last orders to his creature Valtmeyer had been to make that disposition of his prize; and, believing that his wishes in this respect had been complied with, he was actually upon his way to the cavern, when the rumoured approach of Schuyler induced him momentarily to change his destination, and make the best of his way to Sir John Johnson.

Brant, as it appeared, had been misinformed as to Bradshawe's keeping himself aloof from his political friends, and attending to his own concerns in Schoharie. His actual business had been among the Tories in the neighbourhood of Wyoming, whom he succeeded in confirming, and drawing off in a body, to unite their forces with a band of Iroquois which had established a position about the forks of the Susquehanna, upon the confines of New York and Pennsylvania. And this absence in that then unsettled country will account for his ignorance of the projected movement and subsequent march of the patriots upon Johnstown, until he had reached the southwestern settlements of Tryon County.

He had unexpectedly, upon an order from Sir John, started upon his expedition immediately after planning the abduction of Brant's fair captive, which was so ruthlessly consummated by his creature Valtmeyer. He had heard of Valtmeyer's success only through an Indian runner charged with letters from Sir John, by whom Valtmeyer also contrived to transmit intelligence from himself. The tidings from either spoke of the precarious condition of their party, and Bradshawe determined that, whatever course public affairs might take, his own private views should not necessarily be thwarted.

At present he thought only how he could best make sure of the prey which Valtmeyer had thus far secured for him.

That ruffian, immediately upon the seizure of his victim, had, by the aid of confederates, transported her to a lonely cabin upon the skirts of the settlements, where a thrifty innkeeper, privately associated with the outlaw in certain matters of business best known to themselves, maintained a small establishment, which he dignified with the name of his Dairy Farm.

The inn of mine host lay some miles distant from this possession upon the public highway. During the first months of the present troubles it had been used alike by both parties as a rendezvous for their public meetings. But as the cause of the Whigs advanced in popularity, the opposite faction appeared to have withdrawn their patronage from the house, though there were some shrewd surmises that the landlord did not therefore suffer in his coffers. But when it was whispered that the Dairy Farm harboured a nest of Tory spies, and served merely as a sort of scouting-post to collect political gossip from the inn below, the close inquiry that was at once instituted, followed by an examination of the tavern-keeper before a committee of safety, elicited nothing to inculpate that worthy, and, as everyone thought, much-injured individual.

An old black woman and a strapping mulatto lass, whose labours in the dairy were superintended, from time to time, by the pretty daughter of the proprietor, seemed the only permanent or occasional occupants of the place. The old woman was deaf and suffering from rheumatism; the *mulatto* seemed an exception to the generality of her quick-witted race, in being as stolid and stupid of intellect as she was simple and ignorant; and the pretty Tavy Wingear was known the country round as a sprightly, frank, and guileless girl, whom no one would think of making the depositary of a political secret. All suspicions about the Dairy Farm were allayed, and it became nearly as safe a house for the royalist partisans as ever, until the affair of the Hawksnest, subsequent to which the Tories had been shy of holding their secret meetings anywhere in this immediate neighbourhood.

Such was the spot to which Valtmeyer bore his prisoner; and here, having the two Africans to at tend upon her, Alida had passed even months, with no signs of approaching rescue to cheer her solitude. Valtmeyer was often, though never for any length of time, absent from the house; and irksome as this imprisonment became, yet, though he proffered her the full range of the premises whenever his eye was there to watch her motions, this was just the season when confinement to her chamber became most welcome.

Long weeks wore on, and the hope of release became almost extinct in her bosom. The summer was gone; autumn, with its varied tints, made the forests around like one gorgeous bed of tulips to the eye. Winter was at hand, with all its icy rigours; yet the lapse of the seasons and the change of the foliage, as she viewed it from her window, was all that varied the monotonous hours of the unhappy Alida. Once, indeed, and only a few days after she was first immured in this lonely spot, her heart leaped as she heard the blithe tones of a gay young female voice beneath her window. But, flying to the casement, she was scarcely permitted to catch a glimpse of the young woman from whose lips came the cheering sound, before Valtmeyer had rushed into her apartment and rudely drawn her back from the window.

Upon two other occasions she heard the same tones at a distance; and once, before the autumn became sere, she had seen a stranger female afar off, gathering flowers upon the hillside, while a Canadian pony stood grazing near her. The next moment the country damsel leaped into her saddle, and, galloping gayly past the house, guided her active pony amid the stumps of the clearing until she had reached the road, and soon after disappeared to the view of Alida. The sight of that free-limbed courser, and the thought of escape which its appearance suggested, awakened a fresh yearning for freedom that was all but maddening. But neither the horse nor the rider ever appeared again.

As the winter set in, however, a change of scene, if not a release from imprisonment, was soon to be realized by the unoffending captive. Bradshawe, alarmed for the security of his prey, had written to Valtmeyer by the runner who had brought him a missive from that worthy confederate, giving a glowing account of his successful adventure. His letter urged Valtmeyer to lose no time in moving Miss De Roos from so dangerous a neighbourhood. For Alida's friends were scouring the country round for traces of Thayendanagea's captive.

Her fickle-minded but high-spirited brother, so far from slackening in his endeavour to rescue her after the first ill-starred attempt already commemorated, had twice beaten up the Mohawk's quarters with a strong band of border yeomanry; nor did he give up dogging the movements of Brant until the chief had crossed the frontier and passed into Canada for a season. Despairing, then, of recovering his sister by the means hitherto used, Derrick had made his way to the headquarters of the patriot army, where, offering his sword to his country, he lived in the hope of obtaining tidings of the lost Alida through the medium of the first flag of truce that should be sent to the royalist generals in Canada. Balt, too, the humble but zealous friend of the Hawksnest family, adopting less readily the belief that Brant had removed his captive across the frontier, had, after accompanying Derrick in his bootless wildwood quest at the north, renewed a diligent search among the haunts of the Tories nearer home.

It was the restless and prying offices of this faithful fellow—which Valtmeyer, with characteristic hardihood, seemed to make light of when detailing them to his employer—that awakened the anxiety of Bradshawe for the better security of his prize; and his letter designated a remarkable cavern in Schoharie County, well known both to the outlaw and his ruffian principal as the best retreat for security; and it commanded that, as soon as the winter snows should allow of easy and rapid transportation, a covered sleigh should convey Alida, her two attendants, and such furniture as would be indispensable, to this dungeon fastness. A valuable farm on the German Flats, with the promised manumission of the African servants, who were actually the slaves of Bradshawe, was the promised reward for these services if they should be faithfully and effectually rendered.

This letter was the last communication which Bradshawe had held with the lawless instrument of his crimes. He was now about to realize how far his behests had been obeyed. He burned with impatience to ascertain the result of Valtmeyer's machinations, and he ground his teeth in wrath at the thought that the momentary quailing of his spirit before that of Brant had betrayed his secret, endangered his final triumph over Alida, and perhaps compromised the safety alike of his confederate and himself. His horse had long since become way worn and jaded; still it was scarcely possible that Brant, though he might have taken a more direct course for the cavern, could on foot accomplish the journey as soon as himself. His rage and vexation at the bare possibility were for a moment insupportable; and then, as he ferociously vented his feelings upon his tired steed, struggling now with difficulty through the deep snowdrifts, he became calmer the next instant upon remembering that Brant was alone, and that Valtmeyer, in performing his duty of castellan, might possibly despatch the officious and insolent Mohawk.

In the meantime, as the short winter's day approached to a close, Bradshawe himself began to suffer for the want of refreshment; and he was compelled to admit, at last, that it was impossible for his horse to proceed farther, and that he would prove useless on the morrow unless the wants of the animal were soon administered to. And, fortunately for both, an asylum soon presented itself in the deserted cabin of some fugitive settler, whom fear of the Indians had driven from his solitary clearing in the forest to some safer home.

A storm of rain and sleet set in a few moments after the horseman gained this welcome shelter; but he heeded not its peltings without, as, after tethering his horse in one corner of the shanty, he kindled a fire upon the hearth, and by its light discovered a pile of unshocked corn, which he soon laid under contribution, both for himself and his steed. He foddered the horse, while still heated, with the dried blades and husks only, busying himself in the meantime with shelling the ears. The grain thus procured was partly pounded up, and, by the aid of snow-water, converted into hoe-cakes, which were soon roasting by the fire. The rest of it, with a dozen more loose ears, he placed before his horse after this frugal supper was served; nor did Bradshawe resign himself to rest before, like an experienced trooper, he had well groomed his noble steed, by using the husks and cobs of the maize as a substitute for the straw whisp and brush, to which the animal's glossy coat showed he was accustomed. His fire, in the meantime, he fed with an armful of fuel from the same pile which had supplied him with provisions. It blazed up so as to fill the whole cabin with a ruddy light as the dry blades were first ignited, crackled and sputtered for a few moments as the grains of corn became parched and split by the heat, and then subsided into a bed of glowing brands as the dry cobs were seized upon by the element.

"And why," thought Bradshawe, as, wrapped in his cloak, he now stretched himself out for repose, "why may not the burning of this indigenous plant be emblematic of the career of the thousands of my countrymen who are reared almost upon it alone. Here is the quick flash of their first outbreak of rebellion, the noisy sputtering far and wide, in which men more wise than myself thought that it would vent itself and have an end. And here are the live coals at the bottom, that will burn on steady through this long winter's night! Pshaw! what care I, though, if men are such asses as to light the fire, so I only can warm my fingers by the blaze?" And, concluding his unwonted strain of thought with this characteristic reflection, the worthy trooper resigned himself to slumber.

The dawn found Bradshawe again upon his journey. But the rain of the preceding night, followed by one of those mild, foggy days which sometimes occur in midwinter, made his road a difficult one: the half-thawed snow was converted into slush, which, yielding and slipping beneath his horse's feet, made the track at once heavy and insecure. The rivulets upon the hillside too, released for a brief period from their icy fetters, were swollen frequently to torrents, which were absolutely perilous in the passage. The road he was traversing could scarcely, indeed, be dignified with the title of a bridle-path; and though the cavern toward which he was urging his course has of late years been frequently visited by the curious, it would be difficult to designate the route by which Bradshawe had hitherto approached it by any precise geographical data of the present day.

CHAPTER 11

The Cavern of Waneonda

Earth hath her wondrous scenes, but few like this.
The everlasting surge hath worn itself
A pathway in the solid rock; and there,
Far in those caverned chambers, where the warm,
Sweet sunlight enters not, is heard the war
Of hidden waves, imprisoned tempests—bursting
Anon like thunder; then, with low, deep moan,
Falling upon the ear the—mournful wail,
As Indian legends say, of spirits accursed.

Mrs. Ellet.

In the hilly region of Schoharie county, where the Onidegra ridge
of the Helderburg mountains extends its flanking battlements of perpendicular rock along the lovely vale of the Schoharie kill, there ran
in former days an old Indian pathway.

The principal route between Schoharie court house and the ham-
lets to the east and west of that settlement, as well as the great Indian
trail between Catskill and Canajoharie, had a course nearly parallel
with this path, and it had therefore been neglected for so many years
as to be nearly forgotten by everyone, save some roving Indian that
now and then straggled into the settlements, or the white hunter,
who, tired with traversing the forest thickets and rocky defiles of the
adjacent mountains, took his homeward way along this secluded but
well- beaten path.

This trail, where Bradshawe was now travelling it, was walled by
huge buttresses of rock upon the west, while its terraced edge commanded, through the leafless trees, a complete view of the vale of the
Schoharie upon the east; and as a burst of sunshine ever and *anon*

lighted up with smiles that landscape which even in winter is most lovely, even the heart of so reckless an adventurer was touched with the idea of carrying rapine and devastation into a scene so exquisitely calm and rural; "yet such," thought he, with a sternness more in unison with his general character, "such is our only policy, if the king's party ever again get the ascendancy in the district. We must take the hearth-stones from under these people, and then they'll bother us no longer about their parchment privileges."

Alas! did Bradshawe mean to prophesy that Johnson and his bands should sweep, like the besom of desolation, over this fated region within two years afterward? Did he foresee the part which men as ruthless as himself should play in those dark days of monstrous violence?

But now, as he remembers the devious route that he has travelled to avoid the settlements, and looks back upon the road behind him, circling wide to the east and south of his ultimate destination, the *desperado* remembers again that Brant may have reached it before him. He spurs his horse along the narrow path, descends toward the valley, approaches the village, wheels off, skirts the valley, and, ascending once more, tracks his way through a forest of walnut and maples, and arrives at last at the yawning mouth of Waneonda.

A moment sufficed Bradshawe to secure his horse, and then he impatiently hurried to descend. The top of the pit, some twenty or thirty feet in diameter, was wholly hidden from the eye by some huge trees which had probably been felled across it purposely to screen the opening. But their roots were so grown around with thickets, and the trunks lay tossed about in such disorder, that no design was apparent in their arrangement; and they might have been thought to be blown down by the wind, or fallen from natural decay precisely where they now lay.

Below this funnel-like cavity, which was not more than ten feet in depth, there opened a narrow fissure about half that breadth, but extending down ward into perfect darkness. The top of this black chasm was likewise crossed by several sticks of timber; and to the stoutest and longest of these was attached a perpendicular ladder of rope fifty feet in length, secured by the lower end to the rocks below. The ladder was coated with ice, and Bradshawe was compelled to clutch closely the frozen rungs as his feet slipped repeatedly in descending. A sloping declivity of rocks received him; and so rough and precipitous was his pathway, now rendered doubly perilous by the mud and half-frozen slime from the dripping walls above, that he would scarcely have dared

151

to venture farther amid the darkness that reigned below.

But, groping about for a few moments, he felt the broken limb of a tree, and, passing his hand along it toward the trunk, discovered that a new convenience had been provided since last he visited the spot, and he readily perceived that it must have been for the accommodation of Alida that the ponderous piece of timber had been plunged down and placed in its present situation. Lowering himself down the tree in an oblique direction, he soon entirely lost sight of the opening above him; and the temperature of the cave became so mild that traces of ice were no longer discovered. A ladder of wood then gave him a firmer foothold down the third descent; and a fourth declivity of rough rocks brought him to the bottom of the cavern.

The adventurer was now one hundred and fifty feet beneath the surface of the soil; and no one, unless as perfectly familiar with the cave as was Bradshawe, could have safely effected the descent amid the darkness which reigned around him. The horizontal passage in which he now found himself was about ten or twelve feet in breadth, nearly half of which space was occupied by a rivulet running in a southern direction; and, keeping as close to the wall on his left as possible, Bradshawe followed it for a few paces, until the roof of the cavern drooped so low that he could feel it with his outstretched hands as he placed them before him. Dropping now upon his knees, he crawled along for several yards, until his eyes were greeted by a stream of light which came through a narrow aperture on the left. He crawled through the opening, and entered an apartment some thirty feet in diameter by a hundred or more in height.

Had Bradshawe possessed a taste for the grand and beautiful in nature, the appearance of this chamber might have arrested his attention. The ceiling was fretted with stalactites; the walls hung with a rich tracery of spar, which likewise, in a thousand fantastic forms, encumbered the floor upon which, in the course of ages, its broken fragments had fallen. But a solitary lamp, fed with bear's fat, which stood upon a truncated column in the centre, dimly revealing the glistening objects around, seemed only to claim his attention as he eagerly advanced toward it. A bugle lay by the side of the lamp; and, taking the latter only in his hand, he repassed through the fissure which had admitted him into "the Warder's Room," as it was called by his followers, and regained the low-arched passage from which he had temporarily digressed.

Crawling now cautiously a few paces in advance, he paused, and, placing the bugle to his lips, blew a blast which resounded through the cavern. Several minutes now elapsed; the last rumbling echoes seemed to have traversed every chamber of the cavern which could send back a sound, and died away at last in some unfathomable abyss remote from them all. At last a sound like the dip of an Indian paddle was heard. A shred of light then seemed to flicker upon the bottom of the cave, like a glow-worm crawling along its floor toward him. A moment after the feeble ray became stronger, and separated itself into two dots of light, which were still approaching; and then, again, from the brighter reflection upon the water as the taper now neared Bradshawe, it could be seen that he was standing upon the brink of a subterranean lake, and that a canoe, with one solitary voyager, was approaching him.

"Valtmeyer, is he here, my good Charon?" asked Bradshawe of the deformed half-breed that steered the canoe, as the man turned a rocky promontory on the left, and suddenly presented his features in full view by the ruddy torchlight.

"He is here, captain," replied the Indian, respectfully.

"And the lady?"

"I know nothing of the lady since the first day she came down among us, when I carried her along the River of Ghosts to the chamber at the north end of the cavern, which our men call the 'Chapel.'"

"And has no one else been here?"

"Not a soul but Red Wolfert, and he seems to go near her as seldom as possible."

"It is well. Shove off."

There was a silence for a few moments as the shallop kept her way over the deep and mysterious flood; and Bradshawe, as he sat with folded arms in the stern, seemed busied only in trying to pierce with his eye the undiscoverable height of the black vault above him.

"Who of my band are here?" he at length resumed, abruptly.

"Not those whom you value most; and some, perhaps, who should never have been trusted with the secret of the cave. But Syl Stickney says that things are going so badly above, that we must find hiding-places for our friends if we'd have them stick to the cause, and Wolfert therefore forgave him for bringing them down."

"Syl Stickney and be "d——d to him! I must pistol that officious rascal some cold morning," muttered Bradshawe; and then added aloud, "And have these fellows seen the lady?"

"Neither they nor Syl. Syl only guesses that there is some mystery shut up at the other end of the cave; for Wolfert has forbidden that the newcomers should be told there is such a place as the chapel; and he swears he'll cut Syl's throat if he approaches it."

"Admirable Wolfert!" said Bradshawe, mentally; "thou hast thus far been the truest of ruffians, and well earned thy reward."

The boat had now reached the farther shore of this "Black Acheron," where a shelving indentation among the steep rocks affords a landing-place to the voyager, who, having passed the gulf, proposes to penetrate the Cimmerian region beyond. This enterprise, though unattended with danger, is sufficiently awe-inspiring to anyone who has been ferried over that dark, still river, upon which no beam of sunshine has ever fallen. But a man less bold than Bradshawe might have shrunk from adventuring farther, if unfamiliar with the sounds which now met his ear as he scaled a rough ascent leading up from the water side; for never from Tartarus itself arose a wilder discord of horrid blasphemy, intermingled with drunken laughter. The strange, unearthly oaths, echoed from the hollow depths around, seemed to tremble long in air, as if it *thickened* with the damning sounds, and held them, there suspended as in their proper element. The peals of eldritch merriment were first shrilly reverberated as in mockery from the vaulted roof; and then, as if flung back into some lower pit, some burial-house of mirth, died away in a sullen moan beneath his very feet.

This strange confusion of sounds, however, lost its effect upon the ear the moment Bradshawe had entered the outlaws' banqueting hall, where he suddenly presented himself in the midst of his men, who, in every variety of costume, were variously grouped about the vast circular chamber. Some were carousing deeply around a board well filled with flagons; some, seated upon the ground, were deep in a game of cards together; the rattling of a dice-box betrayed the not dissimilar occupation of two others; while some, more remote from the rest, were amusing themselves with jumping for a wager, and other feats of strength and agility. The size of this apartment, which formed a rotunda forty paces in diameter by fifty feet in height, afforded ample room for all this diversity of occupation.

Syl Stickney and others of Bradshawe's Tory followers, who were not willing to identify themselves completely with Valtmeyer's especial band of outlaws, though they had long consorted with them, kept partially aloof; a herd of them being collected around the worthy Sylla himself, who, with a tankard by his side and a pipe in his mouth, sat upon a ponderous fragment of fallen spar, discoursing much to his own satisfaction, if not to that of his hearers.

"Why, do tell!" he exclaimed, breaking off in his discourse, "if there aint the capting now! Bid I ever! Why, capting, I was jist saying to my brother Marius and these gentlemen—"

"Your brother Marius be d——d. Keep your seats, gentlemen. Stickney, where's Valtmeyer?"

"I guess, if you follow the turning to the right, you'll find him in one of the chambers to the north o' this," said the cool Syl, without ever moving from his seat to salute or welcome his officer.

"Nay, my good fellows," said Bradshawe, turning to the others, who were beginning to explain how they had become his guests in his absence, "the king's friends are always welcome to any shelter I can afford them; and I ought, perhaps, to thank our friend Stickney here for gaining such valuable recruits for my band in times like these."

"Ought ye, raaly, capting? Well, now, that's jist what I told Red Wolfert when he showed signs of kicking up a muss, case, when I went up into daylight one day to lift a rebel sheep or two, 'Wolfert,' says I—but, by darn, the capting's cleared out without speaking to one of the company but ourselves." And, true enough, Bradshawe, seizing a torch from a cleft in the rock, had glided out of the apartment, unobserved by all save those who had marked his entrance.

Taking now a northern direction, he soon encountered the outlaw in a long narrow passage leading from some secret chamber where arms and munitions were said to be kept, but which Valtmeyer probably appropriated to the stowage of booty; a matter which Bradshawe, who did not care to mix himself up with the predatory doings of his lieutenant, never inquired into. Valtmeyer, exchanging but few words with his leader for the present, led him back to the Outlaws' Hall, where everyone seemed to be too much engaged in their own pastime to notice them, as, passing along the wall on one side, Bradshawe entered a narrow aperture toward the south, leading to a distinct suite of apartments. Here Valtmeyer soon brought him the refreshment he so much needed after the toils he had undergone.

In one of these chambers, where the air was ever cooled and kept in motion by the dripping of water from above, a thin plate of stone upon which it fell emitted a sound not unlike that which proceeds from the body of a guitar or other stringed instrument when the wooden part is lightly tapped by the finger. These monotonous tones, varying only at times to a higher and wilder key, as if the cords of the instrument were swept by some unseen hand, mingled strangely with the low murmur of their voices as the two adventurers conversed together; while the huge Cyclopean frame of the freebooter, and fiery eye and reckless features of the Tory captain—which looked doubly wan by the blazing torch that the other held before them while sitting in deep shadow himself—formed one of those studies which the old masters so loved to paint.

A few moments sufficed Bradshawe to despatch his hasty meal, and possess himself of all the information which his zealous coadjutor had to impart; and, repassing again through the Outlaws' Hall, without pausing to make himself known to the half-drunken revellers who were still grouped about it much in the same attitudes in which they were first introduced to the reader, he motioned silently to the wierd-looking ferryman who had brought him into these gloomy realms, and once more regained the shores of the subterranean lake.

The black pool was then again crossed; and, passing by the Warder's Room on the right, the two pursued the arched passage which Bradshawe had before traversed, until they came to the open space in the cave where he had first reached the bottom in descending from the region of daylight to these grim abodes.

The cloistered arches above rose so loftily that the roof was shrouded in impenetrable darkness; and here, through a small aperture in the wall on the left, was again heard the sound of water. It seemed not to be a still, sullen lake, like that he had just crossed, but a flowing river, whose waves dashed heavily and slowly against the cavernous rocks which confined them on either side; and now, taking a torch and paddle in his hands, and placing himself in a recumbent posture in a boat barely large enough to admit of its being pushed through the crevice, Bradshawe, by the aid of the half-breed, entered the opening in the curtain of rock, and launched upon the stream beyond.

The subterranean voyager, who first pushed himself along with his hands only, soon found the vault to enlarge above him, so that he could sit erect in the boat and use his paddle. The water, so clear that his torchlight gleamed upon the bottom some thirty feet below him, was only broken at long intervals by a mimic cascade scarcely a foot in height, over which he easily lifted his shallop, and proceeded upon his errand to the distant chamber where Alida was immured. In this spacious apartment Valtmeyer had partitioned off a dry place by erecting a bark shanty over it, and made other provisions for the unhappy female, from whom, in the outlaw's slang, it took its name of "The Lady's Chapel."

But Bradshawe has now gained the threshold of that the dreari-
est bower in which Beauty ever yet received her suitor, and we must
pause before venturing to describe the strange and painful interview
between them.

CHAPTER 12

The Interview

Hernando.   *Thou art here*
    Wholly within my power; now, as a guest,
    Fair cousin, be less scornful.
Izidora.   *Thou wouldst not dare to wrong me!* '
Hernando.   *I would be*
    Loath to do that; I claim thy hand;
    If thou dost scorn me, lady, then beware!
                 Velasco, by Epes Sargent.

The hallowed honour that protects a maid
Is round me like a circle of bright fire;
A savage would not cross it, nor shall you.
I'm mistress of my presence—leave me, sir.—Willis.

The ruffian Valtmeyer had not, as we have hinted, been wholly unmindful of the comfort of his captive when dragging her from the light of day to become the tenant of this dungeon-like abode. Whether this considerateness arose from motives utterly selfish, or whether the outlaw had really some latent sparks of kindness in his rude bosom, it is impossible to say. But certainly he had been at much pains in preparing "the Chapel" for its occupant before he ever brought her to the cave.

The spot which he had selected for her tent or wigwam of birchen bark had been smoothed by filling up its inequalities with dry leaves; and these, when covered by a piece of Indian matting, afforded an elastic and comfortable carpet. Hither he had, too, with much trouble—from the difficulty of transporting articles of any bulk through these sinuous vaults—conveyed bedding, a chair or two, a table—which he was obliged to take to pieces, and which cost him many an oath in reconstructing—and other household articles. Nor had he forgotten even the ordinary kitchen utensils when preparing one corner of the chapel for the accommodation of the two coloured women who were to attend upon Alida.

It was probably owing to these arrangements chiefly that the health of Miss De Roos was not utterly prostrated by the long weeks she was compelled to pass in the gloomy vaults of Waneonda. For though the air of this remarkable cavern is said to be perfectly pure, and the temperature mild and equable, yet such utter exclusion from the light of day must always be more or less prejudicial, especially to one whose anxious spirit is so worn by emotion that the frame needs all fostering care to prevent its giving way and releasing the throbbing tenant.

But the thought of Death, which, to most characters in her situation, would often have suggested itself as a refuge, had perhaps never once occurred to Alida de Roos. She neither wished for it nor feared it. But she did fear that her bodily strength might give way; her mind become enfeebled with the decay of her health; that mind, upon whose in born and conscious energies she so haughtily relied in the last emergency to which she might be driven. She did fear that the greatest trial of its ascendency and its powers—for she knew that she was in Bradshawe's hands—might be deferred till her faculties were impaired by suffering and her hither to indomitable spirit overborne.

The thought that those faculties might fail their mistress, and that she might fall irretrievably into the power of Bradshawe, was maddening to her. She revolted from it whenever it swept athwart her brain. She tried to forget her sorrows; she refused to entertain her griefs; she endeavoured to postpone, as it were, reflecting upon the full horrors of her situation; and she caught at every object within her reach that could occupy her attention, if it did not amuse her mind. She divided their duties with her attendants, and assumed all those which appertained immediately to the care of her own person; she borrowed her needle of the *mulatto*, who was glad of an excuse for remaining unemployed, and sleeping away the indolent and monotonous hours; and, listening for hours to her dotard prating, she drew from the elder negress all the superstitious lore which formed the only furniture wherewith the mind of the decrepit crone was supplied.

Alida unwittingly thus attached these humble companions to her; and as their simple-hearted affection more and more manifested itself, she began at last to derive a certain solace from their sympathy which actually approached to pleasure in their society. The dungeon-doomed captive, who, in his solitary misery, has made friends of animals that belong to the very lowest and most loathsome orders of created beings, can alone, perhaps, appreciate this growth of friendship between a mind the most gifted and refined, and those the least tutored and liberalized.

On the day—if the phrase be allowable in regions where night alone hath, since creation, reigned—on the day that Bradshawe came on his stern errand to the Lady's Chapel, Alida had, from some slight indisposition, remained withdrawn in her tent; and the two blacks, for the purpose of washing some household articles, had kindled a fire upon the brink of the stream, within a few yards of its door, where they sat watching a boiling kettle, and chattering together after the manner of their loquacious race. The sound of their voices prevented their hearing Bradshawe's approach; and as he extinguished his torch the moment he came within the guiding light of their fire, he was wholly unobserved till he stood suddenly before them.

The shriek they simultaneously uttered at the apparition startled Alida from her couch, and she sprang to her feet, lifting, at the same time, the curtain of her tent, so that the light of a lamp suspended from within fell brokenly across her loosely arrayed person.

Bradshawe, motioning with the back of his hand as if he would cuff the negroes aside, pushed his way at once rudely between them. "Shut up, you squalling black brutes," cried the ruffian, in a characteristic tone, which changed on the instant, as if belonging to another voice, as, bowing low, he saluted Alida when he had approached a few paces toward her.

"I have come," said he, pausing in his advance, and casting his eyes, as in respect to her, upon the ground, "I have come, unheralded and unannounced, I fear, no welcome visitor."

"Unheralded? Who but the savage Valtmeyer is *your* fitting herald? Unannounced? What better than the terrors of this hideous dungeon could announce its proper jailer! Waste not the soft speeches that sit so idly on your lips, and are thrown away in my ears. But tell me, tell me, Walter Bradshawe, whence come you, why come you? Tell me why I am here; for what monstrous wickedness have I been kidnapped, kept for months aloof from my friends and family, and brought to this spot? and why do you stand there blasting my eyes with your presence? Speak out, man; out with it all, if words can syllable the foul contrivings of your heart!"

Thus haughtily did Alida confront her spoiler; and as she thus, in

look as well as words, gave vent to her outraged feelings, while Bradshawe, standing on the declivity below her, seemed to stoop and cower before her presence, she looked—half emerging from the drapery
of the tent, with the pale light from within brightening the outlines
of her features and person, and leaving the rest in deep shadow—she
looked like some indignant spirit, who, descending from a brighter
world, had pierced its way into these black realms to rebuke their un
hallowed master.

"By Jove, she'll unhitch lightning against me next," said Bradshawe,
mentally. "She's a great girl, and no mistake, this same Mistress Bradshawe;" and then, still preserving his obsequious and almost reveren-
tial bearing toward her, he rejoined aloud, "I can bear this from you;
this, and more, Alida. My heart has not now, for the first time, to be
schooled in your unkindness. If you call it kidnapping to rescue you
from the horrors of Indian captivity; if you call it outrage to provide
a secluded and safe home for you, when the havoc of civil war has
made thousands shelterless, and your own friends are either scattered
or slain; if you call it wickedness to snatch you from the neighbourhood of these scenes of horror as they thicken through the land, and
provide you here a retreat which, rude and gloomy as I confess it is,
still is not without its comforts and advantages; if these humble, but
zealous and unwearying efforts of one who has long since waived his
right as a husband to win your regard as a friend, can make no amends
for the one rash but well-meant act by which I would have made you
mine—then—then, Alida—then—"

"Then, sir!" said the lady, scornfully, as he paused a moment for a
word; "well, sir, and what then?"

"I'm d——d if I know," said Bradshawe to himself. "The jade looks
so cursed cool that my stump eloquence fails me. I must go it on some
other touch."

"Why don't you finish your speech, sir?" repeated Alida, noticing
his hesitation. "Why stop you so short in your pleadings and specifica-
tions? Even Mr. Bradshawe's enemies allow him the glibness, as well as
the guile, of a county-court attorney."

He did not reply, and the lady went on. "Bradshawe, you are a skilful actor, a most specious hypocrite, though your selfish passions are
too fitful and stormy to make you a consummate one. But you must
deem me credulous indeed when you claim for yourself motives of
disinterested kindness which would give the lie to all I have known of
your character in long years gone by. The very attachment with whose

declaration this cruel persecution began, was—"

"Was true, pure, disinterested, by Heaven!" exclaimed Bradshawe, now really speaking from his heart; "was earnest and devoted as ever mortal man bore toward your sex. No, no, Alida, chafe me not with that. 'Had you but accepted my honourable proposals when first I dared to press my suit, you might have made me what you would. Wild and reckless as men called me, my mother's gentleness seemed born anew in my spirit whenever it turned to you."

"And where," said Alida, not wholly untouched by this natural burst of feeling, yet shuddering as she spoke the words which followed, "where was that spirit of gentleness when those horrid nuptials were forced upon me; when, by your lawless instruments, I was torn from my home, and my hand to you in wedlock made the price by which alone you consented to redeem me from the licentious hands of that young barbarian with whom you, as well as Valtmeyer, were colleagued? That fearful night! oh God! oh God!" And the now agitated Alida covered her face with her hands, as if shutting out some hideous spectre which her imagination had conjured up for the moment.

"You have never had reason," said Bradshawe, coldly, "to believe that I was privy to that deed of violence; and though, for certain valuable political services he has rendered, I have since taken Valtmeyer into my confidence, no man has ever dared to whisper audibly that I was at that time colleagued with him. No, Alida, though you *then* disbelieved the tale, I can now only repeat the same story I told you then. And what are the circumstances? I had been some weeks from home in a remote settlement, and, returning by a short road through the wilderness, I stop to bait my horse at the solitary lodge of an Indian missionary. I find the timid man in the utmost anxiety about a female prisoner that, within an hour, had been brought to the house by a ferocious young savage, whose band is hovering near. His followers have called the spoiler away for a few hasty moments, and left a white desperado to stand guard over the captive. I ask to see her, and, to my horror, discover that it is Alida; she whom, a short month since, I had hoped to call my Alida; she for whom still, as her rejected lover, I cherished the deepest respect, the tenderest affection.

"In my wrath I threaten Valtmeyer for the part he has played in this forced abduction. He derides my anger, and points to the smoke of the Indian fires nearby, as seen through the window. I entreat, I conjure him. I add bribes to my entreaties, and he consents to hear me, but rejects the alternatives of flight or resistance as equally hopeless in rescuing the prisoner. There is but one resort remains. I am not personally unknown to Au-neh-yesh; I must plead to him. But will he hear me in such a cause? He has already avowed to the Catholic missionary his intention to marry the white woman; will he be dissuaded from his course by words, when his deeds have just proved the determination of his character. No! there is no way of rescuing you from the ruthless hands of that licentious son of Brant, but by convincing him that you are already married; that, in a word, you are my wife. Proofs are wanting; for, as you do not bear my name, I must make it appear that the espousals long since took place clandestinely.

"The missionary is the only party at hand whose testimony will be believed; but he refuses to give it falsely. He will not swear that we are married unless the rite be solemnized; but he consents, if we accept his ministry at once, to leave a blank in the marriage certificate, which I can antedate, so that Au-neh-yesh shall have no suspicion of being over reached. What remains to be told? You startle from a stupor as you hear the dreadful sound of his voice approaching from a distance; there is not a moment to be lost; the service is hurried through; you faint at the last response, but the ceremony is finished, and the demi-savage foiled in his claim, before he makes his appearance at the door."

"God of mercy!" passionately exclaimed Alida, clasping her hands together, "*is* Thy truth like human truth? Not one word which that man has spoken can I gainsay; yet, while the very scene he describes passed before my eyes—my own eyes—I feel, I know, that it was all false; false, fiendishly false. A *lie*; a living, breathing, moving lie."

She paused. "Yet I did see that stony-eyed priest; I did hear Bradshawe pleading with Valtmeyer; I do remember leaping forward when I heard the voice of that red barbarian, whose naked arm had been around my waist an hour before.—More I remember not till they showed me that fatal certificate; but even then I did not think that this was all a cruel inveiglement, and Bradshawe a specious villain, a most accursed.—When and whence, then, came this firm conviction that I was foully dealt with—that I was a blind victim in the toils of demons?"

The ill-starred lady, while speaking thus, with eyes intensely fixed on vacancy, pushed back with her fingers the long tresses from her brow, as if her intellectual as well as physical vision could thus be cleared. Then shaking her head, from which the dishevelled hair again fell slowly to her shoulders, she turned and fixed on Bradshawe a look so mournful yet so piercing, that even his features of bronze betrayed the uneasy and painful emotion it awakened. But whether that emotion was one of alarm for the future or of remorse for the past; whether his guilty heart quailed beneath that penetrating glance, or whether the grief-stricken mien of the beautiful woman whom he had reduced to this condition of forlornness touched some latent feeling of pity and regret, it was impossible to say. The slight agitation passed rapidly from his countenance, and, folding his arms with a composed but dejected air, in which something of dignity was not unmingled, he said,

"Madam, it is in vain for me to attempt removing these ungenerous, these monstrous suspicions. I shall never attempt to combat with them more; nor would I now have said what I have said, save that I always attributed your horror of my legal claim upon your hand to some painful impression upon your mind, made during the fits of delirium which marked the long illness that followed those unhappy nuptials. I therefore suspended that claim till years should intervene and efface these frightful imaginings. I for years avoided molesting you with my hateful presence, though, unseen by you, I was often hovering near. I kept secret the bond of union between us. I thought that time might soft en the bitterness of your aversion. I hoped to melt at last that heart of obduracy. But I have reasoned vainly. An opportunity such as I have recently availed myself of to prove my watchful affection and devotedness, may never again occur; and if it does, what will be my reward if I embrace it? Scorn and contempt—ay, those are my wages—scorn for the feelings that prompted the service, contempt for the claim I would thus purchase on your regard."

The lady bowed her head and wept. The borderer saw he was gaining an advantage, and determined to pursue it. She spoke not, and he thus went on:

"Hear me, Alida: there was a time when, in the full tide of youth, madly as I loved you, I would never have taken you as a reluctant partner to my bosom. But years of care and disappointment have sobered this arrogance of all-exacting affection. I am, alas! no longer young; and the freshness of both our lives has passed away forever. I never have loved, I never can love, another than you; and you—you can never belong to another until my death shall set you free. Why, then, oh why shall we both continue to be miserable for our remaining years? Why will you not make it my privilege, as it is my right, to minister to your happiness, by crowning mine? Why not confide in the partner whom Destiny has, for good or ill, allotted you, and permit me to announce you to the world as my wife? These wars must soon be over," pursued the Tory captain, gathering confidence as he proceeded; "the rebels are even now splitting into factions among themselves; and when the king's friends come in for honour and offices, and the forfeited estates of heavy-pursed and rich-landed traitors, Walter Bradshawe's claims for the spoils that are won by loyalty and valour will not be the feeblest among them. Ay, and men do say that titles will not be with held when success shall finally entitle us to the full meed of royal bounty and graciousness. Wilt be my Lady Bradshawe, fair Alida?"

And the wily suitor, dropping not ungracefully on one knee, tried that half frank, half humorous smile which had made more than one village maiden pronounce him positively handsome when his features wore it, and which others of the sex, less innocent, had called "the devil's own trick" when they had learned to rue its influence upon their hearts. But Alida—though she too might, in some sense, be numbered among his victims—was made of different metal from those whom Bradshawe had often moulded to his purpose.

"Kneel not to me," she cried, "thou base and sordid slave! thou wretched minion of power debauched and misapplied! thou most fitting tool of drunken tyranny! Share thy name! thy *loyal* name, thy honours, thy titles, forsooth! Vile parricide, I thank thee for reminding me of my bleeding country, which even now is convulsed with the throe of casting out such wretches as thou from her bosom. By Heaven, Bradshawe, I would rather these rocks should close together and crush me where I stand, or that yon black stream should float my senseless corse to an abyss still lower than that in which your villainy has already buried my living frame; I would, I would, rather than bear the name of your wife before men for a single day!"

"There may be a fate reserved for you in these vaults worse than either," said Bradshawe, in a voice husky with passion, as he regained his feet and stepped a pace or two backward. A sheathed poniard, unnoticed by himself, slipped from his belt as he rose, and lay upon the floor of the cavern midway between him and Alida. Her quick eye caught sight of the weapon in a moment; and, almost ere the dreadful import of the last words had reached her ears, she had sprung forward, plucked the dirk from the ground, and recovered her former position. Bradshawe, recoiling first at the impetuous bound she had made toward him, now actually turned pale when he saw her slowly draw the weapon from its sheath, and gaze with a cold smile upon its gleaming blade. He would have spoken, but horror kept him tongue-tied; he would have leaped forward to snatch the deadly steel from her hand, but the least motion on his part would precipitate the catastrophe which he verily believed was impending. But the next movement of Alida relieved the fearful suspense that agitated him. She calmly, after feeling its point, passed the naked dagger through her girdle, so as to secure it to her person.

"It is small, but it will do," she said, flinging the sheath to the feet of Bradshawe. "Your power over me from this moment has its limit. The instrument of my deliverance is in my own hands; and you can do no more than compel me to use it," she added, with an air of determination, so quiet as sufficiently to speak her resolve, even if the words had not been significant enough to reveal her purpose.

"I meant not—I did not mean—" stammered Bradshawe.

"Our conference is over, sir; and it has a fitting end," interrupted Alida, haughtily, waving her hand. "I would be alone, Mr. Bradshawe."

"Another time, then, when my care for your welfare, so far as I can study it in these dreary re treats, shall have obliterated these ignominious suspicions, this most ungenerous and unjust misinterpretation of every word I utter, I will come, Alida, and in a few days, perhaps, may venture to—"

"Come, sir, whenever you have made up your mind to the moment my doom is sealed; but let the victim be released from the presence of the executioner for the few hours that may yet be allotted her."

The curtain of the tent dropped before her as she pronounced these words; and Bradshawe, too much stupefied by the sudden turn which events had taken, and confounded by the position in which he had placed himself, withdrew sullenly to his boat, without bestowing the least notice upon his gaping slaves, who had been the mute and astonished witnesses of this singular scene.

"What a cursed blockhead I was to threaten a storm, when I had lots of time to circumvent, and a thousand other ways to drive the garrison to surrender. Wat Bradshawe, you are more of an ass than most men believe you. You great boy you, to let your blood get above your brain for a moment, because a theatrical girl is mad enough to scoff at you! She, too, wholly, at the moment, in your power! Zounds! but my henhawk made a gallant thing of it. That cursed dagger, too, slipping away as it did. Well for me it was not a pistol, or the Amazon had done for me at five paces. She's a tall girl; a great piece of woman's flesh, that same Mistress Bradshawe. I don't know whether it be love or hatred that drives me on; but something does drive me. If love, there's certainly a streak of malice in it. If hatred, there must be some wishy-washy drippings of tenderness in the bitter waters, for my heart beat the devil's tattoo when she pointed that infernal bodkin so near to her bosom. Hallo, Charon! mongrel half-breed! bowknot of twisted man's flesh! hither, I say! Ah! my good Charon, I dreamed not you were so near at hand."

And Bradshawe, terminating his amiable soliloquy as his deformed follower joined him at the opening in the rock where they had before separated, the two soon afterward regained the Outlaws' Hall.

BOOK THIRD

CHAPTER 1

The Refugees

There's song and oath, and gaming deep,
Hot words and laughter, mad carouse;
There's naught of prayer and little sleep:
The devil keeps the house.

The Bucanier

An injury may be forgiven by a proud spirit, but an insult never. And what human being is without his share of pride? That miserable deformed half-breed; that crooked mongrel of a man; that dumb and uncomplaining slave of the gloomy mine of Waneonda, had yet his human feelings, had still his modicum of inward self-esteem, which brutal words could wound and outrage. His vocation in those tomb-like cells, though toilsome and humble, was still one of the greatest trust; for he was alike warder and seneschal of that subterranean castle, whose moat and drawbridge were the black stream and tottering skiff of the hunchback ferryman.

With these defences the renegade garrison had always held themselves safe from hostile intrusion. They might be starved out of their stronghold, but it could never be carried by assault. For, however the secret of the cave might become known, its recesses could never be penetrated by a stranger, save through the treachery of the ferryman.

That poor wretch, whom we have only known by the sobriquet of Charon, as Bradshawe had nick named him, had always enjoyed his confidence, and hitherto not undeservedly; though, while Bradshawe regarded himself as the patron of the half-breed, and entitled to his gratitude, the other, perhaps, had merely viewed their relations toward each other as a mutual affair of give and take, which left neither party under special obligations to the other. The half-breed, who

171

had originally been a fisherman by occupation, had, in former years, pointed out the cave to Bradshawe when acting as his guide to the trout-streams among the hills. Bradshawe, learning that the spot had been hitherto known only to the Indians, and, for some motive best known to himself, wishing that a knowledge of it should be extended to those white men only to whom he chose to intrust it, determined instantly to take the half- breed into his service, upon condition of his keeping the secret of the place.

Time passed on; the half-breed, carried to another part of the country, became a useless hanger-on of Bradshawe's establishment; nominally a provider for, but really a pensioner upon, Bradshawe's kitchen; in short, one of that lounging, eel-catching degenerates of the aborigines that may still be found near some of the old families on Long Island, incident, as it were, rather than belonging to the establishment. The abduction of Miss De Roos, which made it necessary for Valtmeyer, who played the part of scapegoat in that affair, to disappear from among men for a time, was the first thing that called the half-breed and his secret into actual use. Since that time he had silently almost passed into Valtmeyer's service, who sometimes for a month together retained him in the cavern, of which he was a perfectly contented tenant, and which grew more and more like a home to him.

Idle by nature, yet always to be relied upon when any duty was required of him, this inoffensive, taciturn creature was one of the few human beings who had never provoked the imperious insolence of Bradshawe's nature when brought in familiar contact with him. But his brutality did break out at last in the hour that, foaming with rage and vexation, he called for the service of the ferryman when returning from his fruitless interview with Alida. The jeer at his deformity was resented by the half-breed even in the moment it was uttered; for the means of vengeance were at hand, and, as we shall soon see, he did not hesitate to embrace them.

The goodly company to which Bradshawe was now about to introduce himself in the Outlaws' Hall might, in the slight glimpse we have had of them in these deep cavern shades, have passed well enough as a redoubtable crew of desperadoes, a real melodramatic set of brigands. But the truth is, that, though felon-loving old Salvator might have picked out a head or two among them for his savage pencil, a majority of these worthies would have formed a more suitable study for some American Wilkie—our own Richard Mount, perhaps—whose canvass, borrowing for the nonce some broader and bolder shadows, might delight in preserving the grotesque array of characters.

Among Valtmeyer's immediate crew there were, indeed, some as hideous-looking gentlemen as ever said stand and deliver upon the highway. Faces stolid yet ferocious; looks blended of sinister malice and sensual audacity; wild, rude, and reckless-featured men, with that dash of the genuine savage in their aspect which is only acquired by pursuing a career of crime upon the extreme borders of society, where the practitioner incessantly vibrates between civilized and barbarian life; a variety of the robber species, in short, such as is only found upon our Indian frontiers; such as the curious may occasionally there light upon even at this day; but such as only existed in perfection when the name of Red Wolfert Valtmeyer was terrible in the land.

But, though these ill-omened visages glowered here and there from beneath the wolfskin cap or chequered handkerchief which swathed around the brows, and, with some tawdry plume or Indian medal stuck in its folds, generally formed the headgear in this portrait-gallery of infernals, yet there was that both in the guise and features of many which was hardly in keeping with their present associations. The complexions and appointments of a few betrayed them as city-bred and of luxurious nurture; they were ill-disciplined youths, whom the mad spirit of loyalty, or some home disgust, or some silly boyish *escapado*, had driven from a parent's roof to the stormy border, where, in the whirl of events, they had been hurled, with the black-bearded men around them, into this place of bad spirits, where so many had huddled together for safety.

Of others, the faces were coarse, but not weather-beaten, and bloated in some instances, as if by the loose debauch of the road-side tippling-house, from which, perhaps, their swaggering air was like wise borrowed.

Here a red flannel shirt, breeches of corduroy, and thick-soled brogans betrayed the quondam village tradesman; while there the coat of foxy black, or tattered blue with tarnished metal buttons, and shrunken underclothes of threadbare gray, might have bespoken some bankrupt peddler (or travelling merchant, as the country folk would more reverentially call him), save that the rusty-hilted small sword by his side, bespeaking his old-fashioned claim to gentility, might induce one to set him down as an absconding attorney.

All of the motley group, however, notwithstanding these little discrepancies, seemed to be close confreres, who were upon the choicest terms of fellowship together; and though Syl Stickney's contribution of newcomers had been received at first rather coolly by some members of the company, they had all, doubtless, in other scenes and places, often consorted in brotherhood of some kind to establish the harmonious sympathy which reigned among them.

The tie of that brotherhood was political faith! They were all possessed by that spirit which, next to the old democrat *Death*, is your only true leveller, bringing all men on whom it seizes, save only kings and demagogues, upon the same platform. *Party spirit* had made them at first co-labourers, and then co-mates together. But what mattered the temporary inconvenience of so incongruous an association? The disagreeableness and evils of their state affected only themselves; and what mattered such transient exposure when the well-being of countless generations was concerned? Were they not loyal subjects, banded together to sustain, not merely the right of a crowned king, but to preserve and fix the blessed precedence of rank, with all its orderly succession of prerogative, by which alone civilization can be sustained?

Thus reasoned some four or five small landed proprietors or gentlemen farmers of undoubted respectability, who, having compromised their safety in the plots of their party by being seen riding home from more than one Tory rendezvous, were now compelled "to take earth" for a season, and share this den with the lowest dregs of the faction to which they belonged. These suffering partisans of the royal cause had been now for so many weeks crowded together in familiar contact with their present comrades, that there was really little in their bearing to distinguish them from the rest, though a gray riding-frock and broad-leafed beaver, with a feather in it of the same colour, or the uniform of the royal Greens, in which some of them, who bore a commission in the yeomanry militia, were dressed, might have marked them as being better apparelled than their comrades.

"Ah! Bradshawe," cried one of these worthies, "Bradshawe, my ace of trumps, I am rejoiced to see you; for there are so few faced cards in our pack here, that some of us would throw up our hands in very disgust were it not for the royal game we're playing. But by what devilish legerdemain are we all shuffled here together?"

"Yes, Bradshawe," exclaimed another, "tell us, is there no chance of our breaking away from this cursed hole till the rebels come to unearth us?"

"If you know of any better *hole* to creep into, gentlemen, there is nothing to prevent our parting company at any moment that suits your pleasure," dryly replied Bradshawe, at the same time saluting the company with a formal courtesy.

His personal retainers, crowding tumultuously around him the moment they heard the sound of his voice, prevented any farther parley with the group of gentlemen who had first accosted him, and with whom, indeed, Bradshawe seemed disposed to converse as little as possible. The truth is, that, though he had been more than once indebted to the hospitality of some of them, and would on no account have been so impolitic as to treat any of them with positive rudeness, yet the presence of these royalists of the more respectable class put a check upon his conduct that filled him with chagrin and vexation.

More than one of these gentlemen had, in less troublous times, been personally acquainted with the family of the unfortunate Alida; and all of them were men of that stamp who would not hesitate to embroil themselves in deadly quarrel to succour a lady so iniquitously dealt with as Miss De Roos had been. Nor would his political faith or loyal services have been any shield to Bradshawe had these country gentlemen dreamed of the villainy he was practising against the daughter of an old neighbour well known, and once universally beloved in the county.

Their wrath, had it been once really awakened, Bradshawe would have laughed to scorn, and would soon have made them feel, in their present situation, the folly of chiding the lion when their heads were in his mouth. But while, for very natural reasons, not wishing that anything should create disunion between himself and his brother partisans, he felt that, however idly their indignation might explode where they could be so easily overmastered by his immediate crew, yet, to bring his affair with Alida to a successful termination, the secret of the cavern must not be extended to more than were at present intrusted with it. It was therefore not without an inward feeling of satisfaction that he listened to a proposition which one of the Tory gentlemen, coming forward in behalf of the rest, made him as soon as he was disengaged from receiving the boisterous welcome that others gave him in the Outlaws' Hall.

"We pardon the coldness of your greeting, Captain Bradshawe," said this gentleman, "in consideration of the kindness we have already received from some of your servants; and because our some days' experience of the difficulty of providing for so many mouths in this place suggests that there must be limits to your hospitality, and—"

"Nay, my dear Fenton," said Bradshawe, seizing both hands of the speaker, "I beg you would not mention—"

"Pardon me, Captain Bradshawe," said the refugee, bowing somewhat stiffly as he withdrew his hands from the familiar grasp of the other, "there are four or five of us here who have made up our minds where to dispose of ourselves; and all that we ask is a couple of your retainers, to act as guides and packmen till we can make our way within the borders of Ulster county, where we are sure of a cordial reception at the house of a royalist gentle man of our acquaintance."

"The men, Mr. Fenton, are entirely at your service, if you insist upon thus abruptly taking leave of the poor entertainment I have to offer you. But why not, gentlemen, at the least, put off your departure till the morrow?"

"We had no idea of starting till tomorrow," rejoined one of the older royalists, bluntly.

"Not at all, not at all," said Fenton, rather hurriedly, and colouring at the same time as he appreciated Bradshawe's readiness to get rid of himself and his friends; "we'll be off within the hour if your men can get ready."

"Within the hour be it, since you *will* go," replied Bradshawe, turning at once upon his heel to give the necessary order.

"The churl!" muttered Fenton.

"What can you expect from a hog but a grunt?" echoed Sylla.

"If you sit down with dogs, you must look for fleas," rejoined his brother Marius, as the classic pair stood listening to this colloquy of their betters.

"I say, Squire Fenton," pursued Syl, "I mistrust Marius and I'll make tracks with you out of this darned hole. A fellow'll turn into a woodchuck if he burrows here much longer."

This accession to his party was gladly welcomed by Fenton at the time, though, as it included several of Syl's immediate friends and cronies, it proved subsequently disastrous from the undue confidence it gave Fenton in his numbers, as will appear in the sequel.

The arrangements for their departure were soon completed. But the final exit of Fenton and his followers was attended by circumstances which can scarcely be understood unless we recur to other actors in the scene, athwart whose shadows a new and strange form is but now flitting to mingle mysteriously with the rest.

We have already spoken of the feeling of bitter exasperation which had been excited in the bosom of the hunchback ferryman by the brutal language of his master, but we have not told that the hour which Bradshawe consumed in the Lady's Chapel had seen a trial of

176

the half-breed's fidelity which, considering his Indian origin, was of the severest kind.

Scarcely, indeed, had the Tory captain passed through the opening in the rock and launched in his boat upon the river beyond, before the hunchback found himself in contact with another authority than that which had posted him there as sentinel. Hearing the fall of a pebble on the bottom of the cavern, he stepped quickly forward, and threw the light of his torch against the walls of the pit by which you first descend into the cave. He could discover nothing. Presently another pebble rolled to his feet. It seemed to bound from a ledge of rock near him. Still he could not fix the direction whence it came; and he climbs half way up the zigzag shaft of the pit to see if it can have been precipitated from without. He lifts his torch aloft, so as to throw its light where the rope ladder is wont to be suspended from the crossed trees above. But all looks quiet there and safe. The ladder has been, as usual, drawn in and secured, a thin tendril of grapevine, passing over a cross timber above, being left hanging to raise it from within to its former place, when necessary. Suddenly he sees the grapevine vibrate. The ladder begins slowly to uncoil, and rise before his eyes. He leaps forward, and with one blow of his hunting-knife severs the vine, and the rope falls by his side.

"*Ugh!*" exclaims an Indian voice without, as the swinging sliver comes burdenless to his hand.

The swart features of the hunchback become radiant at the sound as he tosses his torch above his head, and hails the stranger in the Mohawk tongue. The vine is again let down. The hunchback quickly attaches it anew to the ladder of rope. It is drawn up from above. A towering figure darkens the opening for a moment, and then Brant stands beside the deformed outcast of his tribe.

"My child, how fares he here with his white father?" said the chief, kindly.

"'The Broken Tomahawk,'" said the man, calling himself by his Indian name, "has no father. The Mohawk owns not him, he owns not the white man. He is here on his own bidding, but will do the will of Thayendanagea." And, speaking thus, he was about to usher the chief farther into the cavern; for Brant was known to him as the companion in arms of Bradshawe, and, as such, the hunchback had no hesitation in farthering his ingress. The *sachem*, however, was by no means desirous of the interview which the half-breed thought he was seeking, and his errand here must be a brief one, if he would despatch it at all. He ascertained that Bradshawe had already arrived at Waneonda, and assumed the personal charge of his captive, Brant's only chance, then, of rescuing her, depended upon the aid and connivance of the half-breed; and that aid could only be secured by awakening the fellow's Indian sympathies so strongly in favour of the Mohawk that they should overpower his fidelity to the white man.

But the hunchback, though evidently flattered by the frank confidence which the chief seemed to repose in him, and listening with mute respect to the claims which he urged upon his services, was unflinching in his trust. Brant could wring nothing from him save a promise not to reveal this secret visit to Bradshawe; and even this promise was accompanied with a condition which seemed something like a threat upon the part of the hunchback.

"Let the chief go," said he. "Let Thayendanagea depart in secret as he has come. No bird shall whisper that he has been here, and Thayendanagea will come no more."

There was nothing, therefore, to be done with this stanch *seneschal*, unless Brant had chosen to strangle him where he stood, or hurl him deathward down the black pit whose entrance he guarded. But it was not in the heart of Brant to crush in cold blood a creature always so inoffensive, and now so firm when he stood most exposed and defenceless. Had he debated such a thing in his own mind, however, there was now hardly time to effect it successfully; for at this moment the enraged voice of Bradshawe was heard shouting to the half-breed, who waved his hand to Brant, as if motioning him to ascend and leave the cave at once, and then hurried to wait upon the Tory captain.

Brant seized the opportunity to descend farther into the cavern, with whose peculiarities he was perfectly familiar, and gained a recess of the rock not far from the fallen tree just as Bradshawe brushed by it in traversing the passage. The hand of the Mohawk clutched the belt-knife, which was half drawn from its sheath as the glare of the Hunch back's torch shone full upon him for a moment. The life of Bradshawe turned upon a cast. But, haply, he passed by unheeding the peril at hand; and the person of Brant being thrown the next instant into deep shadow, the knife was shot back into its sheath as he saw the danger of discovery had passed away.

That momentary gleam of light, however, had revealed to Brant the features of the hunchback, and the feelings which agitated them; for he had overheard the contumelious epithets which Bradshawe applied to the unfortunate. Brant scarcely doubted what their effect would be upon the half-Indian nature of the hunchback. If not a provocation to revenge, they would at least cancel all ties of kindness which bound him as a retainer of Bradshawe.

Nor did the sagacious Mohawk err in his judgment; for, following shortly afterward to the spot where the others embarked upon the black lake to cross to the threshold of the Outlaws' Hall, the plashing of the ferryman's paddle had hardly died away upon his ear before he again heard its faint dip approach once more the shore from which he had just parted. The hunchback, neither by look nor word, expressed his surprise at finding the chief awaiting him, but mutely drew up his boat, marshalled Brant forward to the opening in the curtain of rock, and aided him in launching upon the River of Ghosts.

CHAPTER 2

The Rescue

His boat was nigh; its fragile side
Boldly the venturous wanderer tried;
Indeed, it was a full strange sight
To see in the track of the ghostly light
The swarthy chief and the lady bright,
On the heaving waves borne on;
While her wan cheek and robe of white
The pale ray played upon,
And above his dusky plumage shook;
Backward was flung his feathery cloak,
As his brawny arms were stretched to ply
The oars that made their shallop fly.

Sands

Alida, to whom, haply, the story of her family, desolated through the agency of Brant, was yet unknown, did not hesitate to accept the deliverance proffered at his hands; but the noble-hearted girl insisted upon the negroes, to whose kindness she was so much indebted, being first removed from the reach of Bradshawe's cruelty; for she knew that the first outbreak of his wrath would be terrible, and that it was upon these defenceless creatures it would fall. The little shallop would contain but two persons at a time, and many precious moments were consumed in ferrying the whole party to the chamber where the hunchback stood a sullen sentry.

The negroes have already found their way to the outside of the cave without farther peril of discovery; and now the swarthy chief and the bright lady have embarked upon those ghostly waters. Their frail boat has brushed safely through the flinty chasm which walls in the sinuous tide. They have reached the crevice in the curtain of rock, and have gained a footing on the land, when suddenly the distant reverberations of a horn are heard trembling through the shadowy cells around. It is a summons to the hunchback to assume his office of warder in facilitating the egress of Fenton and his followers.

In the scene which followed, even the coolness of Brant, aided as he was by the presence of mind of his companion, would hardly have availed them, were it not for the ready offices of the Hunchback in assisting Alida up the first ascent before the foremost of Fenton's party had fairly reached the spot where the danger of discovery was most imminent.

And now, marshalled by torches formed of the blazing knots of the yellow pine, Bradshawe's parting guests were congregated in the chamber from which first commences the ascent to daylight Bradshawe himself coming last to bid them farewell at their exit from the cavern, and make up, if possible, for previous indifference by the warmth of his adieus.

The two foremost of the party, who seemed more closely muffled than the rest, had already, as it appeared, surmounted the first ascent, and contented themselves with waving him a backward *adieu*, as, mounting beyond his reach, they stepped upon the ladder which led up the second. The rest successively gave him each a hand as they passed up the fallen tree before described.

About half had made the ascent of the first steep, when the half-breed hunchback, exclaiming that he would steady the rope ladder for one of the party who was somewhat infirm, mounted with the agility of a cat to the ledge to which its lower end was attached. Bradshawe took no note of his officiousness, and the rest followed, till the two brothers Stickney alone were left at the bottom.

"Ho! treason!" shouted Bradshawe, seizing the luckless Syl by the collar, and flinging him upon the flinty floor of the cave, as he was in the act of moving forward in his turn. "Charon! Valtmeyer!—ho there! Charon, you humpbacked knave, what means this? Ten men, the number of Fenton's party, have already gone up, yet these two Yankee peddlers are still below."

"Peddler yourself, Captain Bradshawe," cried the sturdy Marius; and, in a moment, the indignant Syl having sprung to his feet, the two New Englanders had rushed together upon the Tory captain, hurled him against the wall of the cavern, and scrambled up to the landing-place where stood the hunchback, flinging his torchlight over the pit below. Bradshawe, recovering himself, cocked a pistol and levelled it at Marius on the instant.

"Hullo! capting," cried the undismayed Syl, pressing down the head of his brother, so that the rays of the torch passed over it, and left only his own arm to aim at. "Don't be such a darned fool, capting, as to throw away your shot upon us, who raaly have had nothing to do with this muss. Humpy here's your man, I reckon; and, if you wait a moment, I'll pitch him down to you."

How far the doughty Syl might have succeeded in a tussle with the active half-breed in such a spot, it is impossible now to say; for the Hunchback was about to prepare himself for the encounter, which he did by quickly flinging the torch from his hands into the abyss below. But the movement that he makes in leaning over to hurl it at Bradshawe exposes the upper part of his person for an instant, and the flash of Bradshawe's pistol illuminates the vault in the moment the blazing missile leaves the hand of the hunchback, who instantly follows it, shot to death, and tumbling from ledge to ledge, a mangled corpse, at the feet of the Tory captain.

"Sylla, Marius," shouted Bradshawe, when the reverberations had subsided, "halt the party, and tell them there is treason among us." But no answer came from the classic pair, who had already made their exit from the cavern. Bradshawe, whose presence of mind seems to have deserted him for a moment, instead of at once following the retiring party, groped his way to the Warder's Room, eagerly seized the lantern which was ever kept burning there, ferried himself across the lake, summoned Valtmeyer, with him recrossed the black pool once more, and, leaving his worthy adjutant in the chamber where the hunchback had found a tomb, launched himself upon the River of Ghosts, and wended his way to the remote cell where Alida was immured.

The bats were now its only tenants, and the voice less spot, with no light save the torch of the gloomy voyager to illumine its dark walls, seemed dreary and chill as it had never seemed before to his eyes.

The baffled Bradshawe rejoined his comrade. "Have that carrion flung out to the wolves; or, stay, it may remain till tomorrow, when we will all move away together."

"Do we carry any woman's baggage with us?" asked Valtmeyer, keenly eying his superior.

"No, Wolfert. I give you those niggers wherever you may find them."

"And the farm?"

"D—n the farm, and you too, sir! Don't you see, man, you are plucking at my heartstrings? The girl's gone; lost to me, perhaps, forever. Is this a moment to remind me of the price I paid for her?" And Bradshawe ground another oath between his teeth that put a summary end to the conversation.

With the morrow's dawn the den of renegades had vomited forth its tenants, a wierd and ghastly crew, with beard unshorn and skin cadaverous from long exclusion from the light of day. A fall of snow had obliterated the tracks of those who had departed the night before; and Bradshawe, unwilling to penetrate with such a body of men into the settled country, where farther pursuit of Alida would most probably lead him, made no effort to recover Fenton's trail, but addressed himself to the task of getting his band of followers out of this Whig district as soon as possible. He then laid his course for Oswego, whither great numbers of Tories had already flocked together, under the lead of Colonels Claus and Butler, and where the royal banner, guarded by a thousand Indian warriors under Guy Johnson, was still kept flying.

The Cave of Waneonda, which had so lately rung with the wild peal of outlaw merriment, was left to echo only the monotonous sound of its black-rolling waters. And though some hard-hunted refugee, from time to time, had sought a shelter there with the handful of outlaws it occasionally harboured, it was not until after years that its hideous cells again were fully peopled. Those dungeon vaults, so silent now, what tales of woe and horror could they tell? Tales of those times when the Johnsons came back on their mad errand of vengeance; when they desolated the vale of Schoharie with fire and sword, and Waneonda again disgorged a felon crew to steep the land in crime and blood.

But let us now return to the wanderers who have last emerged from these shadowy realms.

The surprise of Fenton, when his band was fully mustered on the mountain's side and at some distance from the mouth of the cave, maybe conceived at finding strangers among their number. But Brant, so well known to all the gentlemen of this region from the civil offices he had held previous to the present struggle, had only to reveal himself to be warmly received by his brother partisan.

The winter's night was closing in rapidly, and Fenton—whose indignation against Bradshawe was fully roused upon hearing the story of Alida's forcible detention in the vaults of Waneonda—assisted her down the mountain as they hurried forward on their journey. It was determined that she should at once seek a refuge in the settlement of Schoharie, which was at hand; and the whole party was halted to designate someone who could be trusted with the duty of placing her in the hands of her friends. It would have been madness for Brant, even upon such an embassy, to venture himself in the hands of the patriots; and his own men would not spare Fenton, who, although almost equally obnoxious as a virulent Tory, had still not been charged with any stain of cruelty that would call out personal vengeance.

While this discussion was taking place, the attention of the two leaders was distracted by a sudden outcry near. Several of the more lawless members of the party, as it seemed, had pushed in advance of the rest, for the purpose of driving off some horses that were grazing in a field nearby. The farmhouse to which the field belonged chanced, at the moment, to be occupied by a patrol of villagers; for the Whig militia, since Schuyler's march upon Johnstown, had been industriously employed in scouring the country and arresting every person suspected of Toryism upon whom they could lay their hands. This patrol, hearing the clatter of hoofs, now sallied out. The moon, which shone brightly down over the snow-covered fields, showed that they were a mere handful of men, whom Fenton's followers outnumbered; and, though provoked and incensed at the untimely occurrence, Fenton could not resist the temptation to crush the gang of rebellious boors, as he termed them. He sprang from the side of Alida as Brant attempted to seize his arm to prevent the mad movement, drew his rapier, and rushed into the fray.

Alida, though now not unused to scenes of blood and violence, had never stood before with hopes and fears divided between her friends and countrymen engaged in personal conflict. She covered her head with her mantle and cowered toward the earth. There was a quick, irregular volley of firearms, the shout of a sudden onset, followed by the clashing of swords against the barrels of clubbed rifles; and then came the trampling of many feet, as of men borne down in a struggle or flying along the frozen highway near her. She looked up; Brant had disappeared from her side, and the royalists had been driven back past the spot where she stood. Suddenly the Indian war-whoop arose wild and shrilly from a thicket of evergreens at a turning of the road; and now the patriots, as if seized by a sudden panic, came flying back over the road where they had just pressed the foe.

"That's right, boys; git into kiver as soon as you can; it's a regular ambush," exclaimed a well-known voice near her. "We've peppered 'em enough for one night's work." The spokesman, however, seemed very slow in practising his own recommendation, as, coolly loading his rifle, he trudged along behind the rest.

"Run, Balt, run," shouted a fugitive. "The Red skins are upon us."

"They won't lift my head-thatch this time, howsomedever. I'm looking for the chap whose gourd I smashed so handsomely when he came pushing his skewer through my jacket. By the Etarnal, if it be not Squire Fenton," he suddenly exclaimed, starting back from the body of that gallant and unfortunate gentleman.

"Fenton!" faintly ejaculated Alida, who was not twenty paces distant. But her voice was unheeded by Balt; unheeded, too, were the exclamations of the group who quickly gathered around him, retracing their steps as they saw the last scattered remains of the Tory party, preserved by the ruse of Brant, disappear over the hills.

"Yes, boys, that's Squire Fenton, and no mistake," said Balt, with something resembling a heavy sigh; "and he shall have as decent a grave as ever a Christian laid in, if it took the best acre of ground in the county to hold him. He was as true a gentleman as ever sat in the king's commission of the peace among us. As kind and as brave a heart—"

"He was a d——d Tory," said a ruffian voice among the crew, bringing the butt of his rifle heavily upon the frozen ground as he spoke.

"Mister Bill Murphy," said Balt, no way perturbed, "you'll just please to take liberties with the names of Tories of your own shooting, and let mine alone. The devil knows that you've sent enough on 'em to their last account, what with firing on flags o' truce and sich like, Bill."[1]

Murphy felt the rude compliment rather than the reproach that was blended in this speech, and was silent.

"But who have we here?" said Balt, now for the first time noticing the crouched form of the half-frozen Alida. "Who, in the name of the first mother of gals, is this missus that the Tories have left behind them?"

Alida, who had shrunk from claiming the protection of these rude

---

1. Is not this an anachronism? The famous rifle-shot and *desperado* whom tradition accuses of shooting down the bearers of flags of truce upon several occasions during the relentless conflicts between the Whigs and Tories of this region, is not mentioned as thus feloniously signalizing himself until the last great inroad of the refugees in the subsequent years of the war.—P. D.

and bloodstained men, while still chafing around the warm remains of her friend, so recently slaughtered, now dashed these shuddering impressions from her mind, and gladly revealed herself to Balt.

The joy of the worthy woodsman was boundless at beholding her again, though he would scarcely trust his senses to believe that it was really Miss De Roos who stood alive before him. He approached without uttering a syllable in reply to her, turned her around as he raised her from the fallen tree against which she had been reclining, threw back the hood of the cloak which covered her head, and bared her fair features to the moon; then releasing her hand, he stepped back a pace or two, and, lifting his hat reverentially from his gray head, made a deep obeisance as he exclaimed, "The great God be praised, Miss Alida, it is really you!"

BOOK FOURTH
THE WILDWOOD

Where am I now? Feet, find me out a way
Without the counsel of my troubled head;
I'll follow you boldly about these woods,
O'er mountains, through brambles, pits and floods.

Beaumont and Fletcher.

I know each lane, and every alley green,
Dingle and bushy dell of this wild wood,
And every bosky bourn from side to side,
My daily walks and ancient neighbourhood.

Milton.

Joys unexpected and in desperate plight,
Are still most sweet, and prove from whence they come,
When earth's still moon-like confidence in joy
Is at her full. True joy descending far
 From past her sphere, and from the highest heaven
That moves and is not moved.

Chapman.

——I did not take my leave of him,
But had most pretty things to say: Ere I could tell him
How I would think of him at certain hours,
Such thoughts and such; or ere I could
That parting kiss, which I had set
Betwixt two charming words, comes in my father.

Cymbeline.

Chapter 1

The Wanderers

When those we love are absent far away,
When those we love have met some hapless fate,
How pours the heart its lone and plaintive lay,
As the wood-songster mourns her stolen mate!
Alas! the summer bower—how desolate!
The winter hearth—how dim its fire appears!
While the pale memories of by-gone years
Around our thoughts like spectral shadows wait.

Park Benjamin.

She led him through the trackless wild
Where noontide sunbeam never blazed.

Sprague.

The glad spring has come again over the land, and no where do the flowers spring more joyfully beneath her flushing footsteps than in the lovely valley of the Mohawk. Here the seeds of civil discord lie crushed, or, at least, inert, at present. The storm of war has rolled off to distant borders; or if, indeed, it be lowering near again, its terrors are unfelt, because unseen. The husbandman has once more driven his team afield, free from the apprehension that he may return to find a blazing roof-tree and slaughtered household when the close of the day shall relieve him from his toils. The wife once more has joyed to see him go forth whistling on his way, confident that the protector of her children will not fall slaughtered in the ploughshare's furrow, but re-turn to glad her eyes at nightfall. Alas! these simple people dream not that the present calm is but a breathing-spell in the terrible struggle, which, ere it pass away, shall print every cliff of this beautiful region with a legend of horror, and story its romantic stream with deeds of fiendish crime.

Clad in the deepest mourning, the orphan heiress of the Hawk-snest sits by the trellised window, gazing out upon the lovely fields, of which the supposed death of her lover and relative has made her the possessor. Her wild brother, surrendering his share in the estate to her, has gone to seek a soldier's fortune or a patriot's death by fighting in the armies of his country. The green mound that covers the remains of her last surviving parent and of her only sister is seen through a *vista* of trees upon a swell of land beyond. It is the mellow hour of twilight, when the thoughtful heart loves best to ponder upon such mementoes of the departed. And has Alida, when her eye o'erbrims, and her hands are clasped in agitation at the thoughts of the cruel fate which has overtaken her household—has she no thought, no one woman's regretful tear for the lover who had dared everything to shield those who were dear to her from harm; the lover who had thrown away his own life in the effort to snatch her from a captivity worse than death?

She *had* thought of him. She now thought of him. She had too often and too long thought of him. At least, sometimes she herself so believed, when accusing herself of dwelling more upon his memory than upon that of those who ought to be dearer to her. But, then, was there no excuse for that, which her woman's heart straightway supplied? For her sister and father it was pleasurable, but vain, to grieve. It was challenging the will of Heaven ever to dwell gloomily upon their fate, which Heaven, for good or ill, had fixed for ever. But of Greyslaer she could think hopefully, as of one who might still return to share her friendship and receive her gratitude. "Her *friendship!*" Yes, that was the word, if her thoughts had been syllabled to utterance when she hoped for Greyslaer's return. But there were moments when she hoped not thus; moments of dark conviction that he had ceased to be upon this earth; that death had overtaken him as well as others for whom she was better schooled to grieve.

That black death is a strange touchstone of the human heart. How instantly it brings our real feelings to the surface! How it reawakens and calls out our stiffly ac corded esteem! How it quickens into impetuous life our reluctant tenderness, that has been withheld from its object till it can avail no more!

Strange inconsistency of woman's nature! Alida mourned the dead Greyslaer as if he had been her affianced lover; but hoped for the reappearance of the living one as of a man who could never be more to her than a cherished friend—a brother—a dear, dear brother!

Alack! young Max, couldst thou but now steal beside that twilight window, hear those murmured words of sorrow, and take that taper hand which is busied in brushing away those fast-dropping tears, thy presence at such a melting moment might bring a deeper solace, call out a softer feeling than simple joy at recovery of a long-lost friend. Alack! that moments so propitious to a lover should pass away for naught!

And where, then, is Greyslaer? The autumn was not spent idly by his friends in exploring the wilderness for traces of his fate; and even in mid-winter Balt crossed the Garoga lakes on snowshoes, followed up the cascades of Konnedieyu, and penetrated deep into the Sacondaga country upon the same errand. The spot where Brant once held his secret camp, and to which his captives were carried, had been twice examined since Alida lent her aid to direct Balt to the spot. But the *wigwams* were long since deserted, and the snow which beat down and broke their flimsy frames, obliterated every track by which the migrating Indians could be followed. Balt again took up the search the moment the severity of winter became relaxed. He has now followed the spring in her graceful mission northward; and the lakes of the Upper Hudson, the wild recesses of the Adirondack Mountains, that mysterious wilderness which no white man has yet explored, is said to be the scene of his faithful wanderings. Thither we will soon follow him. But first, however, we must go back some months, and take up the thread of our narrative at the squaw camp of Thayendanagea, if we would follow out the fortunes of Greyslaer from the moment when the *desperado* Valtmeyer so fearfully crossed his path.

The first red streaks of dawn were beginning to dapple the east, when the luckless captive found himself traversing a deep hemlock forest, with "The Spreading Dew" for his guide. The Indian girl, after reviving him from the stunning effects of the blow which had prostrated him, by sprinkling water upon his forehead, had bound up the contusion with a fillet of colewort leaves, which was kept in its place by a strip of strouding torn from her own dress; and, urging her still bewildered patient from the scene of his mishap, had thridded the swamp and guided him to the hills in the rear of the Indian camp. These hills stretch away toward the north, increasing continually in altitude as they recede from the Mohawk, until they finally swell into those stupendous highlands known as the Adirondack Mountains.

Greyslaer, though ignorant of the precise geography of this Alpine region, had still some idea of the vast wilderness which extended toward the Canada border; and when he saw his guide, after reaching a rapid and turbulent stream, turn her face to the northward, and strike up along its banks, as if about to follow the water to the mountain lake in which it probably headed, he paused, and was compelled, for the first time, to reflect upon what use he should make of his newly-recovered liberty, and which way it were best for him now to direct his steps. His first object must be, of course, to reach the nearest body of his friends. But, since the events in which he had been an actor, and those which might have transpired during the weeks that he was ill and a prisoner, he knew not where those friends might be found.

He was ignorant what changes might have taken place in the valley of the Mohawk, or which party might have the ascendency now that the spirit of civil discord was fairly let loose in that once tranquil region. Should he fall into the hands of some straggling band of Tories, or should he even venture to claim the hospitality of those who, but a month since, had stood neutral while the conflict was impending, he might find himself seized upon by some new convert to the royal party, who would gladly afford the most lively proofs of his new-born zeal for the crown by securing so active a partisan of the patriot cause. The city of Albany was, therefore, his only safe destination, if he would preserve that liberty of action, by the preservation of which alone he could hope to succour Alida.

He determined, therefore, not to venture descending into the lower country till he could strike it at least as far east as Schenectady. But how, if he concluded to make this long circuit through the woods, could he find his way amid the wild forests he must traverse? Was this lonely Indian girl, who was little more than a child, to be his only guide? and, if so, how were they to procure subsistence in a journey through the wilderness, where the path was so toilsome that many days must elapse before he could accomplish the distance which, upon an ordinary road, can be traversed in one? Max abruptly broke off these unsatisfactory reflections by asking his companion whither she was now guiding him. The reply of "The Dew" told him that much might be gained by admitting her into his counsels.

The foresight of the Indian maid had anticipated at least the most serious of the difficulties which embarrassed her companion. She was leading him to the Garoga lakes, where her tribesmen had once had a fishing camp, in which they might at least find a shelter from the elements, and where Greyslaer could readily obtain subsistence for himself until "The Dew" could make her way to the settlements and gain some tidings of his friends, or, at least, procure him some more eligible guide than herself from the lower castle of the Mohawks; a small band of that tribe, under their leader Hendrick, being friendly to the patriot cause. Greyslaer hoped, however, that if he could once secure a retreat, where, for a few days, he should be safe from pursuit, he might find means to communicate with his faithful and cherished follower, old Balt, if, indeed, the stout forester had not perished in the fray in which he himself was taken prisoner.

These anxious reflections upon the chances of the future served for a while to turn his thoughts from a more bitter channel. But the recollection of the scene in which Alida had been torn from his side now recurred with all its horrors.

It is a hard thing to love vainly. It is a hard thing for the young heart, that has given its first generous burst of affection to another, to be flung back upon itself, shocked, borne down, blasted upon the very threshold of existence. The growth of the sentiment in some minds— in those which love most deeply—is often the first emotion that has ever compelled them to look into their own souls; that has ever made them fully aware of the sentient and spiritual essence which they bear within this earthly tabernacle. And to surrender that sentiment seems like parting with the vital spirit that animates them. Such surrenderment of their early dreams is, however, the fate of thousands; for love—young love—like the Bird of Lightning in the Iroquois fable, which bears the flame from Heaven to teach men only where first the purifying element had birth, seems to fulfil his mission, reckless where'er his burning wings may sweep, so that his mysterious errand be accomplished.

But Greyslaer's was no common tale of misplaced hopes and un-requited attachment. *He* could not fling from him the image of Alida as an idle vision of his dreaming boyhood. Her sorrows had become his own; and the love which might have perished from hopelessness seemed born anew from sympathy—aye, though he were doomed hereafter to have neither part nor lot in aught else belonging to her, save this share in her sorrows only, yet such community of grief was so dear to him, that the world had now no prize for which Greyslaer would have bartered his gloomy heritage of woe. Alas! what a joyless and barren destiny did he thus embrace! Flinging his fresh and blossoming youth, like a worthless weed, away; grafting upon his ripening manhood a shoot of bitterness, that must dwarf its energies and wither its fruit of promise.

The shrill burst of the Indian war-whoop startled Greyslaer from the stern reverie with which we have ventured to blend our own reflections while detailing its general character. The wild cry seemed to come from beneath his very feet. He recoiled a step, and gazed eagerly down the rocky defile he was descending. The *sumach* and *sassafras* grew thick and heavy, imbowering the broken path below. The Indian girl was nowhere to be seen. He turned and threw a hurried glance along the sides of the glen, where ledges of rock here and there cut the foliage horizontally before him. He caught a glimpse, as of the figure of the light-footed maiden scaling the walls of the glen, and retreating from him. He advanced a pace to see if it were indeed she who was thus flying from him at his utmost need.

On the instant, a tomahawk hurtled through the air, and cleaving the light branches near, buried itself in a maple-tree beside him. Quick as light, Max seized the weapon, and plucked it from the bark in which it quivered. But, instantaneous as was the movement, it did not avail him; for, as he was in the act of wheeling round to confront the peril in the direction whence the hatchet came, he was grappled in the arms of a sinewy Indian. Down they both went together, the Indian uppermost; and so completely did he seem to have Greyslaer at advantage, that he leisurely addressed him while partly raising himself to draw his knife.

"My broder thought it time to leave the camp when Isaac come, eh, my broder? Aha!" And, as the miscreant spoke, he made a motion across the skull of his prostrate prisoner, as if he felt tempted to go through the ceremony of scalping while life, yet vigorous in his veins, should give a zest to the cruelty.

But Max was not the man to be sportively handled in a death encounter. His dark eye followed the gleaming weapon, as the barbarian flourished it above his head, with a glance as keen as that of the hawk-eyed Indian. He had fallen with one arm under him, and happily, it was that which held the tomahawk, which thus escaped the notice of his foe. It was for the moment pinioned to the ground, not less by the weight of his own body than by that of the savage; and the force with which he had been hurled to the earth so paralyzed the strength of Greyslaer, that he did not at first attempt to extricate his hand.

But now, throwing back his head, as if he shrunk from the knife that was offered at it, he suddenly arched his back so as to lift the savage and himself together; and, slipping his arm from under him as the other bore him down again by throwing the full weight of his person lengthwise upon him, he dealt a side blow with the hatchet which nearly crushed the skull of the Indian. The fellow relaxed his grip of Greyslaer's throat in an instant, and rolled over, and lay as if stricken to death upon the spot, while, breathless and disordered, young Max regained his feet.

CHAPTER 2

The March of the Captive

Amid thy forest solitudes he climbs
O'er crags that proudly tower above the deep,
And knows that sense of danger—which sublimes
The breathless moment—when his daring step
Is on the verge of the cliff, and he can hear
The low dash of the wave with startled ear,
Like the death-music of his coming doom,
And clings to the green turf with desperate force,
As the heart clings to life; and when resume
The currents in his veins, their wonted course,
There lingers a deep feeling, like the moan
Of wearied ocean when the storm is gone.

Halleck.

Upon examining the features of the Indian, which were of a singularly brutal cast, Greyslaer felt convinced that he had beheld them before, but where or when it was impossible for him to say.

Bending near to scrutinize them more closely, he observed that life still remained; for the eyes, which were shut, had their lids, not smoothly drooping as when closed in death, but knit and screwed together as when suddenly closed in a paroxysm of rage or pain. They opened now, as a heavy gasp broke from the bosom of the savage. Max instantly possessed himself of the scalping-knife which lay near, and held it, like a dagger of *misericorde*, at the throat of his reviving foe. The slightest thrust would have rid him at once of all further difficulty; but it was not in his heart to slaughter a living man thus laid at his mercy, and he shouted to the girl to bring him a withe that he might bind his prisoner. The Dew replied not to his call. But. he heard a quick trampling near, which he mistook for her approach.

He looked in the direction whence the sound of footsteps came, but the leafy covert was so thick in that direction that he could descry nothing. He listened anxiously; they came nearer, but there was no reply to his repeated calls. The footsteps paused a moment. He leaned forward to peer beneath the heavy branches; and in the same moment that an armed Indian darted from the covert before him, the shadow of another, who was approaching from behind, was cast athwart him. He had not time to spring to his feet before he was again a captive and defenceless.

The two last-comers were soon joined by others, who quickly made a rude litter of boughs for their wounded tribesman, and the whole party then took their way through the woods with their captive. They did not, however, carry their prisoner back to the squaw camp, as he first expected they would, when, under the circumstances, he anticipated the usual wretched doom of an Indian prisoner. But, moving along leisurely until they came to a level and marshy piece of ground, they paused for a moment, and seemed in doubt what next to do, when one, who had aided in carrying the wounded man, gave his place to another, and approached to him who seemed to act as leader of the party. He murmured something, which, from the low tones in which the Indians usually pitch their voice?. Greyslaer could not overhear.

"*Wahss!*" (go!) was the brief reply to his communication.

The man beckoned to two others, and the three, plunging into a copse nearby, appeared the next moment, each with a birchen canoe upon his shoulders. Crossing the trail they had been travelling, the whole party entered a thicket of alders, where a thread of water, scarce three inches deep, crept noiselessly along. The others carefully parted the bushes, so that the canoemen could let down their shallops into this slender rill, which was so narrow that the water was wholly hidden when a canoe was placed upon its surface.

The wounded man was assigned to the forward canoe, and Max, with his arms still pinioned behind him. placed in the centre. The whole party were then again soon in motion. The runnel was too narrow for the use of paddles, and for some time they propelled themselves for ward merely by the aid of the bushes which overreached their heads.

At last they came to a spot where the swamp around them, being confined between two hills, poured its oozing springs more complete-ly into a single current. The water, running deeper and swifter, cut its way down through the black mould until a channel of yellow pebbles was revealed beneath it. The alders were separated more widely from each other, and grew more in scattered clumps, which sometimes formed green islets, circled with a fringe of scarlet, wherever their red roots were washed and polished by the flowing waters.

Now the stream would sweep amid tussocks of long waving grass, crowned here and there by a broad branching elm, whose branches dipped in the tide, that whirled in deepening eddies where its projecting roots overhung the water. Now it rippled for a few yards over a pebbly bottom, and then, turned by a spit of yellow sand—thick trodden with the tracks of deer, of wolves, and not infrequently with those of bears and panthers—it would slide round a point of land black with the shade of lofty pines. A frith of long wild grass, growing evenly as a fresh-mowed meadow, and embayed among the thousand points of a tamarack swamp, received now the spreading river. And now, again, it. was circumscribed once more into a deep, black, formal- looking pool, circled with water-lilies; and henceforth, around many a beetling crag, thick sheathed with laurel and the clustering hemlock, and beneath the shadows of many a tall mountain rising from forests of bass-wood and maple, it marched proudly onward till it expanded into a magnificent lake.

Coasting along the shores of this lake for a mile or two they came to an Indian hunter's camp, which, as it seemed, belonged to a man who furnished the canoes. The place was offensive from the smell of dead animals, such as minks, otters, and musquashes, whose carcasses, stripped of their skins, were suspended from the boughs of trees around the cabin as food for the Indian dogs. But the Indians, notwithstanding their proverbial keenness of scent, seemed no wise molested by this savoury atmosphere.[1]

---

1. A sporting friend, the companion of the author in more than one excursion among these mountain wilds, seeing some Indians with whom he hunted busied in removing these objects of annoyance from the camp as the party approached it, was wholly at a loss to conceive the motive of placing them where they were found, until the sudden appearance of two half-famished dogs revealed the mystery; for it is the custom of a hunter, when leaving his dogs to protect his camp in his absence, to hang the food prepared for them at different heights, so that the animal might not devour all his stores at once, but have to leap higher for it as he grows leaner. These dogs, as one might have supposed from their fatigued appearance, had been off somewhere pursuing the chase for their own amusement. But, upon this being suggested to the old Indian hunter, who spoke a few words of broken English, and was more communicative than most of his race, he was indignant at the idea of an Indian dog deserting his charge. He pointed to a mountain peak at the other end of the lake, and assured our friend that they had been watching for him from its summit, when they saw his boat upon the water and hurried homeward.

Leaving their wounded tribesman under the care of this worthy, who laid claim to some skill as a medicine man, the rest of the party started again with their captive on the following day, and, crossing several mountain ridges, and winding their way among innumerable ponds and lakes, halted near a beautiful sheet of water, which still bears the name of Indian Lake, from its having been a sacred place of resort to the Iroquois.

The outlet of this lake, though it is buried in a region of lofty and sterile mountains, winds through natural pastures of deep grass[2] imbowered with enormous elms, forming a soft and open sylvan landscape, which is in the most delicious contrast to the thick and rugged forests which frown from the adjacent hills. This was the seat of the mysterious *kenticoys*, or solemn meetings of the Mohawks, when, at the opening and closing year, the different tribes of the Iroquois retired, each to some such forest-temple, to worship the Supreme Being, whose power was alike acknowledged by all.

The prisoner, though treated at this sacred season with a degree of mildness and forbearance that was new to him as a trait of Indian character, was only allowed to approach the threshold of the valley, where a guardian was appointed him until the solemn days were over.

The garden-like plain was spread out below the eminence upon which stood the shanty which was his temporary prison-house; and Greyslaer could from time to time discern some plumed band defiling from the hills and losing themselves among the far-reaching groves, to which the Indians repaired from every side. But of the form of their ceremonial or the nature of their worship he could discern nothing. Nor has any white man been able to learn more of these periodical gatherings of the Iroquois, save only their name and their object.[3]

It was two days after these unknown rites were con summated that Greyslaer found himself ascending a rugged mountain under the care of his captors, who still withheld all harsh treatment, while warily watching him as if they only held him in trust as the captive of some one more powerful than themselves. It could scarcely be the wounded

---

2. Called "flys "or "vlies" by our hunters.

3. It is curious to remark, however, how, with the spread of Christianity and civilization along our Indian borders, this custom of retiring away from the haunts of men to worship God among primeval woods, grew up among our frontiers-men; while some might even discover an analogy between the rude but not irreligious feeling which first suggested the ancient *kenticoys* of the Iroquois, and the policy which still keeps alive the practice of "camp-meetings" among a numerous and not unenlightened sect of Christians.—See *Flint's Valley of the Mississippi*.

Isaac, however; for, since his first seizure, Max had been studiously kept out of the sight of that ferocious Indian, whose bloody-minded disposition frequently showed itself during the delirium of fever under which he was left at the hunter's cabin.

Whatever disposition it was ultimately intended to make of the prisoner, his life seemed in little danger during the march; but a measure adopted by his captors as he now reached the highest pinnacle of the mountain appeared to indicate that its crisis was at hand. They led him to the edge of a lofty precipice, which commanded a view almost completely around the compass, and motioned to him to cast his eyes above and below him.

It was the hour of autumn sunset, when the golden air seems to glorify every object on which it rests. Never did it bathe in molten light a lovelier landscape of mountain peaks, interminable to the eye; interlaced by lakes so numerous that, as these last reflect the tints of the glowing sky, the mountains themselves seem, in their autumn livery, like rainbow masses floating in liquid ether. The heart of Greyslaer thrilled within him at the sight; and not the least painful part of the death that seemed to hover near was the thought of closing his eyes for ever upon such a world of glorious beauty. But his struggles to prevent them from bandaging his eyes were vain, for his hands were bound behind him; and now he stood blinded and helpless above the gulf into which each moment he expected to be hurled.

Suddenly he felt a rude hand upon either shoulder, and he gasped the prayer which he believed to be his last—but the next moment the two Indians who had fixed their gripe upon him only turned their captive round several times, fast held between them, and led him away from the precipice. He became then conscious of gradually descending. Again he felt that his path led upward over innumerable obstacles, which his guides patiently aided him in surmounting. Once more, again, he was convinced that he was descending, though his path-way wound so hither and thither that it was impossible to say how steep the slope might be.

At last he heard the sound of water faintly dashing upon the shore. His guides halted and removed the bandage from his eyes. He looked up, and found himself upon the edge of a small lake or mountain tarn, deep set at the bottom of a rocky bowl or hollow less than a mile in diameter, circled around by naked crags and splintered pinnacles of rock, some straggling copse-wood or a blasted tree here and there alone relieving the utter barrenness of the scene, which at once conveyed the idea of the extinct crater of a volcano.

This heart-chilling sterility was, however, somewhat redeemed, when, after circling the lake for a short distance, the Indians came to a few acres of well-wooded land in a recess of the circular valley. Here Greyslaer again heard the voices of women and children from a camp of safety, and resigned himself to the monotony of captivity in a stronghold from which there seemed no escape.

It were bootless to relate the varied sufferings of Max Greyslaer during his long winter of captivity in that dreary mountain, which Indians call "The Thunder's Nest:"[4] to tell how he passed weeks of nearly utter starvation, when fortune failed the two or three Indian hunters upon whose success the whole community depended for subsistence; how eagerly he caught at the relief to his monotonous existence, when his captors ordered him also to turn out and hunt the bear, the lynx, and the panther, the only animals which are found among those high mountain fastnesses in the winter season, while the Iroquois themselves pursued on snow-shoes the moose and red deer in the valleys below; to tell of the harsh treatment he received when, weary and faint, with limbs half frozen and lacerated from toiling through the frozen snow-crust, he returned from a fruitless hunt; of the capricious gleams of kindness of which he was the object when his address and prowess in the chase awakened alike the admiration and the jealousy of those who watched his every motion while pursuing it with him.

But now the spring, which has been long in reaching this highland region, has, while thickening the forest around, brought with it the hope of escape, amid some of those greenwood coverts. It is true that he is no longer permitted to wander as far as when the woods were bare. Yet if he can break his thraldom for an hour, there is one at hand with both the will and the ability to guide him from the wilderness.

There has been an accession of numbers to the Indian camp, bringing rumours that Brant and his warriors have all left the lower country. And The Spreading Dew, who came in with the rest, has even communicated to Greyslaer that Sir John Johnson and his loyalist retainers, both Indian and white, have withdrawn from the Valley of the Mohawk and fled to Canada. The patriots must be in the ascendency! Why is Max Greyslaer not there to share the triumph of his friends?

---

4. Crane Mountain is its present, (as at time of first publication), unmeaning name.

The Foresters

The woodland rings with laugh and shout,
As if a hunt were up,
And woodland flowers are gathered
To crown the soldier's cup.
With merry song we mock the wind
That in the pine-top grieves,
And slumber long and sweetly
On beds of oaken leaves.

Bryant.

There were preparations for a hunter's carousal in the heart of the forest. The scene of their revel was a sunny glade, where a dozen idlers were lounging away the noon tide beneath the dappled boughs. A fire had been kindled upon a flat rock nearby, and from the rivulet that gurgled around its base, the neck of a black bottle protruded, where it had been anchored to cool in the running water. A fresh-killed buck lay as if just thrown upon the sod in the midst of the woodland crew, who stirred themselves from the shade as the hunter who had flung the carcass from his strong shoulders turned to lean his rifle against the fretted trunk of a walnut-tree that spread its branches near. "Why, Kit Lansingh, my boy, you are no slouch of a woodsman to carry a yearling of such a heft as that," cried our old friend Balt, lifting the deer by its antlers partly from the ground. "You must have struck the crittur, too, a smart distance from here, for none of us have heard the crack of your rifle today."

"Somebody may, though you have not, Uncle Balt; for, let me tell you, boys, there's other folks in the woods besides us chaps here."

The hunters started up and were now all attention—for the signs of strangers in the forest is ever a source of keen interest to the woodsman, who, when the frontier is in arms, never ventures to strike the game of which he is in search without remembering that he himself may be, at that very moment, the human quarry of some more dangerous hunter that hovers near.

"Nay, Conyer, go on cutting up the carcass. I've left no trail to guide a redskin to this spot," said the hunter, disembarrassing himself of his powder-horn and shooting-pouch, which he hung upon a wild plum-bush nearby. "We can sit down to dinner without any of Brant's people coming to take pot-luck with us; for I've scouted every rod of ground within miles of the camp. But the redskins are out, nevertheless, I tell ye."

"Where, Kit, where? How know you?" simultaneously cried a dozen voices.

"Why, you see, it must be at least four hours agone since I struck that yearling, which was down in the Whooping Hollow by Cawaynoot Pond."

"Cawaynoot Pond!" ejaculated a hunter. "What, that little bog-bordered lake, with the island that floats loose upon it like a toast in a tankard?"

"Go on, go on, Kit," cried another. "We all know the Whooping Hollow; but you were a bold fellow to strike a deer there."

"Yes, I stirred him first in the mash at this eend of Cawaynoot, and that's a fact. But, instead of taking the water there he puts out westward, and clips it right over toward the river, till he brought me in sight of the Potash Kettle."

"Senongewah—'The Great Upturned Pot'—the Abregynes call it," ejaculated Balt; "I know the mounting."

"Well," pursued Lansingh, "the buck doesn't keep on toward the river, but hooks it right round the rim of the Kettle, and back again toward the east. It was, in course, long afore I could git a shot; and, following hard on his trail along a hillside overgrown with short sprangly bushes, I saw, by the way in which they were trampled down, that a white man must have passed that way before me."

"A white man?" cried several voices, with increasing interest,

"Yes, a white man; and that within no very great time, anyhow."

"How knew you that, Kit?" asked Balt.

"Why, I cleared the bushes aside, looked down, and there, as plain as my Bible, I saw the print of his shoe in the moss."

"Which, in course, would not hold a footprint long if it was fresh and springy. Kit is right, boys," said Balt.

"And that wasn't all, uncle. I saw a shoe-print in the fresh moss, with that of a small Injun *moccasin* treading right in his footsteps. (A little salt, Teunis; now let the gravy of that other slice drip on my corn-cake till I'm ready for it—so fashion.")

"A *moccasin?* Go on, go on, Kit," cried an eager young hunter.

"Let a man eat in whiles, won't you, lads?" said Lansingh, who seemed disposed to make the most of his narrative. "Well, I went on, followed my deer till I got a shot at him from behind a cranberry bush in Whooping Hollow, and just as he was bending his knees to take the water near the very spot where I first started him, (it was nateral. you know, Uncle Balt, for the crittur to go back where he belonged—a drop of that liquor, if you please,) he caught my bullet in the back of his neck, gave a splurge, and was done for.

"So, after pulling him out of the water, I hangs up the carcass out of reach of the wolves, and goes back to look after the white man's trail.

"It kept along the hillside only a short distance, and then struck suddenly off atween two rocks and among some dogbriers, where I nearly lost it, right over the ridge, on the opposite side of which it led right back in the direction from which I had first traced it. Now, says I to myself, says I, it's after all only some fool of a fellow that has lost himself in these woods, which are about the easiest to travel in a human crittur could have, seeing that the hills are so many landmarks all around. Let him go to the old boy, says I, for a dunderhead as he is. No, again says I, here's an Injun moccasin right in his track, and per-haps it's some unfortunate who's been driven to take to the bush by the troubles of the times, and not come here to make a fool of himself for pastime; so, Kit Lansingh, streak it ahead, man, and look after your fellow-crittur."

"I'd a disowned ye for my sister's son had ye done otherwise," in-terrupted Balt.

"Well," pursued the hunter, "I did go ahead, and that though it took me myself out of my way, Uncle Balt. I followed the scent for miles toward the east, till I thought it would take me clean out to Lake George. But at last I saw what paid me for my trouble; for, in crossing a bit of pine barren, I came upon a raal Indian trail, and no mistake about it—where a dozen men or more had streaked it through the sand after my shoe and *moccasin.*"

"Tormented lightning!" cried Balt, rubbing his hands in much ex-citement; "go on, go on, Kit; d'ye say a dozen Injuns?"

"Yes, uncle, not a copperskin less; and let me tell you now that this discovery discomboberated me considerably. Why, says I to myself, says I, why should a dozen redskins be led away thus after one poor wanderer, when they might see already, from the double trail, that he is a doomed man, from the *moccasin* tread that is still fresh in his footfalls; here's something new, now, to study in Injun natur, and I'll see the end of it. So, with that, I ups and ons.

"And now I soon saw, by the way in which the white man's track doubled and doubled again, crossing and recrossing that of the Injuns in one etarnal everlasting snarl, that the fellow could not be cutting such carlicues for nothing. He knows what he's about. He's a chap that understands himself, says I; and I began to have respect for him.

"By this time, though I ought to have said it afore, the trail had led west again; yes, indeed, clean across the river, which I forded in following it, and then up and away over the ridge on the opposite side, striking clean over to the Sacondaga. I mistrusted that it would cross that river, too, as it had the other branch; but no, it follows down to the meeting of the waters, or *Tiosaronda*[1] as the Abregynes call it. There, where the falls of the main river roar through the rocky chasm as it hurries along like mad to join the other fork. And here, says I, the game will either be up with Shoeties, or he will give Moccasin the slip altogether. And raaly, boys, I defy the best woodsman among ye—I defy the devil, or Uncle Balt himself—to find any leavings of that white man around the place.

"You may see there the woods trampled all round by Injuns. You may see where they have slipped down the bank, and where they've clomb up again. You may follow their trail backward and forward along either fork of the stream for a mile, and you may see where they all united again, and trudged off as if to take up the back track once more afresh, and so make a new thing of it; but how or whither that white man cleared himself, you cannot find out!"

"That flogs natur," cried a hunter. "And saw ye no other trace of the critturs anywhere, Kit? Not a hair's ashes of them?"

"Yes! but not thereabouts; and now, boys, I'm about to tell you the curiosest part o' the hull business. For you must know, that, if I had not left my deer where I did, the snarl might have remained without any further clew. But as, after giving up the chase, I made back tracks up the river, recrossed, and struck out again for Whooping Hollow to bring the venison on here to camp, what should I discover but the

1. Now Luzerne, (as at time of first publication).

self-same track of the white man right in the heart of the hollow. I did not look to see whether the floating island was near shore, or if he had stepped aboard and floated off on it; but, 'my friend,' says I to him—I mean, says I to myself—' my friend,' says I, 'had I seen your first track in the Whooping Hollow, and on the very shores of Cawaynoot, you would never have led me sich a Jack-a-lantern chase as this. I'm not a gentleman that keeps company with the Striped Huntsman or Red-heeled Bob, as the Scotch settlers call ye; and, if we are. ever to make acquaintance, your own parlour in the Whooping Hollow is not exactly the place I would choose for an introduction.' With that I cut out in quick order from the hollow, and made clean tracks for camp. And that, boys, is the hull o' my story; and now let's have something to drink."

The woodsmen all listened with deep attention to this long rigmarole narrative as it was slowly detailed by the young hunter. By some it was received merely as an idle tale of wonder, such as those who love the marvellous may often hear from the simple-minded rangers of our forest borders. It was but one of the thousand stories told about the Whooping Hollow, whose mysteries none could, and few cared to solve. (For though the wild, whooping sound, from which, in former times, the hollow took its name, is now never heard, save in echo to a human voice, the floating island is still pointed out to the traveller as his road winds around the basin at the bottom of which reposes the little lake of Cawaynoot.[2]) Others, again, regarded the story of Christian's adventures as affording positive evidence of the neighbourhood of Indians; and though "The Striped Huntsman," as he was called, might be at the bottom of the business, yet it was evident that a considerable band of mortals like themselves had been equally, with young Lansingh, misled by his deviltries and lured into their immediate neighbourhood. This last was, in fact, the view which old Balt took of the matter.

"Not," said the honest woodsman, "that the crittur whom folks call 'The Striped Huntsman' be *i*ther a good sperrit or a bad sperrit, or whether or no there be any sperrit at all about the matter! Nother do I pretend to say, with some people, that the Striped Huntsman is only some roguish half-breed or outlawed Injun Medicine man, who has pitched upon this unsettled part of the patent between the Scotch

2. *Cawaynoot* is the term for "island" in the Mohawk tongue. The lake is now, (as at time of first publication), generally called "Adam's Pond," from the name of a settler upon its banks.

and German clearings and the Mohawk hunting grounds, as the very corner of the airth from which it was the business of no one in partiklar to oust him, whatever shines he might cut up on his own hook. No, I leave it to the domine, whose business it is to settle sich matters. (Pity the good man couldn't catch some droppings o' eloquence from yonder preaching brook to lifen his sarmints!) But I tell ye, boys, that if it be raaly the track of the crittur which lies fresh in our neighbourhood, it's not such an unlikely sperrit after all; for why may we not captivate some of the redskins that it has coaxed towards us, and thus, mayhap, git tidings of the poor lost capting?"

"Old Balt," said a hunter, "you are forever thinking of poor Captain Max, whose bones must be long since cold."

"And for what else, Rhynier Peterson, did we come off on this tramp, if it was not that all of us had some thought of the capting? And born heathens we'd a' been had we not come to look after him," added Balt, indignantly.

"Yes, but Balt," said another, "though we all of us followed you willingly enough at first, yet haven't we all determined long ago that it was a wild-goose chase you were leading us after? Here, now, we've been fifty miles above here, poking about among mountains so big, that, if the summer ever manages to climb them, it is only to rest herself for a week or so, when she slants down the other side, and leaves the snow right off to settle in her place. The old ' North,' too, haven't we followed up the river to where it dodges about, trying to hide its raal head in a hundred lakes? These lakes, moresomever, haven't we slapped through them into five times as many more, and made portages up to the leetlest tricklings of some of them? To be sure we have; and what good has it done us, all this trampoosing and paddling hither and thither in this etarnal wilderness? We are now within ten miles of Lake George, and less than half that distance of the mouth of the Sacondaga, and my say is, either to strike over at once to Fort William Henry, or to cross the river below the forks, and make the best of our way to Saratoga."

"And that's my say too," said a gray-headed hunter who had not yet spoken. "It's a fool's errand looking further for the captain. I don't myself altogether believe that young Max is completely done for in this life; for we found traces enough of him in the deserted squaw camp last autumn; and if the Injuns kept him alive so long, he may yet wear his scalp in safety. But it all comes to the same thing if Brant has carried him off to Canada, where he'll be sure to keep him till these wars are over."

"What! you too, Hank Williams!" replied Balt, with a look of keen reproach at the last speaker; "you who were the first to offer to take to the woods with me, and keep there till, dead or alive, we found the capting! Well, boys, I don't want to get riled with ye, when, mayhap, we are jist upon the pint of a fight, where a man wants all his coolness; but I tell ye one thing, I came out here after young Max, and, dead or alive, I don't go in without him. You may drop off one by one, or go away the hull biling on ye together, ye may; but old Balt will not leave these woods till he gets fairly upon his trail; and, once upon it, he'll follow it up, if he has to streak it again clean through the mountains to Canada. So, now we understand each other, let's eat our dinner without no more words said about the matter, but go and look after these Injuns as soon as may be."

"Why, uncle," said Christian Lansingh, as the rest of the party now addressed themselves silently to the rude meal before them, "I never thought for a moment of giving up the chase as long as you thought it well to go ahead."

"I know'd it, boy, I know'd it; the son of old Christian and my nephew is not the chap to be skeered from his promise by some nigger nurse's gammon about the Striped Huntsman and sich fooleries."

"Oh, our friends don't stickle about the matter we have now in hand," said another young hunter, modestly; "but, you know, Balt, some of them have left their homes and—"

"Their *hums?* And who in all natur wants a better hum nor this? Here are walls that rise straight upward higher than any you see in housen, keeping the wind away, yet letting you step about where you choose without getting out o' doors—for these walls follow you, as it were, and close around you wherever you move; and as for them as wants a fireside, why, aint the woods right full of clean hearth-stones and cosy nestling-places? A *hum?* Tormented lightning! is it a soft bed ye want there, lads? Why, isn't yonder mossy tussock as fresh and springy as e'er a pillow your good woman could shake up for ye—there, I mean, where that woof of vine-leaves, close as an Injun mat, spreads over to keep alike the sun and dews away? Lads, lads, I'm ashamed on ye to talk o' housen in a place like this, where the very' light from heaven looks young and new—you may laugh, Bill, but it does, I say—the light o' God looks bright, and fresh, and tender here, as if it might a' been twin-born with the young Summer this very year—see only—jist see for yourselves how it scatters down through the green thatch of yonder boughs, which lift each moment as if some live and pleasant thing dropped from them on the sod below!"

"It is of those they have left at home," rejoined the young hunter, the moment that Balt, pausing to catch breath, allowed him to put in a word; "our friends have left wives and families at home, whom they must look after in times like these; but here's half a dozen of us use less lads, who will keep the woods with you until you yourself shall say that we have made a clean thing of it."

The doughty Balt seemed to wince a little under the first of these remarks; for he was compelled to admit the force of it. He did not reply, however, save by patting the speaker on the shoulders, and nodding to him kindly as he buried his face in the flagon from which the whole of the company drank in succession. The rest of the meal was despatched in silence, and the party then made their preparations for proceeding to the spot where Christian Lansingh had last seen the mysterious footprints.

Leaving Balt and his crew of foresters to make a cautious and weary reconnaissance of this enchanted ground, let us give our attention to the two wanderers, who the reader may soon have cause to suspect were the real flesh and blood actors in this game of woodland magic.

CHAPTER 3

The Flight From the Thunder's Nest

He has left the green valley for paths where the bison
Roams through the forest or leaps o'er the flood;
Where the snake in the swamp sucks the deadliest poison,
And the cat of the mountains keeps watch for its food;
But the leaf shall be greener, the sky shall be purer,
The eye shall be clearer, the rifle be surer,
And stronger the arm of the fearless endurer
That trusts naught but Heaven in his way through the wood.

Brainard.

Let it bring no reproach to the manhood of Max Greyslaer, that now, in the very prime of youthful vigour, with a frame schooled by hardship to endurance of every kind, he must still depend upon female address to deliver him from bondage,

Twice already had he attempted, at the free peril of his life, to regain his liberty; once, as we have before seen, when, lost in the mazes of the forest, he rushed again unawares directly into the arms of his enemy: and again, during his abode in the Thunder's Nest, he had, when nearly succeeding in the attempt, been overtaken in the deep snowdrifts, amid which he must have perished, even if successful, and carried back in triumph to the Indian camp.

Then, upon his second recapture, he had undergone all the horrors of mind which must precede a death of Indian torture with those who have read or heard of its cruelly ingenious and protracted agonies. He had been subjected to all the savage preparations for the stake, and had then confronted death in its most awful shape. He had seen the flames kindled around him. The fire-tipped arrows had been shot into his body, and torments far more excruciating were about to follow, when, as an Indian *beldame* advanced to tear the only remaining strip of vesture from his body, the *totem* of Brant imprinted upon it was revealed to the hellish crew of executioners around him, and saved him from a death so horrible.

Since that moment, though still strictly guarded, he had been treated with all the forbearance which characterized the conduct of the party which had brought him thither, though they had long since gone off and left him in other hands. But as, though wearing the insignia of an immediate follower of Thayendanagea, he had never undergone the ceremony of being formally adopted into any tribe of the Mohawks, he was conscious that his change of treatment arose only from his being now regarded rather as a slave than a prisoner. He was determined once more to seize an opportunity to escape, and to perish rather than be retaken. He relied much, however, it must be confessed, upon The Dew to make such opportunity for him. Nor was that hope and confidence misplaced.

Max, though still given to that half romantic, half philosophic mood of wrapping one's self up in one's own dreams and speculations, which belongs to that inexperienced season of life when we value our own thoughts far more than the material objects around us, was still not deficient in keen and curious observation of character. And for months it had been one of his chief mental resources to study the personal traits and peculiarities of the singular people among whom his present lot was cast.

He was sitting one morning a little aloof from a group of loungers of all sexes and sizes, listening to a rude legend which an old woman, employed in weaving mats, was relating for their edification. The wild tradition with which she was engaged related to those strange subterranean sounds which are still, from time to time, heard among these mountains. She told of some bold hunter who went out determining to trace the spot whence these groanings of the earth had travelled out. And Greyslaer, who had looked with a curious eye upon the remarkable peculiarities of this volcanic region, bent near to hear how the strange fancy of an Iroquois would account for natural phenomena to whose existence he himself could bear testimony.

At this moment the report of a gun was heard not far off. It probably was discharged by some hunter belonging to the camp, and excited no attention among the listening group. Presently, however, The Dew, who had gone down to the shore of the lake to bring water, appeared, and saying aloud that the hunter who had just fired needed the assistance of the white man in bringing some game to camp, motioned Greyslaer the path in which he should go, which, strangely enough, was in an opposite direction from that whence the sound came. The others were too much engaged with the story-teller to notice the discrepancy, whose purport, however, was intuitively understood by the prisoner; and, before the approaching hunter had reached the camp on the one side, he had gained a considerable distance on the other. He pierced far into the ravine through which the waters of the lake discharge themselves from the hollow, and now only hesitated which way to turn his steps.

The ravine, though at first distinctly defined, had, within a few hundred yards of the lake, so broadened and broken up into a thousand rocky inequalities, that it was impossible, as the forest thickened around him, to tell what route to take in order to descend the mountain. The out let of the lake would seem to have been a sufficient guide; but this, a mere rill at its commencement, was broken up into a hundred slender threads of water, which, losing themselves now among matted leaves, and now creeping beneath the mossy woof which wraps the living rocks and the rotten trunks wedged between them, in the same green vesture, served only to distract the judgment that would lean upon them as a guide. Greyslaer, in fact, had only gained a lower and broader basin than that which held the waters of the lake; and though it likewise was walled round by craggy pinnacles, yet here there was a heavy forest-growth; and these barriers themselves, as well as the passage through them, were wholly screened from view by the intervening foliage.

But now, darting like a bird from the greenwood covert, The Dew suddenly presented herself in the path before him, and beckoned Max onward. As yet there were no signs of pursuit behind: but the moments were precious; for the descent of the mountain abounded in difficulties, and they had still a ravine to gain and a narrow gorge to pass through before gaining the bottom; a gorge so narrow that it might serve as a gateway to this labyrinth of natural fortifications; and here a single armed man might prevent their egress. The maiden now doubted for a moment what path to take. The sides of the ravine might be the safest, if they would avoid any chance wanderers returning to the Indian camp from the valley below. But these were every here and there broken by tall benches of rock too high to leap from, and doubling the toil of those who ever and anon must climb over the loose stones around their base.

The girl, therefore, descended still further into the Hollow, where a sloping pavement of smooth rock, some hundred yards in length, seamed the mountain. It looked as if it had been once overlaid by soil and forest growth like that around; but the stratum of matted roots and earths had been peeled off the steep declivity, and the fountains of a rivulet, oozing out from the compost of leaves and fibres which still overlaid the upper end of the slope, glided with thin and noiseless flow over the naked rock. And now, as the shallow rill deepened into a brook, which gurgled among the loose boulders, they followed it down as it kept its way through an easy swale of less broken land.

The woods upon its banks were here an open growth of ash and maple; and Greyslaer's confidence in the sagacity of his guide was for a moment shaken when he saw her persist in keeping her way along so exposed a path. He thought that they had already gained the base of the mountain, from the lofty and frowning cliffs of rock which now and then he could descry afar off, lifting themselves above the tree-tops around. He would fain have struck off to some thickets which, through these open glades, could be plainly seen crowning the lower and nearer ridges of rock that traversed the hillsides above them.

But the girl directed his attention in advance, and, for the first time, he saw the sunshine playing upon some spruce and cedar tops that were immediately upon a level with his line of vision. She pointed to the brook, still their emulous companion, and he understood at once that it must have some sudden fall where those trees were growing. There must be a change of soil, rocks, and thickets there; a swamp, perhaps, and possibly one or more tributaries to the brook ere it reached the plain below. And, truly enough, the sound of a waterfall soon greeted his ears. The sides of the swale became steeper, and it narrowed at last suddenly, as if the ground had sunk. There were irregular walls of stone on either side, with springs welling here and there from their mossy intervals. Loose boulders clogged up the main current of the brook, which, foaming and fretting for a while, emerged at last from the rocky gorge, and took up a more stately march through the heavy forests that spread themselves over a richer soil below.

The fugitives followed on until that guiding water reached the Upper Hudson, where their toilsome descent from the Thunder's Nest, but not the peril of their flight, was ended.

The spot where they first gained the banks of the wild and romantic river of the north, was a few miles above that beautiful pass called Teohoken by the Indians, where the dark-rolling waters which form the outlet of Scroon Lake, sweep into the Hudson. Here Max quickly constructed a raft from the floating timbers which he found in profusion in the eddies of the stream; and the two voyagers drifted down with the current, till, reaching the rapids at the approach of night, they were compelled to betake themselves to an island which divides the waters of the Hudson just above its junction with the Scroon, at Teohoken.

It was a strange situation for the youthful captain, when he found himself alone at nightfall, with that beautiful, elfish creature, upon an island of the wilderness; but the Indian girl, seeming to take no thought of the peculiarity of her position, relieved him from the embarrassment of his. She pointed him to a mossy bank, where a clump of overshadowing basswood kept off the dew; and, retiring herself to a leafy hollow not far remote, the fatigues they had undergone soon plunged them both in slumber, while the virgin moon, shining down upon an open interval between them, was their only sentinel through the night.

The voyagers gained the western shore with the break of dawn, and, following it down till they had passed the rapids, seized upon and appropriated a canoe which they found at the mouth of a little trouting brook which comes into the Hudson a short distance below the forks. In this they floated down the rushing stream, which, with the Indian girl at the helm, and Greyslaer plying his active paddle at the prow, whirled their frail bark safely over its rocky channel. The rapid windings of the river, and the overhanging woods, which at early day let down only here and there a burst of sunshine on its shadowy bosom, swept them so quickly from alternate light to gloom, that the startled deer drinking from the river's brink, had scarcely time to fix his gaze ere the shifting pageant had passed away.

They came at last within sound of the falls of Tiosaronda, and landing here on the western side of the river, near the base of Senongewoh, they circled the northern side of the hill, and struck into the forest in a direction towards Lake George, where Max hoped to find a military post occupied by his countrymen.

Hitherto our bold voyagers seemed to have been utterly free from pursuit. But now they had not advanced far into the forest, climbing two or three hilly ridges in succession, before Greyslaer's steps were arrested by a startling cry, which seemed to come almost from beneath his very feet. He looked up, and saw The Dew, with one foot advanced, her hands averted, as if motioning him back, while she herself gazed forward, as if trying to pierce a shadowy glen that yawned across her path. The yell was again repeated from below, and the maid, cowering towards the ground, made signs to Greyslaer to imitate her movements. Crouching as she commanded, he ventured, however, to approach with stealthy caution to the place where she stood. The Dew gently moved the tilting boughs of a stunted hemlock which was in the rifted side of the cliff on whose edge she hovered: a sprinkling of light showered upon the bald rock, and, as Max peered through the leafy grating, which the hand of the maid had partially removed, the cause of her agitation was at once revealed to him.

A band of Mohawks were clustered around what seemed to be the fresh track of a white man in the forest. Greyslaer, from the intervening foliage, could by no means distinguish the object at which the Indians pointed, but the significant gestures of the whole party left no doubt upon his mind that the joyful discovery of an enemy's trail had caused the wild yell which first startled him and his companion. The Indians had apparently been pursuing their way through the ravine in a direction nearly parallel to that which he was traversing. The next moment, and the whole band had disappeared from beneath his eye; the Mohawks vanishing behind the gray trees so suddenly and silently, that, as their painted forms and tufted plumage disappeared amid the dark foliage, it seemed as if some wild vision of the forest had melted amid its glooms; and he almost expected them to reappear the next moment by his side from beneath the rugged bark of the huge oaks around him; such as unfolded to release the fabled Dryads of old.

The Dew waited until sufficient time had elapsed for the Indians to gain several hundred yards, and then, motioning to Greyslaer to tread carefully in her footsteps, descended the steep bank a few paces and commenced moving rapidly along the hillside. She had not proceeded far in this direction, however, before, coming to a spot where some huge rocks, covered only with dog-briers, let down the light too broadly into the forest, she turned abruptly from the path, thridded the thorny defile, and, crossing to the opposite side of the ridge, regained the point from which she had recently started. The old path was then followed back for full a mile, and then again as suddenly left as before.

Four distinct trails were thus made to branch out at intervals from that which Max and his guide were actually travelling; and the maid, seeming content with these precautions, now kept the way steadily forward; save that, ever and *anon*, she would pause for a moment in some more open glade, poise herself upon some fallen trunk, throw a keen but furtive glance around her, and then flit lightly as a bird from its perch into the leafy shadows beyond.

A deep swamp received them next; and no youth less light of foot than Greyslaer could have kept up with the forest damsel as she glided from one half-floating tussock to another, her feet scarce touching the black and slippery logs, which, plunged as they were in the slimy mould, afforded yet the firmest stepping-place around.

A *windfall* upon the hillside was to be traversed next. The uprooted trees, wrenched from their ancient seats by the tornado's force, lay with their twisted stems, their boughs fast locked together, their enormous roots turned vertically to the sky, with fragments of rock and clay matted by their fibres, and walling one side of the pit from which they had been upturned, while barriers of rankly- grown briers inclosed the others. But the splintered tree, the thorny copse, the deep pitfalls, the palisade of gnarled roots and jagged rocks protruding from them, offered no obstacle to the fairy footsteps of The Dew. The little crossbill of the mountain, the bird that best loves the "windfall," and whose twinkling form and brown and gray plumage is often the only object that enlivens these ghastly wrecks of the forest, seemed hardly more at home among them.

A tract of level land was gained at last. It was a pine barren, where the trees shot upward, a hundred feet or more, with not a leaf of underwood around their stems, with not a shrub below them, and scarcely a green bough appearing to break the monotonous range of columns, save those which formed the verdant roof which shut in this solemn temple. The brown maid here told her white companion to take the lead. She pointed through an almost straight vista between the interminable trunks; and Max, seeing his way before him, stepped fleetly forward, his companion treading cautiously in his footsteps upon the yielding sand.

They had nearly crossed these dangerously open glades, when Greyslaer suddenly felt a light hand upon his shoulder; he turned and saw the girl pointing, with an agitated look, to an object that was advancing toward them nearly in the direct line they were travelling. It was an Indian just emerging from the thickets of ash and maple that grew upon the edge of the barren. A few moments more, and they would have gained the same leafy covert.

The girl in an instant knew the man for a Mohawk. She waited not to see whether he was followed by others. It might be one of the same band she had seen a few hours before upon the trail of the white hunter; and, if so, all her efforts to avoid them had but involved her friend in their toils. But whether it were the same or another party of her tribesmen, it mattered not; the life of Greyslaer now depended more than ever upon her faithful and sagacious guidance. The Indian paused and looked backward, as if awaiting the coming up of his party. The Dew seized the moment, and, followed by Greyslaer, sped backward on her path. She crossed and recrossed it repeatedly, Greyslaer now in his turn stepping lightly and carefully in her footprints, so as to cover, yet not wholly erase them, while their way yet lay through the sands of the pine barren.

They gained at last the thick greenwood, where the deciduous trees imbowered their path, and the elastic car pet of moss and wild flowers, and spongy trunks over grown with juniper, and tangled thickets of moose-wood and wytch-hopple, gave now the springy footing the tired hunter loves, and now afforded the deep covert where the hounded deer will seek to hide.

Proceeding thus in a westward direction, the fugitives soon found themselves again within sight of the river, and near the very place where they had landed in the morning. The current ran swiftly, but they did not hesitate to ford it, and clamber a mountainous ridge opposite. They paused upon a lofty ledge of rock to look back, and saw their pursuers already in the stream. They crossed the ridge and descended to the other side. They gained the banks of another river not larger than the first, but hesitated to cross; for the yell of the Indians was echoed from the rocks above them, and they feared to be seen while making the passage. Whither shall they now fly? They turn and follow down the stream, though it leads them nearly in the direction from which the pursuit is coming; but their only hope is in doubling thus upon their tracks.

They make the point where the two branches meet and mingle their waters. They turn to leave the stream they have been following, and clamber up the sides of the glen through which it flows, and find themselves upon a narrow isthmus, with another stream, deeper and far more violent, roaring around its rocky base. Max approached the verge of the precipice, and despaired of proceeding further. The cliff opposite was steep as that whereon they stood. The main stream, whose tributary it seemed he had been last traversing, had here cloven its way through a rocky ridge in a channel so narrow that any of the trees around him would span the black chasm. But he had no axe to fell one, nor would he have dared to disturb the echoes of the forest if one were at hand.

At this moment the shrill whoop of the Mohawks rose fearfully behind him. They were near. He spoke a few words to his companion, seized a pendant vine that flourished near the spot, and flung himself out from the face of the cliff, as if determined to drop into the roaring current, and take his chance for escape in its angry bosom. He cast one glance back on the maid ere he let himself drop in the tide below. She had not sprung forward to prevent him, but stood with folded arms and a look of indignant sorrow upon her brow. Was it mingled scorn and pity that he should thus desert his preserver? So thought Greyslaer, as, still holding his grasp on the vine, he permitted himself to swing back by her side. "Surely you can swim, you do not shrink from trying that stream with me," he cried.

"Were my brother an otter, he could not live in that terrible water," replied the maiden.

The whoop was again pealed nearer and more near; it rose, too, this time, from a dozen savage voices. The girl wrung her hands as if in despair, while Greyslaer folded his arms and leaned against a tree, as if moodily resigned to his fate. Suddenly, however, the thought of a new device inspired The Dew. She clambered like a squirrel toward the tree-top from which the vine depended; loosing a long and vigorous tendril from the stem as she ascended, she quickly passed another and a smaller one round it, so as to attach it firmly to a projecting bough; descended a few yards, and, grasping the vine tightly in her hands, darted out from the wall of foliage like a swallow from the face of a cliff, cleared the chasm, and landed safely upon a dizzy ledge opposite.

Greyslaer, who, unappalled for himself, had but a few moments before hung suspended over the gulf below, covered his face with his hands in the instant the daring feat was in the act of being accomplished; and, almost ere he could look again, the maid had recrossed the chasm and dropped nimbly by his side. But why did they still delay? The sound of pursuit grew nigher, yet Max refused to take the chance of escape, of which his noble guide had so daringly set him the example, until she herself was in a place of safety. The breath of an instant was precious, and now The Dew again made the airy passage, and was followed by her friend the instant he could recover the vine as it swung back within his reach.

The Dew, with Indian precaution, seized it once more as he was thoughtlessly about releasing it from his grasp, and, winding the end around a heavy stone, she handed it to Max, and signified to him to throw it into a thicket upon the same side of the stream whereon it grew. The two had then barely time to plunge into the bushes beyond them, when the pursuing Mohawks appeared upon the headland opposite, and they soon after heard their baffled howl of disappointment at the broken and lost trail of the fugitives.

CHAPTER 5

A Night in the Whooping Hollow

Then sweet the hour that brings release
From danger and from toil,
We talk the battle over,
And share the battle's spoil.
                            Song of Marion's Men.

A gentle arm entwines her form, a voice is in her ear,
Which even in death's cold grasp itself 'twould win her back to hear;
Now happy is that Santee maid, and proudly bless'd is he,
And in her face the tear and smile are strangely sweet to see.
                            Simms.

The Whooping Hollow lay now" directly in their route to Fort George, and thither the footsteps of the fugitives were directed. The Dew was faint from hunger, and the weary spirits of Greyslaer were anything but cheered by the desolate scene of that swampy-shored lake, with here and there a dead tree waving the long moss from its gray arms as it stood solitary amid the half-floating bog. All concern for himself, however, was forgotten in distressing anxiety for his companion.

They had still eight or ten miles to travel to reach Fort William Henry, and the day was nearly spent. But now a new source of interest presented itself to stimulate his nerves. He heard a distant volley of firearms, followed by a broken but rapid discharge, as of a running fight beyond the hills. It neared him, and he fancied he could hear the rallying shout of white combatants mingling hoarsely with the shrill yell of Indian onslaught. Unarmed as he was, Greyslaer bounded forward, as if to aid those of his own blood, who, it would seem, were borne down in the battle. He turned to give one look at his companion. The languid eyes of the Iroquois girl kindled with new life as she motioned to him to leave her to her fate and rush forward.

But now, again, another volley, another shout, and then the Indian whoop grew fainter and fainter, as of men scattered and fleeing in pursuit. He listened intently, but the sounds of the battle had died away in the distance.

The twilight has come, the night closes in, and again the moon marches up the heavens to cheer the wanderers, if, indeed, her ghastly light, shining down among those haggard trees, and gleaming upon the pool that has settled in that dreary hollow, have aught of cheering in it. The gentle-souled Greyslaer looks often into the deep and languid eyes of the suffering and innocent-hearted girl who had dared and endured so much for him. He blames himself for having permitted her to encounter the perils they had undergone; not the least of which, that of starvation in the wilderness, they are now beginning to realize. The fort, it is true, is not far; but will The Dew have strength to reach it on the morrow?

He made her a couch of fern and leaves, where the cradling roots of an ancient birch supplied her mossy pillow: and now she shrank not from his ministering care as he sat near, watching till her eyes were closed in slumber. But hark! there are other human sounds in the forest besides the cry of the whooping savage or the distant din of border conflict. Can it be a crew of merry makers, or is it only the echoes of the place which wake in chorus to the song now trolled along the hillside:

Room, boys, room, by the light of the moon,
Oh why shouldn't every man enjoy his own room?
Enough in the greenwood, if not in the hall,
By the light of the moon there's enough for us all.

"Hist! halloo there, white man! where the devil do you come from?" cried the foremost of the forest choir, advancing from under the boughs into the moonlight, and levelling his rifle upon Greyslaer as he spoke. "King or Congress! Speak up, my good fellow, if you've got a tongue."

"De Roos!"

"Whose voice is that? Good God! Max Greyslaer, is it your living self that I hold in my arms?" And the impetuous brother of Alida—for it was no other than Derrick himself—drew back from the embrace of Greyslaer, into which he had thrown himself, to look earnestly into the wan features of his long-lost friend. Their aspect of suffering filled him with emotions which he could only conceal in part, as turning round he shouted to his comrades,

"Balt, Lansingh, Miller, carry on, men, carry on. Here are more wonders in the woods tonight than those we've yet dreamed of."

But Balt had heard the first joyful cry of recognition between the friends, and was already hugging Greyslaer in his arms with an unceremonious vigour, that sensibly reminded Max of De Roos's unfortunate speech, assimilating him to a bear, which had once given such deep offence to the worthy woodsman. The salutations of the other hunters, though, of course, less familiar, were hardly less hearty, as Balt stood by and proudly encouraged them to come up and take the hand of his old pupil.

"Didn't I tell ye, boys," said he, "that young Max would come to hand the right side up? Alive? eh! only look at the young springald. Thin and raw-boned as he is, there's life enough in him to squeeze it out of any of us. Law sorts, Capting Max, how your shoulders have spread; and your face, too, is as brown as Kit Lansingh's here. Kit, you land-lougher, stand up and measure *hathes* with the capting."

But Greyslaer had turned away, and was bending with anxious solicitude over a figure that had hitherto escaped the notice of his friends. "Some water, Balt; quickly, in the name of Heaven, quickly, old man. She faints, she faints," said Greyslaer, in tones of almost agonizing solicitude, as he supported the sinking head of The Dew upon his bosom. "Ah! they'll be an age in returning from the lake. Your canteen, De Roos; a drop from that may yet revive her."

De Roos tore the canteen from his side; and, as Max applied the cordial to her lips, the maid opened her eyes.

"Have you no refreshment—a single biscuit in your pouch?" asked Greyslaer.

"Here's a corn-cake, captain," said a hunter, handing a fragment of the coarse bread to Greyslaer.

"Yes, and we can soon get you up plenty of venison," cried Lansingh, who now returned from the lake-side with the water, for which two or three of his comrades had simultaneously rushed together.

"Off, then, with you at once, Kit," rejoined Balt, who now came puffing and blowing up the hill. "We must needs camp here, I take it; for the gal's state won't allow her removal tonight. Who'd a' guessed, though, of finding a petticoat here with the capting?"

"Carry on, boys, carry on, then; get up your shanties as soon as may be," said De Roos, while those of the hunters who had not gone off with Lansingh after the remains of the deer upon which they had already feasted, bestirred themselves on every side. Some cut stakes and rafters for the frame of the *wigwam*; some peeled the heavy bark from ancient hemlocks, which, though prostrate upon the ground, had not yet mouldered, spreading the broad pieces over the roof and adown the sides; while others strewed the floor of the shanty with the fragrant branches shorn from the living tree, after felling it for the purpose of being thus stripped. Some busied themselves in kindling a fire before the opening of this sylvan shed, while the forest resounded with the stroke of the axe, as others felled the hard-wood trees, chopped them up, and piled them near to feed the growing flame when wanted.

Greyslaer, in the meantime, now that his anxiety about "The Dew" was relieved, summarily detailed his principal adventures, speaking always of the disinterested and heroic Indian girl in terms that would have deepened even the colour of her red cheek could she have understood the language in which they were uttered. De Roos, in return, gave him information of both a public and private nature which claimed his deepest interest. The account which Derrick gave him of Alida's escape from the cavern of Waneonda, though bringing to Max the blessed assurance of her present safety, was anything but satisfactory; for while the hot-headed Derrick inveighed against the whole race of rascally Tories, as concerned in her imprisonment, Greyslaer could not but have his own convictions that this mysterious business was one with which the royalists as a party had but little to do. This, however, was not the moment to dwell upon a subject so painful. Nor was De Roos the character with whom he could venture upon any half-formed surmises, without betraying the confidence of Alida to the full extent that she had intrusted him in her affairs.

"But tell me, De Roos," cried Max, making an effort to dash these bewildering thoughts from his mind, "how came you in these woods with old Balt?"

"With old Balt? Why, an hour since, I believed truly that he was a hundred miles from here, as I did that you, dear Max, were enjoying the hospitality of our refugee friends in Canada. Balt must tell you himself how he came here; for I deferred hearing his story till we gained his camp, whither he was conducting me when I fell in with you."

"But yourself; how came you here yourself?"

"Oh, why, you know, we are only a few miles from the fort; so it's no great wonder that I should be here. Van Schaick sent me yesterday to look after some *batteaux* at Glen's Falls, which are ordered up from below for the transportation of the baggage of the command which, you know, has been relieved."

"I know? How should I know anything about the matter, or imagine, even, that you were at Fort George, or who, indeed, was its commandant?"

"True, ay, true; I forgot how you have been cooped up in these stirring times. Well, you see, as I was about to mention, an incidental part of my duty led me back to the lake by this route, which is only a few miles longer to the fort. Gansevoort, our lieutenant-colonel, got some information from Albany a day or two since about that cut throat Tory, Joe Bettys, who—"

"Joe Bettys, the cut-throat Tory!" cried Greyslaer, echoing his words in astonishment. "What, not Ensign Joe Bettys, who was so ardent a Whig, albeit a boon companion and crony of the Tory Bradshawe?"

"The same man, Max; and a brave Whig, too, he proved himself under Arnold in Canada. But, either from some disgust with our officers, or an original want of principle, he has been won over to the other side, and commenced his Tory career in a dashing style, that must make him long remembered in these parts. He is said to have taken up his quarters here in the Whooping Hollow, and, assuming the disguise of a mongrel mountebank, an outcast Indian vagrant, whom he killed, he has practised so successfully upon the superstitious fears of the people below, that they would make no effort to follow and seize him upon his retreating here after some deed of blood or plunder. So I took an Indian guide, and came poking through here to see if I could beat up his quarters in passing, or, at least, light upon his trail."

"And you fell in with Balt—"

"Just in time to lend a volley which saved him from a devil of a licking; for he and his handful of hunters were mad enough to engage with a score of Mohawks, led on, as I suspect, by Isaac Brant, or Auneh-yesh, as he calls himself."

"Isaac Brant? Why, I have already told you that I left him upon the shores of a lake far west of this a dying man, as I thought, and—"

"Ay, but that was some six months since, if I under stood you rightly; and I assure you he is bloody Isaac Redivivus now. Everybody has nine lives in these times. Isaac I know at least to be alive and kicking; for, with Kasselman, Empie, and other scoundrelly Tories who fight under the disguise of Indians, he makes as much noise in this neighbourhood as his father, with fifty times the number of men, is creating along the Unadilla region. There is, though, a touch of humanity about old Joseph that his son is wholly innocent of."

"And you think, then, that Isaac's tribesmen, who were in pursuit of me, guided him hither tonight?"

"Even so."

"But the friendly Indian who was your pioneer to the Hollow, I don't see him here."

"He loitered behind, where I left my corporal to bury some two or three brave fellows whom I have lost by this night's business. By the way, it is our old boyish friend Teondetha. The Tryon County Committee sent him as a runner to Albany, whence he was despatched with the message to the fort, requiring the presence of our regiment to overawe the Tories on the Mohawk. But here comes Miller and his men. You put those brave boys to bed safely, Miller?"

"Safely and snugly, captain; neither wolves nor Indians will trouble them, I reckon," replied the corporal, touching his hat.

"Where's the Oneida?"

"He cleared out as soon as he had taken the hair of the redskins that fell on the other side. I mistrust he has followed on to see if he couldn't add another scalp to his string."

"It's the natur of all of them," ejaculated Balt; "dog eating dog. He must have had good picking, too, among the dead varmint, Adam; for there they lay on the grass, six big buck Injuns, likely fellows all, besides a withered chap that I clipped over with my hatchet, and left to curl up and die."

"And the boy," said De Roos, without heeding Balt's words, in a slight tone of anxiety; "you saw nothing of the boy, Adam?"

"Nothing, captain! The brat was missing from the moment we came in sight of the enemy. Isaac's people must have swooped him up in a moment; and he doubtless was glad enough to go with them."

"What boy is that you speak of?" asked Greyslaer, with some anxiety.

"Nobody—nothing—only a half-breed brat that we picked up on our march. Near the falls, wasn't it, Miller?"

"Yes, captain, in the shanty at the *batteaux* landing which you visited when we went down afore, you know. That time, I mean, when you had high words with the old woman, because you said you knew better when she declared that the child ought rightfully to belong to Isaac Brant, whose son he was, and when—"

225

"Silence, sir," commanded De Roos, who seemed both irritated and annoyed by the loquacity of his non-commisioned officer. "There was no child there at the time, you know well, Miller."

"*Certin!* there was not, capting; but you know you asked when next he would be there, or his mother, I forget which."

"Well, well, it's no matter what you forget, so you don't, forget your duty, which no one can accuse you of, my brave fellow. And now let your men build another fire for themselves, for here come the hunters with something to make a broil."

Greyslaer, in the meantime, had listened to this dialogue with an interest much beyond that of ordinary curiosity. The early dissipation of Mad Dirk de Roos, as his friend was universally called when they were college mates together, was not unknown to him; for, though younger than Derrick, yet, being of a graver and more earnest character, he had often taken upon himself the duty of an older person in lecturing his hair-brained chum. He recollected well that, during one of their vacation visits to the Hawksnest, the scandal of the country people had associated De Roos's name with that of a beautiful squaw, who, those connected with the Indian office at Guy Park said, was betrothed to Isaac Brant. He remembered, too, that, one Christmas morning. Guy Johnson rode over to the Hawksnest with a magistrate, who was at the Park enjoying the hospitality of the season, and closeted themselves with his guardian, De Roos's father, upon business which, though deemed by the family to be of a political nature, had filled him with anxiety for his friend, who was absent at the time. And more facts and reminiscences equally linked together, and having the bearing of strong circumstantial evidence upon this delicate matter, might have suggested themselves to Greyslaer's mind, had he not suddenly been startled from his painful musings by a wild cry of joy from The Dew as Teondetha suddenly presented himself in the light of the fire before her.

The maid recoiled abashed and agitated the instant she had uttered this natural outbreak of her feelings, while Teondetha, who with noiseless step, had approached to light his calumet by the fire, started erect from his stooping posture, and gazed with eagle glance around. But the girl had sunk back upon the pile of brush upon which she was reclining in one corner of the shanty, and the tall spire of flame which shot up between them prevented her for a moment from being seen by her lover. De Roos, in high spirits, as usual, was busy superintending the preparations for supper at the different fires, and joking with

226

the men grouped around them as he restlessly moved to and fro from one to the other. Greyslaer alone had his eye upon the Indian pair, and, as he now fully understood their language, he was not a little amused with the cool generalship with which the Oneida made his advances.

"My sister," said Teondetha, seating himself on a log near the opening of the shanty, the moment he discovered the vicinity of his lady-love; "how is it with her?"

"As with the bird that has wandered from its nest, and knows not where to alight. As with the sunbeam that drops into the forest, and finds no sister ray to receive and mingle with her beneath its chilling leaves."

"Teondetha is the tree whereon the bird would alight.[1] His heart is the fountain that would send back a ray to mingle with the sunbeam. Teondetha is a great warrior. He must build a lodge of his own, wherein to hang up the scalps of his enemies. Who will be there to light the pipe of the young chief?"

The girl, so far from shrinking at sight of the gory trophies at his belt, gazed now admiringly upon them as her half-savage lover held them up to her eyes.

"The young chief has earned a right to smoke before the women," she said. "The Dew will not extinguish his pipe when he lights it."

"Good!" said the copper-coloured gallant; and, bending over the coals, he carelessly swept up one with his hand, and dropped it into the bowl of his pipe. He puffed away calmly for a few moments, while his thoughts seemed occupied only in watching the smoke-wreaths that circled around him.

"What sees my brother in the smoke?" asked the girl, after watching her taciturn wooer for a while.

"A bird," replied the Indian gravely.

The girl smiled, was silent for a moment, and then looking down rather demurely, and pulling to pieces the twigs whereon she sat, asked:

"What says the bird to my brother?"

"It says that Teondetha is a tree whose leaves will only flourish by The Spreading Dew."

The girl laughed outright, (girls *will* laugh!) but the solemn composure of her companion seemed nowise disturbed by her merriment. The laugh, however, ceased at once, without subsiding into a titter.

"And what does my brother see now?" she resumed, so soon as she

1. The meaning of *Teondetha* is "a fallen tree"

had recovered her sobriety.

"He sees a beaver."

"And what says the beaver?"

"The beaver reminds him of a promise which The Dew made many moons ago, off by the yellow waters that flow from Garoga Lake. The beaver says that those of his tribe who have no lodge become worthless castaways. 'Teondetha,' says the beaver, 'let not The Dew go out of your sight again till you have built one for both of you.'"

"The beaver is never foolish," murmured the girl.

A heavy puff of smoke from the fire at that moment wrapped the lovers from Greyslaer's sight, and he could not see whether the Indian pair sealed this important pas sage of their courtship with the impress that fairer wooers would perhaps have used; but, as the smoke cleared away, he thought that he distinguished The Dew with drawing her little hand from that of Teondetha, who had slightly changed his position.

"Carry on, carry on," cried De Roos, at this moment, inviting all parties to supper in his favourite phrase, which, like the "push along, keep moving," of English farce, or the "go ahead" of modern American slang, served him alike upon all occasions, and was equally in requisition whether at feast or fray.

Max, who had eaten nothing, as yet, save a biscuit which he got from the knapsack of a slain soldier, upon which he had been seated near the fire, was sufficiently sharp-set to fall to with a keen relish of the fare now placed before him.

"There's the cup by your side, capting, if it's that ye're looking for. Lean over, now, with your cracker here, till I put this slice of venison upon it. It's done to a crisis, I tell ye; brown on the outside, and juicy red within. The crittur himself would be tempted to taste one of his own cutlets, if he were of a flesh-faring natur. There, now, add the salt and pepper fixings, and the king himself hasn't a slicker supper. Never mind the squaw, never mind the squaw, capting; Scalpy yonder will look after her." And running on thus while he acted as cook, butler, and waiter for Greyslaer, old Balt, ever on the alert to serve him, eyed his pupil at intervals with an affectionate interest, as if it cheered his very heart to see the half-famished wanderer relishing this rude entertainment.

"Ah, capting," he resumed, "but Miss Alida will be glad to see you. We've had some rare doings in the valley since you were missed from among us. Sir John, as you mayhap know, broke his parole and cleared out for Canada, after being stolen off by old Joseph, who cut his way at midnight through the streets of Johnstown in taking him from the Hall. Folks talk hard of the baronet for leaving as he did; but Balt could have told them something which would prove he was not so much to blame. He thought he wasn't safe, he did, after the killing of Mr. Fenton during the armistice between the Whigs and Tories. But Mr. Fenton, you know, sought his own death; and, sorry as I was for it, how could I help smashing him as I did? You don't think I could, capting."

"It was a bad business, Balt; but, according to the account which Captain de Roos gave me tonight, you were certainly not to blame."

"I mistrust I wasn't—I raaly hope not; but Mr. Fenton was a fine man, a likely man, capting, and it was some comfort to me to give him Christian burial. I sent home his watch, and what little money he had about him, to his family; and the two or three papers I found in his pocket I kept till you should come back to tell me what to do about them. What else could I? I never had book-larnin enough to read written hand, and I didn't know but what the papers might hold political matters of some valw to our friends; yet I was afeared to give them to strangers to read, lest there might be private things in them about Mr. Fenton's folks that the family would not like to have go abroad."

"Where are the papers now?" asked Greyslaer.

"Miss Alida sealed them up for me, and put them away in the old brass *beaufet* at the Hawksnest; but she looked, oh! so sad when I told her that they must stay there till you come hum, that I was sorry I had not still continued to carry them about in my shooting-pouch with me. But how did I know but that I should leave my pouch and scalp both among these wild hills?"

"You did most rightly, Balt," said Greyslaer, not untouched by these proofs of the just sense of propriety which seemed to govern the simple woodsman. "But see, that tired girl has already dropped her head upon her arm, as if sleep had overtaken her. Let us withdraw from the neighbourhood of the shanty to the other fire, and see what disposition of us Captain de Roos proposes for the night."

"Yes, and there's the Oneida stretched like a hound upon the edge of the ashes, so that no one can enter the shanty without stepping over him. It is but judgmatical for us to look for a snoozing-place elsewhere."

De Roos, however, when they joined his party a few yards off. seemed to have no idea of anyone's seeking their rest so soon. He had just relieved the sentinels who had been posted here and there in the woods around, and the rest of his half-disciplined followers were ready enough to unite with Balt's hunters in the chorus, as the mad captain again broke out in the song with which he had first waked the echoes of the forest round about, and which he had originally learned from old Balt himself. Greyslaer, however, borrowing a blanket from one of the soldiers, was permitted to forego a part in this midnight saturnalia of the forest; for his plea of excessive weariness was ad mitted when De Roos remembered that they must reach Fort George early on the morrow, if they would have a place in the column when his regiment took up their line of march. The wayworn heir of the Hawksnest was soon plunged in deep slumber; but the words of the following song ever and anon mingled in his dreams, as the woodland revellers bore down merrily in the chorus.

Song of Balt the Hunter

1

There was an old hunter camped down by the kill,
Who fished in this water and shot on that hill;
The forest for him had no danger nor gloom,
For all that he wanted was plenty of room.
Says he, "The world's wide, there is room for us all;
Room enough in the greenwood, if not in the hall.
Room, boys, room, by the light of the moon,
* For why shouldn't every man enjoy his own room?"*

2

He wove his own mats, and his shanty was spread
With the skins he had dressed and stretched out overhead;
Fresh branches of hemlock made fragrant the floor,
For his bed as he sung when the daylight was o'er,
"The world's wide enough, there is room for us all;
Room enough in the greenwood, if not in the hall.
Room, boys, room , by the light of the moon,
For why shouldn't every man enjoy his own room?"

3

That spring, now half choked by the dust of the road,
Through a grove of tall maples once limpidly flowed;
By the rock whence it bubbles his kettle was hung,
Which their sap often filled, while the hunter he sung,
"The world's wide enough, there is room for us all;

230

Room enough in the greenwood, if not in the hall.
Room, boys, room, by the light of the moon,
For why shouldn't every man enjoy his own room?"

4

And still sung the hunter—when one gloomy day
He saw in the forest what saddened his lay;
'Twas the rut which a heavy -wheeled wagon had made,
Where the greensward grew thick in the broad forest glade—
"The world's wide enough, there is room for us all;
Room enough in the greenwood, if not in the hall.
Room, boys, room, by the light of the moon,
For why shouldn't every man enjoy his own room?"

5

But he whistled his dog, and says he,
"We can't stay; I must shoulder my rifle, up traps, and away."
Next day, through those maples the settler's axe rung,
While slowly the hunter trudged off as he sung,
"The world's wide enough, there is room for us all;
Room enough in the greenwood, if not in the hall.
Room, boys, room, by the light of the moon,
For why shouldn't every man enjoy his own room?"

Chapter 6

Estrangement

Where love, that cannot perish, grows
For one, alas! that little knows
How love may sometimes last;
Like sunshine wasting in the skies,
When clouds are overcast.

Dawes.

Is the prayer rejected—the suit disdained?
The pleadings of love—are they vain?
Has the student no lore, has his voice no skill,
To bring back lost smiles again?

Mrs. Embury

Glad rumours of the success which had finally crowned the hunter Balt in his wild-wood quest preceded the arrival of the popular young Max among his old friends and neighbours. It were difficult to define the emotions of Alida when the news of his deliverance' from captivity and death first reached her ears. For, though joy and delight for Greyslaer's escape first swallowed up all other feelings, yet painful reflections succeeded, and doubts and fears crept into her mind, to alloy this generous burst of heartfelt sensibility.

She felt, she owned to herself, that, were it not for the canker of an old sorrow, she *could* have loved her fresh-hearted worshipper. But this thought had only been admitted into her heart when she believed the barrier of the grave was closed between them. How was it now with her when Greyslaer lived? lived, while a barrier more hideous even than that of the grave must keep them apart forever! But why dwell now upon her past relations with Greyslaer? Why imbitter her hours by musing upon their possible future position toward each other?

Long months had intervened since the passionate declaration of her noble-spirited lover. There was time enough even for him to have forgotten his youthful fancy, or exchanged it for another, if some fair face had presented itself to him when away from her. Besides, had she not revealed that to him which must crush all hope upon the instant? Surely he could not have gone on feeding with vain dreams of what *might* be his misplaced and most unfortunate attachment—he had not consumed a captive's long and lonely hours in such fruitless and imbittered musings upon his baffled affections? His sorrows must have been those only of a young and ardent mind, that grieves to find itself cut off, in the season of its vigour, from the paths of ambition which men so love to tread; his dreams, only those which will crowd into a mind fertile as his when planning his escape from present evil—a prisoner's dream of home and friends, of free will and unrestricted motion, and the bright world which, fresh as ever, was to be enjoyed again.

Alida hoped that it might be so; yet she grew sad even in so hoping! A sensible and modest mind is not merely flattered, but substantially raised in its own estimation by the sincere and unaffected attachment of another as well constituted as itself, even when it cannot return the passion. And though it can hardly with precision be said either to grieve or humble us when that regard passes away, yet there is something of sorrow, something of humiliation, when we become assured of its decay.

In the meantime the presumed heiress of the Hawksnest had not wanted for admirers, though the natural imperiousness of her disposition prepared a haughty rebuff for more than one who made haste to address the beautiful orphan, even in her first secluded months of mourning. The advances of some of these suitors were well known in the neighbourhood, and their supposed rejection, when they successively withdrew from the field, became very naturally the talk of the country people, who, when Greyslaer's return from captivity was bruited abroad, unanimously agreed that Fate had intended that he should be the happy man.

"Surely," they argued, "young Max would never take possession of the estate which Miss Alida had so long enjoyed as his nearest kinswoman, and the co-heir of mad Derrick, without offering first to make her his wife? And where was the girl in the valley that would refuse *him*? Proud and uppish as she was, old De Roos, though a respectable man enough, and the old friend of Sir William, was no such great shakes, after all, that his daughter might turn up her nose upon the only son of Colonel Greyslaer that was."

As for Max himself, it was agreed, without any dissent, that he would seek a wife forthwith. He was the last of his name; and, though sternly republican in his political principles, democracy entered not into his ideas of the social relations, and he was believed to inherit from his stately old father sufficient pride of family not to wish the name of Greyslaer to expire with himself.

Max, in the meanwhile, wholly unconscious that he and his affairs were furnishing the only subject of gossip to the good wives of the neighbourhood, now that the storm of war had rolled away from the valley for a season, and left leisure for such harmless themes, disappointed every one by the quietude of his proceedings. A lawyer from the county town, calling upon Miss de Roos, informed her that Captain Greyslaer, being about to join his regiment, which belonged to a brigade of volunteers that had recently been draughted into the service of Congress, he had no idea of taking possession of the Hawksnest, and that Miss de Roos would add to the obligations which Captain Greyslaer already felt himself under to her late lamented father, if she would continue to preside over an establishment which must otherwise be broken up, and perhaps fall to ruins; for the aged housekeeper was now too infirm for the charge, and Captain Greyslaer was at a loss what disposition to make of his other servants in times so disturbed. "The captain," said the lawyer, looking round upon the ancient furniture, "seems to have his heart bent upon keeping these old sticks together, and there is no one but you, madam, to whom he can look, as one feeling the same sort of interest in the place as that which he cherishes."

The latter part of his agent's statement was enforced by a note from Greyslaer, containing an eloquent appeal to her on the score of their mutual childish associations, and on the impracticability of his making any humane disposition of his black servants; for manumitting them—a resource which had suggested itself—would in the existing state of the country, be, in fact, the cruellest thing he could do, there being now no employment for labourers of that class.

Alida, who had not been left unprovided for by her father, and was, therefore, not thus rendered dependent upon the bounty of a distant kinsman, who stood toward her in the delicate relation of a discarded lover, scarcely hesitated in her determination. "She would remain beside the graves of her father and sister, and consider herself as mistress of the Hawksnest until Captain Greyslaer was prepared to enter into his possessions; but it must be as a tenant, upon the same terms that her father had held the property."

A month or more had elapsed after the adjustment of this delicate matter, and Greyslaer, writing weekly to her from Albany and New York, whither his professional duty had led him, managed always in his letters to preserve a tone of easy friendliness, such as had prevailed between them in the younger days of their intercourse. This composure upon paper, however, vanished entirely when at last they met. The frank cordiality which Max assumed, was rather overdoing nature, as Alida thought when she observed his rapid utterance and restless motions; and Greyslaer was conscious that Alida trembled with agitation when he smilingly proffered the ordinary salute which fashion so inconsistently permitted among the polite, considering the otherwise ceremonious manners of that formal day. They each seemed labouring under a continual exertion to maintain the tone in which Max had so happily commenced their correspondence, and which had hitherto been successfully kept up between them. But the restraint which either felt at heart must soon have convinced them that they mutually stood in a false position toward each other.

A famous modern sayer of apothegms tells us that friendship may sometimes warm into love, but love can subside into friendship never; and of the ancients one goes still further, by making hatred the only change of which love is capable. As indifference will often supervene to the most violent passion, the creed of the latter is manifestly absurd; but there is something of truth in the proverb of the former; for though the sentiment of friend ship, a feeling of the warmest and kindest regard, may indeed exist where love has once been, yet the calm relation of friends, with all its easy and pleasurable frankness of intercourse, can hardly grow up between two parties where love has been the source of interest to either, and that love has been once avowed.

There must be some lurking mortification, if not some secret trace of sorrow, on one side or the other; a jealousy of mutual respect, a quickness to take offence, and, above all, the mournful memory of former passages, endeared only in recollection, perhaps, by their being associated with the halcyon season of youth and hope, but still endeared to it; there must be this memory to come over the spirit amid its gayest sallies, and make the society of the one who has elicited them, saddening, if not oppressive, to the mind for the moment.

What wonder, then, if Greyslaer's visits to the Hawksnest were gradually intermitted? A character so earnest as his cannot always find material for conversation amid themes of passing interest, while one that fills his whole soul is utterly forbidden; for conversation with her, moreover, whose presence unlocked the secret chambers of his mind, and peopled it with thoughts that might not walk abroad.

He had promised Alida never officiously to thrust himself further into her confidence, and he remembered his promise; but the forced durance she had suffered at the hands of Bradshawe was known to him, and he burned to resolve his suspicions concerning that dark and desperate man. He had hoped, in his earlier visits, that their discourse might at some future time lead to Alida's reposing that full confidence in him which he persuaded himself was due to the truthfulness and steadfastness of his attachment, under the changed form in which he was determined she should view it. But the moment did not come; and upon each succeeding visit Greyslaer seemed further from the hope of such a revelation than ever. Alida, in fact, did not dream of making it.

Whether it was that she did not consider Greyslaer, her young friend, the most proper party to interest himself about her affairs; whether she paled at the peril to which Greyslaer her lover would be exposed by the steps he might adopt upon receiving the disclosure; whether she shrank, with true female delicacy, from the further agitation of a subject so painful; or whether she had proudly determined to be herself the arbiter of her own destiny, it is impossible to say. But while there are some circumstances which diminish the force of the last supposition—such as the present banishment of Bradshawe from this region, and the change which seemed to have come over the character of Alida after she came to realize the full extent of her family bereavements—it is probable that all these considerations swayed her by turns, and suggested the reserve of conduct which was the result.

And now Captain Greyslaer has become noted alike among his equals in rank and his superior officers for his rigid and exclusive attention to his military duties. He seldom goes beyond the limits of the post where he is stationed. His visits to the Hawksnest, which is only a few miles off, seem gradually to have ceased altogether; and a book or newspaper from New York, with some pencilled remarks upon the news it contains from the seat of war, is, when transmitted through his orderly, the only intercourse he holds with its inmates.

Alida—though other officers of the garrison sought by assiduous attention to supply the place of Max—Alida, it must be confessed, began soon to miss his accustomed visits. The superior mental accomplishments of Greyslaer the student, would with her have given him but slight advantage over his military comrades; but the character of Greyslaer the soldier, of Greyslaer the young partisan, whose wild adventures and perilous escapes among the Indians were the theme of every tongue, appealed more forcibly to the romantic admiration of Alida; and apart from all tender associations of the past, regarding him only in the light of an acquaintance of the day, she would have felt an interest in the society of Max that no other of his sex whom she had hitherto known could inspire.

There might possibly, too, be something in the altered aspect of Greyslaer which more or less affected the light in which a woman's eye would regard him, now that his cheek had lost its freshness from hardship and exposure; and that almost boyish air which characterized his appearance even in early manhood, had been changed by more recent habits of action, of command, and of self-reliance.

The mother who, welcoming her long-absent son, sighs as she looks vainly in his features for those gentler traits which graced the handsome stripling with whom she parted, smiles the next moment with inward pride at the sentiment of newly-awakened respect with which she is mysteriously inspired toward her own offspring; she startles at the altered modulations of his voice as heard at a distance; she wonders at the changed cadence of his footfalls, as his approaching step, which was ever music to her ear, grows nearer; she marks his graver and more even mien; she gazes upon the brow where manhood has already stamped its lordly impress; yet, even while leaning for counsel upon him who so lately looked to her for care, she can scarcely realize the swift and silent change that is now so fully wrought.

So had it been with Alida. Greyslaer was to her a stripling student no more; and if her own feelings had not taught her thus, the conviction must have been forced upon her by the light in which, as she saw. he was regarded by those far older than herself. His opinions upon all subjects seemed to be quoted by those who were his immediate associates; and she heard continually of grave cases in which Greyslaer's judgment was appealed to by members of the Committee of Safety, and others charged with the various clashing powers of the provisionary government of the period. The friendship of such a man she felt was to be valued, and she even acknowledged to herself that, had not circumstances placed an insurmountable barrier between them, Greyslaer—judging him only by the character he had formed for himself in the world—Max Greyslaer was the man of all others to whom her proud and aspiring heart would have been rendered up.

But, alas! what booted such knowledge now? Of what avail was it that reason reluctantly at last sanctioned the preference which a secret tenderness suggested, when reason was wholly at war with the indulgence of these partial feelings? Reason, though she sustained with the one hand the judgment which guided that partiality, pointed sternly with the other to an abyss of hopelessness. Alida might love Greyslaer, but she never could be his.

With minds of a gentler mould, or even with one lofty as hers, if attempered by the sweet influences of Religion, a quiet and uncomplaining resignation would have been the alternative of one thus weighed down by the hand of fate. But Alida, though her fervid soul was in a high degree characterized by that sentiment of natural piety which, existing in almost every highly-gifted mind, is so often mistaken for the deeper and more permanent principle which alone deserves the name of true religion—Alida had never yet known that sober, and holy-conserving influence by whose aid alone, the preacher tells us, we may possess our minds in peace. She rebelled against the lot to which she seemed doomed as a disappointed, if not broken-hearted woman. She would struggle against the blind pressure of circumstance, and war till the last with the fate which only served to exasperate while it over shadowed her spirit.

It is strange how, while most minds grow haughty, exacting, and imperious from success, misfortune, so far from bringing humility with it, produces precisely the same effect in others; they seem to harden in the struggle with sorrow, and grow insolent as they gain knowledge of their own powers of endurance.

'I'll go no more," said Greyslaer one evening, as throwing himself dejectedly into the saddle, he passed through the gate which opened upon the grounds of the Hawksnest, and turned his horse's head toward the garrison; "I'll go no more. Had her reception been merely cold and formal after the long interval I have ceased visiting her, I should not have complained of such notice of my neglect; for *she*, perhaps, never suspects the cause that keeps me away. But those two fingers so carelessly accorded to my grasp, with that light laugh as she turned round in speaking to that group of idlers, even in the moment that I was expressing my pleasure at seeing her—pshaw! there are no sympathies between that woman and myself; there never was, there never can be any;" and he struck the rowels into his horse almost fiercely, as, thus bitterly musing, one angry thought after another chased through his mind.

"And what if she be?" he exclaimed, reining up suddenly again to a slower pace. "What if she be wayward, fitful, and exacting to me alone of all other men? Forgetful of the devoted and all-absorbing love I have borne her; forgetful of the feelings which, save on that terrible night only, I have always kept trained in obedience to what I deemed her happiness? *She* never attempted to inspire this misplaced and mistaken interest; she never lured me on to the avowal; she never trifled with the emotions that prompted it. What right have I to arraign her conduct, to sit in judgment upon her conduct toward me? Her character is the same that I have ever known it. Her conduct toward me? Am I, then, such an egotist that that is to change my estimation of *her*? She does not love me, she cannot love me; and if she did, is there not this hideous bar between us! What care I, then, for the show of interest, when the reality can never be indulged? No! my part is taken—irretrievably taken, and I would not recall my choice. For me there is no fragment of happiness that I can save from the wreck of the past, but I will still drift with her wheresoever the sea of events may hurl us."

It is well for us that it is only in very early life that we are thus prodigal of our chances of happiness, and willing to concentrate them all upon a single issue. Alas! how soon do we learn, in maturer years, to shift our interest from scheme to scheme; to see wave after wave, upon which the bark of our hopes has been upborne, sink from beneath it, until the very one upon which it was about to float at last triumphantly, strands us upon the returnless shores of the grave!

But, though many a worldling has commenced his experience of life with views hardly less romantic than those of Max Greyslaer, *his* was not the mere wayward devotedness of youth to its first sorrow. The very constitution of his mind was of a loyal, venerating kind; (for, deeply imbued as he was, by the classic culture of his mind, with that ancient, intellectual spirit of republicanism which had at once determined his political position in the present civil struggle, Greyslaer, under another system of education, might possibly have turned out almost a bigoted royalist;) and the sentiment which still attached him to Alida was nearly akin to that which, in another age and under other circumstances, would have inspired his self-devotion to some dethroned and expatriated prince, like him for whom one of his maternal ancestors had suffered upon the scaffold.

Had he never declared his passion for Alida, he might have succeeded in crushing it; he would certainly have attempted to reason it away the moment that he discovered that he must love in vain; but, the avowal once made, he never dreamed of withdrawing the adhesion he had thus given in, much less of transfer ring his affections to another. He had made an error of choice; a most unhappy, a most cruel one; but still he would abide by that choice, whatever consequences might accrue. The part which Max Greyslaer had thus chosen would, in a rational point of view, become only an ill-regulated, almost, we might say, a half-besotted mind. Yet the weakness of choosing such a part is precisely that which has dwarfed the growth and distorted the otherwise noble proportions of minds naturally the most masculine and commanding. There is something of the high Christian daring of wild romance, something of the solemn obstinacy of the classic heathen fatalist, in the proud perversity with which they would beard a Doom and grapple with a Destiny.

But the feelings and reflections of Greyslaer, upon which we have dwelt, perhaps, somewhat too minutely, received a new direction at this moment, as he heard the clatter of a horse's hoofs rapidly approaching in an opposite course to that which he was travelling. The speed of the coming horseman seemed to announce that he was either fleeing from pursuit, or riding upon some errand of the utmost urgency; and, ere Greyslaer could make out the figure of the strange rider amid the darkness, his conjectures as to his character were cut short by an occurrence which may best be told in another chapter.

CHAPTER 7

The Discovery

Colous.   *What kind, indulgent power Has smiled on Calous, that so much bliss At once should dissipate his darkest gloom, And make a noon of midnight!*

Athenia.   *His ways are dark and deeply intricate When Heaven was kindest, innocence was lost, And Paradise gave birth to misery.*

                           Athenia of Damascus.

There was a blacksmith's shop at the forks of the road, a few yards in advance of the spot where Greyslaer, the moment he became aware of the stranger's approach, had reined up to challenge him in passing. For, in these times, when almost every passenger upon the highway was an object of scrutiny, a horseman who journeyed so hotly by night naturally awakened suspicion as to his character.

Max, remembering the neighbourhood of the blacksmith's hovel, thought for a moment that it might be only some farmers boy, who, directing his way thither to have a horse-shoe replaced, was endeavouring by speed to diminish the lateness of the hour in which he must return homeward when his errand was finished. But the toils of the blacksmith seemed already ended for the day, as the sound of his anvil had ceased, and no light hovered around his shanty to tell that the bellows was busy within. The horseman, too, did not check his speed as he approached the smithy, but came thundering on as before, evidently about to pass it.

As it chanced, however, the owner of the premises was still there at work around his smouldering fire; and in the very moment that the stranger passed the large unglazed window of the hovel, a sudden puff of his bellows sent the sparks up from the chimney of the forge, and threw a ruddy strip of light across the road. The horse of the stranger, startled at the sudden glare, shyed, and flung his rider upon the spot.

Greyslaer, who clearly beheld the adventure from where he stood, spurred forward, threw himself from the saddle, and assisted the blacksmith, who had rushed to his door, in raising the fallen man from the ground. The smith, who was none other than the doughty Wentz, mentioned in the earlier chapters of our narrative, uttered a significant cry of surprise the moment he beheld the features of the dismounted traveller; and Max, upon scrutinizing them more narrowly as they together dragged their helpless load to the light, was at no loss to recognize the savage apparition of the Haunted Rock in the bruised, bedraggled, and crestfallen being before him.

"You may look for the master where you find the man," said Hans, shaking his head wisely as he dipped a handful of dirty water from the trough in which he generally cooled his irons, and threw it in the face of the stunned and senseless man.

"His master?" interrogated Greyslaer, a dark chain of suspicious and vengeful thoughts forming in his mind with the rapidity of lightning.

"Well, his leader then his employer, or whatever name you would give him who has always used this chap in his doings when he had work on hand. He, I say, Wat Bradshawe, must be astir when Red Wolfert rides abroad after this fashion. It were a mercy, now, to the whole country, captain, to knock him in the head with this iron."

"What! murder a man that lies helpless before you? Surely, Hans, your heart is not harder than the flinty road which has just spared the wretch's life. Lay those pistols out of his reach, however, and this knife too; he must not handle it on reviving," said Max, as the weapons caught his eye while loosing Valtmeyer's girdle to enable him to breathe more freely.

"Thousand devils! where am I?" muttered the brigand, opening his eyes, and quickly closing them again, as if the glare from the forge offended his sight.

"In safe hands enough, Wolfert," answered the blacksmith, as Greyslaer silently motioned him to reply.

"Aha! whose voice is that?" cried the ruffian, rubbing his bloodshot eyes, but not yet raising his head, as he rolled them from side to side. "Hans Blacksmith, was it you that spoke, good Hans? Thousand devils! where's my mare?"

"Far enough by this time, I guess, from the round rate in which she scoured down the south fork. Are you hurt much?"

"Um————. Has Greyslaer, the rebel captain, passed along here yet tonight?"

"Why do you ask?"

"Because we mustn't let him go by, that's all."

"*We!* Why, you're drunk, Wolfert. Do you think I will aid you in stopping passengers on the people's highway?"

Valtmeyer answered only by raising himself upon the bench whereon he had been laid; but he moved so stiffly and slowly that Greyslaer had time to withdraw a few steps within the deep shadows of the place.

"Drunk, you say, um————" and the *desperado* fumbled around his waist for the arms he generally wore there. "*Dunder und blixem!* who in the name of hell has removed my arms?"

"Your belt must have burst a buckle when you were thrown," replied Hans, calmly.

Valtmeyer fixed a penetrating gaze upon his countenance; but the immobility of the blacksmith's features taught him nothing. He raised himself to his feet with a slight groan, paused, and passed his hands down his sides, as if to feel whether or not his ribs were broken; and then, without saying a word, moved toward the single tallow candle which, stuck into a gourd, stood on the anvil nearby.

"I can't spare my only candle, if it's your arms you want to look for," said Hans, stepping forward; "the night air will flare it all away. Nobody will touch your belt where it lies atween now and tomorrow morning."

The outlaw, glowering upon him, muttered something inaudible in reply; and, without heeding the behest of Hans, seized upon the candle. The first movement he made in lifting it, threw the light full upon Greyslaer. Valtmeyer, in his surprise, let the gourd fall from his hands, and the taper it held was instantly extinguished in the black dust beneath his feet. There was now barely light enough from the forge to distinguish the outlines of his person where he stood, and, by plunging instantly into the surrounding darkness, he might at once have escaped. But, uttering the cry of "Treachery" in the moment he let the candle fall, he snatched from the furnace a red-hot iron—a crowbar, as it seemed from its size—and, swinging it double-handed about his head, made for the door.

The entrance to the hovel lay in deep shadow, but his glowing weapon betrayed his position as he dashed from one side to the other to find the means of exit. Hans struck at him repeatedly with a cold iron which he had caught up at the first onset; but Valtmeyer, at one moment whirling his terrible truncheon like a flail about his ears, and launching it forward like a harpoon the next, not only warded off the attack, but at one of his thrusts fairly bore Hans to the ground; while the leathern apron of the blacksmith, shrivelling up at the contact, alone prevented the red-hot iron from passing through his body.

As Hans stumbled over a billet of wood in falling, Valtmeyer might yet have followed up his advantage; but Greyslaer, who, with drawn sword, had planted himself in the doorway to prevent his escape in the first instance, now rushed forward and dealt a blow which would have smitten any common man to the earth, and even the brawny Valtmeyer went down on one knee beneath it. Another blow with the sabre's edge would here have terminated his career; but Max, seeing him drop the crowbar, as if his right arm had been paralyzed from his shoulder, was thrown off his guard by Valtmeyer's apparently defence-less condition, and in another instant the active ruffian was beyond the reach of his sword.

There was a long, low, open window, such as are usual in a black-smith's shanty, near where Valtmeyer fell, and the sill of which he had grasped with his left hand in falling. Through this he flung himself, unharmed by the pistol shot with which Greyslaer almost simultane-ously accompanied his sudden movement.

Max leaped instantly after him in pursuit; but, as the fugitive be-came invisible in the surrounding darkness, he turned to secure his horse, of which the outlaw might otherwise make prize. Hans ap-peared the next moment with a light. They traced Valtmeyer by the blood from his sword-cut for a few yards only. The dust of the road was spotted with it, but the dew lay heavy upon the grass which bordered it, and there were thickets opposite, into which he must instantly have plunged, after crossing the highway.

Valtmeyer's belt for holding his arms, to which his bullet-pouch was still attached, was the first thing that caught Greyslaer's eye as he re-entered the cabin. The weapons he handed over to Hans, who seemed better contented with the issue of the night's adventure as he scrutinized his share of the spoils with a workmanlike eye. But the seams of the girdle inclosed matters far more interesting to Max than the ammunition with which the pouch was stored. There were letters from some of the leading Tories in Albany, who, as is now well known, maintained throughout the war a secret correspondence, which the sagacious Schuyler, in order to avail himself of the intelligence from

Canada thus procured, wisely permitted to go forward so long as he could successfully counterplot with these subtle traitors. These papers were, of course, to be forwarded at once to the Committee of Safety at Albany. But there were also letters relating to private matters which awakened a deeper personal interest in Greyslaer, and whose contents he did not feel called upon himself to communicate, save to the parties immediately interested. One of them was from the famous Joe Bettys to Bradshawe himself; and the heart of Greyslaer thrilled within him as he read the following passage:

> Wolfert will do all that is necessary among our friends in the Valley. The business on hand in this district will not allow us both to leave it. The best rallying-point is somewhere among the Scotch clearings north of the Mohawk. The Cave of Wane-onda, you may depend upon it, will never do; and that for more reasons than one. Your revival of that c——d D. R. affair must have made it more or less notorious. How the devil did that wench slip through your fingers? Valtmeyer has explained the matter to me a dozen times, but I cannot understand it. Zounds! I would like to make an honest woman of that mettlesome hussy myself. But your claim must ever prevent her becoming Mistress Joe Bettys. By the way, Wat, did she ever suspect who played the parson's part in the beginning of that wild business? The jade must someday know how much she is beholden to me; but the secret, I need hardly tell you, is safe until the endorsement of a genuine black-coat shall make all things secure. Had you been the man I took you for, the girl would have gone on her knees to ask for it before you ever let her escape from Waneonda. But to return, &c.

Greyslaer could read no further. The characters swam before his eyes; his senses became dizzied; and were it not for the support of the workbench against which he leaned, he must have fallen to the ground. It was but for an instant, however, that he was thus unmanned, and it were impossible to say what feeling predominated in the conflicting emotions which for that first moment overwhelmed him; though a wild joy, an eager and confident hope prompted his next movement, as, calling in an agitated voice for his horse, he waited not for Hans to pass out of the door, but, brushing almost rudely past him, threw himself into the saddle, and galloped off in the direction of the Hawksnest.

The astounded smith stood listening for a few moments to his horse's footfalls as they rapidly died away in the distance, shook his head, and touched his forehead significantly, as if he feared that all were not right with his young friend; then slowly withdrawing into his shop, he shot the bolt behind him, extinguished the fires, and, taking up the outlaw's belt, which he paused to examine again for a moment, passed through a side wicket into a log cabin which adjoined the shed, and constituted his humble dwelling.

Greyslaer, before reaching the Hawksnest, was challenged by the party of his friends whom he met returning from their evening visit, and whose approach, though the young officers rode gayly along, talking and laughing with each other, he did not notice till he was in the midst of them. A few hurried words, suggesting on their part that he must have forgotten something of importance, and implying upon his that he would overtake them before they reached the garrison, was all that passed between them as he brushed impatiently by.

The family had all retired when he reached the home stead; but a light still burned in Alida's apartments. He threw his rein over the paling, and, after trying the outer door in vain, stepped back from the verandah, and looked to the only window through which the light appeared. The curtain was drawn, but a shadow, which ever and anon fell across it, showed that the inmate of the chamber had not yet sought her repose. It was with Alida alone that he must secure an interview; and Max, in the agitation of his spirits, did not hesitate at the first means which presented themselves. There was on that side of the house a porch, with a balcony over it, having a single window cut down to the floor. This window opened into Alida's dressing-room, which communicated with her bed chamber. Greyslaer clambered to the top of the balcony, and tapped against the panes of glass in the moment that the light was extinguished.

"Fear not," he said, "it is I, Max Greyslaer. I come with tidings of such import to you that I could not sleep before possessing you of them."

Alida, hastily throwing a loose wrapper around her person, opened the casement. "Heavens! Captain Greyslaer," she exclaimed, "what urgent peril can have my brother Derrick, it is not of him—"

"No, no, no peril—nothing of Derrick—undo the door below—it is of you—it is your concerns alone which have brought me here at this untimely hour."

"Is the matter, then, so pressing? Can we not wait till morning?"

said Alida, in strange agitation.

"I cannot trust it till the morrow. I cannot sleep, I must not move from near you, till you hear it."

"Speak it out at once, then, Max, for my poor nerves will not bear this suspense," said Alida, with increasing tremor of voice.

"I cannot speak it all; I must have light to reveal it by. See here this written paper, Alida."

"And what does it say?" she replied with forced calmness. "Tell me, Max Greyslaer; if it be good or evil, I had rather receive it from your lips than from any other source."

"Heaven bless you for those words. My tidings are far from evil, yet I scarce know how to break them to you. There was a bird—do you remember it, Alida, one day in years gone by? a bird that we watched together as it sat crouched upon the lowest bough of yonder chestnut, while a hawk long hovered mid the topmost branches; it seemed withering in the shadow of those ill-omened wings. A chance shot from Derrick at a distance frighted the falcon from his perch of vantage; but the besieged songster also fell to the ground at sound of the report which drove his enemy from his stooping-place, and seemed like to perish, when you caught up the little trembler and cherished him in your bosom."

"Oh! Max, what mean these wild words, spoken at such a time?" said Alida; for this fanciful allusion seemed so unsuited to the earnest purposes of the moment, and was so unlike the wonted manly directness of Greyslaer's mind, that, coupled with his agitated manner and the other strange circumstances of the interview, Alida was shocked for the moment with the apprehension that his brain might be disordered.

"Nay, but they are not unmeaning, if you will but interpret them, Alida! Have *you* not sat thus beneath the withering wing of sorrow? Have you not been ruthlessly hawked at, and made the prey of villainy the most hideous? And has not chance, or God's own providence call it rather, brought the hour of relief, which is come even now?"

"Is *he* dead, then?" whispered Alida, clasping her hands, as a light seemed to break in upon her from Greyslaer's words.

"Dead? ay!—no, not that; but he is to you as if he never lived. They deceived you, Alida; the supposed ties which so manacled your soul have never yet had an existence; it was a false marriage, a fiend-like and most damnable contrivance to destroy you. Look not so doubtful and bewildered. I have the written evidence of what I say! Alida,

247

dearest Alida, speak—speak and tell me that you doubt not. It is I, Max Greyslaer, who always loved, and never yet deceived you; it is I—"

But Alida was mute and motionless. Her tottering knees had failed to support her, though she clung to the dressing-table near which she stood for support. Greyslaer quickly passed through the window, and, catching her fainting form from the floor, bore her out to the balcony. Supporting her there on one knee, he anxiously chafed her pulses, while the refreshing breeze of night, playing through the long tresses which dropped over her shoulders, aided in reviving his lovely burden.

It was a strange scene that which followed; nor could anyone, however familiar with the proud and wayward spirit of Alida, have divined how it would eventuate. A new crisis in her destiny was at hand; a double crisis, as it seemed from Greyslaer's last words of earnest affection. She was not prepared for either of them; and she endeavoured to avoid the last by overwhelming Max with gratitude for his disinterestedness.

"No. Miss de Roos, no." said Greyslaer, almost fiercely. "I will receive no gratitude, no thanks, no friendship at your hands. There is but one return such love as mine can accept, and if you give me not that we part forever."

"Oh why, kindest of friends, can we not still be to each other as we have been?"

"Alida," cried Max with wild emotion, "you would turn the madness of my nature against, itself."

"What madness? Oh, kind, good, noble Greyslaer, be not so excited."

"Woman, you will infuriate me. I am neither of these. Whatever there seems of good in me springs from my love of you, Alida;" and the tones in which he now pronounced her name thrilled through her very spirit. "Alida, thou knowest that my devotion to you was a madness! Beautiful, oh, bewilderingly beautiful as thou art, what other man breathing, had he known what I know, or believed what I believe, would have lavished his worship on such an idol—would have consecrated his manhood to misery, and left his age without a solace? It was madness in me."

"Could I help it?" gasped Alida, now deadly pale.

"No, you could not," said Max, with a smile of bitter pride; "it was a devotion self-lavished from the fullness of my soul, not wrung from it by the imperious exaction of yours."

"And you believe, Greyslaer," said the girl with a flush of generous disdain, "that I would turn this noble weakness of your nature—if weakness indeed it be—that I would turn it against yourself?"

"Believe it?—I know it," answered Max with eye of open frankness but lip compressed with stern determination.

"Am I so mean of soul then, in Captain Greyslaer's opinion?" said Alida, with flashing eye.

But Greyslaer quailed not, though his voice was hoarse with suppressed emotion, as he replied, "You are a woman, Alida all,—all of woman, or these hungry veins had not wasted in consuming passion for you." The girl trembled, and he paused and pressed his folded arms upon his bosom, as if keeping down emotion, and then, with gaze fixed upon her, and clear, slow enunciation, went on. "You are a woman, and fond of power as are all your sex. You have lived of late, for months, amid its triumphs. Unscathed by one jealous pang, I even joyed to see you thus forget your sorrows; but it was amid your sorrows that I remained your slave."

"I can never be too grateful," said Alida tearfully.

"Grateful! grateful!" responded Max with scorn.

"Indeed, most grateful," repeated Alida with something of demureness.

"Woman, you shall not thus foil me," cried her lover, while his broad brow glistened with the white heat of transcendent passion, illuminating it from within. "You love me, Alida, you know it, you feel it. You dare not look into your heart's core, and say there is not there a love as boundless, an affection as infinite as my own. But you would cover it up—yes, you would cover up the tide of sympathy that surges your soul toward mine, till deep should answer to deep, in exhaustless, never-wearying tenderness."

Alida trembled like an aspen, and Max hesitated. She recovered, and, in reply to a haughty bend of the head, he, under the still haughtier influence of tyrannic passion, went on: "You would—you would stifle, you would turn aside God's blessed current of true emotion—you would forget all—deny all, to me—to yourself deny it. And why?"

"And why, sir?"

"Because, in your unconscious, secret, self-willed arrogance of heart, you would turn the mad devotedness of my nature against itself, and still in your prosperity, drink up the wild homage I gave you in adversity, until my defeated life should be numbered among the triumphs of your woman's power. And then, self-idolizing girl, while

I withered for thee, thou wouldst call thy soul-defrauding ministry, 'Friendship.'"

"Oh God! am I such a thing as that?" cried Alida, borne down by the impetuosity of her lover.

"Alida—noble Alida," said Max, now deeply affected, but still firm, "you are that woman—your lonely wrestling with a terrible sorrow at one time, your reckless efforts to dissipate it at another, have thus made you, un consciously, self-absorbed."

"Oh, Max! I am most unworthy of your love."

"Unworthy? Hear me, Alida; without you I were companionless amid my kind for ever; but I accept your companionship upon no terms of gratitude, of friendship, of sisterly communion. Mine you are; mine you must be; mine—all mine; mine in your heart, in your spirit, in your affections, in your pride—in all the rich abundance of a glorious nature that God sent here for me to idolize in that form of loveliness."

"And could you—could you then leave me, Max, if I do not thus acknowledge thee?"

She spoke these words in a low appealing tone. A convulsive tremor shook the sinewy form of the young soldier as he replied with solemn emphasis:

"God only knows if I *can* give thee up and live. But *I* know that I *will* if here—under these stars tonight—thy soul does not make true and full answer unto mine. I will leave thee, and forever."

"And then we should both be miserable."

The words were few, and she pronounced them calmly like a simple truism; but they told the whole tale of a common sympathy, they acknowledged the full law of a common destiny between them; and she did not with draw her own hand, nor recoil from the light touch of his arm, as Max circled her waist in kneeling.

The moon, which was in its last quarter, at this moment cast above the trees the golden light she loves to shed in waning. The mellow beam caught the eyes of Alida, and a tear—the first tear of affection Max had ever seen her shed—trembled upon their lids as she turned from that soft harbinger of happier days to the soulful face of her lover. The impulse was resistless which made Greyslaer, in that moment, snatch her to his bosom. "Yes, dearest Max, I am yours:" are not those the words she murmurs in reply to the unutterable tenderness of his mute caress?

She paused: and in that pause there was an Elysian moment for them both. But in another instant Alida extricated herself from his embrace; and though she suffered him still to retain her hand, her voice was yet painfully constrained and altered as she spoke what follows.

"Ah! Greyslaer, I fear me this flood of happiness has come in too quickly to last for either of us. That paper may be—nay, look not thus hurt—I doubt not that it contains sufficient to produce entire conviction in your mind as well as mine; for, had it not been for the deep reliance I place upon your judgment, Max—a judgment so far beyond your years—I should never have betrayed the feelings you have beheld this night. But, whatever be the fate of the regard I bear you, Greyslaer, you have won it, and it is yours. No, never would I recall this hour." Max mutely pressed her hand to his lips, and she went on. "But it is a strange and dark story of which we have now the threads in our hands, and I shudder with the fear that, deeming too quickly we have unravelled it all, there may be others interwoven with it not so easy to disentangle. My name must be cleared, not only to your satisfaction, Greyslaer, but to that of all who have ever heard its sound, before I will change it for yours; and in these troubled times it is long before I can hope for such a result."

"Your name, Alida! None have ever, none dare ever, connect that with dishonour. Your name! Why. this terrible secret has been so kept from the world, that I never dreamed of mystery attending you till you yourself revealed that there was one."

"Yes, in the class with which we have most mingled, my story is but little known; but there must be many of the country people of a different grade, though worthy of respect as those who sometimes pretend to engross it all, who cannot but have heard of it; and I would not have the simplest rustic cherish a memory that can do irreverence to the wife of Greyslaer. Let us wait, dearest Max; wait till time—till chance, which has already done so much for me, shall determine still farther. Till then, affianced to you in soul Alida will still remain; and whate'er betide, she will never be another's."

Greyslaer, who knew too well the character of Alida to remonstrate against her purpose when settled, determined at least to defer whatever he had to urge against her resolution until a more propitious season. Besides, with a lover's thoughtful consideration, he feared that the night air might blow too chilly upon the loosely-arrayed person of Alida to render it safe to protract the interview. They parted—not with the prolonged caressing *adieux* of newer and happier lovers, but when the hand which Greyslaer was loath to release trembled in his pressure as he bade farewell, he stooped to print a salute upon the pale cheek which was not withdrawn from him; and in the next instant, seizing her to his bosom as if she would grow there, his lips met hers in one long kiss, as if each then drank in the other's soul forever.

And now, good steed, thou bearest a different man upon thy back from him who has thrice already guided thee over the same road to-night. The stern and disappointed man that, with firm hand and even rein, bent his twilight course hither; the moody and abstracted lover that loitered homeward at a fitful pace; the wild-riding horseman, who spurred ahead, as if each moment were of importance to solve the riddle he had already read—were not each and all of these a different being from the buoyant cavalier who now, with ringing bridle, gallops gayly over hill and dale, leaning forward now to pat thy glossy neck and speak cheering words of encouragement, and now rising in the stirrup as if his happy spirit vaulted upward at each gallant bound beneath him? Surely there is a music in the good horse's motions which times itself ever to our mood, whate'er the changes be.

Alas! many were the changes of mood that Greyslaer was yet doomed to know ere the story of his strange loves was ended. But of the delay that sickens hope, the doubt that withers it; of the chilling thoughts, the shadowy fears of the future, he dreamed not, cared not now, more than he did for the clouds which crept over the skies and obscured the path before him. His mind was filled with but one idea, which excluded all others. He knew—what once to know or once to believe, in that first hour of belief or knowledge, makes all the world a Paradise around—*He knew that he was BELOVED.*

Shall we pause to paint the next interview between Max and Alida—when the happy lover won from her lips the final words of her full betrothal to him? Shall we describe those which followed, when Max, with arguments she did not wish to answer, convinced her that there was now no real bar to their wedded happiness, and she yielded up all thought of seeking redress for her wrongs, save through him who was shortly to become the rightful guardian of her honour; to the friend who had already become dearer to her than her life? Shall we tell how the softening influence of love gradually melted the Amazonian spirit of her earlier day, until the romantic dream of retribution, which had so sternly strung the soul of the once haughty Alida, became lost at last in the loving woman's tender fears lest Bradshawe, now so far removed from the vengeance of her lover, should yet cross his path? Shall we dwell upon the transports of feeling which agitated the soul of Max, now burning with impatience to exact such retribution, and now absorbed in a wild confusion of delight as the day approached which should make Alida his forever?

Or shall we rather describe his chafing vexation and her mute forebodings when the call of military honour, abruptly summoning him away to distant and dangerous duty, deferred that blessed expectation of their union to a period which the fearful chances of civil war only could determine?

Shall we follow the patriot soldier in his bright career of achievement, as, courted and caressed by the glowing eyes and chivalrous spirits of the South, he measures his sword with the boldest of his country's invaders, or mingles with few superiors in council among the noblest of his country's defenders? Shall we survey him in that broader field of action, where the indulgence of personal animosity and schemes of vengeance against a low adventurer like Bradshawe are forgotten and swallowed up in the more general and nobler interests that press upon him; but where the image of Alida is still as dear to his mind as when last he waved a reluctant adieu to his native valley?

But no, young Max, it is not for us to track the meteor windings of thy soldierly career amid those thrilling scenes which *Lee, Sumter, Pickens, Marion,* and *Tarlton* their gallant foe, have since immortalized in guerilla story, and made the heritage of other names than thine. The record of thy exploits is fully chronicled, mayhap, in one true heart only, and that grows daily sadder as it counts the hours of thy absence and dreams of the friend who is far away.

BOOK FIFTH
INVASION

Then comes a power
Into this kingdom, who already,
Wise in our negligence, have secret feet
In some of our best ports, and are at point
To show their open banner.

King Lear.

The fatal Time
Cuts off all ceremonies and vows of love
And ample interchange of such discourse
Which so long sundered friends should dwell upon.

Richard III.

On the stage
Of my mortality my youth hath acted
Some scenes of vanity, drawn out at length
By varied pleasures, sweeten'd in the mixture,
But tragical in issue.

The Broken Heart.

Thus to rob a lady
Of her good name is an infectious sin
Not to be pardoned.
Be it false as hell,
'Twill never be redeemed if it be sown
Among the people, fruitful to increase
All evils they shall hear.

Love Lies A-Bleeding.

How has kind Heaven adorn'd the happy land,
And scatter'd blessings with a wasteful hand!
But what avail her unexhausted stores,
Her blooming mountains, and her sunny shores,
With all the gifts that Heaven and Earth impart,
The smiles of nature and the charms of art,
While proud oppression in her valleys reigns
And tyranny usurps her happy plains?

Addison.

CHAPTER 1

Rangers' Revels

Round with the ringing glass once more,
Friends of my youth and of my heart,
No magic can this hour restore;
Then crown it ere we part.

Ye are my friends, my chosen ones,
Whose blood would flow with fervour true
For me; and free as this wine runs,
Would mine, by Heaven! for you.

                                Hamilton Bogart.

A year has passed away—the second year of the Revolution—and Greyslaer is not nearer the fruition of his hopes than in the hour when they first dawned anew upon his soul. The calls of military duty have, in the meantime, carried him far from his native valley, to which, with a sword whose temper has been tried on many a Southern field, he is now returning; for New York at this moment needs all her children to defend her soil. Burgoyne upon the Hudson, and St. Leger along the Mohawk, are marching to unite their forces in the heart of the province, and sweep the country from the lakes to the seaboard.

The ascendency which, upon the first outbreak of hostilities, the Whigs of Tryon county attained over the opposite faction, seemed, at this period of the great struggle, about to be wrenched from their hands. The conspiring bands of Tories which had been driven out or disarmed when Schuyler marched upon Johnstown and crushed the first rising of the royalists, had lifted the royal standard anew upon the border, and rumours of the thousands who were flocking to it struck dismay into the patriot councils. Brant and his Mohawks had always kept the field in guerilla warfare, and the frontiersmen were habituated to the terror of his name; but now Guy Johnson, who had been stirring up the more remote tribes, was said to have thickened his files with a cloud of savage warriors. The combined Indian and refugee forces had rendezvoused at Oswego, thoroughly armed and appointed for an efficient campaign; and Barry St. Leger, who took command of the whole, boasted confidently that he would effect a conjunction with Burgoyne, if that leader could make good his march upon Albany.

Availing himself of the numerous streams and lakes of the country to transport his artillery and heavy munitions, St. Leger advanced with forced marches from the wilds of the north and the west, and, penetrating into the Valley of the Mohawk, invested Fort Stanwix, the portal of the whole region beyond the Hudson. The province far and wide was alarmed at this bold and hitherto successful invasion; and some of the sturdiest patriots of Tryon County stood aghast at the incoming torrent which threatened to overwhelm them. But the anxiety of the mass was more akin to the alarm that rouses than to the terror which paralyzes action. There was a spirit abroad among the people; a spirit of determined resolve, of vengeful hatred against those who had come back to desolate the land with fire and sword. Sir John Johnson, who stood high in the councils of the invading general, had approached the threshold of his forfeited patrimony; but the arrogant though brave baronet, had he penetrated as far as the broad domain over which his family once exercised an almost princely sway, would have found that strange changes had taken place among his rustic and once humble neighbours.

The march of armies, the pomp and parade of martial times, with many of the dark incidents of civil feud shad owing the pageantry of regular warfare, had been beheld in the Valley of the Mohawk, and the lapse of a short two years had markedly altered the character of the district in which the principal scenes of our story are laid. The inhabitants no longer gathered together in village or hamlet to reason calmly about their rights, and pass formal resolutions upon the conduct of their rulers. The reckless assertion, the hot and hasty reply, the careless laugh or fierce oath which cut short the laggard argument, showed that men's tempers had altered, and the times of debate had long since given way to those of action.

The soldier had taken the place of the civilian; the military muster supplanted the political assemblage; and the plain yeomanry of a rural district were no longer recognizable in the gay military groups that seemed to have usurped their place at the roadside inn. And when the proclamation of the commandant of the district summoned every male inhabitant capable of bearing arms to the field, the highways were filled with yeomanry corps, battalions of infantry, volunteers from the villages, and squadrons of mounted rangers from the remote settlements, all urging their way to the general rendezvous at Fort Dayton.

Hitherward, too, occasionally, intermingled with these raw levies, were likewise marching bodies of experienced partisan troops, which, as the scene of war shifted from one part of the northern frontier to another, had kept the field from the first. Armed and trained to serve as either cavalry or infantry, the "Mohawk Yaegers," as they called themselves, were found acting now as videttes and foraging parties for the Congressional forces; fighting now by themselves with the Indians in guerilla conflict, and now again co-operating with the Continental army in regular warfare. The public house of Nicholas Wingear, which lay immediately upon the road to Fort Dayton, was at this time a favourite stopping-place of refreshment with the different corps which composed this motley army, and a small command had halted there for the night at the time we resume the thread of our story.

The old stone-built inn, with its ruined sheds and out houses of half-hewn logs, which used to stand somewhere about midway upon the road between Canajoharie and German Flats, has probably long since given place to some more modern hostelry. Mine ancient host, too, the worthy Deacon Wingear—unless the flavour of his liquor lives in the memory of some octogenarian toper—is perhaps likewise forgotten. It is not less our duty, however, to chronicle his name here while opening this act of our drama beneath the hospitable roof of Nicholas.

The apartment in which the ranger corps were carousing was large and rudely furnished, containing only—besides the permanent fixture of a bar for the sale of liquors, which was partitioned off under the staircase at one end of the room—a small cherry-wood table and a few rush-bottomed chairs as its customary movables. Temporary arrangements seemed, however, to have been lately made for a greater number of guests than these would accommodate. An oaken settle had been brought from its place in the porch, and arranged, with several hastily-constructed benches, around a rude substitute for a dining-table, formed by nailing a pair of shutters upon a stout log placed upright upon the floor; the convenience being eked out in length by some unplaned boards resting upon an empty cask or two.

The rudeness of this primitive banqueting furniture could hardly be said to be smoothed away by a soiled and crumpled tablecloth which scantily concealed less than half of its upper surface. It appeared, however, to answer the purpose with the bluff campaigners who were now seated around it, filling beaker after beaker from a huge pewter flagon which rapidly circulated around the board. Nor did they, while making the most of these ungainly appliances for their comfort, envy the burly and selfish lounger who occupied and monopolized two or three of the chairs, as well as the smaller and neater table in one corner of the apartment. Of this privileged and loutish individual we shall speak hereafter. A heavy black patch covered one of his eyes; but the curious glances which he with the other ever and anon cast upon the carousing soldiery would appear to intimate that they were worthy of a more minute description than we have yet given of them.

Their stacked arms and knapsacks flung carelessly in the corners might indicate that they were only some fatigue party of militia that had stopped here for refreshment; or it might be a detachment from some larger body of light troops which had halted for the night upon their march through the country. The absence of all military etiquette, and the free and equal tone of their intercourse, as they sat all drinking at the same board, would imply that they were only privates of some volunteer company of foot. And yet, if his sabre and spurs were wanting, there was still that in the appearance as well as the equipments of more than one of their number which would anywhere have distinguished him from the common soldier of a marching regiment, much more from an ordinary militia-man. His looks were too intelligent for those of a mere human machine, accustomed only to act in mechanical unison with others. His features were earnest, but not rigid. His air was martial, but yet not strictly military. It betrayed the schooling of service rather than the habit of discipline. It bespoke the soldier, who had been made such by circumstances rather than by the drill sergeant. In a word, it was the air of a guerilla, and not of a regular.

But listen; the partisan grows musical in his cups. There is a grave pause in his wild wassail; he has linked hands with his comrades; and now, with one voice, they raise their battle hymn together. It is that half-German gathering song which, in the days of the Revolution, used to stir the Teuton blood of "The old Residenters," as the men of the Mohawk called themselves.

1

Raise the heart, raise the hand,
Swear ye for the glorious cause,
Swear by Nature's holy laws
To defend your fatherland!
By the glory ye inherit,
By the deeds that patriots dare,
By Columbia's freedom, swear it:
By YOUR COUNTRY this day swear!
Raise the heart, raise the hand,
Fling abroad the starry banner,
Ever live our country's honour,
Ever bloom our native land.

2

Raise the heart, raise the hand,
Let the earth and heaven hear
While the sacred oath we swear,
Swear to uphold our fatherland!
Wave, thou lofty ensign glorious,
Floating foremost in the field;
While thine eagle hovers o'er us
None shall tremble, none shall yield.
Raise the heart, raise the hand,
Fling abroad the starry banner,
Ever live our country's honour,
Ever bloom our native land.

3

Raise the heart, raise the hand,
Raise it to the Father spirit,
To the Lord of Heaven rear it,
Let the soul tow'rd HIM expand!
Truth unwavering, faith unshaken,
Sway each action, word, and will;
That which man hath undertaken,
Heaven can alone fulfil.
Raise the heart, raise the hand,
Fling abroad the starry banner,
Ever live our country's honour,
Ever bloom our native land.

The solitary lounger, who sat aloof from the soldiers, exhibited every sign of boorish impatience short of being directly offensive, as each new verse followed the repetition of the chorus from the other table. He was a strong-featured, bull-necked fellow, whose slouched drab beaver, huge loaded whip, and blanket-cloth overcoat indicated the occupation of a teamster or drover. A pipe and pot of beer had been placed before him while the soldiers were in the midst of their song; with whose soothing luxury he seemed not fully content, however, judging by the growling impatience with which, ever and *anon*, he now asked about some toasted cheese that it appeared was preparing for him in the kitchen. His remarks were addressed to mine host, a thin-faced, lank-haired worthy, in a complete suit of black velveteen, who stood behind the bar with slate in hand, ready to make any addition to his reckoning at the first call for replenishing the jorum of the soldiers; and partly to a tight lass that glided to and fro through the room, on the alert to receive the orders of the company.

"Why, Tavy, gal," said the drover, "I shall have drank up all my ale before that cheese is forthcoming. Your mammy ought to be able to toss up such a trifle at five minutes' notice. I must ride far tonight and that right soon, to overtake my cattle, which must be driven to Fort Dayton before breakfast tomorrow. And here one moment—I would tell you something, my pretty Tavy."

"Octavia—Sarah—Ann," cried a shrewish female voice from the kitchen.

"Go, Tavy, my good girl, to your mother," said mine host, evidently uneasy to get the girl out of the way of the cheese customer. "Your call shall be obeyed in a moment, worthy sir; only have a little patience. We are anything but strong-handed in this house just now. My son Zachariah went off with the Congress soldiers yesterday, and Scotch Angus stole away to join the king's people last week. The niggers are all sorting the horses that came in tonight, and my good woman has no one to split a stick for her till Zip comes in from the stable."

"Well, Bully Nick, you might have spared all that long palaver if you had left spry-tongued Tavy to tell me the same thing in three words, instead of squinting and blinking to her to clear out, as you did just now. Hark ye, Nicholas, I would say a word to you ;" and the man, whose lawless features put on a scowl, as if some angry thought had struck him, beckoned to the innkeeper to approach near enough for them to exchange a whisper together. But this mark of confidence Wingear seemed sedulously to avoid; and the traveller, at last rising abruptly from his seat, strode up to the bar, and flinging down his reckoning, stalked out of the apartment; not, however, before he had leaned over the counter, and catching the shrinking Nicholas by the collar of his coat, muttered in his ear,

"I see you know me, worthy Nick! and, seeing that you do, I've half a mind to split your weasand for fighting so shy of an old acquaintance. *Schinos!* breathe but a syllable to this rebel gang, and I'll roast you and your household among these rotten timbers before morning. Remember! I have an eye upon you, even among that batch of fools yonder."

"I say, deacon," cried one of the *Yaegers*, as the inn keeper, stooping down behind the bar, as if busied in arranging something, managed thus to conceal the terror which this formidable speech had inspired, "I say, deacon, my boy, who the devil's that surly chap who's just left us?"

"That's more than I can tell you, Captain de Roos," replied Wingear, with difficulty mastering the trepidation into which he had been thrown, and still averting his face as he plied his towel industriously along the shelves over which he leaned. "The man's in the cattle business, I believe, sir, as he talked of driving some critturs to Fort Dayton for the troops there."

The officer paused for a moment in mere idleness of thought, as it seemed from the intentness with which he watched the smoke-wreaths from his mouth curling up ward toward the rafters; and then knocking the ashes from his segar, he resumed abruptly, before replacing it in his lips,

"Did you ever see anything of Wolfert Valtmeyer in these parts, Nicky?"

"Oh yes, sir," answered Octavia, who that moment entered with a fresh flagon from the cellar; "he stopped here about harvest time two years ago with Mr. Bradshawe, just as the troubles were beginning. They went off in a hurry; folks said because old Balt the hunter came down here to look after their doings."

"You are mistaken, Tavy," said her father, uneasily; "Bradshawe and the drover—and Valtmeyer I mean—put down the pitcher, gal, and don't stand gaping at me so. The drover and Brad—I mean Wolfert—"

"You mean! and what the devil do you mean?" said the soldier, turning round fiercely, and fixing a stern eye upon the innkeeper. "Keep a straight tongue between your teeth, Nick, or you may wish it bitten off when too late."

The abashed publican, quailing beneath the penetrating glance of De Roos, was glad of any excuse for remaining silent, while the other, addressing the girl, thus pursued his inquiries:

"And so, my pretty Tavy, you saw Valtmeyer about two years since, eh? About the time of Greyslaer's fight, wasn't it?"

"Yes, sir, either just before or just after Brant carried off Miss Alida."

The features of the gay soldier darkened as she spoke; but quickly resuming his air of unconcern, he continued his questions by asking,

"What kind of a looking fellow was Wolfert then? Did he bear any resemblance to the drover that was here but now?"

"He was about as tall as the drover, sir, but not so fleshy. When the drover had his back turned I almost mistrusted it was Mr. Valtmeyer; but then the drover was much younger and rounder-faced, and, in spite of the black patch over his eye, altogether more likely looking than Mr. Valtmeyer, who looked mighty homely with his great sprangly beard, he did;" and the girl smoothed down her apron, and cast a glance over her shoulder at a bit of looking-glass stuck against a post of the bar, as if she questioned the taste of the unshorn Wolfert in having by his toilet shown such indifference to her charms.

"He was thinner, and wore a long beard, eh? a razor and good quarters would easily make all the difference," soliloquized De Roos. "But the impudent scoundrel would scarcely dare thus to put his head in the lion's mouth. Yet I must have an eye to the puritanical curmudgeon that this simple lass has the courtesy to call father." And then resuming aloud, he added, "Did your father ever know—"

"Octavia—Sarah—Ann," interrupted the shrill voice from the kitchen.

"Curse the *beldam!*" muttered De Roos, as the nuisance was instantly repeated.

"Octavia—Sarah—Ann, come take this toasted cheese to the cattle merchant."

"Yes, mother, yes, I'm coming! Had you any more questions to ask me, captain?"

"Go, gal, go," growled old Wingear, in a low voice. "You are too fond, young missus, of keeping here among the sogers."

"Any more questions? no—stay one moment, sweet Tavy, my blooming Tavy. Where got you those gay ribands which lace that bodice so charmingly?"

"Law, sir," replied the girl, bashfully retiring a step or two as the gallant soldier stretched out his hand as if to draw her near and examine the trim of her tasteful little figure more curiously; "law, sir, it's only the blue and buff, the Congress colours, you know, that old Balt brought me, with other fixings, from Schenectady."

"Octavia—Sarah—Ann, if ye're not here in the peeling of an inion, 'twill be the worse for you," screamed the virago mother.

"You see, captain, I *must* go."

"Zounds! what a tight ankle the girl has too," quoth the captain, as she tripped out of the apartment. "And so that queer quiz, old Balt, has induced her to mount the patriot colours! Well, I hope a finer riband will not induce her to change them for the blue and silver of 'The Royal New Yorkers,' as Johnson's motley gang call themselves. For 'Bold and true, in buff and blue, &c.;'" and the mercurial ranger strolled off to the stables, humming some verses of an old song, which was quickly taken up and echoed by his comrades.

Oh bold and true,
In buff and blue,
Is the soldier-lad that will fight for you,
In fort or field,
Untaught to yield
Though Death may close his story—
In charge or storm,
'Tis woman's form
That marshals him to glory;
For bold and true,
In buff and blue,
Is the soldier-lad that will fight for you.

In each fair fold
His eyes behold
When his country's flag waves o'er him—
In each rosy stripe,
Like her lip so ripe,
His girl is still before him.
For bold and true,
In buff and blue,
Is the soldier-lad that will fight for you.

"There he goes—God bless him—singing for all the world like a Bob-a-linkum on the wing—a crittur whose very natur it is not to keep still for a moment, and to make music wherever he moves."

"And what mare's nest has our singing bird found now, corporal?"

"Well, I don't know, sargeant; only, if the captain has got upon the trail of Wild Wolfert, as his words belikened, it would be a tall thing for us boys to seize that limb o' Satan, and carry him along with us to the German Flats."

"Ay, ay, it would indeed; but though our scouts would make us believe that both he and Bradshawe are snooping about the country among the Tories, I rather guess that they are both snug in St. Leger's lines before Fort Stanwix."

"No doubt, no doubt," said a trooper, rapping an empty flagon with the hilt of his sabre, as if tired of the discussion of so dry a subject. "Butler could never spare such an officer as Bradshawe at such a time as this."

"Yes," rejoined another, "and if he were really skulking about among the Tories, the hawk-eyed Willet must have lighted upon him while screwing his way through such a ticklish region to come down and alarm the lower country as he did."

"Come, lieutenant," cried one who had not yet spoken, "give us another song; and be it a merry or droll one, if it suits you; this is the last night we are to mess together like gentlemen volunteers. Tomorrow we shall be mustered with the old Continentals, and then the cursed etiquette of army discipline puts an end to all fun among us. It takes Captain Dirk a whole campaign to thaw out into a clever fellow after passing a week with his company in the regular lines; and as for you, Tom Wiley, who've sat the whole evening—"

"Spare me, worthy Hans; I hate to find myself under the command of a Congress officer as much as you do, only you know that, for the honour of the corps, we *Yaegers* should keep up the observances of military rank when acting with the government forces."

"That's a fact, boys," said the corporal. "What! would you have your free companies confounded with the common-draughted milishy, and laughed at by all the Continentals as *they* be? No, no; I may wince as much as any on ye when I feel the screws o' discipline first beginning to set tight, but I like to see our captain take airs upon himself with the best on 'em when it's for the honour of the corps. There now's the Refugee partisans that fight on their own hook just like ourselves—Johnson's Greens and Butler's Rangers, Tories though they be—toe the mark like raal sodgers upon a call of duty. Oh, you should have been in Greyslaer's company to see discipline, and that, too, jist when the war was breaking out; only ask Cornet Kit Lansingh, when the poor boy comes safe to hand again from that wild tramp of hisn! As sure as my name's Adam Miller, if Major Max ever comes back from the South—"

"It will be to haunt you, Adam, for prosing about these gloomy byegones instead of drinking your liquor. Major Greyslaer has been dead these six months, and his ghost ought to be laid by this time. As for poor Cornet Kit, the only service we can render him is to drink his memory all standing."

"Don't tell me that," said the corporal, his face reddening with indignation. "You can't riley me about the major. Tom Wiley; for, though folks would make out that he fell at Fort Moultrie, I knows what I knows about *him!* As for Kit Lansingh, you needn't waste liquor by drinking to his memory yet a while; for hasn't old Balt got scent of him clean off in the Genesee country? and aint he upon his living trail by this time with the friendly Mohegan that I myself heerd tell about having seen Kit with his own eyes among the Oneidas last winter?"

"What, Balt try to carry his scalp safely through the Seneca nation, not to mention the Onondagoes and Cayugas, through all of which he'll have to run the gauntlet before reaching the Genesee? Pshaw, man, the old hunter is as cold as my spurs long before this."

Though the reckless trooper spoke thus only for the sake of teasing his comrade, yet the partisan corporal was familiar enough with the dangers of the wilderness not to fear that what Wiley said was true. But, as if to shake off the ungrateful conviction, he emptied his beaker at a draught, shook his head, and was silent, while another of the *Yaegers* changed the subject by saying:

"Well, well, let's have Wiley's song. Come, Wiley, if it must be the last time we have a bout of free and equal fellowship like this together, just tune up something we can all join in."

The vocalist began to clear his throat, filled a bumper, threw himself back in his chair, and had got more than half through the usual preliminaries with which most pre tenders to connoisseurship chill and deaden the impulsive flow of festive feeling, (in instantaneous sympathy with which their song should burst forth if they mean to sing at all,) when he was suddenly superseded in his vocation.

"Tavy, my light lass! Tavy, my border blossom!" cried the gay voice of De Roos without; and then, as entering the room from one door, while the girl peeped shyly in from the other: "Come hither—hither, my flowering graft of a thorny crab; come hither, my peeping fawn, and learn news of the kind old forester who has always played the godfather to you. They have succeeded, boys. Kit Lansingh lives and thrives. Here's a messenger from Fort Dayton, bringing the news from Balt himself, now at that post. Carry on, carry on, and tell us your tidings; but hold, the poor fellow's athirst, perhaps. Wash the dust from his mouth with a cup of apple-jack, Adam, and then he'll speak."

The countryman, who, entering the room at the heels of De Roos, had cast a wistful eye upon the table from the first, advanced without saying a word, and tossed off the liquor which the corporal filled out for him, smacked his lips, wiped his mouth with his coat-sleeve, and thus delivered himself:

"All I have to say, gentlemen, is nothing more or less than what I was telling the capting here when he broke away from me like mad at the stable door; where, who should I first happen upon but the capting when I went to put up my pony, before looking round for him here. 'Is there anything astir among the people?' says the capting, says he, when I delivered him that note from Colonel Weston, which he holds in his hand, and which, if I don't make too bold, is an order—"

"Yes, yes, an order for me to move forward tonight. Carry on, man, carry on with your story," cried the impatient De Roos.

"Well, as I was saying, ' Is there anything astir?" says the capting, says he. 'Why, to be sure there is,' says I; 'and a mighty pretty stir it is, too,' says I. 'Hasn't old Balt got back from his wild tramp, and doesn't he bring the best of news for us in times as ticklish as these? I guess he does, though,' says I. 'There's the young chief Teondetha and a white man he rescued from the Cayugas, and took home among his people for safety, are coming down to help the country, with three hundred Oneida rifles at their backs,' says I; 'and didn't they send Balt a short cut ahead to warn our people not to move upon Fort Stanwix until they could have time to crawl safely round the enemy and join old Herkimer at the German Flats? To be sure they did,' says I; and then the capting, what does he do but, instead of hearing me out, he ups at once and asks me the name of the white man as furiously as if it was for dear life he spoke; and when I told him it was Mr. Christian Lansingh, the likely young nephew of old Balt, he tore away from me as if I had the plague; and I—I ups and follows at once to see the end of his doings; and there, now, gentlemen, you have the hull history o' the matter, so I'll jist put another drop o' liquor in this glass and drink sarvice to all on ye, not for getting that right snug young woman, whose colour has been coming and going like all natur while I told my story—meaning no offence whatever, miss."

"Offence to Tavy, my lad! no one suspects you of that. There are mettlesome chaps enough here to take care of her," said a soldier.

"Ay," echoed another, "she has a brother in every man in the troop."

"And she shall choose a husband among the best of ye, when the wars are over," cried De Roos. "But carry on, men, carry on; we must sound for the saddle in twenty minutes; and, unless you would leave your liquor undrunk, carry on, carry on."

"Ay, ay, fill round for our lust toast," said the serjeant, rising: "*War and woman*—wassail we've had enough of tonight—war and woman—the myrtle and steel."

"The myrtle and steel," echoed a dozen voices. "Your song, your song now, Wiley."

"War and woman—the myrtle and steel," shouted De Roos; and then, before the twice-foiled lieutenant could collect his wits for the occasion, the spirit of the wild partisan broke forth in the song with which we close this record of the rangers' revels.

1

One bumper yet, gallants, at parting,
One toast ere we arm for the fight;
Fill around, each to her he loves dearest—
'Tis the last he may pledge her! tonight.
Think of those who of old at the banquet
Did their weapons in garlands conceal,
The patriot heroes who hallowed
The entwining of Myrtle and Steel!
Then hey for the Myrtle and Steel,
Then ho for the Myrtle and Steel,
Let every true blade that e'er loved a fair maid,
Fill around to the Myrtle and Steel.

2

'Tis in moments like this, when each bosom
With its highest-toned feeling is warm,
Like the music that's said from the ocean
To rise in the gathering storm,
That her image around us should hover,
Whose name, though our lips ne'er reveal,

We may breathe through the foam of a bumper,
As we drink to the Myrtle and Steel.
Then hey for the Myrtle and Steel,
Then ho for the Myrtle and Steel,
Let every true blade that e'er loved a fair maid,
Fill around to the Myrtle and Steel.

3

Now mount, for our bugle is ringing
To marshal the host for the fray,
Where our flag to the firmament springing
Flames over the battle array:
Yet gallants—one moment—remember,
When your sabres the death-blow would deal,
That MERCY wears her shape who's cherished
By lads of the Myrtle and Steel.
Then hey for the Myrtle and Steel,
Then ho for the Myrtle and Steel,
Let every true blade that e'er loved a fair maid,
Fill around to the Myrtle and Steel.

CHAPTER 2

The Soldier's Return

Home of our childhood! how affection clings
And hovers round thee with her seraph wings!
Dearer thy hills, though clad in autumn brown,
Than fairest summits which the cedars crown;
Oh happy he, whose early love unchanged,
Hopes undissolved, and friendship unestranged,
Tired of his wanderings, still can deign to see
Love, hopes, and friendship centring all in thee.

Holmes.

It was a summer's evening, when Max Greyslaer, returning, after a long absence, to his native valley, left his tired horse at the adjacent hamlet, and hurried off on foot to present himself at the Hawksnest. The sun of a fiercer climate, not less than the unhealthy swamps of the South, had stolen the freshness from his cheek; and the arduous campaign in which he had lately signalized himself, had left more than one impress of its peril upon his manly front. But the heart of the young soldier was not less buoyant within him because conscious that the comeliness of youth had passed away from his scarred and sallow features. He had learned, before reaching its neighbourhood, that the beloved inmate of the homestead was well; and, breathing again the health-laden airs of his native north, he felt an elasticity of feeling and motion such as he had not known in many a long month before. The stern realities of life which he had beheld, not less than the active duties in which he had shared, had long since changed Max Greyslaer from a dreaming student into a practical-minded, energetic man; but his whole moral temperament must have been altered completely, if the scene which now lay around, and the circumstances under which

271

he beheld it, had not called back some of the thoughtful musings of earlier days.

The atmosphere, while slowly fading into the gray of evening, was still rich in that golden hue which dyes our harvest landscape. The twilight shadows lay broad and still upon the river which glided tranquilly between its overhanging thickets; but, while those on the further side were purpled with the light of evening, the warm hues of lingering sunset still played upon the canopy of wild vines which imbowered those that were nearer, touching here and there the top of a tall elm with a still ruddier glow, and bathing the stubble field on some distant hill in a flood of yellow light. But, lovely and peaceful as seemed the scene, there was something of sadness in the deep silence which hung over it.

The whistle of the ploughboy, the shout of the herdsman, the voices of home-returning boors loitering by the roadside to chat for a moment together when their harvest-day's work was over—none of these rustic sounds were there. The near approach of invasion had summoned the defenders of the soil away from their native fields, and the region around was almost denuded of its male inhabitants; infirm age or tender youth alone remaining around the hearths they were too feeble to protect. The deep bay of a house-dog was the first thing that reminded Greyslaer that some sentinels at least were not wanting to watch over their masterless homesteads.

The young officer, fresh from the animated turmoil of a camp-life, had ridden all day along highways bustling with the march of yeomanry corps, crowding into the main route from a hundred farm-roads and by-paths, all hastening toward the border, and the air of desertion in the present scene could not but strike him by the contrast. It was with a heart less light and a step less free than they were an hour before that he now wended his way among the shrubbery in approaching the door of the Hawksnest. The sound of music came from an open window in the wing which was nearest to him, and his heart thrilled in recognition of the voice of the singer as he paused to listen to a mournful air which was singularly in unison with his feelings at the moment. The words, which were Greyslaer's own, had, indeed, no allusion to his own story, but they had been thrown off in one of those melancholy moods when the imprisoned spirit of sadness will borrow any guise from fancy to steal out from the heart; and coming from the lips they did, they were now not less apposite to the passing tone of his mind than in the moment they were written.

1

We parted in sadness, but spoke not of parting;
We talked not of hopes that we both must resign,
I saw not her eyes, and but one teardrop starting
Fell down on her hand as it trembled in mine:
Each felt that the past we could never recover,
Each felt that the future no hope could restore;
She shuddered at wringing the heart of her lover,
I dared not to say I must meet her no more.

2

Long years have gone by, and the springtime smiles ever,
As o'er our young loves it first smiled in their birth.
Long years have gone by, yet that parting, oh! never
Can it be forgotten by either on earth.
The note of each wild-bird that carols toward heaven,
Must tell her of swift-winged hopes that were mine,
While the dew that steals over each blossom at even,
Tells me of the teardrop that wept their decline.

The song had ceased, but Greyslaer, before it was finished, had approached near enough to hear the sigh with which it ended; for how much of the past did not that single sigh repay him, even if his long account of affection had not been already balanced by the true heart that breathed it! In another moment Alida was folded to his bosom.

******

"My own Alida was hard to win, but most truly does she wear. Do I not know who was in your thoughts, beloved, in the moment that my rustling footsteps made you rush to the verandah to greet me?"

"I heard not your footsteps, I *felt* your presence, dearest Max; yet was I strangely sad in the instant before you came."

"And I, too, Alida, was sad, I scarce know why, save from that mysterious sympathy of soul with soul you have almost taught me to believe in. But now—"

"Now I know there should be no place for gloom, yet why, Max, should melancholy thoughts in the heart of either herald a moment of so much joy to both?"

Max, who had often playfully philosophized with her upon the tinge of superstition with which the highly imaginative mind of Alida was imbued, now attempted to smile away her apprehensive forebodings. But as she knew, in anticipation, that he was on his way to the seat of war, and could only have snatched this brief interview in passing to the post of peril, the task of cheering her spirits was a difficult one.

"Not," said she, rising and pacing the room, while her tall figure and noble air seemed to gather a still more queenly expression from the feelings which agitated her, "not that I would have the idle fears of a weak woman dwell one moment among your cares—for your mind, Max, must be free even of the thought of me when you go where men are matched in war or counsel against each other—but something whispers that this meeting, that this parting is—is what your own words, which I sung but now, may in spirit be prophetic of."

"Nay, nay, Alida," said Max, smiling, "that foolish song has already more than answered its purpose in serving to while away a lonely moment of yours, and I protest against my rhymes being perverted to such dismal uses. You may change your true knight into a faithful trouba dour or humble minstrel of your household, if you will; but I protest against your making him play the musty part of old 'Thomas the Rhymer,' merely because he has once or twice offended by stringing verses together."

"Why will you always jest so when I feel gravest?" said Alida, half reproachfully, as she placed her hand in that which gently drew her back to the seat which she had left by Greyslaer's side.

"It is gravity of mood, and not of thought, dearest, that I would fain banter away; for surely my Alida would not call these vain and idle fancies *thoughts?* Why should 1 deal daintily with things so troublous of her peace? Out upon them all, I say. The future has no cloud for us, save that which will continue to hover over thousands till peace return to the land; why should we study to appropriate more than our proper share of the general gloom? As for this Barry St. Leger," said Max, with increasing animation, "St. Leger is a clever fellow to have pushed his brigand crew thus far into the country; but gallant Gansevoort still holds him stoutly at bay, and if Herkimer and his militia fail to bring him to a successful account, we have fiery Arnold and his Continentals already on the march to beat up his quarters and drive the Tories back to Canada."

As the young soldier spoke, Alida caught a momentary confidence not less from the tone of his voice than from the look of his eye. The proud affection with which she now gazed upon the manly mien of her lover seemed more akin to her natural character than did the anxiety of feeling which again resumed its influence in her bosom;

an anxiety which continually, throughout the evening, lent a shade of sadness to her features, and which Greyslaer, remembering long months afterward, had but too much reason to think proceeded from one of those unaccountable presentiments of approaching evil which all have at some time known.

Since the memorable night when Greyslaer's providential discovery of the real position in which Alida stood toward Bradshawe had won from her the first avowal of her regard, this painful subject had been rarely alluded to by either; nor, closely as it mingled with the story of their loves, will it seem strange that a matter so delicate should be avoided by both in an interview like the present.

The joy of their first meeting had banished it alike from the hearts of either; and Alida, as the painful moment of parting grew nigh, could not bring herself to add to her present sorrows by recalling those which seemed all but passed away entirely, though their memory still existed as a latent cause of disquiet to herself. As for Max, his spirits seemed to have imbibed so much vigour and elasticity from the stirring life he had lately led, that it was almost impossible for Alida not to catch a share of the confidence which animated him. But though the state of the times and the duties which called Greyslaer to the field, and which might still for a longer period defer their union, seemed, as they conversed together, the only difficulties that obstructed their mutual path to happiness, there was in the heart of Alida a vague apprehension of impediments yet undreamed of and far less easy to be surmounted.

The moments of their brief converse were sweet, deliciously sweet to either; but the banquet of feeling was to Alida like the maiden's feast of the Iroquois legend. Her bosom was the haunted lodge, where ever and anon a dim phantom flitted around the board, and withered, with his shadow, the fruits and flowers which graced it.

In the meantime there was one little circumstance, which, calling up a degree of thoughtfulness, if not of pain in the mind of Greyslaer, would alone have impaired the full luxury of the present hour. Some household concerns had called Alida for a few minutes from the room in which they were sitting, and Max, to amuse himself in her absence, turned over a portfolio of her drawings which chanced to be lying upon a table near. The sketches were chiefly landscape views of the neighbouring scenery of the Mohawk, which is so rich in subjects for the pencil; but there were several studies of the head of a child interspersed among the rest, which, after the recurrence of the same features sketched again and again with more or less freedom and lightness, finally arrested the earnest gaze of Max as he viewed them at last in a finished drawing, which was evidently intended for a portrait. He felt certain that he had seen the face of that young boy before, yet when or where it was impossible for him to remember. There was an Indian cast in the physiognomy, which for a moment made him conceive that it must have been during his captivity among the Mohawks that he had seen the child. Yet, though a close observer of faces, he could recall no such head among the bright-eyed urchins he had often seen at play around his wigwam.

"I am puzzling myself, Alida," said he, as Miss de Roos returned to the room, "to remember where it is that I have seen the original of this portrait; for certain it is, the style of the features, if not the whole head, is perfectly familiar to me;" and Max, shading the picture partly with his hand, looked up for a moment as Alida approached him while speaking. "Good heavens!" he added, in a tone of surprise, "how much it resembles yourself as the light now falls on your countenance."

"Do you think so?" cried Alida; "that is certainly very odd. for I have always thought that poor little Guise bore a wonderful resemblance to my brother Derrick, notwithstanding his straight black Indian locks are so different from Dirk's bright curls. Your remark confirms the truth of the likeness I discovered between them; for Derrick and I, you know, were always thought to resemble each other."

"And who, if I may ask," rejoined Greyslaer, gravely, "is this 'poor little Guise,' who is so familiar a subject of interest to you?"

"Oh! I should have told you before of our little *protégé*, but my thoughts have been so hurried tonight," replied Alida, blushing. "You must know, then, that Derrick takes a vast interest in this forlorn little captive, who is neither more nor less than a grandson of Joseph Brant, that was left behind in an Indian foray when Derrick's band had driven back or dispersed his natural protectors."

"What, a childlike that accompany an expedition of warriors across the border! a child of Isaac Brant, too; for he, I believe, is the only married son of the chief! Who gave you this account, Alida?"

"Dear Max, you look grave as well as incredulous. I tell only what Derrick imparted to me when he brought that friendless boy hither, and begged me to assume the charge of him for a short season. I conjured my brother to return him to his people, but he would not hear of it. He only answered that, as the boy was an orphan whose mother had perished in the fray in which her child was taken, and whose father was off fighting on another part of the frontier, it was a mercy to keep him here. I saw Derrick for scarcely an hour at the time he made the re quest. He came galloping across the lawn with the child on the pommel of his saddle Before him; scarcely entered the house, except to exchange a joke or two with the old servants who crowded around him; took Guise with him to the stable to look at the horses, and then hurried off to join his troop, which, he said, had made a brief halt while passing through the country toward Lake George."

"And has he given you no further particulars since?"

"Not a word. He has written once or twice, inquiring how I liked his dusky pet, as he calls him; but he says not a word of his ultimate intentions in regard to him. It was only the other day that, in marching through from the Upper Hudson toward Fort Stanwix, he paid me a visit; but he stopped only to breakfast, and came as suddenly and disappeared almost as quickly as before; and though he caressed and fondled the child while here, yet, when I attempted to hold some sober talk with him about his charge, he only ran on in his old rattling manner, and said there was time enough to think of this when the St. Leger business was over."

"Can I see the child?" said Greyslaer, with difficulty suppressing an exclamation of impatience at the levity of his friend.

"He sleeps now, dear Max. He has been ill today, and when I left the room it was only to see whether or not the restlessness of my little patient had subsided into slumber."

"Does this picture bear a close resemblance to his features?" rejoined Max, taking up the drawing once more from the table.

"I cannot say that; yet I have tried so often, for my amusement, to take them, that I ought at least to have partially succeeded in my last effort. The wild, winning little creature is so incessantly in motion, though, that a far more skilful hand than mine might be foiled in the undertaking. But, Max, if you really feel such a curiosity about my charge, I must show him to you; wait but an instant till I return."

Alida, taking one of the lights from the table as she glided out of the room, reappeared with it, a moment afterward, in her hand. "Tread lightly, now," she said, "while following me, for he still sleeps most sweetly, and I would not have him disturbed for the world."

Greyslaer, who seemed to be actuated by some more serious motive than mere curiosity for holding this inquisition over the sleeping urchin, followed her steps without speaking. Alida, entering the dressing-room—into which, as the reader may remember, the eyes of her lover had once before penetrated—made a quick step or two in advance, and closed the door leading into the chamber beyond; then turning round, she pointed to a little cot-bedstead which seemed to have been temporarily placed there for greater convenience in attending upon her patient.

Max took the candle from her hand, and, shading the eyes of the infant sleeper with his broad-leaved beaver, bent over, as if in close scrutiny of its placid features; while Alida, touched by the sympathizing interest which her lover displayed in her charge, and dreaming not of the cause which prompted that interest, gazed on with a countenance beaming with sensibility. At first the deep sleep in which the child was plunged left nothing but the lovely air of infantile repose in its expression; but—whether from being stirred inwardly by dreams, or disturbed by the light which penetrated its fringed lids from without, or touched, perhaps, by the drooping plume with which the soldier shaded its brow—it soon began to move, to grasp the coverlet in its tiny lingers, and, turning over petulantly even in its slumbers, to work its features into something more of meaning.

It was a child of the most tender years; but, though scarcely four summers could have passed over its innocent head, the lineaments of another, less pure than it, were strongly charactered in its face. Something there was of Alida there, but far more of her wild and almost lawless brother. There seemed, indeed, what might be called a strong family resemblance to them both; but while the darker hue of Alida's hair might have aided in first recalling her image to him who gazed upon the sable locks of the Indian child, yet her noble brow was wanting beneath them; and the mouth, which earliest shows the natural temper, and which most nearly expresses the habitual passions at maturity—the mouth was wholly that of her wayward and reckless brother. The features were so decidedly European, that the tawny skin and the eyes, which were closed from Greyslaer's view, were all, he thought, that could proclaim an Indian origin for this true scion of the Mohawk chieftain's line, as Derrick had represented him to his sister.

"It is the mysterious instinct of blood, then, as well as the natural promptings of her sex's kindness, which has elicited Alida's sympathy for this wild offshoot of her house. But she should have a more considerate protector than this giddy brother, who, even in assuming the most sacred responsibility, must needs risk mixing up a sister's name with his own wild doings."

"You do not tell me what you think of my *protégé*," said Alida, as

278

Greyslaer, musing thus, was silent for a moment or two after they returned to the sitting-room. "I declare your indifference quite piques me. You have no idea of the interest poor forlorn little Guise excited when I took him with me to Albany on my last visit to our family friends there."

Max had it upon his tongue to ask her in reply if she thought that the child bore any resemblance to Isaac Brant, its reputed father, whom Alida must have seen in former years; but, at once remembering how closely that individual was connected with Bradshawe's misdeeds, he stifled the question, and, passing by her last observation as lightly as possible, changed the subject altogether. The whole matter, however, left a disagreeable impression upon him, and he was provoked at the importance it assumed in his thoughts, when, after the thrilling emotions of a lover's parting had passed away, it recurred again and again to his mind during his long walk back to the inn where he was to pass the night.

The dawn of the next morning found Greyslaer again upon the road toward Fort Dayton, where a pleasurable meeting with more than one old comrade awaited him, and where a military duty devolved upon him which, slight in its character as it first appeared, was destined, in its fulfilment, to have a most serious bearing upon his own happiness and that of Alida.

CHAPTER 3

The Conspirators

Euphion.   It now remains
To scan our desperate purpose. Senators,
Let us receive your views in this emergence;
Only remember, moments now are hours.

Colous.   For me, I hold no commerce with despair.
Your chances of success are multiplied;
Even now, while they expect your suppliant suit,
Pour out a flood of war upon their camp,
And crush them with its weight. Meanwhile, perhaps,
The imperial forces may fresh succour bring.

The reader has perhaps gathered from the interview between
Greyslaer and Alida last described, that the characters of both had undergone no slight change since the period when they were first introduced into our story: that Max, as the successful wooer and the travelled soldier who had seen the world, was a somewhat different being
from the visionary student, the fond-dreaming and willow-wearing
lover, whose romantic musings have heretofore, perhaps, called out,
at times, a pitying smile from the reader: that Alida, the once haughty
empress of his heart, whose pride, though utterly removed from ordinary selfishness, had still a species of self-idolatry as its basis, had been
not less affected in her disposition by the softening influences of love
and sorrow, and that patient realization of hope deferred which tam-
eth alike the heart of man or woman. Yet these changes were merely
those which time and circumstance will work in all of us, and Max
and Alida were still the same in every essential of character.

The change in Greyslaer was one that all men more or less under-
go as the sobering influence of riper years steals over them, and their

minds are brought more in contact with the practical things of life; when, having tested their powers in the world of action, the frame of the mind becomes, as it were, more closely knit and sinewy, and seeks objects to grapple with more substantial than the shadowy creations of the ideal world in which erst they dwelt. Now, while the success which had hitherto crowned the early career of Max Greyslaer alike in love and arms, was one of the most active elements in rapidly effecting this change from wild, visionary youth, to dignified, consummate manhood, the emotions and cares of Alida were precisely those which would dash the Amazonian spirit and humble the arrogance of self-sustainment in a proud and beautiful woman, once the petted inmate of a bright and happy home, and intrenched in all the advantages that family and station could confer.

The half-insane idea of righting in person the wrongs which she had received at the hands of Bradshawe, had been long since dispelled by the realization of more irremediable sorrows in the death of her nearest relations; and as her woman's heart awoke for the first time to the graces of woman's tenderness, and her spirit grew more and more feminine as it learned to lean upon another, she even shuddered at remembering the strange fantasy of revenge that was the darling dream of her girlhood. It is true, that in the hour of her betrothal to Greyslaer she had listened with the kindling delight of some stern heroine of romantic story to the deep-breathed vengeance of her lover against the man who had plotted her ruin. But as time wore on, and the fulfilment of the vow grew less probable from the prolonged exile of Bradshawe, which might ultimately result in total banishment from his native land; and as Max, who was soon afterward called away by his military duties to a distant region, grew more and more dear to her in absence, she gradually learned to shrink as painfully from the idea of a deadly personal encounter between him and Bradshawe, as she lately had from her own unfeminine dream of vengeance.

Nor had the views of Greyslaer, though affected by different causes from those which swayed Alida, altered less in this respect. Max, though his well-ordered mind was in the main governed by high religious principle, was certainly not in advance of those opinions of his day which held a fairly-fought duel as no very serious offence against Heaven; and indeed he had betrayed, upon more than one occasion, while serving with the hot-headed spirits of the South, that no scruple of early education interfered to prevent him from calling an offender to account after the most punctilious fashion of the times.

But, since he had mingled more among men of the world, he had learned enough of its customs to know that Bradshawe was rather a subject for the punishment of the criminal laws than for the chastisement of a gentleman's sword; and that, while wiping away an insult with blood was a venial offence according to the fantastic code to which, as a military man, he was now subject, to spill the same blood in cutting off a felon was unofficer-like indeed, as it was unchristianlike in spirit to thirst after it. These sentiments, which his camp associations had gradually, and almost unknowingly to himself, infused into the young soldier, were more than redeemed from trivial-mindedness by those more extended views of action which, growing up at the same time with them, merged the recollection of personal grievances in the public wrongs, to whose redress his sword was already devoted.

The scenes he was now about revisiting served to re call the distempered counsels of former times: when, after his betrothal to Alida, he had meditated throwing up his commission, and dogging Bradshawe with the footsteps of an avenger until the death of one of them were wrought; and when his being ordered unexpectedly upon dangerous duty to a remote district happily interposed the point of honour as a stay to such mad procedure. But these scenes, with their attendant associations, revived no feeling in Max's bosom nearer akin to personal hostility toward Bradshawe than any earnest and honest mind might entertain toward a low-lived and desperate adventurer, whose mischievous career would be shortened with benefit to the community. If, then, either the fortune of war or a higher Providence should seem at any time to single him out as the appointed instrument of Bradshawe's punishment, let it bring no reproach to the chivalrous nature of Greyslaer if he should fulfil his stern office with the methodical coldness of the mere soldier.

The order which Captain de Roos had received to hurry forward with his comrades was prompted by intelligence which had been received at Fort Dayton of a secret movement among the disaffected in the neighbourhood. The rapid advance of Barry St. Leger into the Valley of the Mohawk, together with his formidable investiture of Fort Stanwix, while far and wide it called out the valour and activity of the patriots to resist the invasion, was viewed with very opposite feelings by the remains of the royalist party which were still scattered here and there throughout Tryon county. These disaffected families, taught, by the events which followed Schuyler's march upon Johnstown in the earlier days of the war, that their lives were held by rather a precarious tenure, and that both their property and their personal safety de pended upon their abstaining from all political agitation, hesitated long to venture upon any new overt acts of treason.

The Johnsons and their refugee adherents, however, had not, in the meantime, been idle in scattering the proclamations of the British ministry, and attempting, by every means in their power, to keep up an intimate connection with their political friends who were within the American lines. The provincial government was fully aware of the existence of these intrigues, which were so daringly set on foot and indefatigably followed up by the Tories; and a military force, consisting of the first New York regiment and other troops, had at an early day been posted at Fort Dayton on the Mohawk, in order to over awe the loyalists, and prevent any sudden rising among them.

So bold a Tory as Walter Bradshawe, however, was not to be paralyzed in his plans by such impediments to their success. His emissary, Valtmeyer, whom we have Already recognized under his disguise at the roadside inn, had appeared among his old haunts on the very day that St. Leger sat down before Fort Stanwix; and, by the aid of letters and vouchers both from Bradshawe and his superiors, had successfully busied himself in leaguing the Tories together for sudden and concerted action. But, before openly committing themselves in arms, it was deemed necessary that a meeting should be held at the house of one of their number for the purposes of general consultation.

Within a few miles of Fort Dayton resided a Mr. Schoonmacker, a disaffected gentleman, who, previously to the breaking out of the war, had been in His Majesty's commission of the peace. This individual, a man of extensive means and influential connections, had of late exerted himself effectually in rekindling the spirits and hopes of his party in the neighbourhood. The address with which he managed his intrigues for a long time preserved him from all suspicion of taking an active part in the affairs of the times, though his political tenets were well known in the country round. Grown rash by long impunity, however, or rather, perhaps, incited by the blustering proclamations with which St. Leger flooded the country to give confidence to the king's friends, Schoonmacker now ventured to commit himself completely by offering his house for the accommodation of the clandestine meeting.

His generous zeal was warmly praised by the loyalists, already in arms under St. Leger; and their commander promised that an officer of the crown should be present at the assemblage to represent his own views, and aid and encourage Schoonmacker's friends in their under taking. Walter Bradshawe, who was now in command of one of the companies of refugees enrolled with the forces that beleaguered Fort Stanwix, eagerly volunteered upon this perilous agency, stipulating only that, a small detachment should accompany him to the place of rendezvous, in order to cut his way back to the besieging army in case the projected rising should prove a failure.

Taking with him a dozen soldiers and the like number of Indians, the Tory captain withdrew from the lines of Fort Stanwix and approached the rendezvous of the conspirators upon the appointed evening. His white followers, though they had been mustered in St. Leger's army as regular soldiers, consisted chiefly of those wild border characters who, throughout the war, seem to have fought indifferently upon either side, as the hope of booty or the dictates of private vengeance prompted them to adopt a part in the quarrel. One of these last, a man whose powerful frame seemed of yet more gigantic proportions, clad as he was in the loose hunting-shirt of the border, arid armed to the teeth with knife and tomahawk, two brace of pistols, and a double-barrelled fusee, presented the appearance of a walking armoury as he strode along in earnest conversation with his leader.

"Well, Valtmeyer," said Bradshawe, as they approached their destination, "I do not order you upon this duty, which I think one of my light-armed Indians could perform better, perhaps, than yourself; but, if you choose to reconnoitre the fort while we are engaged in counsel, you have full liberty to do so, only—"

But, before he could add the precautions he was about to utter, Valtmeyer, simply exclaiming—"Enough!" turned shortly into an adjacent thicket, where the sound of his footsteps upon the rustling leaves was soon lost to the ear of his officer.

Though the hour was late, yet the party collected at Schoonmacker's were still seated at table when Bradshawe, having stationed his sentries, prepared to join them. The carousing royalists had evidently drunk deep during the evening. The health of "The King" was pledged again and again; and their favourite toast of "Confusion to the Rebels" was floating upon a bumper near each one's lips when Bradshawe entered the apartment.

"You are loud in your mirth, gentlemen," cried the Tory officer, returning their vociferous greeting with some sternness, and impatiently waving from him the glass that was eagerly proffered by more than one of the conspirators. "Do I see all of our friends, Mr. Schoonmacker, or have these loyal gentlemen brought some retainers with them?" added Bradshawe, with more blandness, bowing at the same time politely to three or four of the company, as he recognized them individually either as influential characters well known in the county, or as old personal acquaintances of his own. "I was told, Major Mac-Donald," continued he, turning to a noble-looking, gray-headed man of fifty, "I was told that you, at least, could bring some twenty-five or thirty of your friends and dependants to strengthen our battalion of Royal Rangers."

"Twenty-six, sir, is the number of followers which I have promised to add to the royal levies; but, in lending my poor means to aid the cause of the king, I was not aware that my recruits were to be mustered under the command of a stranger; nor did I understand from General St. Leger that we were to serve in the Rangers. There are certain forms, young sir, to be observed in such proceedings as those in which we are engaged; and it may be well for you to produce certain missives, with which you are doubtless furnished, before we proceed directly to business."

Bradshawe—who, by the way, was hardly of an age to be addressed as "young sir" without some offence to his dignity—bit his lip while observing the coolness with which the worthy major knocked the ashes from his segar while tranquilly thus delivering himself. He, however, repressed the insolent language which rose to his lips in reply, and, placing his hand in his bosom, contented himself with flinging contemptuously upon the table a bundle of papers which he drew forth, exclaiming, at the same time,

"You will find there my warrant, gentlemen, for busying myself in these matters."

As he spoke he threw himself into a chair and poured out a glass of wine, with whose hue and flavour he tried to occupy his attention for the moment; but he could not conceal that he was somewhat nettled by the coolness with which the veteran turned over and examined the documents one after another, passing the captain's commission of Bradshawe, with the other papers, successively to those who sat near him. Bradshawe moved uneasily in his chair as this examination, which seemed to be needlessly minute and protracted, was going forward; and it is impossible to say what might have been the result of so severely testing the patience of his restless and overbearing spirit, if the phlegmatic investigation of the worthy major had not been interrupted by a noisy burst of merriment from another part of the house, which instantly called the partisan captain to his feet.

"For God's sake, Mr. Schoonmacker, what means this revelry? Do those sounds come from the rebels, who lie near enough and in sufficient force to crush us in a moment, or is it our own friends who play the conspirator after such a fashion? Who the dev—"

"Your zeal is too violent—pardon me, my worthy friend," interrupted the amiable host. "The revellers you hear are only the good country people whom our friends have brought with them to honour my poor house, and who are making themselves a little merry over a barrel of cider in the kitchen. We could not, you know, Mr. Bradshawe," he added, in an insinuating, deprecatory tone, as the other raised his eyebrows with a look of unpleased surprise, "we could not but give them the means of drinking the health of the king, and all are so well armed that we dread no surprise from Colonel Weston."

A shade of chagrin and vexation passed over the haughty features of Bradshawe as he compared in his mind more than one orderly and stern assemblage of the Whigs, to which he had managed to gain access, with the carousing crew with whom he had now to deal. "The fools, too!" he muttered, "sending my countrymen to drink with their servants! Do they think that is the way to confirm the loyalty of American yeomen?" Then addressing himself to the company with that urbane and candid air which he knew so well how to assume, and by which he had often profited when before a jury in other days, he said, "I was too hasty, gentlemen; but I was afraid, from the noise I heard, that a body of Indians that I have brought with me had in some way got access to liquor; and, to prevent the possibility of so dangerous a circumstance, I think we had better at once call our friends together, and let the proclamation of General St. Leger, with the accompanying letter from Sir John Johnson, both of which lie before you, be read aloud for the benefit of all."

The suggestion, which could not but have weight with all parties, was instantly adopted. A meeting was soon organized by calling Major MacDonald to the chair, and appointing Mr. Schoonmacker secretary; and the more humble adherents of the royal cause being summoned from the other parts of the house, the proclamation and letter were duly read by the latter.

The appeal of Sir John to the timid and disaffected in habitants of Tryon County to follow his example, and, abandoning their present neutral position, take up arms for their lawful sovereign, was received with warm approbation. Nor was there less enthusiasm upon hearing the proclamation from St. Leger read, inviting all true subjects of the king, and all violators of the laws, who hoped pardon for past offences from his majesty's goodness, to come and enrol themselves with his army now before Fort Stanwix. Bradshawe then moved a resolution, beginning with the customary preamble: "At a meeting of the loyal gentry and yeomanry of Tryon County, convened," &c., and by way of clinching matters while they seemed in such capital train, he mounted a chair and commenced haranguing the assemblage, urging the importance of immediate action in the cause to which every man present had now fully committed himself.

His adroit, and withal, impassioned eloquence, was ad dressed chiefly to the common people; and the generous boldness with which he committed his and their property to the chances of a civil war, in which either had but little or nothing to lose, elicited their rapturous admiration; particularly when he set forth, in glowing terms, how much they were to expect from the exhaustless bounty of their sovereign. In the midst of his harangue, however, and while all parties were warmed up to the highest pitch of loyal enthusiasm, he met with an interruption, the cause of which may be best explained by looking back a few pages in our narrative.

CHAPTER 4

The Spy

On him did passion fasten, not to roam,
And love and hate alike might find a home;
And burning, bounding, did their currents flow
From the deep fountain of the heart below.
Many a year had darkly flown
Since passion made this heart its own;
Fit dwelling for the scorpion
Revenge, to breathe and riot on;
Fit, while the deep and deadly sting
Of baffled love was festering.

Brooks.

The outlaw Valtmeyer, after parting with his officer in the manner already described, had proceeded at once, agreeably to the permission he had obtained, toward Fort Dayton, which had been for some time garrisoned by a battalion of Continental troops under the command of Colonel Weston, but where several detachments of other corps had recently taken up their temporary quarters. The object of Valtmeyer was partly to reconnoitre the outworks of the fort for future attack, and partly to spy out any movement upon the part of Weston and his people which might indicate that Bradshawe's mission in the neighbourhood was suspected, and give him and his friends timely warning of the danger.

A well-trained Indian warrior would, as Bradshawe had hinted, have better performed this duty than the wild borderer to whom it was now intrusted; for the character of Valtmeyer, whose vindictive daring and brutal courage has made his name terrible in the tradition of this region, was even less suited than that of a wild Indian to the duties and responsibilities of a regular soldier. The Indian warrior, though he insists upon encountering his enemy wholly after his own fashion, is still amenable to certain rude laws of discipline, for whose observance he may be relied upon; but the white frontiersman who has led the life of a free hunter, perhaps of all other men shrinks most from every form of military subordination. And, indeed, Valtmeyer, though to answer his own selfish purposes, he had so often been a mere tool in the hands of Bradshawe, already regretted having taken service with the Royal Rangers, and consenting to act under the command of any person save that of Wolfert Valtmeyer.

Being now wholly withdrawn from the surveillance of his officer, the worthy Wolfert, somewhat oblivious of his military duties, bethought himself how he could turn the occasion to the best account, by what a similar combatant in the battle of Bennington afterward called *making war on his own hook*. In other words, he determined to amuse himself for an hour or so within the purlieus of Fort Dayton, by carrying off or slaying some of the sentinels; a species of entertainment in which he thought there would be no difficulty in indulging himself. This seizing of opposite partisans, and holding them to ransom, was always a favourite feat with Valtmeyer and his compeer Joe Bettys; and the annals of the period make it of so common occurrence in the province of New York, that one would almost think that man-stealing was the peculiar forte of its inhabitants.

Had Wolfert, in approaching the fort, got his eye upon any of the picket-guard, he might very possibly have successfully effected his purpose. But, ill-practised as he was in the regulations of a well-ordered garrison, the adventurous hunter had not the least idea how far the line of out posts extended; and, like many a cunning person, he over reached himself while trying to circumvent others. In a word, he got completely within the line of defences, without being at all aware of their position.

With the stealthy art of a practised deer-stalker, he managed to creep, alike unobserved by others and himself unobserving, within the outer line of pickets, which was posted in the deep shadow of a wood, to a thicket of briers, where he paused. The gleam of a sentinel's musket above the bushes had lured him thus far, and he halted to see if the sentinel himself were now visible. It seemed that he could make out nothing satisfactory as yet; for now, throwing himself upon his chest, he continued lowly to advance, crawling through the long grass until he gained a copse of dog-wood and *sumach* bushes within half pistol-shot of his victim. The soldier was now fully displayed to view; Valtmeyer could see his very buttons gleam in the light of the moon as the planet from time to time shone through the clouds which traversed her face. Another moment, and the seizure was fully accomplished. The brigand, crumpling his worsted sash in his hands, leaped upon the sentinel just as he was turning in his monotonous walk, and bore him to the ground, while adroitly gagging his mouth before he could utter a cry.

"Pshaw! what a cocksparrow!" muttered Wolfert, when, having dragged his captive within the bushes, he for the first time observed that it was but a stripling recruit of some sixteen or eighteen years. "I must carry away with me something better than a boy."

With these words he hastily secured the lad to a sapling by the aid of a thong which he cut from his leather hunting-shirt, and then prepared to make a similar onset upon the next sentinel in the same line.

This man had paused for a moment at the end of his walk, waiting for a glimpse of moonlight to reveal his comrade, whom he had missed in his last turn. A straggling beam fell at last upon the path before him, and the soldier, resting on his musket, leaned forward, as if trying to pierce the gloom. The side of his person was turned toward Valtmeyer, and his head only partially averted; but Wolfert preferred seizing the present moment rather than to wait for a more favourable one, which might not come. Clasping his hands above his head, he leaped forward with a sudden bound, and threw them like a noose over the neck of the other, slipping them down below the elbows, which were thus pinioned to the side of his prisoner, whose musket dropped from his hands.

"Wolfert Valtmeyer, by the Eternal!" ejaculated the man, instantly recognizing his assailant from the well-known trick which they had often practised upon each other in the mock-wrestling of former days.

"Exactly the man, Balt; and you must go with him."

"Not onless he's a better man than ever I proved him," said Balt, struggling in the brawny arms of his brother borderer, who held him at such disadvantage.

"*Donder und blixem,* manny, you would not have me kill a brother hunter, would ye?" growled Valtmeyer, whose voice thickened with anger as he felt himself compelled to use every effort to maintain his grip.

"There's—no—brother—hood—atween—us—in—this—quar'l,"

panted forth the stout-hearted Balt, without an instant relaxing his endeavour.

"Then die the death of a rebel fool," muttered the other, hastily drawing his knife, and raising it to strike. The blow, as driven from behind by so powerful a hand, must have cut short the biography of the worthy Balt, had it fairly descended into the neck at which it was aimed. But the intent of the Tory desperado was foreseen in the very instant that the former released his grip with one hand in order to draw his knife with the other; and Balt, dropping suddenly upon his knees as Valtmeyer, who was full a head taller than his opponent, threw the whole weight of his body into the blow, the gigantic borderer was pitched completely over the head of his antagonist, and measured his length upon the sod. The clanging of his arms as he fell raised an instant alarm among those whom the deep-breathed threatenings of these sturdy foes had not before aroused. But Valtmeyer was upon his feet before Balt or the other sentinel, who rushed to the spot, could seize him. Indeed, he brought the former to the ground with a pistol-shot, stunning, but happily not wounding him, as he himself was in the act of rising. The other sentinel, who ought to have fired upon the first alarm, made a motion to charge upon him, and then threw away his shot by firing just at the instant when Valtmeyer parried the thrust of the bayonet with his knife, and, of course, simultaneously averted the muzzle of the gun from his body.

While this was passing, the guard turned out; but though Valtmeyer received their fire unharmed as he rushed toward the wood, he escaped one danger only to fall into another. Ignorant of the existence of the outer line of sentinels, he was seized by the picket-guard in the moment that, thinking he had escaped all dangers, he relaxed his efforts to make good his advantage.

The prisoner being brought before Colonel Weston, that sagacious officer lost no time in a fruitless examination of so determined a fellow taken under such circumstances. The redoubtable Valtmeyer was well known to him by fame, and Balt fully established his identity. Weston was before aware that the noted outlaw had taken service with one of the different corps of Butler's Rangers, and he readily conceived that he had been but now acting as the scout for some predatory band of Tories. Captain de Roos, who, as an active and efficient partisan officer, had been summoned to the fort for the very purpose of scouring the country for such offenders, was sent off with his command to make the circuit of the neighbourhood, and another detachment of troops was instantly despatched to the suspected house of Mr. Schoonmacker. The latter duty was one of some delicacy, and requiring a cooler judgment than that of De Roos; and Weston selected Major Greyslaer as the officer to whom it might best be intrusted.

De Roos, rashly insisting that he could squeeze something out of the sulky villain, was permitted to take Valtmeyer with him as a guide to the whereabout of his friends; and Valtmeyer, after fooling with him for a season, and leading his party in every direction but the right one, finally succeeded in saving his own neck from the gallows by giving them the slip entirely. The expedition of Greyslaer had a different issue.

Ever cool and steady in his purposes when duty called upon him to collect his energies, this officer advanced with speed and secrecy to the goal he had in view. The grounds around Schoonmacker's house were crossed, and every door beset by a party of armed men in perfect quietness. Balt—who had soon recovered from the stunning effects of the pistol-shot that grazed his temple—availed himself of the lesson in soldier-craft which he had just received from his brother woodsman, and secured the only sentinel that was upon his post. The temptation of the cider-barrel in the kitchen proved too strong for the Indians and their newly-levied white comrades to permit of their keeping a better watch. The house was, in fact, fairly surrounded by the Whig forces before a sound was heard to interrupt the harangue which Bradshawe was perorating within. MacDonald alone sprang from his seat, and, darting into an adjacent closet, made his escape through an open window in the moment that Greyslaer entered the room with a file of bayonets.

"In the name of the Continental Congress, I claim you all as my prisoners," cried Max, advancing to the table, and with great presence of mind, seizing all the papers upon it, including the commission of Bradshawe.

That officer, who had stood for the moment astonished at the scene, now made a fiery movement to clutch the papers from Greyslaer as the latter quietly ran his eye over their superscription; but he instantly found himself pinioned by two sturdy fellows behind him.

"See that you secure that spy effectually, my men."

"Spy, sir!" cried Bradshawe, with a keen look of anxious inquiry, while he vainly tried to give his voice the tone of indignant disclaimer to the imputed character.

"Spy was the word, sir," answered Max, gravely; "and, unless these documents speak falsely, as such you will probably suffer by dawn tomorrow. This paper purports to be the commission of Walter Bradshawe as captain in Butler's regiment of Royal Rangers; and the promised promotion in this note, for certain service to be rendered this very night, leaves no doubt of the character in which Captain Bradshawe has introduced himself into an enemy's country. Lansingh, remove your prisoner to the room on the other side of the hall, and see that he be well guarded!"

It is astonishing how invariably the success of an individual, whether in good or evil undertakings, affects his character with the vulgar; a term which, both in its conventional as well as its primitive sense, includes, perhaps, the majority of mankind. Certain it is, that, in this instance, the very associates and complotters of the prisoner, who but an hour before had hailed his appearance among them with such cordial greetings, now slunk from his side as if he had been a convicted felon. Indeed, some of the meaner minds present even attempted to conciliate the successful party by exhibiting the strongest, signs of personal aversion to Bradshawe, and of coarse gratification at the mode in which his career seemed suddenly about to be brought to a close.

These miscreants were scattered among others of both parties who were collected in the hall and grouped around the open door of the apartment in which Bradshawe, guarded by a couple of sentinels, was pacing to and fro. And while Mr. Schoonmacker and others of the leading Tories in the opposite room were listening in dignified dejection to the measures which Greyslaer stated, in the most courteous terms, it was his painful duty to adopt in regard to them, their followers were exchanging tokens of recognition with old neighbours and former comrades of the opposite party.

"Jim, you've done the darn thing agin us tonight, and no mistake," said one. "But if the Injuns hadn't got as drunk as fiddlers, you couldn't have popped in upon us as you did."

The Congress soldier made no reply; but the demure gravity of him and his comrades did not prevent others of the Tory militia from attempting a conversation with them.

"Well, Mat," said a second, "if I'm to be taken by the Whigs, I'm only glad that you happened to come up from the fort along with them; for you are just the man to say a good word for an old friend. All this muss is of Wat Bradshawe's cooking."

"Yes," cried a third, "the friends of the king only met to drink his health and have a little social junketing together; and if bully Bradshawe had not come among us, things would have gone off as quietly as possible. All the harm I wish him is, that he may get paid off for his old scrapes with a halter, and rid the country of such a pest; there's the affair, now, of old De Roos's daughter, for which he ought to have swung eight years since."

"Eight years!" rejoined the other. "No, the scrape you speak of is hardly a matter of six years by gone. But give the devil his due. The few folks that knowed of it talked hard about wild Wat for his share in that business. But things could not have gone so far, after all, or the Rooses would never have refused to appear against him, much less would the gal herself have rejected his offer when he wanted to make an honest woman of her."

Bradshawe betrayed no agitation during this discussion, which took place so near to him that, though the speakers lowered their voices somewhat, it must have been at least partially overheard by himself as well as by others. But when another of the rustic gossippers pointed significantly toward the room in which Major Greyslaer was engaged, while whispering that Miss de Roos had now "a real truelove of her own, and no mistake," the features of the Tory captain writhed with an expression almost fiendish.

"Yes! I must live," he muttered internally. "I cannot, I will not die. I have too many stakes yet in the game of life to have the cards dashed thus suddenly from my hands. My scheme of existence is too intimately interwoven with that of others to stop here, and stop singly. I know, I feel that Alida's fate and that of this moonstruck boy is interwoven with mine. *I* only can redeem her name, or blast it with utter infamy; and their peace or my revenge—whichever is ultimately to triumph—were both a nullity if I perish now." Alas! Walter Bradshawe, dost thou think that Providence hath but one mode of accomplishing its ends, if innocence is to be vindicated, and that only through so foul an instrument as thou!

Thus thought, or "thought he thought," this iron-hearted *desperado*. But there were other distracting feelings in his bosom which it was impossible for him to analyze. Though hatred had long since predominated over love in the warring passions of his stormy breast, yet that hatred was born only of the indignation and horror with which his attempts to control Alida's inclinations had been received, and his admiration had increased from the very circumstances which chilled his love; but now the subtle workings of jealousy infused a new element among his conflicting passions, which quickened both love and hatred into a more poignant existence.

Few, even of the most ignoble natures, are *wholly* base; and Brad-shawe, though he could not imagine, much less realize, one generous emotion that belongs to those dispositions which the world terms chivalrous, still possessed some of the qualities that keep a man from becoming despicable either to himself or to others. He had both bravery and ability, and he knew it. Incapable of one magnanimous thought, indeed he might still be great! And determined in purpose as he was loose in principle, he believed that he was a man born for the very time and country in which his lot was cast; for, regarding all others as senseless zealots, he deemed that every man of abilities en-gaged in the present political struggle was an adventurer like himself, having his own selfish views as the ultimate objects of his dangers and his toils.

If the aspiring aims, then, of a reckless ambition, backed by no ordinary talent and courage the most unflinching, can redeem from ignominy a mind otherwise contracted, coarse, and selfish, Bradshawe may be enrolled upon the same list with many a hero, not less mean of soul, whom the world has consented to admire; for the majority of mankind always look to the deeds of those who distinguish themselves beyond the herd, without much regard to the feeling which actuated or the moral end which those deeds were intended to promote; and one brilliant invading campaign of Napoleon is more dazzling to the mind than the whole military career of *him* who fought only to pre-serve his country! whose Heaven-directed arms triumphed ultimately over thousands as brave as Walter Bradshawe in the field; whose god-like counsels discomfited thousands more gifted, if not more unprin-cipled, in the cabinet.

But, awarding whatever credit we may to Bradshawe for his aspira-tions after fame, let us leave him now to awaken from the vague dream which, almost unknown to himself, had at times passed through his brain—the dream of sharing his future renown with Alida; and, while wiping off, in honourable marriage, the reproach which he had at-tached to her name, of gratifying, at last, the passion which was rooted in his heart. Let us leave the search ing pang of jealousy to reveal to him first the existence of this lingering touch of tenderness amid feelings which he himself thought had become only those of hatred. Let us leave him with that utter desolation of the heart's best earthly hope, which would prompt most men to welcome the grave upon whose brink he stood, but from which he, fired with a burning lust of vengeance, shrunk as from a dungeon where the plotting brain and relentless hand of malignity would lie helpless forever.

How little they read the man who deemed that terror of his fate had stupefied him, when, obedient to the order of his captor, he moved off, with stolid and downcast look, amid the guard which conducted him to durance at the quarters of the patriots.

CHAPTER 5

The Field of Oriskany

Strike—till the last armed foe expires,
Strike—for your altars and your fires,
Strike—for the green graves of your sires,
God! and your native land!

Halleck.

It *shouted to the mountain and the wave,*
That fetterless were left—the wild old woods,
And the free dweller there—to winds that go
And wist no bidding. 'Twas the uncurbed voice
Of Nature calling fiercely for her own.
It was the beating of the human mind
Against the battlements of power.
Then were ye marshalled forth!

Mrs. E. Oakes Smith.

The doom which Greyslaer had, with military sternness, predicted, was formally, by a military court, pronounced upon Bradshawe that very night; but when the hour of execution arrived on the morrow, events were at hand which, postponing it for the present, gave him, in fact, the advantages of an indefinite reprieval.

Some Continental officers, of a rank superior to that of the commandant, who arrived at Fort Dayton during the night, suggested doubts as to the policy of thus summarily executing martial law upon the prisoner. In the morning a message arrived from the beleaguered garrison of Fort Stanwix, urging the Whig forces to press forward to the scene of action, and attempt raising the siege at once, or their succour would come too late to save their compatriots. All was then bustle and motion. The greater part of the troops at once hurried forward to join Herkimer's forces, which had already taken up their line of march for Oriskany, while a detachment was sent down the river to speed on those who still loitered on the road to the border. When this last was about to depart, the opportunity was deemed a good one of getting rid of Bradshawe, by sending him to head-quarters at Albany, where his sentence could either be enforced or remitted, as a higher military authority should decide; and he was accordingly marched off, strictly guarded by the detachment.

Of the use that Walter Bradshawe made of this reprieve to carry into effect his meditated vengeance against Alida and her lover, we shall see hereafter. We must now return to other personages of our story, who have been, perhaps, too long forgotten.

It has been already incidentally mentioned that Brant and his followers were playing a conspicuous part in the bold invasion which now threatened to give the royalists possession of at least two-thirds of the fair province of New York, if, indeed, they should not succeed in over running the whole. Brant, who had brought nearly a thousand Iroquois warriors to the standard of St. Leger, was indeed the very soul of the expedition; for, if there be a doubt of his devising the scheme itself, he certainly planned some of its most important details; and the zeal with which he executed his share of the undertaking proved how thoroughly his heart was engaged in it. The Johnsons, indeed, had come back to struggle once more for a noble patrimony which had been wrested from them, and many of their refugee friends were animated by the hope of recovering the valuable estates they had forfeited; but Brant fought to recover the ancient seats of his people, whose name as a nation was in danger of being blot ted out from the land.

When, therefore, he learned, through his scouts, that Herkimer was approaching by forced marches to break up the encampment of St. Leger, relieve Fort Stanwix, and repel the advance of the invaders through the valley of which it was the portal, he instantly suggested measures for his discomfiture, and planned that masterly ambuscade which resulted in the bloody field of Oriskany.

There is, within a few miles of Fort Stanwix, a deep hollow or ravine which intersects the forest road by which Herkimer and his brave but undisciplined army of partisan forces were approaching to St. Leger's lines. The ravine sweeps toward the east in a semicircular form, either horn of the crescent thus formed bearing a northern and southern direction, and inclosing a level and elevated piece of ground upon the western side. The bottom of the ravine was marshy, and the road crossed it by means of a causeway. This was the spot selected by Brant for attacking the column of Herkimer; and hither St. Leger had sent a large force of royalists to take post with his Indians on the morning of the fatal sixth of August.

The white troops, consisting of detachments from Claus's and Butler's Rangers and Johnson's Greens, with a battalion of Major Watts's Royal New Yorkers, disposed themselves in the form of a semicircle, with a swarm of red warriors clustering like bees upon either extremity; and it would seem as if nothing could save Herkimer's column from annihilation, should it once push fairly within the horns of the crescent thus formed. The fortunes of war, however, turn upon strange incidents; and in the present instance, the very circumstance which hurried hundreds of brave men among the patriots upon their fate was a cause of preservation to their comrades.

The veteran General Herkimer, who was a wary and experienced bush-fighter, aware of the character of this ground, had ordered a halt when within a few hundred yards of the spot where the battle was ultimately joined; but irritated by the mutinous remonstrances of some of his insubordinate followers, several of whom flatly charged the stout old general with cowardice, he gave the order to "march on" while his ranks were yet in confusion; and eagerly was the order obeyed by the rash gathering of border yeomanry.

"March on," shouted the fiery Cox and ill-fated Eisenlord. "March on," thundered the Gardinier and Samson-like Dillenback, whose puissant deeds at Oriskany have immortalized their names in border story. "March on," echoed the patriotic Billington and long-regretted Paris, and many another brave civilian and gallant gentleman, whom neither rank, nor station, nor want of skill in arms had prevented from volunteering upon this fatal field—the first and last they ever saw! "March on," shouted the hot-headed De Roos, catching up the cry as quickly it ran from rank to rank, and dashing wildly forward, he scarce knew where.

And already the foremost files had descended into the hollow, and others, pressing from behind, were pouring in a living tide to meet the opposing shock below.

The impatience of Brant's warriors did not allow them to wait until the Whig forces had all descended into the ravine; but, raising their well-known war-cry, the Mohawks poured a volley, which nearly annihilated half of Herkimer's foremost division, and wholly cut off the remainder from the support of their comrades. Uprising then among the bushes, they sprang with tomahawk and javelin upon the panic-stricken corps, already broken and borne down by that first onslaught. The refugees pushed forward with their bayonets to share in the massacre of their countrymen. But now fresh foes were rushing upon them in turn. Headstrong and impetuous themselves, or urged on by the fiery masses that pressed upon them from behind, they descended like an avalanche from the plain above, and filled that little vale with carnage and destruction; now swooping down to be dispersed in death, and now bearing with them a resistless force that hurled hundreds who opposed it into eternity.

The leaders of both parties soon began to see that this indiscriminate melee could result in no positive advantage to either, while involving the destruction of both; and, in a momentary pause of the conflict, the voices of Herkimer's officers and of the opposing leaders were simultaneously heard calling upon their men to betake themselves to the bushes and form anew under their cover. And now the fight was somewhat changed in its character. Major Greyslaer, seeing the causeway partially cleared of its struggling combatants, rallied a compact band of well-disciplined followers, and charged the thickets in advance. But the throng through which he opened a passage closed instantly behind him, and with the loss of half his men, he was obliged to cut his way back to his comrades, where the chieftain Teondetha, with his Oneida rifles, covered the shattered band till Greyslaer could take new order.

The Whig yeomanry, in the meantime, had for the most part taken post behind the adjacent trees, where each man, as from a citadel of his own, made war upon the enemy by keeping up an incessant firing. But Brant, whose Indians were chiefly galled by these sharpshooters, gave his orders, and the Mohawks, wherever they saw the flash of a rifle, would rush up, and, with lance or tomahawk, despatch the marksman before he could gain time to reload. Balt, whose unerring rifle had already made many a foeman bite the dust, had ensconced himself behind a shattered oak, a little in advance of a thicket of birch and juniper, from which Christian Lansingh, with others of Greyslaer's followers, kept up a steady fire, and thus covered Balt's position. The worthy hunter absolutely foamed with rage when he saw several of his acquaintance, who were less protected than himself, thus falling singly beneath the murderous tomahawks of Brant's people; but his anger received a new turn when he beheld Greyslaer breaking his cover and rushing with clubbed rifle after one of the retreating Mohawks, who had despatched an unfortunate militiaman within a few paces of him.

"Goody Lordy!" he exclaimed, "the boy's mad! He'll spoil the breaching or bend the bar'l of the best rifle in the county. Tormented lightning! though, how he's buried the brass into him."

Greyslaer, as Balt spoke, drove the angular metal with which the stock of the weapon was shod, deep into the brain of the flying savage, while Balt himself, in the same moment, brought down a javelin man who was flying to the assistance of the other.

"Aha! ain't that the caper on't, you pizen copperhead! Down, major, down," shouted the woodsman, as his quick ear caught the click of a dozen triggers in the opposite thicket, and Max, obedient to the word, threw himself upon his face, while the fire of a whole platoon of Tory rangers, that was instantly answered by a volley from his own men, passed harmlessly over him.

The dropping shots now became less frequent, for the borderers on either side were so well protected by wood land cover, that, though the clothes of many were riddled with bullets, yet the grazing of an elbow or some slight flesh-wound in the leg was all the execution done by those who were as practised in avoiding exposure to the aim of an enemy, as in availing themselves with unerring quickness of each chance of planting a bullet.

General Herkimer, who had already seen Greyslaer's spirited effort to cut his way through the enemy with a handful of men, deemed this the fitting time to execute the movement upon a larger scale. The fatal causeway was again thronged by the patriots in the instant they heard the voice of their leader exhorting his troops to force the passage in which their bravest had already fallen. But, even before they could form, and in the moment that those closing ranks exposed themselves, a murderous fire was poured in upon them on every side; every tree and bush seemed to branch out with flame.

Thrice, with desperate valour, did Herkimer cross the causeway and charge the thronged hillside in front; and thrice the files who rushed into the places of the fallen were mowed down by the deadly rifles from the thickets, or beaten back by the cloud of spears and toma-hawks that instantly thickened in the path before them. In the third charge the veteran fell, a musket-ball, which killed his horse, having shattered his knee while passing through the body of the charger.

But the fall of their general, instead of disheartening seemed only to nerve his brave followers with new determination of spirit, as placed on his saddle beneath a tree, the stout old soldier still essayed to order the battle. His manly tones, heard even above the din of the conflict, gave system and efficacy to the brave endeavour of his broken ranks. The tree against which he leaned became a central point around which they rallied, fighting now, not for conquest—hardly for self-preservation—but only in stubborn resistance of their fate. And now, as the enemy, impatient of this long opposition, concentrated round them, they formed in circles, and received in silence the furious charge of their hostile countrymen. Bayonet crossed bayonet, or the clubbed rifle battered the opposing gunstock as they fought hand to hand and foot to foot. Again and again did the royalists recoil from the wall of iron hearts against which they had hurled themselves. But though the living rampart yielded not, it began to crumble with these successive shocks; the ranks of the patriots grew thinner around their wounded general, where brave men strewed the ground like leaves when the autumn is serest.

The Indian allies upon either side had in the meantime suspended their firing. In vain did the voice of Brant encourage his Mohawks to strike a blow which should at once decide this fearful crisis. In vain did the gallant shout of Teondetha cheer on the Oneidas to rescue his friends from the destruction that hedged them in. Not an Indian would move in that greenwood. The warriors of the forest upon both sides had paused to watch this terrible death-struggle between white men of the same country and language. They had already ceased to fire upon each other; and now, gazing together upon the well-matched contest of those who involved them in this family quarrel, they would not raise an arm to strike for either party.

A storm, a terrific midsummer tempest, such as often marks the sudden vicissitudes of our climate, was the Heaven-directed interposition which stayed the slaughter of that battlefield. The breath of the thunder-gust swept the rain in sheets of foam through the forest, and the hail burst down in torrents upon those warring bands, whose arms now flashed only as they glinted black the lightning's glare.

There was a pause, then, in the bloody fight of Oriskany; but the battle, which seemed but now nearly ended in the overthrow of the patriots, was soon to be resumed under different auspices. The royalists had withdrawn for the moment to a spot where a heavier forest-growth afforded them some protection from the elements. The republicans had conveyed their wounded general to an adjacent knoll, from which, exposed as it was to the fire of the enemy, he insisted on ordering the battle, when it should be resumed; and here, in the heat of the onslaught which succeeded, the sturdy old border chief was observed, with great deliberation, to take his flint and tinder-box from his pocket, light his pipe, and smoke with perfect composure. The veteran bush-fighter, who missed many an officer around him, grieved not the less for more than one favourite rifle-shot who had perished among his private soldiers; and, in order to counteract the mode of warfare adopted by Brant, when, in the early part of the battle, the Indian spears and tomahawks made such dreadful havoc among the scattered riflemen, Herkimer commanded his sharpshooters to station themselves in pairs behind a single tree, and one always to reserve his fire till the Indians should rush up to despatch his comrade when loading.

In the meantime, while the different dispositions for attack and defence were thus making by their leaders, the rude soldiers on either side, hundreds of whom were mutually acquainted, exchanged many a bitter jeer with each other, while ever and anon, as some taunting cry would rise among the young warriors of Brant's party, it was echoed by the opposing Oneidas with a fierce whoop of defiance that would pierce wildly amid the peltings of the storm.

An hour elapsed before an abatement of the tempest allowed the work of death to commence anew. A movement on the part of the royalists by Major Watts's battalion, first drew the fire of the patriots; and then the Mohawks, cheered on by the terrible war-whoop of Brant, and uttering yell on yell to intimidate their foes, commenced the onslaught, tomahawk in hand. But the cool execution done by the marksmen whom Herkimer had so wisely planted to sustain each other, made them quickly recoil; and the Oneidas, eagerly pressing forward from the republican side, drove them back upon a large body of Butler's rangers. Many of this corps had been so severely handled by Greyslaer's men in the first part of the battle, that they had fallen back to take care of their wounded.

But Bradshawe's company, which had suffered least, was now in advance. These fierce men brooked no control from the young subaltern who was now nominally their commander. Headed by the terrible Valtmeyer, whose clothes were smeared with the gore from a dozen scalps which dangled at his waist, they broke their ranks, rushed singly upon the Oneidas, who had intruded into their lair, and, driving them back among their friends, became the next moment themselves mixed up in wild melee with partisans of the other side. This onslaught served as a signal for a rival corps in another part of the field; and Claus's Rangers broke their cover to battle with their foemen hand to hand.

This corps of refugee royalists consisted of men enlisted chiefly from the very neighbourhood where they were now fighting. They had come back to their former homes, bearing with them the hot thirst of vengeance against their former friends and neighbours; and when they heard the triumphant shout of the Whigs at a momentary recoil of their friends, and perhaps recognized the voices of some who had aided in driving them from their country, their impatience could not be restrained; they rushed forward with a fiendish yell of hatred and ferocity, while the patriots, instead of awaiting the charge, in obedience to the commands of their officer, sprang like chafed tigers from their covert, and met them in the midst. Bayonets and clubbed muskets, made the first shock fatal to many; but these were quickly thrown aside as the parties came in grappling contact, drawing their knives and throttling each other, stabbing, and literally dying in each other's embrace.[1]

And thus, for five long hours, raged this ruthless conflict. All military order had been lost in the moment when the wild bush-fighters first broke their cover and rushed forward to decide the battle hand to hand. Men fought with the fury of demons; or if, by chance, a squad or party of five or six found themselves acting together, these would quickly form, rush forward, and, charging into the thickest of the fight, soon be lost amid the crowd of combatants. At one moment, the tomahawk of some fierce red warrior would crash among the bayonets and spears of whites and Indians as he hewed his way to rescue some comrade that was beset by clustering foes; at another, the shattering of shafts and clashing of steel would be heard where a sturdy pioneer, with his back to a tree, stood, axe in hand, cleaving down a soldier at every blow, or matching the cherished tool of his craft with the ponderous mace of some brawny savage. Now the groans of the dying, mixed with imprecations deep and foul, rose harshly above the din of the battle, and now the dismal howl or exulting yell of the red Indian was mocked by a thousand demoniac voices, screeching wild through the forest, as if the very fiends of hell were let loose in that black ravine.

The turmoil of the elements has long since subsided. The sky is clear and serene above. Happily, the forest glooms interpose a veil between its meek, holy eye, and this dance of devilish passions upon the earth.

---

1. Stone, Campbell, Gouverneur Morris.

CHAPTER 6

The Issues of the Battle

Let me recall to your recollection the bloody field where Herkimer fell. There were found the Indian and the white man, born on the banks of the Mohawk, their left hand clenched in each other's hair, the right grasping in the gripe of death the knife plunged in each other's bosom. Thus they lay frowning.— *Discourse of Gouvrneur Morris before the New York Historical Society, 1812.*

An accomplished statesman and eloquent writer has, in the passage which heads this chapter, well depicted the appearance which the field of Oriskany presented when the fight was over. The battle itself, while the most bloody fought during the Revolution, is remarkable for having been contested exclusively between Americans, or at least between those who, if not natives of the soil, were all denizens of the province in which it was fought. And though its political consequences were of slight moment, for both parties claimed the victory, yet, from the character of the troops engaged in it—from the number of Indian warriors that were arrayed upon either side—the protracted fierceness of the action, and the terrible slaughter which marked its progress, it must be held the most memorable conflict that marked our seven years' struggle for national independence.

Of the field officers that fell, it is true that most, like the brave Herkimer himself, were only militiamen, and of no great public consideration beyond their own county; but with these gallant gentlemen were associated as volunteers more than one military man of rank and repute that had been won upon other fields; and many a civilian of eminence, who, at the call of patriotism, had shouldered a musket and met his death as a private soldier. The combatants upon either side consisting almost exclusively of inhabitants of the Mohawk Valley, there were so many friends and neighbours, kinsmen, and even brothers arrayed against each other, that the battle partook of the nature of a series of private feuds, in which the most bitter feelings of the human heart were brought into play between the greater part of those engaged.

And when the few who were actuated by a more chivalric spirit like the gallant Major Watts of the Royal New Yorkers, and others who might be designated among his hostile compatriots—met in opposing arms, they too fought with a stubborn valour, as if the military character of their native province depended equally upon the dauntless bearing of either party. The analyst has elsewhere preserved so many minute and thrilling details of Herkimer's last field,[1] that it hardly becomes us to recapitulate them here, though we would fain recall some of those traits of chivalrous gallantry and generous daring which redeem the brutal ferocity of the contest.

The deeds of the brave Captain Dillenback, though his name is not intermingled with the thread of our story, are so characteristic of the times in which its scenes are laid, that they can hardly be passed over. This officer had his private enemies among those who were now arrayed in battle as public foes; and Wolfert Valtmeyer, with three others among the most desperate of the refugees, determined to seize his person in the midst of the fight, and carry him off for some purpose best known to themselves. Watching their opportunity, these four *desperadoes*, when the tumult of the conflict was at the highest, cut their way to the spot where Dillenback was standing; and one of them succeeded in mastering his gun for a moment.

But Dillenback, who caught sight of Valtmeyer's well-known form pressing forward to aid his comrades in the capture, knew better than to trust himself to the tender mercies of his outlaw band. He swore that he would not be taken alive, and he was not. Wrenching his gun from the grasp of the first assailant, he felled him to the earth with the breech, shot the second dead, and plunged the bayonet into the heart of the third. But in the moment of his last triumph the brave Whig was himself laid dead by a pistol-shot from Valtmeyer, who chanced to be the fourth in coming up to him.

But perhaps as true a chevalier as met his fate amid all that host of valiant hearts was a former friend of Balt the woodsman, an old Mohawk hunter, who bore the uncouth Dutch name of *Bronkahorlst*.

2. See Stone's *Border Wars of the American Revolution*.

It was in the heat of the fight, when Brant's dusky followers, flitting from tree to tree, had at one time almost surrounded Greyslaer's small command, that Balt, in the thickest of the fire, heard a well-known voice calling him by name from behind a large tree near; and, looking out from the huge trunk which sheltered his own person, he recognized the only Indian with whom his prejudices against the race had ever allowed him to be upon terms of intimacy.

"Come, my brother," said the Iroquois warrior, in his own tongue. "come and escape death or torture by surrendering to your old friend, who pledges the word of a Mohawk for your kind treatment and protection."

"Rather to you than to anybody, my noble old boy; but Balt will be prisoner this day to no mortal man. My name is *Nozun Dofji*—he that never shirks."

"And my name," cried the Indian, "is *The Killer of Brave Men*; so come on; we are happily met." With these words both parties threw down their rifles, and, drawing their knives, rushed upon each other.

The struggle was only a brief one; for Time, who had nerved the brawny form of the white borderer into the full maturity of manly strength, had dealt less leniently with the aged Indian, who was borne at once to the ground as they closed in the death-grapple. It was in vain that Balt, mindful of other days and kinder meetings in the deep woodlands, attempted to save his opponent's life by making him a prisoner; for, in the moment that he mastered the scalping-knife of the Indian and pinioned his right arm to the ground, the latter, writhing beneath his adversary with the flexibility of a serpent, brought up his knee so near to his left hand as to draw the leg-knife from beneath the garter, and dealt Balt a blow in his side which nothing but his hunting-shirt of tough elk-hide prevented from being fatal. Even as it was, the weapon, after sliding an inch or two, cut through the arrow-proof garment that ere now had turned a sabre; while Balt, feeling the point graze upon his ribs, thought that his campaigning days were over, and, in the exasperation of the moment, buried his knife to the hilt in the bare bosom of Bronkahorlst.

"We are going together, old boy," he cried, as he sank back with a momentary faintness. "I only hope we'll find the game as plenty in your hunting-ground of spirits as we have on the banks of the Sacondaga; God forgive me for being sich a heathen!"

But while this singular duel, with personal encounters of a similar nature, were taking place in one part of the field, others more eventful in their consequences were transpiring elsewhere. The puissant deeds of Captain. Gardinier, like those of Dillenback, have given his name a place upon the sober page of history; but, as they involved the fate of more than one of the personages of our story, we have no hesitation in recapitulating them here.

One principal cause, perhaps, why the Whigs maintained their ground with such desperate tenacity, was the hope that, so soon as the sound of their firearms should reach the invested garrison of Fort Stanwix, a sally would be attempted by the besieged to effect a diversion in their favour. That sally, so famous in our Revolutionary history, and which gave to *Willet*, who conducted it, the name of "*the hero of Fort Stanwix*," did, in fact, take place before the close of the Battle of Oriskany, and was, as we all know, attended with the most brilliant success. But, long before the performance of that gallant feat of Willet's, the Tory partisan, Colonel Butler, aware of the hopes which animated his Whig opponents at Oriskany, essayed a *ruse de guerre*, which had well nigh eventuated in their complete destruction.

This wily officer, withdrawing a large detachment of Johnson's Greens from the field of action, partially disguised them as Republican troops by making them change their hats for those of their fallen enemies; and then adopting the patriot colours and other party emblems so far as they could, they made a circuit through the woods, and turned the flank of the Whigs in the hope of gaining the midst of them by coming in the guise of a timely reinforcement sent from the fort.

The hats of these soldiers appearing first through the bushes, cheered Herkimer's men at once. The cry was instantly raised that succour was at hand. Many of the undisciplined yeomanry broke from their stations, and ran to grasp the hands of their supposed friends.

"Beware! beware! 'tis the enemy; don't you see their green coats?" shouted Captain Gardinier, whose company of dismounted rangers was nearest to these newcomers. But, even as he spoke, one of his own soldiers, a slight stripling, recognizing his own brother among the Greens, and supposing him embarked in the same cause with himself, rushed forward to embrace him. His outstretched hand was seized with no friendly grasp by his hostile kinsman; for the Tory brother, fastening a ferocious gripe upon the credulous Whig, dragged him within the opposing lines, exclaiming only, as he flung him backwards amid his comrades, "See, some of ye, to the d——d young rebel, will ye?"

"For God's sake, brother, let them not kill me! Do you not know me?" shrieked the youthful patriot, as he clutched at one of those amid whom he fell, to shield -him from the blows that were straight-way aimed at his life.

But his brother had other work to engage him at this instant; for the gallant Gardinier, observing the action and its result, seized a partisan from a corporal who stood near, and wielding the spear like a quarter staff, dealt his blows to the right and left so vigorously that he soon beat back the disordered group and liberated his man, who, clubbing his rifle as he sprang to his feet, instantly levelled his treacherous brother in the dust. But Gardinier and his stripling soldier were now in the midst of the Greens, unsupported by any of their comrades; and the sturdy Major MacDonald, who this day had taken duty with a detachment of Johnson's men, rushed forward sword in hand to cut down Gardinier in the same moment that two of the disguised Greens sprang upon him from behind. Struggling with almost superhuman strength to free himself from their grasp, the spurs of the Whig Ranger became entangled in the clothes of his adversaries, and he was thrown to the ground. Both of his thighs were instantly transfixed to the earth by the bayonets of two of his assailants, while MacDonald, presenting the point of his rapier to his throat, cried out to "Yield himself, rescue or no rescue." But Gardinier did not yet dream of yielding.

Seizing the blade of the sword with his left hand, the trooper, by a sudden wrench, brought the Highlander down upon his own person, where he held him for a moment as a shield against the assault of others. At this moment, Adam Miller for the first time saw the struggle of Gardinier against this fearful odds. His sword was already out and crimson with blood of more than one foe; and now, rushing forward, he laid about him so industriously, that the Greens were compelled to defend themselves against their new adversary. Gardinier, raising himself to a sitting posture, bore back MacDonald; but the gallant Scot, still clinching the throat of his foe with his left hand, braced himself firmly on one knee, and turned to parry the frenzied blows of Miller with his right.—Gardinier had but one hand at liberty, and that was lacerated by the rapier which he had grasped so desperately; yet, quick as light, he seized the spear which was still lying near him, and planted the barb in the side of MacDonald. The chivalric Highlander expired without a groan.

The Greens, struck with dismay at the fate of this veteran officer, the near friend of Sir John Johnson, fell back upon those of their comrades who had not yet broken their ranks; while those lookers-on, stung with grief for the loss of such an officer, rallied instantly to the charge, and poured in a volley upon the Whigs, who had just succeeded in dragging the wounded Gardinier out of the *mêlée*. Several fell, but their death was avenged on the instant; yet dearly avenged, for the blow which followed, while it terminated the battle, concluded the existence of one of the most gallant spirits embarked in it.

Young Derrick de Roos on that day had enacted wonders of prowess. And though the rashness he exhibited made his early sobriquet of "Mad Dirk" remembered by more than one of his comrades, yet he seemed to bear a charmed life while continually rushing to and fro wherever the fight was hottest. At the very opening of the conflict, when most of the mounted Rangers threw themselves from their saddles and took to the bushes with their rifles,[2] De Roos, with but a handful of troopers to back him, drew his sword and charged into the thickets from which came the first fire of the ambushed foe.

"It is impossible for cavalry to act upon such ground," exclaimed an officer, seeing him about to execute this mad movement. De Roos, who, on the march, was leading his horse, did not heed the remark as he threw himself into the saddle. "Your spurs—where are your spurs, man?" cried another, as the horse, flurried by the first fire, rose on his hinder legs instead of dashing forward. "Charge not without your spurs, captain!"

"I'm going to win my spurs," shouted Mad Dirk striking the flanks of the steed with the flat of his sabre, which the next moment gleamed above his head as the spirited animal, gathering courage from his fiery rider, bounded forward in the charge.

In the instant confusion that followed, De Roos was no more seen; the smoke, indeed, sometimes revealed his orange plume floating like a tongue of flame amid its wreaths; and his "Carry on, carry on, men," for a few moments cheered the ears of the friends who could distinguish his gay and reckless voice even amid the earnest shouts of the white borderers, mingled as they were with the wild slogan of the Indian warriors. But De Roos himself appeared no more until, in the

---

2. The horses of mounted riflemen are generally, during a frontier fight, secured to a tree in some hollow or behind some knoll, which protects them from the enemy's fire. Not infrequently, however, the sagacious animal is trained, in obedience to the order of his master, to crouch among the leaves, or couch down like a dog behind some fallen tree, while the rider, protected by the same natural rampart, fires over his body.

pause of the battle already mentioned, he presented himself among his compatriots, exclaiming,

"I've used up all my men! Is there no handful of brave fellows here who will rally under Dirk de Roos when we set-to again?"

The fearful slaughter which, as is known, took place among Herkimer's officers at the very outset of the fight, and almost with the first volley from Brant's people, yet left men enough among these undisciplined bands to furnish forth a stout array of volunteers, who were eager to fight under so daring a leader; and when the battle was renewed, the wild partisan went into it with a train more numerous than before. But his horse had long since been killed under him; the followers upon whom he was in the habit of relying had fallen, either dead or disabled, by his side; and Derrick, somewhat sobered in spirit, became more economical of his resources. And, though still exposing his own person as much as ever, he was vigilant in seeing that his men were well covered, while he hoarded their energies to strike some well-directed blow which might terminate the battle.

With the last volley of the Greens he thought the fitting moment had come. His bugle sounded a charge, and on rushed his band with the bayonet.

"Carry on, carry on!" shouted De Roos, who charged, sword in hand, a musket's length ahead of his foremost files.

It seemed impossible for the weary royalists to stand up against this column; for small in number as were the men who composed it, they were comparatively fresh, from a short breathing spell which they had enjoyed; while their spirits were excited to the utmost by their having been kept back by their officer, as he waited for the approaching crisis before permitting a man to move. But the line of the royalists, though broken and uneven, was still so much longer than that of the patriots, that, out flanking their assailants as they did, they had only to permit their headlong foe to pass through, and then fall upon his rear.

This movement the Greens effected with equal alacrity and steadiness. Their ranks opened with such quickness that they seemed to melt like a wave before De Roos's impetuous charge; but, wavelike too, they closed again behind his little band, which was thus cut off from the patriot standard. Furious at being thus caught in the toils, the fierce republicans wheeled again, and madly endeavoured to cut their way back to their friends; but the equally brave royalists far outnumbered them, and their fate for the moment seemed sealed, when suddenly another player in this iron game presented himself.

Max Greyslaer, who, from a distance, had watched the movement of his friend with the keenest anxiety, saw the unequal struggle upon which the fortunes of the whole battle were turning. He had fought all day on foot, and wounded and weary, he seemed too far from the spot upon which all the chances of the fight were now concentred to reach it ere they were decided. He looked eagerly around for assistance; he shouted madly to those who were closer to De Roos to press forward; and, bounding over a fallen tree near him, he stumbled upon the trained horse of a rifleman, which had been taught to crouch in the thickets for safety. The *couchant* steed but now so quiet when masterless rose with a grateful winnow as Max seized his bridle; and, gladly yielding his back to so featly a rider, he tossed his head with proud neighing as he felt himself no longer a passive sharer in the dangers of the field. On came the gallant horse. The rider gathered new life from the fresh spirits of his steed. He swept—'twas thus the warlike saints of old swept before the eyes of the knightly combatants—he swept meteorlike across the field, and charged with his flashing brand, singly against the royal host. Down went the green banner of the Johnsons; down went the sturdy banner-man, shorn to the earth by that trenchant blade.

The Greens, attacked thus impetuously in their rear, turned partly round to confront this bold assailant; but Greyslaer had already cloven his way through their line, and Christian Lansingh, with a score of active borderers, had rushed tumultuously into his wake. The royalists were broken and forced back laterally on either side of the pathway thus made; but either fragment of the disjoined band still struggled to reunite with desperate valour. The republicans, concentrating their forces upon one at a time, charged both parties alternately. Thrice, wheeling with the suddenness of a falcon in mid air, had Greyslaer hurled himself upon their crumbling ranks; and now, as one division was nearly annihilated by that last charge, De Roos, emulous of his friend, headed the onslaught against the remaining fragment of the royalists. His orange plume again floated foremost; and loud as when the fight was new, his cheering voice was heard,

"Carry on, men, carry o—" [4]

An Indian whoop—the last that was heard upon the field of Oriskany—followed the single shot which hushed that voice and laid

---

4. In the action in which the United States Frigate *President*, was captured by a British squadron, off Sandy Hook, Lieut. Hamilton expired with this catchphrase upon his lips. It was his cant expression, at "*feast or fray.*"

that orange plume in the dust.

Both Mohawks and royalists had already mostly with drawn from the field; and the remainder of the Greens, who had contested it to the last so stubbornly, retired when they saw De Roos fall.[5]

---

5. Brant and his Tory confederates carried off so many prisoners with them from the field of Oriskany, that the battle is often spoken of as a defeat of the Whigs. But as these prisoners were taken in the early part of the action, and during the first confusion of the ambuscade, the meed of victory must be accorded to the patriots, who were left in possession of the battlefield; fearful, however, as was the general slaughter, the loss of life upon the Royalist side seems to have been chiefly among the Indian warriors, while on the Republican side the whites suffered far more than did their Oneida allies.

CHAPTER 7

The Doubtful Parentage

True joy, still born of heaven, is blessed with wings,
And, tired of earth, it plumes them back again:
And so we lose it. A sad change came o'er
The fortunes of that pair, whose loves have been
Our theme of story—a sad change, that oft
 Comes o'er love's fortunes in all lands and homes.

Simms.

They were busy making rude litters for the wounded upon that field of slaughter. The brave Herkimer, who so soon died of his injury, was already borne off; but most of his surviving followers yet remained. There were groups of mournful faces around the dying, and here and there a desolate-looking man was seen stalking over the field, pausing from time to time in his dreary quest, looking around now with quick and painful glances, and now, with a half-fearful air, stooping over some gory corse, as if seeking some near friend or kinsman among the fallen.

By the root of a dusky tamarack lay a bleeding officer, whose pale features showed that he was yet young in years; while another of similar age was busied in stanching the blood which oozed in torrents from his side. A kneeling soldier offered a vessel of water; a grizzly hunter held the feet of the dying man in his bosom; as if to cherish the extremities that were rapidly growing cold. A grave Indian stood mutely looking on. If he indeed sorrowed in heart like the others, his smooth cheek and quiet eye betrayed not the agitation which painted their faces with emotion.

It was of no avail, the kindness of that ministering group of friends. The dying man, indeed, once opened his eyes, and he seemed to murmur something, which the other officer bent forward with the most earnest solicitation to hear. He seemed to have some charge or bequest of wishes to make to his friend; but his thoughts could not syllable themselves into connected utterance. His wound seemed to gather virulence from each successive effort; yet still he squandered his remaining strength in futile attempts to communicate with his friends. Alas! why did he not speak before, that luckless soldier, if life's last moments were so precious so him?

"I know—I know—it is of Guise, the Indian child, you would speak," cried the agonized friend, as the sudden thought started into his mind. "It is the mystery of his birth—it is your wishes about your own offspring that you would declare. God of heaven, pardon and spare him for a moment. Press my hand, Derrick, if I have guessed truly that the child is yours; make any—the least, the feeblest sign, and your boy shall be as dear to Greyslaer as his own."

But Derrick died and *gave no sign!* His last breath went out in the moment that his agitated friend, for the first time, conjectured what he intended to reveal.

They buried him beneath that dusky tamarack; and there let him lie, a gallant, frank-hearted soldier, whose bravery and generosity of disposition were remembered in his native valley long after the blemishes, or, rather, the inherent defects of his character were forgotten; a character not altogether inestimable, far less unloveable, at that graceful season of life when the wildest sallies of youth are forgotten in the generous impulses which seem to prompt them, but which, unregulated by one steadfast principle, was, perhaps, of all others, the most likely to degenerate into utter profligacy and selfishness when age should have chilled the social flow of its feelings, and habit confirmed the reckless indulgence of its own humours.

It was well, then, perhaps, for the memory of the gay and high-spirited De Roos, that his career closed when it did; but the sorrowing group who were now retiring from his hastily-made grave, would have spurned the solace which such a reflection might have imparted. The three white men scattered twigs and tufts of grass over the spot before they left it; and they turned to see why the Indian still lingered behind them; an exclamation of displeasure, as at beholding some heathen rite, burst from the lips of Greyslaer as he saw a column of smoke arise from a pile of brush which Teondetha had already heaped together.

"The pagan redskin, what is he doing?" muttered Christian Lansingh.

"Teondetha is wise," said Balt, sadly, in the only words of kindness he had ever spoken to the young chief. "He has preserved all that remains of poor Captain Dirk; for the wild beasts will never scratch through the ashes to disturb him."

The Indian replied not, and they all left the battlefield in silence.

Tradition tells of the horrid spectacle which that field exhibited three days afterward, when the wolves, the bears, and the panthers, with which the adjacent forests at that time abounded, had been busy among the graves of the slain; but the simple precaution of Teondetha preserved from violation the last resting-place of the friend of his boyhood.

Of the others that fell in this ensanguined conflict, it be longs to history rather than to us to speak. The analyst of Tryon County[1] tells us, that in the whole Valley of the Mohawk, there was scarcely a family which had not lost some member; scarcely a man, woman or child who had not some relative to deplore after the fatal field of Oriskany. Brant's warriors had suffered so severely, that his immediate band of Mohawks was nearly all cut to pieces; but, deeply as the chieftain grieved for the loss of his brave followers, he had still room in his heart to lament his friend MacDonald. At this point we shall probably take leave of the famous sachem whose career, though it grows more and more thrilling in interest through the successive scenes of the civil war along this border, is haply no farther interwoven with the thread of our narrative.

Teondetha, too, though he may possibly again flit across our page, we must now dismiss with his Oneidas to the ancient seats of his people, where they finally halted after cruelly harassing the rear of the flying St. Leger. That officer, as is known, broke up his lines before Fort Stanwix upon Arnold's approach to Fort Dayton, and effected a most disastrous retreat to the wilds from which he had emerged with such boastful anticipations. Of the officers to whom the arduous duty of pursuing him into the wilderness was intrusted, few were more distinguished for zeal and efficiency than Major Greyslaer, whose knowledge of forest life enabled him to co-operate with the greatest advantage with the Oneida allies of the patriot cause.

Returning from this arduous and perilous service, Greyslaer, when halting to refresh his men at the Oneida Castle, had an opportunity of witnessing the wedded happiness of "The Spreading Dew," who was long since united to her true warrior, and who welcomed him with

1. Campbell.

proud feelings of gratification to her husband's lodge. He sympathized with the fortunate issue of their simple loves, even while he sighed to think that the course of his own, which had never run too smoothly, was still far from bright.

It was impossible for him to be near Alida in the first days of her grief, when the tidings should reach her that her only brother, the last male of her family, the last near relation she had on earth, had been taken away; but he had promised himself that many weeks should not elapse before she should find a comfort in the society of one who would leave no means untried that kindness could suggest to alleviate her sorrows; who would in all things endeavour to supply the place of him who could return no more. And, truly, if the ever-watchful consideration, the tender and fostering care, the minute and gentle offices of affection suggested by a heart of inborn delicacy and feeling—if these cherishing ministrations at the hands of a stranger to our blood can ever supply the loss of a natural tie, Max Greyslaer was the man of all others whose sympathies would be most balmful at such a season.

Alida herself, though in the first agony of her grief she would have shrunk from communion even with Greyslaer, yet, when the paroxysm had passed away, looked naturally to her lover—the earliest and closest friend of the brother she had lost—as her best consoler; and she yearned for his appearance by her side with that impatience of disappointment or delay which, though chiefly characteristic of poor Derrick's impetuous and irrestrainable disposition, was in no slight degree shared as a family trait by his sister. But the day was far distant when the lovers were again to meet; and destiny had strange things in store for them ere that meeting, now so eagerly desired by both, was to be brought about.

The greater part of the patriot troops employed against St. Leger had been marched off to oppose Burgoyne, whose invasion along the Hudson was destined to be equally unsuccessful with that upon the Mohawk. The fate of Major Greyslaer did not lead him to have a share in the glorious operations of Schuyler and Gates; while the large force which had thus been withdrawn from the Valley of the Mohawk, rendering the utmost vigilance necessary in those who were left to guard it, made it impossible for an officer of his standing and importance to be absent on furlough at such a season.

As the autumn came on, he found himself posted at Fort Stanwix, where new works were to be erected to strengthen a frontier position which late events had proved to be all-important to the preservation of the province.

The winter set in, and his prospect of seeing Alida was still further postponed. The spring arrived at last; and what were the hopes it brought with its blossoms, when Greyslaer was about to avail himself at last of a long-promised furlough?

The letters of Alida, meanwhile, had long breathed a spirit which filled him with anxiety. They had become more and more brief; and, though not cold precisely, there was yet something formal in their tenor, as if their writer were gradually falling back upon the old terms of friendship which had so long been their only acknowledged relation of regard. It seemed as if some new and deeper sorrow had fixed upon her heart; some weight of misery which even he could not remove. She did not complain; she made no mention of any specific cause of grief, but she spoke as one whose hopes were no longer of this world.

At first Greyslaer thought that it was the death of her brother which had thus preyed upon her spirits; and his replies to her letters bore the tenderest sympathy with her sorrows as he united in mourning over the early-closed career of his gallant and high-spirited friend. But, dearly as she loved Derrick, his name now was never mentioned by Alida! Could it be that her health was failing? Was the grave, then, about to yawn between Greyslaer and his hopes, to swallow them up forever? And did Alida wish thus gradually to wean him from the wild idolatry which had been the passion of his life? to prepare him for the passing away of his idol?

He thought, with terror, that it must be so. There was a tone of serious religious sentiment, a character of meekness and humility in some of her letters, wholly foreign to her once proud and fervid spirit. It was the tone of one who had ceased to struggle with and rebel against her lot; who had yielded her spirit to the guidance of Him who gave it, and who waited in humble patience for the moment of its recall.

"Yes," said Greyslaer on the day that he was at last to be relieved from his military duties, as he read one of those passages in an agony of emotion, with which something of solace was still intermingled, "yes, she feels herself fading into the grave. Consumption—yet Alida's is not the soul to crumble beneath disease! This new-born gentleness can only have been imparted from above. Her bright spirit is gathering from on high the only grace it lacked to fit it for that blessed sphere. She is fading—fading away from me forever." His eyes were strained on vacancy as he spoke, and he stood with arms wildly outstretched, as if to arrest some beloved phantom which seemed melting before them.

The starting tears had scarcely filled those eyes, when a comrade, abruptly breaking into his quarters, told a tale which congealed them with horror where they stood. The whole nature of Max Greyslaer, the gentle, the high-minded, was changed within him from that very moment.

And what was the monstrous tale that wrought this change upon a mind so well attempered, a soul so steadfast, a heart so true in all that can approve its worth as was that of Greyslaer? Had fortune still a test in store to prove the love that never wavered? Had fate, from her black quiver, thrown a shaft that even love itself, in all its panoply, could not repel?

We are now approaching a part of our story that we would fain pass over as rapidly as possible, for the details are most painful; so painful, so revolting, in fact, that we cannot bring ourselves to do more than touch upon them while hurrying on to the catastrophe which they precipitated.

Walter Bradshawe, as we have seen, was convicted as a spy, and received sentence of death; but a mistaken lenity prompted his reprieve before the hour of execution arrived. When removed to Albany, he was at first closely imprisoned for several months; but the secret Tories, with whom the capital of the province at that time abounded, found means of mitigating the rigor of his confinement, and even of enlisting a strong interest in his behalf among some of the most influential inhabitants. Bradshawe, before the Revolution, had mingled intimately in the society of the place, and his strongly-marked character had made both friends and enemies in the social circle. His present political situation increased the number of both, and both were now equally active in the endeavour to preserve or crush him. The royalists, willing to keep politics entirely out of view, appealed only to private and personal feelings of old association in pleading for his safety.

Some of the patriots sternly rejected all reference to a state of things which had passed away, and would see only a Tory malignant and detected spy in their former neighbour. But others accepted the issue which was offered by the friends of the criminal, and indignantly insisted that there was nothing in his private character which should make him a fit subject for mercy. The whole career of his life was ripped up from the time when, as a law student at Albany, he was known as one of the most riotous and reckless youths of the period—through the opening scenes of the Revolution, when his insolent and scandalous conduct, on more than one occasion, had exasperated the minds of men against the official profligate—through those which followed the outbreak of civil discord, when his aid or connivance was more than suspected to many a deed of ruthless violence, of midnight burning, of bloodshed and cruelty—down to the present time, when he stood a convicted criminal, whose life had been most justly forfeited.

Men stop at nothing when their minds are once excited in times so frenzied as these; and the whole story of the abduction of Miss de Roos was brought up as testimony against Bradshawe's character, with every particular exaggerated, and the outrage painted in every colour which could inspire horror at its enormity.

Rumours of Greyslaer's approaching nuptials with the unhappy lady who was thus made the general subject of conversation, reached the ears of Bradshawe while chafing beneath these charges, and the thought of the misery they would inflict upon his victims might have been sufficient even for his revengeful spirit; but he determined, with a hellish ingenuity, to fling the imputation of the outrage from himself, and, at the same time, to plant its stigma in an aggravated form upon her whose name had been so recklessly dragged in by his persecutors. He first set afloat insinuations in regard to the parentage of the half- blood Indian boy who had long been an inmate of the family at the Hawksnest, and who had more than once visited Albany under the care of Alida, whom the child so much resembled! And then he boldly proclaimed, that, so far from instigating the alleged abduction of Miss de Roos, he had only, out of respect for her connections, aided in withdrawing her from the protection of Isaac Brant, to whom she had fled from her father's halls!

A conviction of the nature of the feelings the tortured and blasted feelings—which had prompted the tone of Alida's letters, flashed electric upon the mind of her lover at this horrid recital; and at thought of his betrothed—that soul-stricken and cruelly injured girl—that lady, most deject and wretched—his noble and most sovereign reason—to which religion had ever been the handmaid—was quite o'erthrown. The soldier's, scholar's eye, tongue, sword, quite—quite down.

In a word, Max Greyslaer, as we have already said—Max, the gentle, the high-minded, became changed in soul on the instant. The prayerful spirit of one short hour ago vanished before the new divinity that usurped its place upon the altar of his heart. His dream of submission to the will of Providence—the tearful resignation which his belief in Alida's illness inspired, was over, lost, swallowed up, obliterated in the wild tempest of his passions. The fierce lust of vengeance shot through his veins and agitated every fibre of his system; a horrid craving seized his heart—the craving for the blood of a human victim! And had Bradshawe stood near, gifted with a hundred lives, Greyslaer could, one by one, have torn them all from out his mortal frame.

The object of his vengeance was far away, but Max Greyslaer from that moment was not less in thought—a *MURDERER*

BOOK SIXTH
RETRIBUTION

Think my former state a happy dream
From which awaked the truth of what we are
Shows me but this. I am sworn brother now
To grim necessity, and he and I
Must keep a league with death.

Shakespeare.

Miserable creature,
If thou persist in this 'tis damnable.
Dost thou imagine thou canst slide on blood
And not be tainted with a shameful fate?
Or, like the black and melancholy yew tree,
Dost hope to root thyself in dead men's graves
And yet to prosper?

Webster.

Prosper me now my fate, some better genius
Than such as wait on troubled passions,
Direct my courses to a noble issue.
. . . I am punished
In mine own hope by her unlucky fortune.

Ford.

A sin! a monstrous sin! Yet with it many
That did prove good men often have been tempted;
And though I'm crooked now, 'tis in your power
To make me straight again.

Massinger.

CHAPTER 1

The Avenger's Journey

His face was calmly stern, and but a glare
Within his eyes—there was no feature there
That told what lashing fiends his inmates were,
Within—there was no thought to bid him swerve
From his intent; but every strained nerve
Was settled and bent up with terrible force
To some deep deed far, far beyond remorse;
No glimpse of mercy's light his purpose cross'd,
Love, nature, pity, in its depths were lost;
Or lent an added fury to the ire
That seared his soul with unconsuming fire.

Drake.

An acute observer of human nature has remarked, that there are seasons when a man differs not less from himself than he does at other times from all other men; and certain it is that passion will often, with the magic of a moment, work a change in the character which the blind pressure of circumstances throughout long years—the moulding habits of an ordinary lifetime, with all their plastic power above the human heart, could never have wrought in the same individual who undergoes this sudden transformation.

An hour had passed away with Greyslaer; an hour of frenzied emotion. And one such hour is enough, with a man of deep, intense, and concentrated feelings, for the gust of passion to subside into the stern calmness of resolve. The soldier who was sent to summon him to the mess-table reported that Major Greyslaer's quarters were vacant. The soldier had passed the major's servant on his way thither to pack up and put away his things, as if his master were likely to be long absent. The servant himself came the next moment to say, that his master, being suddenly called away from the post, would not dine with the mess that day. His brother officers, though knowing that their popular comrade had lately received a long-expected furlough, were still surprised at this abrupt departure; and one or two of them left their seats and hurried out to the stables. Greyslaer stood there with a cloak and valise over his arm, superintending in person the equipment of his horse for a long journey. His cheek was pale, his eye looked sunken, and his aspect altogether was that of one who had for the first time ventured forth after a long and serious illness; yet there was no fever about his eyes; they were rather, indeed, dull, cold, and glassy.

The officers, who simultaneously uttered a cry of surprise at the strange alteration in the appearance of their friend since the morning, were—they hardly knew why—instantly silenced by Greyslaer's manner as he turned round to answer their salutation. They had come there, impelled by motives of friendly curiosity, to ask why he broke away so suddenly from their society. They now stood as if they had forgotten their errand; mute lookers-on, whom some mysterious influence withheld from expressing their emotions even by a sympathetic glance with each other. When all was ready, Greyslaer threw himself into the saddle, murmured something about his having already taken his leave of the colonel, and, as the two officers thought they remembered afterward, left some words of kind farewell for others of the mess.

But the ghastly appearance of Greyslaer, the icy coldness of the hand he gave them to shake, and his strangely unnatural and statue-like appearance as he slowly moved off unattended, struck a chilling amazement into the hearts of his friends, that left them perfectly stupefied for the moment. They had broken away from the table to take a cordial farewell of one whose generous, soldierly temperament, not less than his brilliant social qualities, had made him the pride and delight of the mess. The marble figure with which they but now parted wore, indeed, the lineaments of their friend, but was a perfect stranger to their hearts. The very voice, they swore, never did belong to Max Greyslaer. As for the soldiers, many of whom were recruited from among the superstitious Scotch and German settlers of the neighbouring mountains, they fully believed that some evil spirit of the heathenish Indians had wrought this sudden and mysterious change in the whole look and bearing of their favourite officer; and, alas! it was but too true that the direst of pagan deities had taken up her abode in the heart of Max Greyslaer.

In the meantime, the horseman who furnished so earnest a theme for those whom he had left behind, slowly but steadily pursued his journey. His horse, from the regular, mechanical gait he adopted, seemed to know that a long road was before him. The patient roadster and his motionless rider were long seen from the battlements of Fort Stanwix, though the evening shadows of the adjacent woods snatched them more than once from view before they finally glided like an apparition into the silent forest.

There was no moon, but the stars shone brightly above him as Greyslaer crossed the fatal field of Oriskany. His horse snuffing the air, which, in the warm, moist night of teeming springtime, stole out from the tainted earth, first reminded him of the scene of slaughter over which he was riding. He passed the tree beneath which the remains of De Roos had been laid. He did not shudder. He gave no tear to the recollection of the past, neither did one thought arise to rebuke the memory of his early friend for present sorrows. He did not even envy him the repose of his woodland grave. He only looked coldly upon the spot as a mere landmark of Fate, where one breathing being, warm with life and intelligence, had found his allotted bourne; and why ponder upon a doom common to all fixed, predetermined, and to which he himself, as he believed, was then moving at such a cold, passionless pace?

It was long after midnight before Greyslaer halted, and it was then only for the purpose of refreshing his steed. The dawn found him again upon his journey, and, by changing his horse for a fresher one, he reached the Hawksnest before evening. His original determination led him direct to Albany, where Bradshawe was still under durance; but when he found himself in the neighbourhood of his homestead, and obliged to halt for a few hours from the impossibility of getting another relay, he felt himself irresistibly prompted to make a secret visit to the premises. He did not intend to have an interview with Alida, but he must look upon the house which held her.

He approached the domain, and all was silent. It was too early yet, perhaps, for lights to show through the casement; but, if there had been any there, Greyslaer could not have seen them, for every shutter was closed. There was no smoke from the chimneys, around which the swallows clustered, as huddling there to an unmolested roost. Max had never seen the home of his fathers look so desolate. With quickening pace he advanced to the hall door and tried the latch; but in vain, for the bolts had been drawn within. He knocked, and the sound came hollowly to his ears, as we always fancy it does from an untenanted mansion. He walked to the end of the verandah, and, glancing rapidly round among the outhouses, which stood off at one wing of the main building, observed some poultry at roost among a cluster of pear and locust trees which nearly encircled the kitchen. Their presence suggested him to apply to the only spot where these feathered dependants could now look for their food. He approached the kitchen—a small, Dutch-built building of brick—and rapped against the window before trying the door. A gray-headed negress, protruding her head through a narrow window in one of the gables, at length greeted his ears with the sound of a human voice.

"Who's dere?" she cried, in a quick tone of alarm.

"It is I—Master Max, Dinah."

"Lorrah, massy, be't you for sartain, or only your spook?"

"No spook, my good Dinah, but my living self. Come down and let me in."

"Me mighty glad to see you, massy," said the negress, lighting a candle, after she had unbolted the door to Greyslaer; "for Dinah go to bed when they leib her all alone, so that she not see the spook. But, Lorrah, Mass Max, how berry old he look. He pale, too, as spook," added the slave, shading the candle partly with her hand as she peered into her young master's features.

"But where are all my people? Where is Miss—"

"De boys—all de boys, massy, has gone to de village to hold a corn-dance for seed-time. De housekeeper, you know, lib at de oberseer's down in the lane eber since she shut up the great house after Miss Alida went away."

"And where has Miss Alida gone?" said Greyslaer, with unnatural calmness, as he caught hold of the back of a chair to steady himself; for, of a truth, he for a moment feared that Alida, stung to madness by the cruel nature of her sorrows, might have hurried upon some tragic fate, he scarcely knew what.

The answer of the old servant took an instant load from his bosom. Miss Alida, she said, had taken the little boy with her and gone to Albany near a month since. "She grew thin and looked mighty sorrowful before she went, and it made our hearts bleed to see her, Mass Max," said the faithful black; "and, though we were all cast down like when we saw her pack up her things to go away, yet we thought it might be better for young missus to go where there were more white folks to cheer her up."

Greyslaer made no answer, but, asking for the key of the house, lighted a stable-lantern, and telling Dinah that he should not want her attendance, entered the deserted house. He gained the parlour, which had beheld the last ill-omened parting of the lovers, so sad yet so sweet with al. The room looked much the same as when last he left it, save that there were no fresh-gathered flowers upon the mantelpiece, and some few slight articles belonging to Alida had been removed. He placed the lantern upon a table and opened its door; for the flickering light, dancing upon one or two portraits with which the walls were hung, gave them a sort of fitful life that was annoying. He wished to realise fully that he was alone. He looked around to see if there were no memento or trace of the last hours which Alida had passed in the same chamber.

A little shawl, thrown carelessly across the arm of a sofa, met his eye. He took it up, looked at it, and knew it to be Alida's. It had probably been flung there and forgotten in the hasty moment of departure. Greyslaer had never been what, in modern parlance, is called "a lady's man;" and though he could sometimes tell one article of dress from another, he was wholly unskilled in the effeminate knowledge and toilet-like arts which distinguish that enviable class of our sex. It was curious, therefore, to see him stand and fold this scarf with the utmost nicety and neatness. He handled it, indeed, like something precious; and, from the delicacy with which he pressed it to his lips before placing it in his bosom, he seemed to imagine the senseless fabric imbued with life; but all his motions now were like those of one who moves in a dream.

At last he took up the lantern to retire from the apartment, so desolate in itself, yet peopled with so many haunting memories. A letter, which had been unobserved when he placed it there, lay beneath it. Max read the superscription; it was addressed to himself, and in the hand writing of Alida. He broke the seal, and read as follows:

You will probably, before reading this, have surmised the cause why I have withdrawn from beneath a roof which has never sheltered dishonour. Oh! my friend—if so the wretched Alida may still call you—you cannot dream of what I have suffered while delaying the execution of a step which I believe to be due alike to you and to myself; but the state of my health would not sooner admit of putting my determination into execution, and I knew there would be full time for me to retire before you could come back to assume the government of your house hold. That determination is never to see you more. Yes, Greyslaer, we are parted, and forever. The meshes of villainy which have been woven around me it is impossible to disentangle.

My woman's name is blasted beyond all hope of retrieval, and yours shall never be involved in its disgrace. I ask you not to believe me innocent. I have no plea, no proof to offer. I submit to the chastening hand of Providence. I make no appeal to the love whose tried and generous offices might mitigate this dreadful visitation. I would have you think of me and my miserable concerns no more. God bless you, Max! God bless and keep you; keep you from the devices of a proud and arrogant spirit, which Heaven, in its wisdom, hath so severely scourged in me; keep you from that bitterest of all reflections, the awful conviction that your rebellious heart has fully merited the severest judgment of its Maker. God bless and keep you, dearest, dearest Max. A. D. R.

The features of Greyslaer betrayed no emotion as he read this letter the first, the second, and even the third time, for thrice did he peruse it before he became fully master of its contents; and even then, from the vacant gaze which he fixed upon its characters, it would seem as if his mind were by no means earnestly occupied with what it contained. He laid it down upon the table, paced to and fro leisurely through the chamber, paused, took up some trivial article from the mantelpiece, examined it, and replaced it as carefully as if his thoughts were intent only upon the trifles of the moment. He returned to the table, yet again took up the letter, and slightly shivering as he came to the close of it, turned his eyes upward, while the paper, which he held at arm's length, trembled in his hands, as if he were suddenly seized with an ague-fit. "God of Heaven!" he cried, "I cannot, I dare not pray; yet thou only—" he paused, and shuddered still more frightfully, as his lips seemed almost unwittingly about to syllable the prayerful thoughts which, rising from a heart tenanted as his was by a *murderer's vow,* would be a mockery, an insult to Heaven.

Tears—the first resource of woman, the last relief of man—burst that moment from his eyes, and alleviated a struggle so powerful as to threaten instant madness to its half-convulsed subject. The sufferer buried his face in his hands, and, throwing himself on the sofa, wept long and passionately. Let no man sneer at his weakness, unless he has once loved as did Greyslaer; unless that love has been blasted as his was; unless he has felt himself the victim of an iron destiny, when the heart, softened by years of unchanging tenderness, was least fit ted to bear up under the doom to which he must yield! Greyslaer knew the singular firmness, the inflexible determination of Alida's character. He believed, as she did, that it was now impossible to wipe away the reproach that attached to her name. She had declared her resolution. He felt that he would see her no more.

And was there, then, it may be asked, no doubt in the mind of Max, no shadowy but still poignant doubt, no latent and subtle suspicion of the truth of his mistress? No momentary weighing of testimony as to what might be the real circumstances of Alida's story?

Not one! even for a moment—not one disloyal thought to the majesty of her virtue; not one blaspheming doubt to the holiness of her truth; no, never—never for the breath of an instant, had an un-hallowed suspicion of Alida's maiden purity crossed the mind of her lover! Greyslaer himself was all truth and nobleness! How could so mean and miserable a thought have found entrance into a soul like his, regarding one as high-strung as itself, and with which it had once mingled in full and rich accord? Besides, the love of a feeling and meditative mind; the love that, born in youth, survives through the perilous trials of early manhood, with all the warm yet holy flush of its dawn tincturing its fondness, and all the soberer and fuller light of its noontide testing without impairing its esteem—such a love becomes as much a part of a man's nature, mingles as intimately with his being, as the very life-blood that channels through his veins; and to doubt the purity of her who inspires it were as deathful as to admit a poison into the vital fluids of his system. Such love may languish in hopeless-ness, may wither in despair, may die at last—like the winter-starved bird of Indian fable, who melted into a song, which, they say, is still sometimes heard in his accustomed haunts—but it never can admit one moment's doubt of the worthiness of its object.

The gush of passionate emotion to which the unhappy Max had abandoned himself, had at last its end. And as these were the first tears which he had shed in years—for his frenzied ravings in the hour when he first received the cruel blow to his happiness had had no such re-lief—they were followed by a calmness of mind far more natural than that which he had recently known. Even the old negress, who had sat up watching for him, pipe in mouth, by the kitchen fire, where she had raked a few embers together, could not but observe the difference in his appearance while commenting upon the fixed air of sadness which her young master still wore.

Greyslaer, who, even at such a time, was not forgetful of the humble dependants upon his bounty, handed the old woman a few shillings to replenish her store of tobacco, the only luxury left to her age and infirmity; and, leaving a trifle or two for the other servants, took a kind leave of old Dinah, and returned to the inn where he had left his horse. The gray of the morning found him once more upon the road; and before sunset the spires of Schenectady, the last village he was to pass through before reaching Albany, rose to his view. But we must now leave him to look after other personages of our story.

CHAPTER 2

The Night Attempt

This rope secures the boat. Be still,
Though sounds should rise the heart to chill
If coming feet should meet thine ear,
And I am silent, do not fear;
For I've another task in view.

J. K. Mitchell.

Walter Bradshawe, whose long incarceration at Albany has been already commemorated, had, through the intercession of friends and the clemency of those in power, been transferred from the common jail of the town where he was first imprisoned, to a sort of honorary durance in the guarded chamber of an ordinary dwelling-house.

The building in which he was now confined was situated near the waterside, in the upper part of the town, having a garden in the rear running down to the quay. The room appropriated to Bradshawe was in the second story, at the back of the house, and immediately at the head of the first flight of stairs. At the foot of this staircase, and within a few yards of the outer door, which opened upon the street, was posted a sentinel.

As month after month flew by, and still greater indulgences were granted to Bradshawe with the prolongation of his imprisonment, the duty of this sentinel became at last so much a matter of mere form, that it was customary often to place a new recruit with a musket in his hands in the place which was, in the first instance, occupied by some veteran soldier of trust and confidence. This relaxation of vigilance was, of course, not unobserved by the friends of the prisoner, if, in fact, it was not procured by their agency; and, upon intelligence being conveyed to Valtmeyer how things were situated, he immediately planned the escape of Bradshawe, and selected a shrewd and trusty follower (an old acquaintance of the reader) to assist him in the project.

Syl Stickney, therefore, according to previous arrangement, succeeded in making his way into the city of Albany in the guise of a Helderberg peasant; and, after lounging about the streets for a few days, he allowed himself to be picked up by a sergeant's patrol, and carried to a recruiting station, where, without much difficulty, he was persuaded to enlist in the patriot army. Valtmeyer, in the meantime, hovered around the outskirts of the town, and was advised of all Stickney's movements through the agency of several disaffected persons of condition, who, though in secret among the most active partisans of the royal cause, still kept up appearances sufficiently to enjoy an easy position in society, and who had almost daily access to the prisoner upon the mere footing of former general acquaintance.

Many days had not passed before the Helderberg recruit was placed as sentinel before the door of Bradshawe's quarters, and it was easily ascertained when his tour of duty would come round a second time. Valtmeyer was on the alert to avail himself of the opportunity.

Entering the city of Albany by the southern suburbs, this daring partisan succeeded one night in throwing himself, with a party of followers as desperate as himself, into a stable which stood near the edge of the river, where they lay concealed in the hayloft through the whole of the following day. With the approach of the next evening—the time fixed upon for the proposed rescue—a canoe, paddled by a single negro, crept along the bank of the river from the islands below, and was moored within a few yards of the stable. This canoe was appropriated to the escape of Bradshawe; but the plotting brain of Valtmeyer, which could not remain idle during the long hours that he was obliged to lie quiet in his lurking-place, contrived a still further use for it.

The stable in which he chanced to have taken post was situate at the foot of a garden upon the premises occupied by a zealous Whig, and one of the most efficient members of the Albany Council of Safety, being a man, indeed, whose firmness, vigilance, and unwearied activity in the Whig cause made him second only to General Schuyler among the most valuable citizens of Albany in those times. Mr. Taylor—for that energetic Revolutionary partisan and subsequently distinguished civilian was the person in question—was particularly obnoxious to the Johnson family for the part he had acted in expelling some of its members from the province: and the daring genius of Valtmeyer kindled with the idea of conveying him off a captive to Sir John. In fact, though the success of Bradshawe's escape must be endangered by connecting it with such an attempt, yet Valtmeyer, when, from his lurking-place, he several times throughout the day caught sight of the Whig councillor moving about, unconscious of danger, over his own grounds, could not resist the temptation.

The famous Joe Bettys, who had associated himself with this expedition, did his best to dissuade his daring comrade from this project until they got the head of Bradshawe fairly out of the lion's mouth; but Valtmeyer insisted that no time was so fit as the present; for, the moment Bradshawe was missed, such precautions would be taken that they could not venture into so perilous a neighbourhood again. He knew, he said, that Bradshawe would damn him if he let such a chance go by. It was agreed, therefore, that Bettys should go alone to guide Bradshawe down to the boat, where Valtmeyer promised that he would meet him with his prisoner when the turning of the tide should enable them to drop down the stream most easily.

The attempt to seize Mr. Taylor—as we know from the annals of the period—failed through one of those incidents which, seeming so trivial in themselves, are still so important in their consequences that they cannot but be considered providential. But the results of that failure are most intimately connected with the course of our story.

The clock of the old Dutch church which stood in the centre of State street, struck the hour of midnight when Bettys departed to attend to his share in the perilous operations of the night. Leaving him, for the present, to make his way to the quarters of Bradshawe, we must in the meanwhile attend to the proceedings of his brother brigand.

It was the intention of Valtmeyer to effect an entrance into Mr. Taylor's house with as little disturbance as possible, and to seize and bear away the master of the house hold to the canoe at the foot of his garden. But, though the family had, from appearances, already retired for the night, he meant to defer the attempt until Bettys had made good his retreat to the water-side with Bradshawe. It chanced, however, that scarcely ten minutes after Bettys had left his comrades, their attention was excited by a noise at the door in the rear of the house which precipitated their movements.

A chain falling, the clanging of an iron bar, and the grating of a heavy bolt as it was withdrawn, showed that the only door through which they could hope for ingress was guarded and secured by precautions which, though not unusual in private buildings at that period, seem not to have been anticipated by Valtmeyer in the present instance. There was evidently someone about to come out into the yard. Valtmeyer hoped that it might be the councillor himself; if not, he determined, in any event, that the occasion must not be lost of effecting an entrance through the open door.

Age or caution seemed to make the forthcoming person very slow in his movements; but the door moved at last upon its hinges, and the dull light of a stable lantern falling across the threshold, revealed only the form of an old black servant, who, with creeping step, was moving forward into the yard.

The Tories, thinking the moment for action had arrived, sprang impetuously forward to seize the negro. But, though the sudden rush had nearly effected their object, the movement was premature; for the negro, startled at the first noise of their onset, dropped his lantern, scuttled back across the threshold, and shot the bolt of the door just as the foremost assailant reached it. Valtmeyer gnashed his teeth with rage as he heard the faithful fellow tugging at the chain and bar, still further to secure it within, while his cries at the same time summoned the family to his aid. The next moment there came a pistol-shot from a window; and the Tories, seeing now that the whole neighbourhood would be alarmed, retreated to their boat as rapidly as possible.

The canoe was easily gained; but now what to do in the predicament in which he had placed himself puzzled even the fertile brain of Valtmeyer. To remain where he was, exposed all his party to seizure, for the whole town must be alarmed in a very few moments; yet to depart at once must jeopard, fatally perhaps, the lives of both Bradshawe and Bettys, not to mention that of the false sentinel, who, it was supposed, would come off with them. Valtmeyer did not hesitate long; and his decision, though attended with no benefit to his absent allies, was still the best that could be made in the premises. He determined to lighten his canoe, and, at the same time, effect a diversion in case of pursuit, by sending all his followers, save himself, to make their retreat along the river's bank by land, in the same way they had entered the town. He then, with wary paddle, commenced creeping along shore up the river, so as to approach the place of Bradshawe's confinement, which was toward the other extremity of the town.

Let us now follow the doughty Joe Bettys upon his mission.

The duty of this worthy *confrère* of Valtmeyer, though perilous, was sufficiently plain. He had only to ascertain that the Tory sentinel was at his post, and make him aware that he himself was near, when Bradshawe, who knew the minutest arrangement of the plot for his relief, would at once emerge from his quarters and follow Bettys' guidance. Their first movement would be to make for the river; for there lay their means of escape, and there the piles of timber, of which Albany was ever a great mart, afforded the best opportunity for present concealment, if it should be necessary.

And thus, indeed, every circumstance, like those of a well rehearsed play, might have succeeded each other, were it not for the intrusion of a most unexpected actor upon the scene.

The first intimation which Bettys had of such interference was from the stupid exclamation of surprise which his appearance drew from the disguised sentinel as he en countered him upon entering the hall. Stickney, who might have just awakened from a nap upon a bench which stood near, was supporting his staggering limbs against the banister, and seemed to be listening, half awake, to some noise in the room at the head of the stairs. Upon the entrance of Bettys, he turned round sharply, and, catching at his musket, which leaned against the wall, seemed disposed to dispute the passage with him.

"Softly, Syl," cried the wary Joe; "you needn't act the drunken man so far as to run me through by mistake. Why, zounds! the infernal rascal's dead drunk in earnest; sewed up completely, by—" he added, with an angry oath, as he advanced and collared him.

"Aint in liquor—more—than—my—duty—requires," hiccoughed Sylla; "for didn't I see—you—with my—eyes—shut—come in that door and go upstairs—but ten minutes—ago?"

"Me—me, you lying, drunken rascal! Saw me? Answer quickly, or I'll shake the life out of you."

"If I didn't, may I never—touch—a drop of good liquor again. By Goy!" ejaculated Stickney, finishing his as severations with a stupid stare,"! believe I am drunk; for, if this be raally Leftenant Joe Bettys, I've seen double at least once tonight. The fellow that went upstairs—"

Bettys waited to hear no more, but hurled his sottish follower from him with a force that sent him reeling to the farther end of the hall. The noise the man made in falling brought the owner of the mansion instantly to his door; but he only opened it far enough to thrust out his head, and cast a furtive and anxious glance at Bettys as the latter rushed up the stairs, when, seeming to think for the moment that all was right, he drew back and locked his apartment. And we too must now leave Bettys upon the threshold of Bradshawe's room, to look after another of those who were most deeply concerned in the deeds of this eventful night.

CHAPTER 3

The Rencontre

Ay, curse him—but keep
The poor boon of his breath
Till he sigh for the sleep
And the quiet of death!
Let a viewless one haunt him
With whisper and jeer,
And an evil one daunt him
With phantoms of fear.

Whittier.

It chanced, then, that, in the very hour appointed for carrying into execution the bold project which we have thus far traced, Max Greyslaer, bent on his errand of murderous vengeance, entered the city of Albany by the Schenectady road, and, leaving his horse at a wagoner's inn in the suburbs, penetrated on foot into the heart of the town. He had possessed himself, while at Schenectady, of every particular relating to the place of Bradshawe's imprisonment, and of the nature of the guard that was kept over him; and fevered with impatience to accomplish the one fatal object which had brought him hither, he proceeded at once to reconnoitre the prisoner's quarters. Greyslaer, in all his movements that night, acted like one who was impelled in a dream by some resistless power within him; and he *was* spell-bound—if the icy wand of demon passion hath aught in it of magic power above the human heart.

He approached the house, and discovered, by the glimmer of a dull lamp within the entry, that the street door was ajar. He reached the door itself, and, opening it still further with a cautious hand, beheld the sentinel stretched upon a bench in the hall, and snoring so obstreperously, that, if his slumbers were not feigned, they must be the effect of deep intoxication. An empty flagon, which lay on the floor just where it had rolled from the drunken hand of the sleeper, seemed sufficiently to prove that the latter must be the case; and, indeed, we may here mention, in passing, that Stickney, who played the part of the Helderberg recruit so successfully, subsequently escaped the extreme penalty of military law by pleading that his neglect of duty arose from intoxication produced by a drugged mixture administered by the family upon whom the prisoner and his sentinel were alike quartered—their real connivance in the escape of Bradshawe being known only to Stickney's superiors.

Greyslaer paused a moment to discover if there were no greater obstacle to his ingress to the premises than those which had hitherto presented themselves. Suddenly he heard a step in the room nearest to the street door; it showed that the family which occupied the lower floor of the house had not yet retired. Greyslaer started slightly, (did the guilty soul of a murderer make him thus tremulous ?) and, turning round at the noise, the scabbard of his sword rattled against the bench whereon reposed the sleeping soldier. A light flashed momentarily through the keyhole of the door opposite; and then, as it was straightway extinguished, all became still as before.

Had Max's mind not been wholly preoccupied by one subject, his suspicions must now have been fully aroused, that the occupants of the mansion were quietly colluding in the escape of the prisoner. But now he had ascended the staircase, and, pausing yet a moment to loosen his rapier in its sheath, he gave a low tap at the door of the room in which Bradshawe was quartered.

"Enter, my trusty Joseph, most adroit and commend able of burglars," said Bradshawe, scarcely looking up from the table at which he was writing by the fickle light of a shabby taper. "Hold on but a single instant, Bettys," he continued; "I am only scratching off some lines to exculpate my worthy host from any share in this night's business, in case the wise rebels should think fit to seize him. There, 'Walter Bradshawe,' that signature will be worth something to an autograph-hunter some of these days; and now—"

"And *now*," echoed a voice near him, in tones so freezing, that even the heart of Bradshawe was chilled within him at the sound; "and now prepare yourself for a miscreant's death upon this very instant."

Bradshawe looked up in stupefied amazement.

"Do you know me, Walter Bradshawe?" cried Greyslaer, raising his hat from his brow, and making a stride toward the table.

"We're blown, by G—d!" ejaculated the captive Tory. "Know you? to be sure I do. You're the rebel Greyslaer, who, having got wind of this night's attempt, have come mousing here after further evidence to hang me. But you'll find it devilish hard to prove that I meant to abuse the clemency of Lafayette," added the prisoner, tearing to pieces the note he had just written.

"I come on no such business," said Greyslaer, smiling bitterly. "I come—"

"And if you are not here in an official capacity, sir, how dare you intrude into my private chambers?" cried Bradshawe, springing to his feet and confronting Max with a look of brutal insolence.

"Bradshawe, you cannot distemper me by such a tone of insult. Your own heart must suggest the errand which brought me hither." (The countenance of Bradshawe for the first time fell.) "I might have slain you as I entered; murdered you as you sat but now with your eyes bent upon the paper that you have since torn; but my vengeance were incomplete, unless you knew by whose hand you fell."

The passionless, icy tone in which Greyslaer spoke, seemed to unnerve even the iron heart of Bradshawe. He tried to return the steadfast gaze of that fixed and glassy eye, but his glances involuntarily wandered, his cheek grew pale, his soul wilted before the marble looks of his mortal foe. "He must have the strength as well as the look of a maniac," he murmured, catching at the back of a chair which stood near him whether to seize it as a weapon of defence or merely to steady himself by its support, we know not. But Max seemed to put the last construction upon the act, as, with a discordant laugh, he cried,

"Aha! he shrinks then, this truculent scoundrel—"

"I'm unarmed, I'm defenceless—a prisoner. If it's satisfaction you seek of me, Major Greyslaer," cried Bradshawe, hurriedly, as, holding the chair before him, he backed toward a corner of the apartment—

"Satisfaction, felon?" thundered Max, interrupting the appeal by springing furiously across the room. The strength of Bradshawe seemed to wither beneath the touch of the icy fingers that were instantly planted in his throat. "Oh! felon—damned felon! what satisfaction can *you* make to man—to God, for driving me to an accursed deed like—this?"

His sword leaped from its scabbard as he spoke, and Bradshawe involuntarily closed his eyes as the gleaming blade seemed about to be sheathed in his bosom.

But suddenly the hand of Greyslaer was arrested by an iron grip from behind; he turned to confront the assailant who had thus seized him, when Bradshawe, quickly recovering himself, dealt a blow with the chair—of which he had not yet released his hold—a blow that brought Greyslaer instantly to the ground. Wounded, but not stunned, Max quickly regained his feet, and made a pass at the intruder, which only inflicted a slight flesh wound, but not before Bradshawe had thrown open a window, through which, followed by Bettys, he leaped upon a shed and dropped into the garden below. Greyslaer hesitated not to follow; but the mutual assistance which the fugitives rendered each other, enabled them to scale the garden-wall more quickly than their pursuer, and their receding forms were swallowed up in the surrounding darkness, before Greyslaer had gained the quay to which they had retreated.

The reviving air of night, the inspiring consciousness of freedom after so long incarceration, brought back at once to Bradshawe his wonted energy and hardihood of character; and when Bettys provided him with a weapon to use in any extremity to which they might be reduced in accomplishing the final steps of their escape, the bold Tory could scarcely resist the impulse to turn back and take signal vengeance upon the man who had momentarily humbled his haughty spirit; but every instant was precious, and the fugitives paused not in making their way to the point where they expected to find Valtmeyer's boat waiting them.

They followed down the water's edge nearly to State street, as it is now called, and must have been within a few hundred yards of the canoe—for the garden of Mr. Taylor, near which it was moored, lay close upon the south side of this broad avenue—when suddenly the report of a pistol fired from the house arrested their steps.

They faltered and turned back. Bradshawe, hurriedly telling his companion to leave him to his fate, turned the angle of a street, and struck up from the river toward the heart of the town. He approached Market street, which runs parallel with the Hudson, and, hearing the tramp of an armed patrol upon its side-walks, concealed himself behind a bale of merchandise, which afforded the only shelter near. It seemed an age before the city guard had passed by; and Bettys, who, in the meantime, had thridded the piles of staves and lumber upon the quay, and visited the place where he expected to find the canoe, returned to Bradshawe's side just as the patrol had passed the head of the street, and whispered that the boat was gone.

Not an instant was to be lost if they would now make their way to the suburbs, through which was their only hope of escape into the open country beyond. They crossed Market street—though at the widest part—fled up the dark and narrow passage of Maiden Lane, and gained the outskirts of the town near the top of the hill, where the old jail, till within a few years, stood frowning. The sight of the grated cells in which he had been immured for so many long months, lent new life to the exertions of Bradshawe; and, with the agile Bettys, he soon reached the nodding forests, which at that time still in broad patches crowned the heights in the rear of the ancient city of Albany.

Let us now return to Greyslaer, whom we left groping his way among the midnight shadows upon the river's bank when the fugitives escaped from his pursuit, and flitted along the water-side while he was scaling the walls of the garden.

The escape of Bradshawe, under all the circumstances which attended his imprisonment, wrought up his pursuer to a pitch of frenzy that completely bewildered him. It was not merely that he was thus foiled in his meditated vengeance on the instant when the cruel slanderer of Alida seemed placed by fate completely in his hands, but the idea that Bradshawe should make good his retreat within the lines of the royalists, and thus triumphantly leave the stigma which he had planted to work its dire consequences, when he himself was secure and far away from his victims, made Greyslaer frantic; and Max, scarce knowing whither he hurried or what he could hope for in this wild pursuit, darted hither and thither amid the labyrinth of lumber which was heaped up along all the busy quays of Albany.

Now it chanced that, at the very moment that Bettys was, with whispered curses, deploring to Bradshawe the absence of the canoe, upon which the safety of all seemed to depend, Valtmeyer, whom the intervening piles of boards upon the shore had alone screened from the view of Bettys, was stealthily gliding around the head of the pier at the foot of the street where the two fugitives had halted until the patrol should pass by. The outlaw, too, as well as they, heard the tramp of armed men in the silent streets of the city; and, pausing for a moment until the sounds of alarm swept further toward the northern part of the town, he plied his paddle with fresh industry until he could run his shallop into a slip or dock near the foot of the garden where Max had first lost sight of the fugitives. Here he landed, in the hope of still being in time to prevent Bradshawe and his comrade from seeking the boat at a point further down the quay, and taking them off from the shore the moment they should make good their escape from the rear of the house.

In the meantime, the darkness of the night, and the other obstructions to pursuit already mentioned, soon cut short the frantic search of Greyslaer, who, emerging from the heavy shadows of the place, thought that he again had caught sight of the fugitives as Valtmeyer suddenly confronted him in his path.

"*Dunder und blixem*, capting, I was afeard you were a goon coon, and was on the point of shoving off without you. Where's Bettys? We must be off in haste! A rebel *luder!*" he exclaimed, as Max sprang forward and attempted to collar him. "*Der Henker schlag herein!* The hangman strikes in it, but Red Wolfert's rope is not yet spun."

And, muttering thus, the giant, quick as light, shook off the grasp of the young officer, and leaping backward a pace or two, presented a pistol at his head.

"Miss me, you scoundrel, and your fate is certain," cried the undaunted Max; but Valtmeyer had no idea of further compromising the escape of himself and his friends by the report of arms at such a moment; and, seeing that the attempt to awe his foeman into silence had failed, he drew his hanger and rushed upon Greyslaer; the sword of Max was already out, and the ruffian strength of Valtmeyer found an admirable match in the skill, the steadiness, and alertness of movement of his opponent, though the darkness amid which they fought deprived Greyslaer of much of his superiority as a fencer.

Thrice did the outlaw attempt, by beating down the guard of his opponent, to fling his huge form upon Max and bear him to the earth; and thrice did the sword of Greyslaer drink the blood of the brawny borderer as he thus essayed a death-grapple with his slender foe.

And now Greyslaer, who had hitherto yielded ground before the furious onslaught of the other, began to press him backward foot by foot, until the edge of the quay, upon which Valtmeyer stood, permitted him to retreat no further. He ground his outlandish oaths more savagely between his teeth as he felt his life-blood failing him, and, conscious that his hour had come, seemed bent alone upon bearing his gallant foeman with him to destruction. He heard the sullen dashing of the waves at his feet, and glared furtively around; whether from now first realizing the double danger near, or to distract for a moment the attention of his antagonist, it mattered not; for now, quickly dropping his weapon, he sprang forward and clutched Max in his arms in the same moment that a final thrust passed through his own body.

The wound was mortal, but still the bold outlaw struggled. He had borne his foeman to the ground, and, pierced through as he was, with the steel still quivering in his vitals, he floundered with his grappled burden toward the water's edge. The life of Greyslaer hung upon a hair, as with knee planted against the breast of Valtmeyer and one hand at his throat, he clung with the other to the topmost timber of the pier; when, suddenly, the mortal grip of the dying ruffian was relaxed. There was a heavy plashing in the dark-rolling river, and now its current swept away the gory corse of Valtmeyer.

But the perils of this eventful night were not yet over for Max Greyslaer.

The town, as we have already noted, had been alarmed by the scene near Mr. Taylor's premises, and the streets were now patrolled in every direction, either by a military guard or by the bold *burghers*, who rushed armed from their houses at the first sound of danger. Amid the excitement of a fight so desperate, neither Max nor his redoubted foe had noticed the turmoil that was rising near. But the clashing of their swords had not escaped the ears of the patrol, who hurried toward the spot whence came the sounds just as the conflict was terminating; Greyslaer had scarcely regained his feet before he was in the hands of the guard—a prisoner.

CHAPTER 4

The Dungeon Tenant

Daughter of grief! thy spirit moves
In every whistling wind that roves
Across my prison grates.
It bids my soul majestic bear,
And with its sister spirit soar
Aloft to Heaven's gates.

J. O. Beauchamp.[1]

Max Greyslaer the tenant of a dungeon? and placed there, too, as the murderer of Walter Bradshawe? It was but too true! The fatality was a strange one; yet there are turns in human destiny far more singular.

Had Greyslaer been recognized in the moment that, covered with dust and gore, he rose breathless from the embrace of the dying Valtmeyer, and was seized by the party of Whig soldiery, the charges that were that very night preferred against him by the Tory friends of Bradshawe, in order to conceal their share in the escape of that partisan, had never been listened to; nor could their successful attempt at criminating him have made the head it did. But, now, before the Whig officer could call upon a single friend to identify his character, the suspicion of murder had been fixed upon him, and, by the time his name and rank became known, his enemies were prepared with evidence which made that name a still further proof of his guilt.

The disaffected family to whose care Bradshawe was intrusted, deposed to the fact of a muffled stranger having passed into his quarters at midnight. The head of the household averred that it was a man of Greyslaer's height and general appearance. He had heard his step

---

1. *Vide A Winter in the West*, vol. ii.

in the entry, unlocked his door, and looked out to see who it might be; but the stranger having already reached the staircase and begun ascending, his face was averted from deponent, who could see only the general outline of the stranger's figure. The deponent did not call upon the stranger to stop, nor address him in any way; for he took it for granted that the stranger had been challenged by the sentinel, and must therefore be provided with a permit or pass to visit the prisoner at that unusual hour. He had himself already retired for the night.

The deponent had subsequently heard a tumult, as of men struggling together, in the room above. He leaped from his bed, and, hastening to ascend the stairs, stumbled over the sentinel who lay stretched at their foot, as if struck down and stunned a moment before. As he stooped a moment to raise the man, he heard a noise, as of a heavy body falling, in the room above. He hurried onward to the room, but its occupant had already disappeared. There was blood upon the floor; a broken chair, and other signs of desperate conflict. A window that looked into the garden stood open, and there was fresh blood upon the window sill.

Other members of this deponent's family here supplied the next link in the testimony, by stating that they had heard the window above them thrown open with violence, and the feet of men trampling rapidly over the shed beneath it, as if one were in ferocious pursuit of the other.

As for the sentinel, he seemed ready to swear to anything that would get himself out of peril. He could not account for the stranger making his way into the house unnoticed by himself, save by the suspicion that his evening draught must have been drugged by somebody. He certainly was not sleeping upon his post, but his perceptions were so dulled that he was not aware of the presence of an intruder until he felt himself suddenly struck from behind, and cast nearly senseless upon the ground. But he too, when raised to his feet by the first witness, had followed him to the chamber already described, of whose appearance at the time the former deponent had given a true description.

The testimony of the night patrol—less willingly given—proved the condition in which Greyslaer was found, with dress disordered and bloodstained, as if fresh from some deadly encounter. The marks of blood, too, were found spotted over the timbers of the pier, while the footprints leading down to the water's edge; the steps dashed here and there in the blood-besprinkled dust; the light soil beaten down and flattened in one place, and scattered in others, as if some heavy body had been drawn across it—all marked the spot as the scene of some terrible struggle, whose catastrophe the black-rolling waves at hand might best reveal.

There was but one circumstance which suggested another agency than that of Greyslaer in the doings of this eventful night, and that was the attack on Mr. Taylor's premises, which had first alarmed the town. But this, again, took place at the opposite side of the city, and could have had no connection with Bradshawe; for Mr. Taylor's people had seen the ruffians flying off in a contrary direction from that where Bradshawe resided.

But, then, what motive could have hurried on a man of Greyslaer's habits and condition of life to a deed so foul as that of murder?

His habits, his condition? Why! was not the supposed murderer no other than the wild enthusiast, who, in some besotted hour of passion, had betrothed himself to the abandoned offcast of an Indian profligate? And had not Bradshawe been compelled, by the venomous assaults which had been made upon his own character, to rip up that hideous story, and publish to the world the infamy of Greyslaer's mistress? Was it not, too, through the very instrumentality of this unhappy person that Bradshawe's life had, under colour of law, been previously endangered; that the felon charge of acting as a spy had been got up and enforced against the much-injured royalist? a charge which, even after sentence of death had been pronounced upon the Tory partisan, the stanchest of the faction hesitated to acknowledge was sufficiently sustained to war rant his execution. No, the murderer of Bradshawe could be no other than the betrothed lover of Alida! Such was the testimony and such the arguments which had lost Greyslaer his personal liberty, and which now threatened him with a felon's fate upon the scaffold!

And where now was that unhappy girl, whose sorrows had so strangely reacted upon her dearest friend? whose blighted name carried with it a power to blast even the life of her lover?

It is the dead hour of midnight, and she has stolen out from the house of the relative who had given her shelter and privacy, to visit the lonely prisoner in his dungeon. The prisoner starts from his pallet as the door grates on its hinges, and that pale form now stands before him.

Let the first moments of their meeting be sacred from all human record. It were profane to picture the hallowed endearments of two

347

true hearts thus tried, thus trusting each other till the last.

"Oh, Max," murmured Alida, when the first moments of their meeting were over, "oh, how little did I dream, when I wrote that you should see me no more, that love and duty again might lead me to you; that God's providence would place you where no woman's doubt could prevent me from—"

"God's providence! Speak not those words to me," said Greyslaer, withdrawing from her as if some shuddering recollection hurried over his soul.

Alida answered only with a look of perplexed, wildly appealing anxiety; while the features of her lover became set and moody, as if from some suddenly occurring internal consciousness that their identities of sympathy were no longer the same.

"You loved me once, Alida," said Greyslaer, his stolid look not changing.

"Oh God! he's mad, he's mad! Loved you once, dearest! When could those days be, time gone by? Loved you once, Max!" She wept bitterly.

Greyslaer looked on unmoved. "Was I worthy of your love? Did my devotion satisfy the imperious needs of a soul like yours?" he asked with mechanical coldness.

"*Did* it satisfy? Oh Heaven, what means this, Greyslaer? my life, my more than life! Thou knowest, thou knowest thy love has been to me more than fancy had conceived—more than hope had whispered. Have I not lived in the atmosphere of thy exhaustless tenderness, when thou wert near; and when defrauded of thee—when shut from thy dear presence, has not my spirit still drank from the unfathomable depths of thine? Satisfy? My own, my proud, my noble Greyslaer, is not thy nature as wildly affluent, as burning, as headstrong as my own—and have I not witnessed thy high will in curbing it, and then adored thee for thy nobleness? Loved thee once, Greyslaer?— ever, ever. Thou dost satisfy the restless cravings of thought; thou dost content the spiritualism of sentiment; thou dost gratify the dreams of imagination; thou dost fill the sense of the manly and the beautiful; thou dost flood with content all yearnings of affection; all cravings of tenderness; all rapturous dreams of sympathy—the mightiest!

"Thy love not satisfy me, Max? Oh, if I had died and left this doubt upon thy soul! this dreadful scepticism of faith in me and in thyself—" and the impassioned being wrung her hands in anguish at the thought she had conjured up; "but I would not—I could not have died without thee, Max.—Max, I deceived myself when I left thee.—I am a woman, a poor weak woman.—I am no heroine at the call of duty, as I thought myself.—If not thy wife, thy mistress then, thy thrall; I would nestle in thy bosom, I would share thy councils, I would comfort, I would sustain thee; or if not that, I would sit at thy feet, clasp thy dear hand, and look into thy noble face, and read all of heaven there.— Thou wert made for worship, for me to worship, and when my heart overflows in its fullness of love for thee, we would kneel down and bless God each for the gift of the other.—Speak to me, speak to me now—now, my noble, my beautiful, my grand—speak to me, and say thou believest I am so wrapped in thy being I would be absorbed into thy very self.—Tell me, oh, tell me, but that my love has been worthy of thine own, as deep, as boundless, as unutterable."

It was a terrible joy that which thrilled the bosom of that dungeon prisoner as his betrothed the next instant throbbed against his delirious heart. But Greyslaer's concentrated passion supplied no terms of rhapsody through which to pour itself. "Alida," said he, speaking at last, and the cold drops stood on his forehead as he pronounced the words, and his voice was hard and husky, as if delivering the doom of his worldly honour—"Alida, wert thou as base as Bradshawe would make thee out to be, ere accepting my love, mine thou shouldst be— mine. I would still uphold thee, peerless in womanhood, oh most angelic in thy devotedness—heeding not, believing not, recking not how, or when, or where—mine only, mine all—thy glorious soul did fall from its appointed sphere of purity and reverence, I would pluck thee from the scorners, and buckler thy name with mine against a world of obloquy—most loved, most dear, most radiant one, as Heaven hears me now, I would!" .

Ashen pale was the cheek of Alida, as thus he spoke. "Thou *shouldst NOT*, Greyslaer," was her firm reply. "My pride in thee is at the root of all my love. Never shouldst thou bate thine honour one jot to share my sorrows or console me in despair."

"Honour!" said Max bitterly—"Alida, Alida, know you not that, in the eye of Heaven, I am this moment the thing that men would make me out to be?"

"Oh, no, no, no!" she shrieked, starting back with fear tares which, for a single instant convulsed with horror, were changed to more than woman's tenderness as again she caught the hands of Max in both hers, "you are not, you cannot be a—a—no, Greyslaer, no, you cannot be a—murderer. You fought with him, you met him singly—sinfully, in the eye of Heaven, but not with brutal intent of murder—you did—in single combat—'twas in a duel he fell."

"Hear me, hear me, my loved one; it was—"

"No, no, I will not hear; I know 'twas so; and I—*I* was the one whose guilty dream of vengeance first quickened such intention into being, and sharpened your sword against his life."

"Alas! Alida, why torture yourself by recalling the memory of that wild hallucination of your early years? That shadowy intention of avenging your own wrongs was but the darkly romantic dream of an undisciplined mind preyed upon and perverted by disease and sorrow; and many a prayerful hour has since atoned to Heaven for those sinful fancies. But my conscience is loaded far more heavily, and with a burden that none can share; a burden," he added, smiling with strange meaning on his lip, "that mayhap it hardly wishes to shake off."

"You slew him not at vantage; he fell not an unresisting victim to your vengeful passions," gasped Alida.

"The man that I slew yesternight fell in fair and open fight, Alida. There is no stain upon my soldier's sword for aught that happened then." The words had not passed the lips of her lover ere Alida was on her knees. "Nay," cried Max, catching her clasped hands in his, "blend not my name in your prayer of thankfulness to Heaven; 'twill weigh it down and keep it from ascending; for, surely as thou kneelest there, I am in heart a murderer. 'Twas Bradshawe's life at which I aimed; 'twas Bradshawe's death, his murder that I sought, when Valtmeyer crossed my path and fairly met the punishment of his crimes. A mysterious Providence made me the instrument of its justice in exacting retribution from him; and the same Providence now punishes in me the foul intention which placed me there to do its bidding."

If there was something of bitterness in the tone in which Max spoke these words, which gave a double character to what he said, Alida did not notice it, as passionately she cried,

"Kneel, then, Greyslaer, kneel here with me; kneel in gratitude to the Power that preserved thee from the perpetration of this wickedness, and so mysteriously foiled the contrivings of thy heart; kneel in thankfulness to the chastening hand that hath so soon sent this painful trial to punish this lapse from virtue—to purge thy heart from its guilty imaginings; kneel in prayer that this cloud which we have brought upon ourselves may in Heaven's own time pass away; or, if not, *ITS* will be done!"

"I may not, I cannot kneel, Alida," said Max, in gloomy reply to her impetuous appeal. "No! though I own the chastening hand which is even now stretched out above me, my heart still refuses to cast out the design that brought me hither. I will not, I must not kneel in mockery to Heaven!"

"And thou—thou wouldst still—*murder* him!" shrieked Alida.

"Leave me, distract me not thus," cried her agonized lover, leaning against the wall as if to steady himself, and covering his face with his hands to shut out the earnest gaze she fixed upon him.

"Speak to me, look at me, Max," implored Alida, in tones of wild anguish, as she sprang forward and caught his arm. "Thou wouldst—thou wouldst!"

A cold shiver seemed to tremble through the frame of her lover; but his voice, though low and husky, had an almost unearthly calmness in it, as dropping his hands and fixing his looks full upon her, he said,

"I would, though hell itself were gaping there to swallow both of us! Hear me, Alida; it is the hand of Fate—it is some iron destiny that works within my heart—that knots together and stiffens the damned contrivances it will not forego. Why should I deceive you when I cannot deceive myself? Why insult Heaven with this vain lip-worship when no holy thought can inhabit here?—here," he repeated, striking his hand upon his bosom, "here, where one horrid craving rages to consume me—the lust of that man's blood!"

"Oh God! this is too horrible!" gasped Alida, as, shuddering, she sank upon the prisoner's pallet and buried her face in her hands.

Max made no movement to raise her, but his was the mournful gaze of the *doom-stricken*, as, standing aloof, his lips moved with some half-uttered words, which could scarcely have reached the ears of Alida.

"Weep on," he said, "weep on, my love—my first, last, my only love. Those bursting tears do well become her, a child of sorrow from her earliest youth. Those tears! Mine is not the hand to stay them, mine the heart to mingle with them in sympathetic flow; for I—I can weep no more!"

"Alida, sweet Alida," said he, advancing at last toward her; "Alida, my best, my loveliest—she hears me not; she will not listen to me. Oh God! why shudder you so, and withdraw your hand from my touch?"

But Alida has sprung to her feet, has dashed the tears from her eyes, and her clear voice thrills in the ears of her lover as thus she speaks to him:

351

"Hear me, Greyslaer: 'twas I first infused these fell thoughts into your bosom; 'twas I, in the besotted season of youth, and folly, and girlish fantasy *I* that taught you this impious lesson of murderous retribution. It is my wrongs, my individual and personal injuries, whose recent aggravation has revived the mad intent, and stamped it with a character of blackness such as before you never dreamed of. Now, by the God whom I first learned to worship in full, heart-yielded reverence, from you, Max Greyslaer—by *HIM* I swear, that, if you persist in this, I—I myself, woman as I am—will be the first to tread the path of crime, to which you point the way, and forestall you in perdition of your soul. I am free to move where I list, and work my will as best I may; *your* will is but that of a dungeon prisoner, and Bradshawe's life, if it depend upon the murderous deed of either, shall expire at my hand before you pass these doors."

The fire of her first youth flashed in the eyes of Alida as she spoke, and there was a determination seated on her brow, such as even in her haughtiest mood of that arrogant season it had never worn. But the next moment all this had passed away entirely, and it was only the broken-hearted, the still loving, the imploring Christian woman that kneeled at the feet of Greyslaer.

"Max—Max—dearest Max," she said, while sobs half suffocated her utterance, "it is Alida, your own, your once fondly loved Alida, that pleads to you, that kneels here imploring you to rend this wickedness from your breast, and ask Heaven for its pardon. It is she who has no friend, no relative, no resting-place in any heart on earth save that from which you would drive her to make room for images so dreadful. Surely you did love me once; surely you have pity for my sorrows; you will not, you cannot persist in thus trebling their burden. Ah! now you weep; it is Heaven, not I, dearest Max, that softens your heart toward your own Alida. Blessed be those tears, and—nay, raise me not yet—not till you have knelt beside me."

★★★★★★

The cell is narrow, the walls are thick. There is no sound of human voice, no shred of vital air can pass through the vaulted ceiling which shuts in those kneeling lovers! Can, then, the subtle spirit of prayer pierce the flinty rock, mount into the liberal air, and, spreading as it goes, fill the wide ear of Heaven with the appeal of those two lonely human sufferers?

The future may unfold.

CHAPTER 5

Wayfarers in the Forest

Now stay, thou ghostly traveller, stay;
Why haste in such a mad career?
Be the guilt of thy bosom as dark as it may,
'Twere better to purge it here.

The Dead Horseman, by Mrs. Sigourney.

The mingled yarn of our story is now becoming so complex, that, to follow out its details with clearness, we must pause to take up a new thread which at this moment becomes interwoven with the rest.

The faithful Balt had been almost the only visitor admitted to the Hawksnest during the last few months that immediately preceded the withdrawal of Miss de Roos from her home. The old forester seemed to have conceived a kind of capricious liking for little Guise, the half-blood child; and as his visits were really paid to that ill-omened urchin, though his excuse for coming was to ask after the health of Miss Alida, and to inquire if she had any news of the major, Miss de Roos never thought it worthwhile to deny herself to her humble friend, even while practising the strictest seclusion in regard to her other neighbours.

Balt, in the meantime, was too observing a character not to notice that some secret grief must be preying upon Alida; and his new-sprung interest in little Guise soon became secondary to the feelings of concern which her fast fading health awakened in the worthy woodsman.

It chanced one day that Alida, who not infrequently took occasion to employ his services in some slight task, which, while remunerating his trouble, would give him occupation while lounging about the premises, pointed out a magnolia which she wished removed to

353

another part of the shrubbery, in the hope that a more favourable situation might revive its drooping condition. Balt readily under took the task of transplanting it, while Alida looked on to direct him during the operation.

"Now, Miss Alida." said the woodsman, striking his spade into the earth, "I don't know much of the natur of this here little tree, seeing as I never happened on one in any woods I've hunted over; but I rayther mistrust the winds have but little to do with its getting kinder sickly as it were, in its present situation, I do."

"And why, Balt?"

"Why. you see now, ma'am, if the tree were attacked from the outside, it's the outside would first feel it; the edges of the leaves would first crumple up and turn brownish like, while the middle parts of them might long remain as sleekly green and shiny as the edges be now. There's something, Miss Alida, at the heart, at the root, I may rayther say, of that tree; something that undermines it and withers it from below. And these sort o' ailings, whether in trees or in human beings, are mighty hard to get at, I tell ye." As the woodsman spoke he leaned upon his spade, and looked steadfastly at Miss de Roos, who felt conscious of changing colour beneath the earnest but respectful gaze of her rude though well-meaning friend.

She did not answer, but only motioned him to go on in his digging; and Balt, seeing that he had in some way offended, resumed his work with diligence. But the next moment, forgetful wholly of the figurative use he had made of his skill in arboriculture, and speaking merely in literal application to the task before him, he exclaimed triumphantly,

"There, you see, now, it's jist as I told ye, Miss Alida; there *has* been varmint busy near the roots of this little tree. Look but where I put my spade, and see how the field-mice have more than half girdled it. The straw and other truck which that book-reading Scotch gardener put around the roots, has coaxed the mice to make their nests there in the winter, and they've lived upon the bark till only two or three fingers' breadths are left."

"I hope there's bark enough left yet to save it," said Alida, now only intent upon preserving the shrub.

"There's life there, Miss Alida—green life in that narrow strip; and, *while there's life, there's hope;* and old Balt, when he once knows whence comes the ailing, is jist the man to stir himself and holp it from becoming fatal."

As the woodsman spoke he again ventured an earnest though rapid glance at the face of the young lady; but this time she had turned away her head, and, hastily signifying to Balt that he might deal with the magnolia according to the best of his judgment, she strolled off as if busied for the moment in examining some other plants and soon afterward withdrew into the house, without again speaking to him.

The worthy fellow, who, on his subsequent visits to little Guise, had never again an opportunity of seeing the protectress of the child alone, was deeply hurt at the idea o this conversation having put Alida upon her guard against listening to more of these hinted suspicions that she needed his sympathy. His natural good sense, however, pre vented honest Balt from apologizing for his officious kindness, or showing in any way that he was conscious of having offended. He was, however, from this moment fully convinced that some mysterious sorrow was the latent cause of Miss de Roos's rapidly failing health, and he determined to leave no proper means untried to get at the real source of her mental suffering.

His first desire was to communicate instantly with Greyslaer; but he had never been taught to write, and his mother wit suggested the impropriety of trusting matters so delicate to a third party by employing an amanuensis. In the meantime, the cruelly slanderous story of Bradshawe reached at last the sphere in which Balt was chiefly conversant. The first mysterious affair about Miss de Roos had, as we have seen, been known almost exclusively to the simpler class of her country neighbours; but the dark tale, as now put forth by Bradshawe and his Albany friends, originating in the upper classes of society, soon descended to the lowest, and became alike the theme of the parlour and the kitchen, the city drawing-room and the roadside ale-house.

A heartless female correspondent of Alida had first disclosed it to that unhappy lady, when alleging it as an excuse for breaking off their further intercourse; but it was not till after her departure from the Hawksnest that Balt heard the tale, as told in all its horrid enormity among the coarse spirits of a village bar-room. His first impulse was to shake the life out of the half-tipsy oracle of the place, who gave it as "the latest news from Albany; but, upon someone exclaiming, "Why, man, this is fiddler's news, that we've all known for a month or more," while others winked and motioned toward Balt, as if the subject should be dropped for the present, he saw that the scandal had gone too far to be thus summarily set at rest. There was but one other move which suggested itself to him, and that was to take instant counsel with the party chiefly interested in the fair fame of Alida. And Balt, within the hour, had borrowed a horse from a neighbour, and started for Fort Stanwix.

Pressing forward as rapidly as possible, he continued his journey through the night, and thus passing Greyslaer on the road, arrived at his quarters just four-and-twenty hours after Max had so hurriedly started for Albany. Balt surmised at once what must be the cause for his abrupt departure, and, as soon as possible, took horse again and re-traced his steps; borrowed a fresh nag from the same farmer who had lent him the first, and pushed forward toward Albany.

His journey was wholly uneventful until he had passed Schenectady and entered upon the vast pine plains which extend between that city and the Hudson. But, fitly to explain what here occurred, we must go back to Bradshawe and his comrade Bettys, and trace their adventures from the place where last we left them in the immediate suburbs of Albany.

To enter a farmer's stable and saddle a couple of his best horses was a matter of little enterprise to two such characters as Bradshawe and his freebooter ally; and now the pine plains, that reach away some fif-teen miles toward Schenectady, had received the adventurous fugitives beneath their dusky colonnade's.

The remains of this forest are still visible in a stunted undergrowth, which, barely hiding the sandy soil from view, gives so monotonous and dreary an appearance to the continuous waste. But at the time of which we write, and even until the steam-craft of the neighbouring Hudson had devoured this, with a hundred other noble forests in its greedy furnaces, there was a gigantic vegetation upon those plains which now seem so barren.

The scrub oak, which is fast succeeding to the shapely pine, had not made its appearance; and the pale poplar, whose delicate leaves here and there quivered over the few runnels which traversed the thirsty soil, was almost the only deciduous tree that reared its head among those black and endless arcades of towering trunks, supporting one unbroken roof of dusky verdure.

Bold and expert horsemen as they were, Bradshawe and his com-rade soon found it impossible to pick their path amid this cavernous gloom in the deep hour of mid night. They were soon conscious of wandering from the highway, which, from the impossibility of seeing the skies through the overarching boughs above it, as well as from the absence of all coppice or undergrowth along its sides, was easily lost.

They therefore tethered their steeds and "camped down," as it is called in our hunter phrase, upon the dry soil, fragrant with the fallen cones of the pine-trees which it nourished.

So soon as the morning light permitted them to move, they discovered, as they had feared, that they had lost the highway without the hope of recovering it, save by devoting more time to the search of a beaten path than it were safe to consume. They knew the points of the compass, however, from the hemlocks which were here and there scattered through the forest whose topmost branches, our woodsmen say, point always towards the rising sun, and resumed their journey in a direction due west from the city of Albany.

An occasional ravine, however, which, though at long intervals, deeply seamed this monotonous plateau of land, turned them from their course, and thus delayed their progress; and, with appetites sharp-set by their morning ride, they were glad to arrive, about noon, at the earthen hovel of one of that strange, half-gipsy race of beings known by the name of *Yansies*, which, even within the last twelve or fifteen years, still had their brute-like bur rows in this lonely wild. Even Bettys, little fastidious as he was, recoiled from the fare which these "Dirt Eaters," as the Indians called them, placed before him. But Bradshawe, while declining their hospitality with a better grace, procured an urchin to guide him to the highway, which he was glad to learn was not far from the hovel.

They emerged, then, once more upon the travelled road within a few miles of Schenectady, and at a point where they would soon be compelled to leave it to make the circuit of that town. Their horses were weary and in need of refreshment; and, with their various windings through the forest, they had spent nearly twelve hours in accomplishing a journey which, by a direct route, the time-conquering locomotive now performs in one.

The Yansie boy had left them; for the red hues of the westering sun, streaming upon the sandy road, made their way sufficiently plain before them. Their jaded horses laboured through the loose and arid soil, but still they urged them forward to escape from the forest before the coming twilight. They had ridden thus for some time in perfect silence, when, upon a sudden exclamation from Bettys, his comrade raised his eyes and looked anxiously forward in the long *vista* before him. The road at this place ran perfectly straight over a dead level for a mile or more. The setting sun poured a flood of light upon the yellow sand, from which a warm mist, that softened every object near, seemed to be called out by its golden beams. Bradshawe shaded his eyes with his hand to see if he could descry an approaching object, while Bettys, who had already drawn his bridle, motioned impatiently for him to retire among the trees.

"Give me one of your pistols, Joe," cried Bradshawe. "It is but a single mounted traveller; I can make him out now clearly, and I'm determined to put a question or two to the fellow."

"Well, captain, you know best; only I thought it might be a pity to slit the poor devil's throat to prevent his carrying news of us to Albany; and that, you know, we must do if we once come to speech of him."

"How know you but what he may be a king's man, and assist us— or a mail-rider, and give us some rebel news of value? Draw off, Joe, and leave me to fix him." But Bettys had already trotted aside into the wood, where he managed to keep nearly a parallel route with Bradshawe, who, clapping Bettys' pistol in his bosom, and loosing in its scabbard the sword with which that worthy had provided him in the first hour of his escape, now jogged easily forward to meet the traveller.

As they approached each other more nearly, and Bradshawe got a closer survey of the coming horseman, there seemed something about him which promised that he might not be quite so easily dealt with as the Tory captain had at first anticipated.

His drab hat and leather hunting-shirt indicated only the character of a common hunter of the border or frontiersman of the period. But though he carried neither rifle on his shoulder nor pistol at his belt, and while the light cutlass or *couteau de chasse* by his side seemed feebly matched with the heavy sabre of the Tory captain, there was a look of compact strength and vigour—a something of military readiness and precision about the man, which stamped him as one who might often have borne an animated share in the fierce personal struggles of the times; a man to whom, in short, an attack like that meditated by Bradshawe could bring none of the confusing terrors of novelty.

The stranger, who seemed so occupied with his own thoughts as scarcely to notice Bradshawe in the first instance, now eyed him with a curious and almost wild gaze of earnestness as they approached each other.

Bradshawe, on the other side, surveyed the borderer's features with a stern and immovable gaze, till his own kindling suddenly with a strange gleam of intelligence, he plucked forth his pistol and presented it within a few feet of the other horseman.

"The rebel Balt, by G—d!" he cried. "Dismount, or die on the instant."

The back of the woodsman was toward the sun, and his broad-brimmed hat so shaded his features that his assailant could scarcely scan them to advantage; but if the suddenness of the assault did in any way change the evenness of his pulse, not a muscle or a nerve betrayed the weakness.

"I know ye, Lawyer Wat Bradshawe," said he, calmly, "but I don't know what caper ye'd be at in trying to scare an old neighbour after this fashion—I don't noways."

A grim smile played over the harsh features of Bradshawe, as if even his felon heart could be touched by admiration at finding a foeman as dauntless as himself.

"Real pluck, by heavens!" he ejaculated. "Balt, you're a pretty fellow, and no mistake; had you trembled the vibration of a hair, I should have shot you dead; but it's a pity to spoil such a true piece of man's flesh if one can help it. Give me that fresh gelding of yours, my old cock, and you shall go free."

"Tormented lightning! Give you Deacon Yates's six-year-old gray? That indeed! And who in all thunder, squire, would lend Uncle Balt another horse, if I gin up this critter for the asking?"

"Pshaw, pshaw! Don't think, old trapper, you can come over me with your mock simplicity. I don't want to make a noise here with my firearms, so save me the trouble of blowing you through by dismounting instantly."

As Bradshawe spoke thus, the pistol, which, ready cocked, he had hitherto kept steadily pointed at the breast of his opponent, suddenly went off. The ball grazed the side of the woodsman with a force which, though it did not materially injure him, yet fairly turned him round in the saddle.

The swords of both were out on the instant, while their horses, plunging with affright, simultaneously galloped along the road in the direction in which Balt was travelling. With two such riders, however, they were soon made obedient to the rein. Balt, in fact, had his almost instantly in hand, while Bradshawe's tired steed was easily controlled. But their training had never fitted them for such encounters; and the gleaming of weapons so terrified the animals, that it was almost impossible for their riders to close within striking distance of each other.

Balt, who had the advantage of spurs in forcing his horse forward and keeping his front to his opponent, had twice an opportunity of plunging his sword into the back of Bradshawe, as the ploughman's nag of the latter reared and wheeled each time their blades clashed above his head; and it is probable that the wish to make prisoner of Bradshawe, rather than any humane scruple upon the part of the worthy woodsman, alone prevented his using the unchivalrous advantage.

But now Balt, if he would keep his life, must not again forego such vantage. A third horseman gallops out from the wood, and urges forward to the aid of the hard-pressed Bradshawe; and shrewdly does the Tory captain require such aid; for his horse, backed against a bank where the road has been worn down or excavated a foot or more in depth, stands with his hind legs planted in a deep rut, and, unable to wheel or turn, must needs confront the stouter and more active steed of the opposing horseman, whose fierce and rapid blows are with the greatest difficulty parried by his rider. But the third combatant is now within a few yards of the woodsman, who, as he hears the savage cry of this new assailant behind him, wheels so quickly that he passes his sword through the man in the same instant that a pistol-shot from the other takes effect in the body of his charger.

"Oh! captain, the d——d rebel has done for me," cried Bettys, tumbling from his horse in the same moment that Balt gained his feet, unhurt by the fall of his own charger, and sprang forward to grasp the bit of Bradshawe's horse; but that doughty champion had already extricated himself from the ground where he fought to such disadvantage. He met the attempt of Balt with one furious thrust, which happily failed in its effect; and, seeing a teamster approaching in the distance, darted into the woods, and was soon lost to the eyes of his dismounted opponent.

"Are you much hurt, Mr. Bettys?" said Balt, not unkindly, as he now recognized the wounded man while approaching him.

"Hurt?" groaned Bettys. "I'm used up completely. That cursed iron has done for me in this world, Uncle Balt."

'And I fear," said the woodsman, gravely, "you've done for yourself in the other."

"No! by Heaven," said the stout royalist; "there's not a rebel life that I grieve for having shortened.—No! as a true man, there's but one deed that sticks in my gizzard to answer for, and that, old man, is a trick I played long before Joe Bettys thought of devoting himself to the king's lawful rights—God save him."

"Pray God to save yourself, rayther, while your hand's in at praying, poor benighted critter," said Balt, in a tone of commiseration, even while an indignant flush reddened his swarthy brow. "Let every man paddle his own canoe his own way, is always my say, Mr. Bettys; but you had better lighten yours a little while making a portage from this life to launch upon etarnity."

"Yet I meant it not—I meant it not," said the wounded man, unheeding Balt. "Wild Wat swore it was but a catch to serve for a season; that he would make an honest woman of her afterward. But this infernal story that boy too—oh—"

Balt, with wonderful quickness, seemed instantly to light upon and follow out the train of thought which the broken words of the wounded man thus partially betrayed; and yet his aptitude in seizing them is hardly strange, when we remember that it was the full preoccupation of his thoughts with the affairs of Alida which enabled Bradshawe to take him at disadvantage so shortly before. He saw instantly, or believed he saw, that Bettys' revelation referred to her; but having as yet only the feeblest clew to her real story, it behooved him to be cautious in betraying the extent of what he knew. He did not attempt, therefore, to question the wounded man as to what he had first said, but only to lead him forward in his confession.

"Yes, the boy—the poor boy—and his father—" said he, partly echoing the words of Bettys as he bent over him.

"His father? Yes, Dirk de Roos left mischief enough behind him to punish his memory for that wild business. But we were all gay fellows in those days—" some pleasant memories seemed to come over Bettys as he paused for a moment; but he groaned in spirit as he resumed, "And Fenton, too, Squire Fenton, who took the deposition of the squaw—they're gone both of them—they are both gone now, and I—I too am going where—where—"

The loss of blood here seemed to weaken Bettys so suddenly that he could say no more. The approaching wagoner had by this time reached the spot; and when Balt had lifted the fainting form of the wounded Tory into his wagon, and bound up his wounds as well as he was able, the teamster willingly consented to carry Bettys to the nearest house on the borders of the forest.

In a few moments afterward, Balt, having caught Bettys' horse, which was cropping the herbage near, threw himself into the saddle, made the best of his way back to Schenectady, got a fresh nag, and hurried with all speed to the Hawksnest.

CHAPTER 6

The Trial

Loredano.   Who would have thought that one so widely trusted,
A hero in our wars, one who has borne
Honours unnumbered from the generous state,
Could prove himself a murderer?

Padoero.   We must look
More closely ere we judge—
Be it ours to weigh
Proofs and defence. We may not spill the blood
Of senators precipitately, nor keep
The axe from the guilty, though it strike the noblest.

Mrs. Ellet.

At this distant day, when we can calmly review all the facts which led to Max Greyslaer's being put upon trial for his life, there would hardly seem to be sufficient evidence against him even to warrant the indictment under which he was tried. It must be recollected, however, that the force of circumstantial evidence is always much enhanced by the state of public opinion at the time it is adduced against a culprit; nor should we, whose minds are wholly unbiased by the fierce political prejudices which clouded the judgment and warped the opinions of men in those excited times, pass upon their actions without making many charitable allowances for the condition of things which prompted those actions.

The clemency which the noble-hearted *Lafayette*—who, being then in charge of the northern department of the army of the United States, had his headquarters at Albany—the clemency which this right-minded leader and statesman exercised toward Walter Bradshawe, by ameliorating the rigors of his confinement, and even (if tradition may be believed) permitting him to be present at his levees, affords sufficient proof how public opinion may be perverted in favour of a criminal by the subtle arts and in defatigable labours of a zealous faction working in his behalf. If one so keenly alive to everything that was just and honourable as Lafayette, could be blinded as to the real character and deserts of a detected spy like Bradshawe, is it wonderful that the intrigues of the same faction which reprieved his name from present infamy, should for the time awaken the popular clamour against the be sotted admirer of a woman whose fair fame was already blasted by its association with that of an Indian paramour?

How far the grand jury which returned the indictment against Greyslaer were influenced by that clamour, and what underhand share the great portion of its members may have had in first raising it, we shall not now say. Those men, with their deeds, whether of good or evil, have all passed away from the earth; it is not our duty to sit in judgment upon them here, nor is it necessary for us to examine into the feelings and principles, whether honest or otherwise, by which those deeds were actuated.

Something is due, however, to the leading Whigs of Albany, who allowed the issue of life and death to be joined under the circumstances which we have detailed; something to extenuate the cold indifference with which they appear to have permitted the proceedings to be hurried forward, and the life and character of one of their own members, not wholly unknown for his patriotic services, to be thus jeoparded; and, happily, their conduct upon the occasion is so easily explained that a very few words will possess the reader of everything we have to say upon the subject.

The horrid crime of assassination was in those days of civil discord but too common, while each party, as is well known, attempted to throw the stigma of encouraging such enormities upon the other. The life of General Schuyler, of Councillor Taylor, and of several other Whig dignitaries of the province of New York, had been repeatedly attempted; and when the outrage was charged upon the Tory leaders, their reply was ever that these were only retaliatory measures for similar cruelties practised by the patriot party; though the cold-blooded murder of a gallant and regretted British officer by a wild bush-fighter on the northern frontier was the only instance of this depravity that is now on record against the Republicans.

Still, as the Whigs had always claimed to be zealous supporters of all the laws which flow from a free constitution, they were galled by

this charge of their opponents; and the desire to wipe off the imputation from themselves, and fix the stigma where alone it should attach, rendered them doubly earnest in seeking to bring an offender of
their own party to justice. They were eager to prove to the country
that they were warring against *despotism* and not against *law*; and that,
wherever the Whig party were sufficiently in the ascendency to regulate the operation of the laws, they should been forced with the most
impartial rigor against all offenders. In the present instance, these rigid
upholders of justice, as old Balt the hunter used afterward to say, "*stood
so straight that they rayther slanted backwards.*"

The appearance of Greyslaer upon the eventful morning of his
trial was remembered long afterward by more than one of the many
females who crowded the court room on the occasion; but when long
years and the intervention of many a stirring theme among the subsequent scenes of the Revolution had made his story nearly for gotten,
the antiquated dame who flourished at that day would still describe
to her youthful hearers the exact appearance of "young Major Max"
as his form emerged from the crowd, which gave way on either side,
while he strode forward to take his place in the prisoner's box.

The gray travelling suit in which he came to Albany, and which
he now wore, offering no military attraction to dazzle the eye, the
first appearance of the prisoner disappointed many a fair gazer, who
had fully expected to see the victim of justice decked out with all
the insignia of his rank as a major in the Continental army. But his
closely-fitting riding dress revealed the full proportions of his tall and
manly figure far better, perhaps, than would the loose habiliments,
whose broad skirts and deep flaps gave such an air of travesty to the
unsoldierlike uniforms of that soldierly day. And the most critical of
the giddy lookers-on acknowledged that it would be a pity that the
dark brown locks, which floated loosely upon the shoulders of the
handsome culprit, should have been cued up and powdered after the
fashion which our Revolutionary heroes copied from the military
costume of the great Frederic. But, however, these trifling traditional
details may interest some, we are dwelling perhaps too minutely upon
them, when matters of such thrilling moment press so nearly upon
our attention.

Before the preliminary forms of the trial were entered upon, it
was observed by the officers of the court that the prisoner at the
bar seemed wholly unprovided with counsel; and the presiding judge,
glancing toward an eminent advocate, seemed about to suggest to

Major Greyslaer that his defence had better be intrusted to a more experienced person than himself. Greyslaer rose, thanked him for his half-uttered courtesy, and signified that he had already resisted the persuasions of the few friends who were present to adopt the course which was so kindly intimated; but that he was determined that no means but his own should be used to extricate him from the painful situation in which he was placed. His story was a plain one; and when once told, he should throw himself upon God and his country for an honourable acquittal.

The words were few, and the tone in which the prisoner spoke was so low, that nothing but the profound silence of the place, and the clear, silvery utterance of the speaker, permitted them to be audible. Yet they were heard in the remotest corner of that crowded court; and the impression upon the audience was singularly striking, considering the commonplace purport which those few words conveyed.

There is, however, about some men a character of refinement, that carries a charm with it in their slightest actions. It is not that mere absence of all vulgarity, which may be allowed to constitute the negative gentleman, but a positive spiritual influence, which impresses, more or less, even the coarsest natures with which they are brought in contact.

Max Greyslaer was one of the fortunate few who have possessed this rare gift of nature, and its exercise availed him now; for, ere he resumed his seat, every one present felt, as by instinct, that it was impossible for that man to be guilty of the brutal crime of *murder!*

The trial proceeded. The jury were impannelled without delay, for there was no one. to challenge them in behalf of the prisoner; and he seemed strangely indifferent as to the preliminary steps of his trial. The distinguished gentleman who at that time filled the office of attorney-general for the State of New York, was absent upon official duty in another district. But his place was supplied by one of the ablest members of the Albany bar, who, though he had no professional advocate to oppose him, opened his cause with a degree of cautiousness which proved his respect for the forensic talents of the prisoner at the bar. His exordium, indeed, which was conceived with great address, consisted chiefly of a complimentary tribute to those talents; and he dwelt so happily upon the mental accomplishments of the gentleman against whom a most unpleasant public duty had now arrayed his own feeble powers, that Greyslaer was not only made to appear a sort of intellectual giant, who could cleave his way through any meshes of the law; but the patriotic character, the valuable military services, and all the endearing personal qualities of the prisoner, which might have enlisted public sympathy in his favour, were lost sight of in the bright but icy renown which was thrown around his mental abilities.

In a word, the prisoner was made to appear as a man who needed neither aid, counsel, nor sympathy from anyone present; and the jury were adroitly put on their guard against the skilful defence of one so able, that nothing but the excellence of his cause would have induced the speaker, with all the professional experience of a life passed chiefly in the courts of criminal law, to cope with him. He (the counsel for the prosecution) would, in fact, have called for some assistance in his own most difficult task, in order that the majesty of the laws might be asserted by some more eloquent servant of the people than himself, but that some of his most eminent brethren at the bar, upon whom he chiefly relied, were absent from the city; and, though the evidence against the prisoner was so plain that he who runs may read, still his duty was so very painful that he felt that he might not set forth that evidence with the same force and circumspection that might attend his efforts under lass anxious circumstances.

Having succeeded thus in effecting a complete revolution as to the different grounds occupied by himself and the unfortunate Max, the wily lawyer entered more boldly into his subject. And if Greyslaer, who as yet had hardly surmised the drift of his discourse, blushed at the compliments which had been paid to his understanding, he now reddened with indignation as the cunning tongue of detraction became busy with his character; but his ire instantly gave way to contempt when the popular pleader.came to a part of his speech in which, with an ill-judged reliance upon the sordid prejudices of his hearers, he had the audacity to attempt rousing their political feelings by painting the young soldier as by birth and feeling an *aristocrat*, the son and representative of a courtier colonel, who in his lifetime had always acted with the patrician party in the colony. The allusion, which formed the climax of a well-turned period, brought Greyslaer instantly to his feet; and he stretched out his arm as if about to interrupt the speaker. But his look of proud resentment changed suddenly into one of utter scorn as he glanced around the court. His equanimity at once returned to him; and he resumed his place, uttering only, in a calm voice, the words, "You may go on, sir."

The shrewd lawyer became fully aware of his mistake from the suppressed murmur which pervaded the room before he could resume.

He had, by these few last words, undone all that he had previously effected. He had caused every one present to remember who and what the prisoner was up to the very moment when he stood here upon trial for his life.

The experienced advocate did not, however, attempt to eat his words, or flounder back to the safe ground he had so incautiously left, but hurried on to the next branch of the subject as quickly as possible; and now came the most torturing moment for Greyslaer. The speaker dropped his voice to tones of mystic solemnity; and almost whispering, as if he feared the very walls might echo the hideous tale he had to tell if spoken louder, thrilled the ears of all present with the relation of the monstrous loves of Alida and Isaac Brant, even as the foul lips of Bradshawe had first retailed the scandal.

The cold drops stood upon the brow of Greyslaer; and as the low, impassioned, and most eloquent tones of the speaker crept into his ears, he listened shuddering. Fain would he have shut up his senses against the sounds that were distilled like blistering dew upon them, but his faculty of hearing seemed at once sharpened and fixed with the same involuntary intenseness which rivets the gaze of the spellbound bird upon its serpent-charmer. And when the speaker again paused, he drew the long breath which the chest of the dreamer will heave when some horrid fiction of the night uncoils itself from his labouring fancy.

The advocate ventured then to return once more to the character of the prisoner himself ere he closed this most unhappy history. He now, though, only spoke of him as the luckless victim of an artful and most abandoned woman. But he had not come there, he said, to deplore the degradation which, amid the unguarded passions of youth, might overtake a mind of virtue's richest and noblest promise. The public weal, alas! imposed upon him, and upon the intelligent gentlemen who composed the jury before him, a far sterner duty—a duty which, painful as it was, must still be rigidly, impartially fulfilled. And no matter what accidents of fortune may have surrounded the prisoner—no matter what pleading associations, connected with his youth and his name, might interpose themselves—no matter what sorrowful regrets must mingle with the righteous verdict the evidence would compel them to give in, they were answerable alike to God and their country for that which they should this day record as *the truth*.

The testimony, as we have already detailed it, was then entered into; and, as the reader is in possession of the evidence, it need not be recapitulated here.

Greyslaer seemed to have no questions to put in cross-examination of the witnesses for the prosecution, and this part of the proceedings was soon disposed of. The impression made by the testimony was so strong, that the prosecuting attorney scarcely attempted to enforce it by any comments, and now the prisoner for the first time opened his lips in his own defence. Greyslaer said:

> I come not here to struggle for a life which is now valueless; and, though there are flaws in the evidence just given which the plain story I might tell would, I think, soon make apparent to all who hear me, I am willing to abide by the testimony as it stands. I *mean* the testimony immediately relating to the transaction which has placed me where I am. *But*, regardless as I may be of the issues of this trial as respects myself, there is another implicated in its results whom that gentleman—I thank him for the kindness, though God knows he little meant it as such—has given me the opportunity of vindicating before the community where she has been so cruelly maligned. Death for me has no terrors, the scaffold no shame, if the proceedings by which I shall perish shall providentially, in their progress, make fully clear her innocence."

The counsel for the prosecution here rose, and suggested that the unfortunate prisoner had better keep to the matter immediately before the court. He saw no necessity for making a double issue in the trial, &c., &c. The spectators, who were already impressed by the few words which Greyslaer had uttered, murmured audibly at the interruption. But Max only noticed the rudeness by a cold bow to the opposite party, as, still addressing the court, he straightway resumed:

> The learned advocate, who has given such signal proofs of his zeal and his ability in this day's trial, has directed his chief efforts to prove a sufficient motive for the commission of the act with which I am charged. In the attempt to accomplish this, the name of a most unfortunate lady has been dragged before a public court in a manner not less cruel than revolting. I have a right to disprove, if I can, the motive thus alleged to criminate me; and the vindication of that lady's fame is thus inseparably connected with my own. But, to wipe off the aspersions on her character, I must have time to send for the necessary documents. The court will readily believe that I could never have

anticipated the mode in which this prosecution has been conducted, and will not, therefore, think I presume upon its lenity
in asking for a suspension of the trial for two days only.

The court looked doubtingly at the counsel for the state, but
seemed not indisposed to grant the privilege which the prisoner asked
with such confidence; but the keen advocate was instantly upon his
feet, and, urging that the prisoner had enjoyed every opportunity of
choosing such counsel as he pleased, insisted that it was too late to
put in so feeble a plea, merely for the purpose of gaining time, in the
vain hope of ultimately defeating justice. The calmness of Greyslaer,
the apparent indifference to his fate which had hitherto been most
remarkable, vanished the instant the bench had announced its decision
against him; and his voice now rang through the crowded cham ber in
an appeal that stirred the hearts and quickened the pulses of everyone
around him. He said:

What! is the life of your citizens so value less that the hollow
forms of the law—the law, which was meant to protect the
innocent, shall thus minister to their undoing? Does the veil
of justice but conceal a soulless image, as deaf to the appeal of
truth as she is painted blind to the influence of favour? Sir, sir,
I warn you how you this day wield the authority with which
you sit there invested. You, sir, are but the servant of the people;
and I, though standing here accused of felony, am still one of
the people themselves, until a jury of my peers has passed upon
my character. An hour since, and irregular, violent, and unjust as
I knew these precipitate proceedings to be, an hour since, and
I was willing to abide by their result, whatever fatality to me
might attend it. I cared not, recked not for the issue.
But I have now a new motive for resisting the doom which
it seems predetermined shall be pronounced upon me; a duty
to perform to my country, which is far more compulsory than
any I might to myself. Sir, you cannot, you shall not, you dare
not thus sacrifice me. It is the judicial murder of an American
citizen against which I protest. I denounce that man as the instrument of a political faction, hostile to this government, and
plotting the destruction of one of its officers. I charge you, sir,
with aiding and abetting in a conspiracy to take away my life. I
call upon you to produce the evidence that Walter Bradshawe
is not yet living. I assert that that man and his friends know well

that he has not fallen by my hands, and that they, the subtle and traitorous movers of this daring prosecution, have withdrawn him for a season only to effect my ruin. Let the clerk swear the counsel for the prosecution; I demand him to take his place on that stand as *my* first witness in this cause.

Had a thunderbolt crashed in the midst of that assemblage, it could not have produced a greater sensation than did this master-stroke of intellectual audacity. There was none of the grimacing impudence of vulgar villainy facing down truth, in the heroic assurance of the man who thus, in haughty strength, challenged and dragged down his persecutors into the lists prepared for his immolation. The act sprung only from the instant resolve of a daring, a direct, and powerful mind, confident that if was surrounded with an atmosphere of duplicity, and roused to a sublime self-reliance, a Samson-like antagonism against the monstrous odds of a vile, an unscrupulous, and seemingly overwhelming opposition; and the look, not less than the voice, of Greyslaer, was majestic, as he stood there defiant.

As we have said, then, the effect of this brief and bold appeal upon every one present was perfectly astounding. But its influence in our time can only be appreciated by remembering how generally the taint of disaffection attached to the upper classes of society in the province of New York, and how withering to character was the charge of Toryism, unless the suspicion could be instantly wiped away. It would seem, too—though Greyslaer had only ventured upon this desperate effort to turn the tables upon his persecutors from instinctive conviction that in a general way he was unfairly dealt with—it would seem that there was really some foundation for the specific charge of secret disaffection which he so boldly launched against his wily foe. For the lawyer turned as pale as death at the words wherewith the speech of Max concluded; and he leaned over and whispered to the judge with a degree of agitation which was so evident to everyone who looked on, that his altered demeanour had the most unfavourable effect for the cause of the prosecution.

What he said was inaudible, but its purport might readily be surmised from the bench announcing, after a brief colloquy:

. . . . . that the prisoner was in deep error in supposing that the counsel for the prosecution was animated by any feeling of personal hostility toward him. That learned gentleman had only attempted to perform the painful duty which had de-

370

volved on him, to the best of his ability, as the representative of a public officer now absent, who was an immediate servant of the people. As an individual merely, the known benevolence of that gentleman would induce him to wish every indulgence granted to the prisoner; and, even in his present capacity, he had but now interceded with the bench for a suspension of the trial until time might be given for the production of the documents which the accused deemed essential to his defence. The court itself was grieved to think that the prisoner at the bar had forfeited all title to such indulgence by the unbecoming language he had just used in questioning the fairness with which it came to sit upon this trial; but the situation of the prisoner, his former patriotic services, and his general moderation of character, must plead in excusing this casual outbreak of his feelings, if no intentional indignity or disrespect to the court was intended. These documents, however, it is supposed, will be forthcoming as soon as—

"Jist as soon, yere honor—axing yere honour's pardon—jist as soon as those powdered fellows with long white poles in their hands will make room for a chap to get through this 'tarnal piling o' people and come up to yon der table."

"Make way, there, officer, for that red-faced man with a bald head, who is holding up those papers over the heads of the crowd at the door," cried the good-natured judge to the tipstaff, the moment he discovered the source whence came the unceremonious interruption.

"Stand aside, will ye, manny?" said Balt, now elbowing his way boldly through the crowd; "don't ye see it's the judge himself there that wants me? Haven't ye kept me long enough here, bobbing up and down to catch the eye of the major? Make way, I say, feller citerzens. I'm Mowed if I wouldn't as lief run the gauntlet through as many wild Injuns. Lor! how pesky hot it is," concluded the countryman, wiping his brow as he got at last within the railing which surrounded the bar.

"Come, come, my good fellow," said the judge, "I saw you holding up some papers just now at the door; why don't you produce them, and tell us where they came from?"

"Came from? Why, where else but out of the brass *beaufet* where I placed 'em myself, I should like to know! and where I found this pocket-book of the major's, which I thought it might be well to bring along with me, seeing I had to break the lock, and it might, therefore, be no longer safe where I found it."

"The pocket-book! That contains the very paper I want," cried Greyslaer.

"It doesn't hold all on 'em you'd like to see though, I guess, major," said Balt, handing him a packet, which Max straightway opened before turning to the pocket-book, and ran his eye over the papers:

"Memorandum of a release granted by Henry Fenton to the heirs of, &c.; notes of land sold by H. F. in town ship No. 7, range east," &c. &c., murmured Max; and then added aloud, "these appear to be merely some private papers of the late Mr. Fenton, with which I have no concern; but here is a document—" said he, opening the pocket-book.

"One moment, one moment, major," cried Balt, anxiously; "I can't read written-hand, so I brought 'em all to ye to pick out from; but I mistrust it must be there if you look carefully, for I made out the word Max, with a big G after it, when I first took those papers from the clothes of Mr. Fenton."

Greyslaer turned over the papers again with a keener interest, and the next moment read aloud:

In the matter of Derrick de Roos, junior, and Annatie, the Indian woman; deposition as to the parentage of Guise or Guisebert, their child, born out of wedlock, taken before Henry Fenton, justice of the peace, &c., certified copy, to be deposited with Max Greyslaer, Esquire, in testimony of the claim which the said child might have upon his care and protection as the near friend and ward of Derrick de Roos, senior, who, while living, fully acknowledged such claim, in expiation of the misdeeds of his son.

   Witness,   Henry Fenton.

N. B.—The mother of the child has, with her infant, disappeared from the country since this deposition was taken. She is believed, however, to be still living among the praying Indians of St. Regis, upon the Canada border.

                 H. F.

The deposition, whose substance was given in this endorsement, need not be here recapitulated; and the reader is already in possession of the letter from Bettys to Bradshawe, sufficiently explaining their first abduction of Miss de Roos, which letter Greyslaer straightway produced from the pocket-book, and read aloud in open court. The strong emotion which the next instant overwhelmed him as he sank back into his seat, prevented Max from adding any comment to this unanswerable testimony, which so instantly wiped every blot from the fair fame of his betrothed.

As for Balt, he only folded his arms, and looked sternly around to see if one doubting look could be found among that still assemblage; but the next moment, as he rightly interpreted the respectful silence which pervaded the place, he buried his face in his hat, to hide the tears which burst from his eyes and coursed down his rude and fur rowed cheeks.

The counsel for the prosecution—who, with an air of courtesy and feeling, at once admitted the authenticity of these documents—was the first that broke the stillness of the scene. And his voice rose so musically soft in a beautiful eulogium upon the much-injured lady, whose story had for the moment concentrated every interest, that his eloquence was worthy of a far better heart than his; but, gradually changing the drift of his discourse, he brought it back once more to the prisoner, and reminded the jury that the substantial part of the evidence upon which he had been arraigned was as forcible as ever. The motive for Bradshawe's destruction at the hands of the accused was proved even more strongly than before.

There was no man present but must feel that the prisoner had been driven to vengeance by temptation, such as the human heart could scarcely resist. But, deep as must be our horror at Bradshawe's villainy, and painfully as we must sympathize with the betrothed husband of that cruelly outraged lady, there was still a duty to perform to the law. The circumstances which had been proved might induce the gentlemen of the jury to recommend the prisoner to the executive for some mitigation of a murderer's punishment, but they could not otherwise affect the verdict which it was their stern and sworn duly to render.

"And you don't mean to let the major go, arter all?" said Balt, addressing himself to the lawyer with little show of respect, as the latter concluded his harangue.

"Silence, sir, silence; take your seat," said a tipstaff, touching Balt on the shoulder.

"And why haven't I as good a right to speak here as that smooth-tongued chap?"

"You must keep silence, my worthy fellow," said the judge. "I shall be compelled to order an officer to remove you if you interrupt the proceedings by speaking again."

"But I will speak again," said Balt, slapping his hat indignantly upon the table. "I say, you Mister Clark there, take the Bible and qualify me. I'm going into that witnesses' box. You had better find out whether Wat Bradshawe is dead or no afore you hang the major for killing on him."

But the relation which Balt had to give is too important to come in at the close of a chapter, and it may interest the reader sufficiently to have it detailed with somewhat more continuity than it was now disclosed by the worthy woodsman.

CHAPTER 7

Conclusion

And thus it was with her,
The gifted and the lovely—
And yet once more the strength
Of a high soul sustains her; in that hour
She triumphs in her fame that he may hear
Her name with honour.
Oh let the peace
Of this sweet hour be hers.

Lucy Hooper.

Leaving Balt to tell the court in his own way the particulars of his first encounter in the forest, we will take up his story from the moment when the broken revelation of the wounded Bettys prompted the woodsman to hurry back to the Hawksnest, where he had deposited the papers of the deceased Mr. Fenton, as previosly mentioned in this authentic history.

As Balt approached the neighbourhood of the Hawksnest, he found the whole country in alarm. A runner had been dispatched from Fort Stanwix, warning the people of that bold and extraordinary inroad of a handful of refugees which took place early in the summer of 1778, when, swelling their ranks by the addition to their number of more than one skulking outlaw and many secret Tories, who had hitherto continued to reside upon the Mohawk, the royalists succeeded in carrying off both booty and prisoners to Canada, disappearing from the valley as suddenly as they came.

Teondetha was the agent who brought the news of the threatened incursion, but the movements of the refugees were so well planned that they managed to strike only those points where the warning came too late. They were heard of at one settlement, when they had already slaughtered the men, carried off the women and children, and burned the dwellings of another; and, indeed, so rapid were their operations, that the presence of these destroyers was felt at a dozen different points almost simultaneously. They were first seen in their strength near Fort Hunter; they desolated the farm-houses between there and "Fonda's Bush," swept the remote settlements upon either side of their northern progress, and finally disappeared at the "Fish-house" on the Sacondaga.

The historian seems to have preserved no trace of their being anywhere resisted, so astounding was the surprise of the country people at this daring invasion; but tradition mentions one instance at least where their inroad received a fatal check.

Balt, who, as we have said, was hurrying to the Hawksnest to procure the papers which, while clearing the fair fame of Alida, have already given so important a turn to the trial of Greyslaer, instantly claimed the aid of Teondetha to protect the property of his friend in the present exigence; and, with Christian Lansingh and two or three others, these experienced border warriors threw themselves into the mansion, and prepared to defend it until the storm had passed by.

Nor was the precaution wasted; for their preparations for defence were hardly completed, and the lapse of a single night passed away, when, with the morrow's dawn, a squad of Tory riders was seen galloping across the pastures by the riverside, with no less a person than Walter Bradshawe himself, now well mounted and completely armed, riding at their head. He had fallen in with these brother partisans while trying to effect his escape across the frontier, obtained the command of a dozen of the most desperate among them, and readily induced his followers, by the hope of booty, to make an attack upon the Hawks nest. Whether the belief that Alida was still dwelling there induced him to make one more desperate effort to seize her person, or whether he only aimed at striking some daring blow ere he left the country in triumph—a blow which would make his name a name of terror long upon that border—it is now impossible to say. But there, by the cold light of early dawn, Balt soon distinguished him at the head of his gang of *desperadoes*.

Early as was the hour, Teondetha had already crept out to scout among the neighbouring hills; and Balt, aware of his absence, felt now a degree of concern about his fate which he was angry with himself at feeling for a "Redskin," though somehow, almost unknowingly, he had learned to love the youth. He had, indeed, no apprehension that the Oneida had been already taken by these more than savage men; but as the morning mist, which rolled up from the river, had most probably hitherto prevented Teondetha from seeing their approach, Balt feared that he might each moment present himself upon the lawn in returning to the house, and catch the eye of Bradshawe's followers while unconscious of the danger that hovered near.

The scene that followed was, however, so quickly over, that the worthy woodsman had but little time for further reflection.

Bradshawe had evidently expected to obtain possession of the house before any of the family had arisen or warning of his approach was received; and, dividing his band as he neared the premises, a part of his men circled the dwelling and galloped up a lane which would lead them directly across the lawn toward the front door of the house, while the rest, wheeling off among the meadows, presented themselves at the same time in the rear.

The force of Balt was too small to make a successful resistance against this attack, had the Tories expected any opposition, or had they been determined to carry the house even after discovering that it was defended. His rifles were so few in number that they were barely sufficient to defend one side of the house at a time; and, though both doors and windows were barricaded, the woodsman and his friends could not long have sustained themselves under a simultaneous assault upon each separate point.

Balt, however, did not long hesitate how to receive the enemy; his only doubt seemed to be, for the moment, which party would soonest come within reach of his fire.

"Kit Lansingh," he cried, the instant he saw the movement from his lookout place in the gable, "look ye from the front windows, and see if the gate that opens from the lane upon the lawn be closed or no. Quick, as ye love yere life, Kit."

"The gate's shut. They slacken their pace—they draw their bridles—they fear to leap," shouted Kit the next instant in reply. "No—they leap; ah! it's only one of them—Bradshawe; but he has not cleared it; the gate crashes beneath his horse; his girths are broken; and now they all dismount to let their horses step over the broken bars."

"Enough, enough, Kit. Spring now, lads, to the back windows, and each of you cover your man as the riders from the meadow come within shot. But no! never mind taking them separately," cried Balt, as his party gained the windows. "Not yet, not yet; when they double

377

that corner of the fence. Now, now, as they wheel, as they double, take them in range. Are you ready? *Let them have it.*"

A volley from the house as Balt spoke instantly emptied several saddles; and the on-coming troopers, recoiling in confusion at the unexpected attack, turned their backs and gained a safe distance as quickly as possible.

"Now, lads," shouted Balt, "load for another peppering in the front;" and already the active borderers have manned the upper windows on the opposite side of the house.

But the assailants here, startled by the sound of firearms and the rolling smoke which they saw issuing from the rear of the house, hung back, and would not obey the behests of their leader, who vainly tried to cheer them on to the attack. In vain did Bradshawe coax, conjure, and threaten. His followers caught sight of their friends drawing off with diminished numbers toward the end of the house. They saw the gleaming rifle-barrels protruding through the windows. They clustered together, and talked eagerly for a moment, unheeding the frantic appeals of their leader; and now, with less hesitation than before, they leaped the broken barrier of the gate, and were in full retreat down the lane.

"One moment, one moment, boys; it's a long shot, but we'll let them have a goodbye as they turn off into the pasture. Ah, I feared it was too far for the best rifle among us," added Balt, as the troopers, apparently untouched by the second volley, still galloped onward.

"God's weather! though, but that chap on the roan horse has got it, uncle," cried Lansingh, the next moment, as he saw a horseman reel in the saddle, while others spurred to his side, and upheld the wounded man. "My rifle against a shotgun that that chap does not cross the brook!"

"To the window in the gable, then, boys, if you would see the Tory fall," exclaimed Balt, as the flying troopers became lost to their view from the front windows. "Tormented lightning! you've lost your rifle, Kit; they are all over the brook."

"No, there's a black horse still fording it," cried Lansingh, eagerly. "'Tis Bradshawe's horse; I know it from the dangling girths he drags after him. He has gained the opposite bank; his horse flounders in the slippery clay; no, he turns and waves his hand at something. He sees us; he waves it in scorn. Oh! for a rifle that would bring him now."

And, even as Lansingh spoke, the sharp report of a rifle, followed by a sudden howl of pain and defiance, rang out on the still morning air. The trooper again rose in his saddle and shook his clenched fist at some unseen object in the bushes. The next moment he disappeared in a thicket beyond; and now, again, the black horse emerged once more into the open fields; but he scoured along the slope beyond, bare-backed and masterless; the saddle had turned, and left the wounded rider at the mercy of that unseen foe!

Not five minutes could have elapsed before Balt and his comrades had reached the spot where Bradshawe disappeared from their view; but the dying agonies of the wounded man were already over; and, brief as they were, yet horrible must have been the exit of his felon soul. The ground for yards around him was torn and muddled with his gore, as if the death-struggles of a bullock had been enacted there. His nails were clutched deep into the loamy soil, and his mouth was filled with the dust which he had literally bitten in his agony. The yeomen gazed with stupid wonder upon the distorted frame and muscular limbs—so hideously convulsed when the strong life was leaving them and one of them stooped to raise and examine the head, as if still doubtful that it was the terrible Bradshawe who now lay so helpless before them. But the crown of locks had been reft from the gory skull, and the face (as is said to be the case with a scalped head) had *slipped down*, so that the features were no longer distinguishable.

The next moment the Oneida emerged from the bushes with a couple of barbarous Indian trophies at his belt; and subsequent examination left not a doubt that both Bradshawe and the other wounded trooper had been dispatched by the brave but demi-savage Teondetha.

Such were the essential particulars of Bradshawe's real fate, as now made known by him who beheld his fall.

The court had given an order for the instant release of the prisoner, and the clerk had duly made it out long before the narrative of the worthy woodsman was concluded; but the relation of Balt excited a deep sensation throughout that crowded chamber, and the presiding judge for some moments found it impossible to repress the uproarious enthusiasm with which this full exculpation of the prisoner at the bar was received by the spectators. Those who were nearest to the prisoner—the members of the bar and other gentlemen—the whole jury in a body, rose from their seats and rushed forward to clasp his hand; and it was only Greyslaer himself who could check the excitement of the multitude and prevent them from bearing him off in triumph upon their shoulders. His voice, however, at last stilled the tumult, so that a few words from the bench could be heard. They were addressed, not to the prisoner, but to Balt himself.

"And pray tell me, my worthy fellow," said the judge, with moistened eyes, "why you did not, when first called to the stand, testify at once to the impossibility of this Bradshawe having fallen by the hand of our gallant friend, for whose unmerited sufferings not even the triumphant joy of this moment can fully compensate? Why did you not arrest these most painful proceedings the moment it was in your power?"

"And yere honor don't see the caper on't raaly? You think I might have got Major Max out of this muss a little sooner by speaking up at onct, eh? Well, I'll tell ye the hull why and wherefore, yere honour;" and the worthy woodsman, laying one brown and brawny hand upon the rail before him, looked round with an air of pardonable conceit at finding such a multitude of well-dressed people hanging upon his words, cleared his throat once or twice, and thus bespoke himself:

"I owned a hound onct, gentlemen, as slick a dog as ever you see, any on ye, for the like o' that brute was not in old Tryon; and one day, when hunting among the rocky ridges around Konnedieyu,[1] or Canada Creek, as some call it, I missed the critter for several hours. I looked for him on the *hathes* above, and I clomb down into the black chasm where the waters pitch, and leap, and fling about so sarcily, and sprangle into foam agin the walls on airy side. It was foolish, that's a fact, to look for him there; for the eddies are all whirlpools; and if by chance, he had got into the stream, why, instead of being whirled about and chucked on shore, as I hoped for, the poor critter would have been sucked under, smashed on the rocky bottom, and dragged off like all natur. And so I thought when I got near enough for my eyes to look fairly into those black holes, with a twist of foam around them, that seemed to screw, as it were, right down through the yaller water of Konnedieyu.

"But now I hears a whimper in the bushes above me. I looks up to the top of the precipice against which I'm leaning, and there, on a ledge of rock about midway, what do I see but the head of the very hound I was in search of peering out from the stunted hemlocks that grew in the crevices. To holp him from below was impossible; so I went round and got to the top of the hathe. The dog was now far below, and it was a putty risky business to let myself down the face of the cliff to the ledge where he was. The critter might get up to me full as

1. Now Trenton Falls.

easily as I could get down to him; for here and there were little sloping zigzag elects of rock broad enough for the footing of a dog, but having no bushes near by which a man could steady his body while balancing along the face of the cliff. They leaned over each other, too, with breadth enough for a dog to pass between, but not for a man to stand upright,

"I whistled to the dog: 'Why in all thunder does the old hound not come up when I call?' says I to myself, says I. 'By the everlasting hokey, if he hasn't got one foot in a painter[2] trap,' said I the next moment, as I caught sight of the leather thong by which some Redskin had fixed the darned thing to the rock. I ups rifle at onct, and had hand on trigger to cut the string with a bullet. 'Stop, old Balt, what are ye doing?' says I agin, afore I let fly. 'The dumb brute, to be sure, will be free if you clip that string at onct, as you know you can. But the teeth of the trap have cut into his flesh already; will you run the chance of its further mangling him, and making the dog of no valu to an one by letting him drag that cursed thing after him when he gets away? No! rayther let him hang on there a few moments as he is, till you can go judgmatically to work to free him.' With that I let the suffering critter wait until I had cut down a tree, slanted it from the top of the cliff to the ledge where he lay, got near enough to handle him, uncoiled the leather thong that had got twisted round him, sprung the trap from his bleeding limb, and holped him to some purpose.

"Now, yere honour, think ye that, if I had not waited patiently till all this snarl about Miss Alida had been disentangled afore Major Max got free, he would not have gone away from this court with something still gripping about his heart, as I may say; something to which the steel teeth of that painter trap, hows'ever closely they might set, were marciful, as I may say? Sarting! sarting he would. But now everyone has heard here all that man, woman, and child can say agin her. And here, in open court, with all these book-larnt gentlemen, and yere honour at their head, to sift the business, we've gone clean to the bottom of it, and brought out her good name without a spot upon it."

We will leave the reader to imagine the effect which this homely but not ineloquent speech of the noble-minded woodsman produced upon the court, upon the spectators, and upon him who was most nearly interested in what the speaker said.

The reader must imagine, too, the emotions of Alida when Max

2. Panther.

and she next met, and Greyslaer made her listen to the details of the trial from the lips of his deliverer; while Balt, pausing ever and anon as he came to some particular which he scarcely knew how to put in proper language for her ears, would at last get over the difficulty by flatly asserting that he "*disremembered* exactly what the bloody lawyer said jist at this part, but the major could tell her that in by-times."

Those *by-times,* as Balt so quaintly called them, those sweet and secret interchanges of heart with heart, and that full and blessed communion of prosperous and happy love, came at last for Max and Alida.

They were wedded in the autumn, at that delicious season of our American climate when a second spring, less fresh, less joyous than that of the opening year, but gentler, softer, and—though the herald of bleak winter—less changeable and more lasting, smiles over the land; when the bluebird comes back again to carol from the cedar top, and the rabbit from the furze, the squirrel upon the chestnut bough, prank it away as merrily as when the year was new; when the doe loiters in the forest walk as the warm haze hides her from the hunter's view, and the buck admires his antlers in the glassy lake which the breeze so seldom ripples; when Nature, like her own wild creatures, who conceal themselves in dying, covers her face with a mantle so glorious that we heed not the parting life beneath it. They were wedded, then, among those sober but balmy hours, when love like theirs might best receive its full reward.

Thenceforward the current of their days was as calm as it had hitherto been clouded, and both Max and Alida, in realizing the bounteous mercies which brightened their afterlives, as well as in remembering the dark trials they had passed through; the fearful discipline of the character of the one, the brief but bitter punishment of a single lapse from virtue in the other—that Heaven-sent punishment, which but heralded a crowning mercy—both remained henceforth among those who acknowledge

There is a Divinity That Shapes Our Ends.
Rough Hew Them How We Will.

★★★★★★

Our story ends here. The fate of the other characters who have been principally associated in its progress is soon told. Isaac Brant, as is related in the biography of his father, perished ultimately by the hand of that only parent, whose life he had several times attempted, and who thus most singularly wrought out the curse which the elder

De Roos had pronounced against him in dying. Of Thayendanagea, or Brant himself, we need say nothing further here, as the full career of that remarkable person is sufficiently commemorated elsewhere. The two Johnsons must likewise at this point be yielded up to the charities of the historians who have recorded their ruthless deeds throughout the Valley of the Mohawk in the subsequent years of the war.

The redoubtable Joe Bettys did not close his career quite so soon as might have been expected from the disastrous condition in which we last left him; but, recovering from his wound under the care of the presumed teamster to whom Balt had intrusted him, and who turned out to be a secret partisan of the faction to which Bettys belonged, the worthy Joe made his escape across the frontier. He lived for some years afterward, and, after committing manifold murders and atrocities, he finally finished his career upon the scaffold at the close of the war. The striking incidents of his capture are told elsewhere with sufficient minuteness.[3] Old Wingear was attainted as a traitor, and died of mortification from the loss of his property.

Syl Stickney, the only Tory, we believe, yet to be disposed of, attempted once or twice to desert to his old friends, considering himself bound for the time for which he had enlisted, though both Bradshawe, his leader, and Valtmeyer, who had enlisted him, were dead. When the term expired, however, he did not hesitate to join the Whigs, with whom he fought gallantly till the close of the war, and received a grant of land in the western part of the State for the active services he rendered in Sullivan's famous campaign against the Indian towns. It was doubtless this Sylla and his brother Marius, who, calling each a settlement after themselves, set the example of giving those pedagogue classic names to our western villages, which have cast such an air of ridicule over that flourishing region of the State of New York.

It remains only to speak of the affectionate-hearted Balt, whose only foible, if so it may be called, was, that he never could abide a *Redskin*. His nephew, Christian Lansingh, marrying the gentle Tavy Wingear, succeeded to the public-house of her father after the attainder of the hypocritical deacon had been reversed in his favour. And there, by the inn fireside, long after the war was over, old Balt, with his pipe in his mouth, used to delight to tight his battles over for the benefit of the listening traveller. The evening of his days, however, was spent chiefly at the Hawksnest.

Greyslaer, soon after his marriage, had embraced the tender of a

3. See *Stone's Life of Brant*, vol. ii.

mission to one of the southern courts of Europe, with which government honoured him. The health of Alida had been seriously impaired
by her mental sufferings; and though loath to relinquish the active part
he had hitherto taken in the great struggle of his country, Max was
glad to be able to devote himself in a different way to her interests,
where Alida would have the benefit of a more genial clime. But in the
peaceful years that followed his return, many was the pleasant hunt,
many the loitering tour that he and old Balt had together among the
romantic hills and bright trout-streams to the north of his demesnes;
and many the token of kindness from Alida to the Spreading Dew,
which Max carried with him on these excursions, when the rapid
disappearance of game in his own level country induced Teondetha to
shift his *wigwam* to these mountain solitudes.

ALSO FROM LEONAUR

AVAILABLE IN SOFTCOVER OR HARDCOVER WITH DUST JACKET

THE CIVIL WAR NOVELS: 1 *by Joseph A. Altsheler*—*The Guns of Bull Run &
The Guns of Shiloh*—the first and second novels of a series of eight adventures which
follow the momentous events, campaigns and battles of the great American Civil War
between the Northern and Southern states.

THE CIVIL WAR NOVELS: 2 *by Joseph A. Altsheler*—*The Scouts of Stonewall
& The Sword of Antietam*—the third and fourth novels of a series of nine adventures
which follow the momentous events, campaigns and battles of the great American
Civil War between the Northern and Southern states.

THE CIVIL WAR NOVELS: 3 *by Joseph A. Altsheler*—*The Star of Gettysburg
& The Rock of Chickamauga*—the fifth and sixth novels of a series of nine adventures
which follow the momentous events, campaigns and battles of the great American
Civil War between the Northern and Southern states.

THE CIVIL WAR NOVELS: 4 *by Joseph A. Altsheler*—*The Shades of the Wilderness & The Tree of Appomattox*—the seventh and eighth novels of a series of nine
adventures which follow the momentous events, campaigns and battles of the great
American Civil War between the Northern and Southern states.

THE CIVIL WAR NOVELS: 5 *by Joseph A. Altsheler*—*Before the Dawn: a Story
of the Fall of Richmond*—the last of a series of nine adventures which follow the momentous events, campaigns and battles of the great American Civil War between the
Northern and Southern states.

THE FRENCH & INDIAN WAR NOVELS: 1 *by Joseph A. Altsheler*—*The
Hunters of the Hills & The Shadow of the North*—In this three volume, six novel set the
story of the war, with many of its real life characters, is told through the adventures
of its principal characters, Robert Lennox, the hunter Willet and his Indian companion Tayoga.

THE FRENCH & INDIAN WAR NOVELS: 2 *by Joseph A. Altsheler*—*The
Rulers of the Lakes & The Masters of the Peaks*—In this three volume, six novel set the
story of the war, with many of its real life characters, is told through the adventures
of its principal characters, Robert Lennox, the hunter Willet and his Indian companion Tayoga.

THE FRENCH & INDIAN WAR NOVELS: 1 *by Joseph A. Altsheler*—*The Lords
of the Wild & The Sun of Quebec*—In this three volume, six novel set the story of the
war, with many of its real life characters, is told through the adventures of its principal
characters, Robert Lennox, the hunter Willet and his Indian companion Tayoga.